NO HOLDING
BACK

LORI FOSTER

NO HOLDING BACK

HQN

ISBN-13: 978-1-335-25097-1

No Holding Back

HQN
22 Adelaide St. West, 40th Floor
Toronto, Ontario M5H 4E3, Canada
www.Harlequin.com

Printed in U.S.A.

Very special thanks to army ranger master sergeant Shayne Laflin for answering the million and one questions I had on army rangers.

To amazing author Pamela Clare, and wonderful reader Kim Potts, thank you for sharing info on the Colorado landscape, highways, the front range and small towns along the Rockies.

I also want to share my heartfelt gratitude and deep respect to all who serve in our armed forces, and the families who love and support them.

And to the special police task forces fighting daily against human trafficking and forced labor, thank you. I know you see things no one should have to, and that your job is incredibly difficult on so many levels. Thank you for still doing it. You're making the world a better place.

Any and all errors, either on Colorado, rangers or task forces, are entirely my own!

NO HOLDING
BACK

CHAPTER ONE

Shivers racked her body as she watched him drink. Curled in the corner, waiting, dreading the inevitable—even breathing was difficult with so much fear crowding in around her. She wanted to cry but knew it wouldn't help. She wanted to let in the hysteria, but she hadn't quite accepted her fate…not yet.

She couldn't.

Outside the room, two other men stood guard. They'd told her she'd be forced to do this up to ten times a night, and she wasn't sure she'd even survive this first time.

She wanted to go home.

She wanted to curl up and die.

Mostly she wanted to fight—but how?

Amused by her fear, the man watched her while tossing back another shot. He enjoyed her terror—and that amplified everything she felt.

What to do, what to do, what to do?

Her gaze frantically searched the second-story room. One small window, opened to let in a breeze, led to a sheer drop

onto a gravel lot. Would she survive going out that window?
At the moment, did it really matter?

The man stood near the door. He'd slid a metal bar into
place, locking her in, ensuring she couldn't get past him. But
also ensuring no one else could get in. Not until he'd finished.

He'd paid for two hours but now didn't seem in any rush to
get started.

To the right of the door, a tiny table held a bottle of whis-
key and a single glass. To the left, an empty wooden coat tree
stood as a place for him to hang his clothes.

A bare mattress on a small bed occupied a wall.

Nothing else.

Only her fear, the reality, the terror, her hatred, the cruelty…
her will to survive.

When his loose lips stretched into a smug grin, she braced
herself—and noticed that he stumbled a little as he stepped toward her.

Her heart punched painfully. Slowly, she slid up the wall to
her feet. An invisible fist squeezed her throat, but she sidled
sideways, toward that barred door.

Toward the little table.

From the hallway, loud music played. Whatever happened in
this room, they didn't want to be bothered with it.

She kept her gaze locked on his, her hands clammy with
sweat, so afraid that her limbs felt sluggish.

"Thinking to run?" he asked, his grin widening with anticipation.

"I… I was hoping I could have a drink, too?"

"You want to numb yourself? No, I don't think so."

He wanted her afraid. He wanted her to feel every awful second of this degradation. With a lot of effort, she tamped down
the need to vomit and managed to ask, "Then…should I pour
you another?"

Snorting, he propped a shoulder to the wall. "Want to get me drunk, huh? Sure, go ahead and try it, but you'll see, I know how to hold my liquor." Tipping his head, he narrowed his eyes and the grin turned into a sneer. "Alcohol makes me mean."

Refusing to dwell on that possibility, she forced a nod, reaching for the bottle anyway, letting him see how badly she trembled. She filled the small glass, then lifted it...while keeping the bottle in her other hand.

The obnoxious brute paid no attention; he focused on watching her quake as she came to him, the glass held out as a feeble offering.

Instead of taking it, he caught her wrist in a painful grip, jerking her toward him, laughing as she cried out.

She swung the bottle with all her might.

Sterling jerked awake with a start, her heart racing and her throat aching with the need to scream.

She didn't. She never did—no matter what. Silence kept her safer than a scream ever could.

In just seconds, she absorbed the low light of the bar, the ancient rock and roll playing on the jukebox, the clamor of a few dozen voices talking low to one another.

God. She swallowed heavily, looking around at the familiar sights. Her gaze landed on the bartender.

He watched her. *Always.*

Nothing got by that man.

He could pretend to be an average guy, he could wear the trappings of a simple bar owner, but she knew better. He hid something, maybe something as monumental as her own secrets, but she wouldn't ask. The Tipsy Wolverine bar was her haven from the road. She could sleep in her truck, and sometimes did, but she didn't truly rest.

Here, in the little Podunk bar in the small mountain town of Ridge Trail, Colorado, she knew no one would bother her.

Because of *him*.

Again her eyes sought him out. She guessed him at six feet five. *Really* big, but solid head to toes. Posture erect. Awareness keen. He wore his glossy dark hair neatly trimmed, precisely styled…but it was those piercing blue eyes that really caught and held her attention.

His gaze had veered away from her, but that didn't make him unaware. Sterling pegged him as ex-military, or maybe something deadlier. He was too damn physically fit to be anyone ordinary.

Her nostrils flared a little as she looked him over. In the seedy area of town where locals slumped in their seats and laughed too loudly, he was always…mannered. Contained. Professional but not in the way of a suited businessman.

More like a guy who knew he could handle himself in any situation. A guy who easily kicked ass, took names and did so without a scratch. Those thick shoulders… Studying his body left a funny warmth in Sterling's stomach, sending her interested gaze to his pronounced biceps, watching the fluid bunch and flex of them with the smallest movement. His pullover shirt fit his wide chest perfectly, showing sculpted pecs and, letting her attention drift downward, a flat, firm middle.

Lord, the man was put together fine. Add in a lean jaw, a strong but straight nose, and those cool blue eyes fringed by dark lashes, and she assumed he broke hearts on a daily basis.

Not *her* heart. She wasn't susceptible to that kind of stuff. She could take in the exceptional view and stay detached. *She could.*

Only…this time she had to really concentrate to make it true.

His gaze locked to hers, catching her perusal, and his firm lips quirked in a small "you're not immune" smile.

It made her mouth go dry.

He couldn't know that, could he? Yet he looked as if he'd just read her every admiring thought.

Feeling oddly exposed, she held up her glass, realized it was still full and hastily mouthed, "Coffee?"

With a nod, he moved away to a service counter behind the bar. Less than half a minute later, he strode over in his casual yet confident way with a steaming cup.

He knew how she took it, with one sugar and a splash of creamer. He knew because he missed nothing. Ever.

Setting it before her, he asked, "Done with this?" indicating the shot she'd ordered—and hadn't touched.

Usually, to justify her lengthy naps, she bought a couple of drinks. This time, exhausted to the bone, she hadn't lasted long enough.

"Thanks." Sterling sipped her coffee.

That he didn't move away set her heart tripping. Defiant, she glanced up and caught a slight frown carved from what appeared to be concern. She was good at reading people—except for him. Most of the time she didn't know what he was thinking, and she didn't like that.

Suspicion prickled. "What?"

Heavy lashes lowering, he thought a moment before meeting her gaze again. "I'm worried that anything I say might put you off."

Sterling stiffened with accusation. "What do you have to say?"

"Such a lethal tone," he teased—as if they knew each other well. "You don't have to order drinks just to be in here. You want a place to kick up your feet—"

Abruptly, she dropped her feet from the seat of the chair across from her. She unconsciously braced herself—to act, to react, to protect herself if necessary.

"Or to rest without being disturbed," he continued, ignoring her tension. "You're always welcome." As if he knew her innate worry, as if he could see her automatic response to his nearness, he took a step back. "No questions asked, and no drink order necessary."

Before she could come up with a reply, he walked away.

For twenty minutes, Sterling remained, but he didn't look at her again.

Not until she walked out. He watched her then. Hell yeah, he did. She felt his gaze burning over her like a physical touch. Like *interest*. It left her with heightened awareness.

Of him.

Damn, damn, damn.

Cade wanted to kick his own ass.

She'd been coming into the bar for months now. She hadn't yet given her name, but he knew it all the same. He made a point of knowing everyone in the bar, whether they were important to his operation or not.

Sterling Parson. Star for short.

Privately, he called her Trouble.

At a few inches shy of six feet, her body toned, she walked with a self-possessed air that he recognized as more attitude than ability. She wore that swagger like a warning that all but shouted *Back off*.

Her long wavy brown hair was usually in a ponytail, occasionally in a braid and sometimes stuffed under a trucker's cap.

Despite the loose shirts she wore with straight-legged jeans and mean lace-up black boots in an effort to disguise her body, she'd be hard to miss. For sure no one in his bar had missed her.

The woman was unique in so many ways. Bold but somehow vulnerable. Composed, yet temperate. Beautiful...but only to a discerning eye, because she did all she could to blend in.

The big rig she drove had SP Trucking emblazoned on the side, yet she was far from the usual trucker they got as customers.

The day she'd first walked in, heads had swiveled, eyes had widened and interest had perked—but after Cade swept his gaze around the room, everyone had gotten the message.

The lady was off-limits.

Cade hadn't bothered to explain to anyone. He never did…
except occasionally to family. Then only when pressed.

From the moment he'd first spotted Sterling, he'd sensed the
emotional wounds she hid, knew she had secrets galore and understood she needed a place to rest.

She needed *him*.

Star didn't know that yet, but no problem. In his bar, in this
shit neighborhood, he'd look out for her anyway—same as he
did for anyone in need.

Moving to the window, he watched her leave. Her long stride
carried her across the well-lit gravel lot, not in haste but with
an excess of energy. He couldn't imagine her meandering. The
woman knew one speed: full steam ahead.

After unlocking the door, she climbed into her rig with
practiced ease. Head tipped back, she rested a moment before
squaring her shoulders and firing the engine. She idled for a
bit, maybe checking her gauges, then eased off the clutch and
smoothly rolled out to the road. Cade watched until he couldn't
see her taillights anymore.

Where she'd go, he didn't yet know—but he wanted to. He
wanted to introduce himself, ask questions, maybe offer assistance.

Her preferences on that were obvious.

Except that tonight she'd watched him a little more.

Actually, she often noticed him, in a cautious, distrustful
way. And she always came back.

Sometimes she'd sleep for an hour, sometimes longer. Tonight, she'd dozed for two hours before jerking awake in alarm.

A bad dream?

Or a bad memory?

If she kept to her usual pattern, she'd be back tomorrow night
on her return trip. Maybe, just maybe, he'd find a chink in her
armor. He glanced at the little table she always chose.

Tomorrow, he'd offer her something different.

★ ★ ★

After too much driving, sitting through endless traffic in Colorado's summer heat and going without enough rest, Sterling returned to the bar. Aching from her eyebrows to her toes, it was a relief to pull in to the lot a littler earlier than usual.

She'd thought about finding another place to rest. Bars and truck stops riddled this side of the Rockies. Before discovering the Tipsy Wolverine, she'd often crashed in a different location each time, but here... For some reason she was mostly comfortable here. *Mostly.*

It was the bartender, she knew. He didn't say much, didn't thump his chest like an ape—because he didn't have to. His commanding presence let everyone know that he was the one in charge.

She knew it. In that bar, no one could hurt her because he wouldn't let them.

Sterling shook her head. It was a crazy conclusion, but she trusted her instincts. So far, they'd served her well.

Grabbing her discarded jacket, she climbed out of the truck. Higher in the mountains, the chill could seep into her bones, but here in the valley, it had to be in the midnineties. The temperature in Colorado was all about elevation. The higher you went, the colder it got. She'd learned that her button-up shirt would be fine in the valley, but if the road climbed—and it sometimes did—she needed warmer clothes. The air-conditioning in the bar often chilled her, too, especially when she napped.

Her long sloppy ponytail bounced and her heavy boots crunched on gravel when she strode across the lot. Some strange sensation sizzled inside her.

She refused to acknowledge it as anticipation.

The minute she walked through the door, she knew something was different. Two men, regulars that she recognized, sat at her customary table. That hadn't happened since her third visit months ago. The table was usually saved for her. Without pausing, she continued into the dim room, giving a casual glance around.

No, it wasn't extra crowded.

Yes, there were other tables available.

So why, then…

The bartender stepped in front of her, his nearly six and a half feet of muscle drawing her to a sudden stop. "Could I have a word?"

Almost plowing into him sent her heart shooting into her throat. She was tall enough that few men made her feel small, but this one towered over her.

Damn it, she hadn't even noticed him approach before he was just…there, standing too close, crowding her with his size and strength. In a nanosecond, her body jolted into defense mode.

She hid her unease even as she considered her options of fight or flight.

And damn him, he *knew* it. She saw it in the way his gaze sharpened, how his mouth softened.

In sympathy?

Screw that. Sterling took a step back, ready to retreat. Not like fighting was an actual option.

Raising his hands, his expression impassive, he said, "At the bar would be fine, if you have just a minute. I'm still on the clock."

Her gaze skipped to her table, and seconds ago she'd anticipated resting her bones in that well-worn seat. Now some of her exhaustion had lifted.

"I can move them if you want me to," he offered quietly. "After I've explained."

She had no interest in conversing with him, being drawn to him in any way. Familiarity worried her, yet curiosity won out. To cover her caution, she offered a casual shrug and indicated he should lead the way.

No way did she want him at her back.

He gifted her with that brief smile again.

Such a nice mouth, she couldn't help noticing. Not that she cared. Nice or not, she refused involvement.

He turned and headed for the bar.

Drawing in a bracing breath, she followed. Nice back, too. And forearms. And his backside in those jeans…

Sterling frowned at herself and vowed none of it mattered.

No one else sat at the far end of the scarred, polished wood counter, and once she'd taken the last stool, he circled around.

"Coffee? Cola?"

"Coke is fine."

"I can throw you together a sandwich if you want."

In most cases, she refused food when offered to her, but here, from him, it seemed okay—especially with her stomach grumbling. "Sure, thanks."

He went through a half door that led to the kitchen behind the bar and returned a minute later with a ham-and-cheese sandwich and chips. After setting the food before her, he filled a glass with ice and poured her a Coke.

Sterling realized he must have coordinated this little meet and greet, because one of his workers took over filling orders without being asked.

Obviously he was up to something—but what?

Watching her a little too closely, he leaned a hip against the bar. "You don't miss much, do you?"

Her gaze shot to his. She had a mouthful and had to chew and swallow before she could answer. "Should I?"

"No, but few people are as aware as you are." He opened his own cola, drinking straight from the bottle. "My name is Cade McKenzie, by the way."

"I didn't ask."

"I know. But I thought if you knew more about me, you'd—"

"What?" Panic, maybe anger, sharpened her tone. "Loosen up? Like you more? Get friendly?"

"Stop distrusting me."

Had her wariness been so noticeable? Apparently. "I'm eating your sandwich. What is that if not trust?"

Her reasoning made him grin, showing straight white teeth, and good God, when he did that, he was too damn gorgeous. The amusement softened his granite edge, made him feel approachable.

And damn it, it sparked something deep inside her.

She concentrated on her sandwich.

"My brother owns a gym in town," he continued. "You've probably noticed him in here a few times."

Of course she had. The family resemblance was unmistakable. "He's younger, different-colored eyes."

Nodding at this additional sign of her awareness, he explained, "Different mothers, but we were raised together. I have a sister, too. She's the baby at twenty-six."

"Does she look like you, as well?" She hadn't seen any women at the bar that she'd have pegged as a relation.

"Similar features, only more feminine. Same-colored eyes as my brother, but her hair is lighter than ours."

It struck Sterling that she was chatting. Casually, easily. When had she last done that? The shock of it put her on edge. "I didn't ask for a family rundown."

"I know. Other than your usual table and an occasional drink, all you ask for is to be left alone."

"Yet here we are." Not that she could entirely blame him for that. She'd chosen to accept the food, the conversation. Nothing would come of it, though. Not more familiarity. Not friendship.

Definitely nothing beyond that.

He leveled that electric-blue stare on her. "I wanted to show you that I have roots here, that I'm not a threat in any way."

Refusing to lower her guard, she asked, "But *why*?" She didn't trust goodwill. A motive generally followed close behind.

"Because you're a good customer, a regular, and I get that

you want your space—no problem with that—but I thought I could help."

Slowly, she ate another bite of the sandwich while considering him. The urge to walk away was strong.

Oddly enough, an equally compelling urge had her asking, "Help how?" Then she thought to add, "With *what*?"

He propped his elbows on the bar, leaning toward her as he eased into his topic. "So your table… I can keep it open for you if that's what you want. That isn't a problem. But since you usually catch a nap, I wanted to offer my office."

One of the chips caught in her throat, making her cough.

Thankfully, he didn't reach around to pat her on the back. He seemed to know touching her would be a very bad move.

Instead, he nudged her glass toward her.

It took three gulps before she could catch her breath. Then she gasped, "Your office?"

A big old *no* to that. Not in a million years.

"It locks from the inside, so you wouldn't have to worry about customers stumbling in on you."

Would she have to worry about him?

"I have a key," he said, using his uncanny mind-reading superpower. "But you could hold on to it while you're in there."

The offer so surprised her that she couldn't find the right words to refuse him. She settled on shaking her head. "No thanks." She preferred to be out in the open. Not that the public option always equaled safety—she'd learned that the hard way. But at least this space was familiar to her. She'd memorized it in detail and knew the exits, the number of tables to the door, that the big front window was tempered glass and that Cade McKenzie kept a few weapons behind the bar—but generally wouldn't need them to restore order if it came to that.

That line of thinking took her attention to his hands. Big hands. Hands that would feel like sledgehammers if he made a fist.

No, he didn't need a weapon. He *was* a weapon.

Not deterred by her refusal, he continued explaining. "I only use the office before we open and after we close. Besides my desk and chair, there's a love seat, a few throw pillows. A private landline." His gaze searched hers. "You'd be more comfortable."

Suddenly, it struck Sterling as funny. Here they were, tiptoeing around the obvious: she *knew* he wasn't just a bartender. And somehow he *knew* she wasn't just a trucker.

Grinning, she sat back and studied him.

"That's nice," he said.

Taken off guard, she asked, "What?"

"Your smile."

Stymied by that, it took her a second to regroup. "Look, I haven't even given you my name."

"I'm aware."

"But you know it anyway, don't you?" She expected him to lie, and when he did, she'd have solid reason not to trust him. She'd pay for her food, walk out and drive away—never to return.

Doing his own thorough study, he let his gaze move over her face as if cataloging each feature...and liking what he saw. "I can't go into details, or explain, but yes, I know your name."

Her heart skipped a beat. He'd admitted it! What did that mean for their association? Part of her shivered with alarm, but another part, a part she'd like to deny, suffered the strangest sort of...relief.

If someone actually knew her, then she was no longer alone. She existed. She *mattered*.

Sterling shook her head. Maybe he wasn't as good as she assumed.

Caught between conflicting emotions, she narrowed her eyes. "Fine. Let's hear it."

Straightening, Cade did a quick check to ensure no one listened to them, then casually dropped his research bombshell.

"Sterling Parson, but you used to go by Star. You're twenty-nine, got your commercial driver's license when you were barely twenty-two, worked for Brown Transportation for a while, then bought your own rig when you were twenty-six."

Her jaw literally dropped. Dear God, he knew so much. *Too* much. She'd been right to fear him—no, damn it. *Not* fear. Just good old caution, the same caution she used with everyone. The caution that kept her alive. He wasn't different, wasn't special, and she couldn't—

"My sister," he offered with grave seriousness, interrupting her private castigation. "She's a research whiz, and I was curious."

"About me?"

"About you," he concurred.

No apology, but an explanation? "You had no right," she whispered through stiff lips.

For a moment he looked away while using one long, blunt finger to trace a bead of condensation on his cola bottle. "You can call it second nature." He rolled a thick shoulder. "Or instinct." Tension ratcheted up when he looked into her eyes, making them both a little breathless. His voice sounded like a soft growl when he added, "I felt it was important to know."

Dazed, confused and, damn him, disappointed, Sterling shook her head. "Now I have to find a new place to go."

His focus never wavered from hers. "Whatever you're up to, Star, you'll be safer here. Give yourself a minute to think before you react, and you'll admit it."

"What?" she asked with a sneer. "You don't know what I'm doing? You don't know why? How…incomplete of you."

"I tried not to overstep too much."

That made her laugh, but not with any humor.

"You're drawing attention when I assume you'd rather not. No," he said when alarm stiffened her neck, "not from anyone dangerous. Actually, all the customers have been curious about you at one time or another. I don't think any of us have ever heard you laugh."

"You can't know who's dangerous and who isn't." More than most, she'd learned that it was sometimes impossible to tell.

Softly, he insisted, "Yes, I can. I know everyone who comes here. You can trust me on that."

She snorted. She wouldn't trust anyone ever again.

"Right now there are only locals, a few truckers and a few vacationers, but it's still better not to be noticed, right? In case anyone comes around asking questions?"

Regret froze her to the spot, leaving her a little sick to her stomach, full of angst. And yearning.

God, she had so much yearning.

This bar had begun to feel like…home? How absurd. It wasn't in any way special, and it wasn't even in a good part of town. It was just a place where she could relax, and she hated to lose it.

The location was ideal for her, being only thirty minutes from I-25 with plenty of places to hide in between, and closer still to other venues known for seedier practices.

She didn't want to give it up, but what choice did she have now?

Cade made a small sound of frustration, there and gone. "Your table is empty now," he pointed out.

Yes, she was aware of that. Standing, she pulled out some cash to toss on the counter, but Cade stopped her with a shake of his head.

"This one was on the house. Go get some rest—and think about my offer."

She really didn't feel like leaving yet. Now that she'd eaten, lethargy gripped her. Finally she nodded. "All right, I'll think about it."

"Thanks, Star. I appreciate it."

"As you pointed out, I *used* to go by that name. Now I'm more comfortable with Sterling."

"I don't think you're ever really comfortable, so let's not nit-pick on the name yet."

Teasing again? The man had a dimple. How unfair! He was always so attractive, but now with satisfaction in his gaze and his sexy mouth curved? Devastating.

She didn't understand him. She didn't understand herself with him, either. Rather than let him see her confusion, she headed to the table, ignoring the curious glances from the regulars who knew it was unusual for her to chat up anyone.

Despite her new caution, the feeling of security remained. Within minutes of sitting down, she dozed off.

Cade knew the second she nodded off. She sat facing the rest of the bar, her long legs stretched out to the chair opposite her, her arms folded over her chest. Uncaring what anyone thought, she slumped in the seat, more reclining than otherwise, let her head rest back against the wall and closed her eyes. Long lashes sent feathery shadows over her cheekbones.

He admired her nose, narrow with the slightest arch in the bridge; he considered it perfect for her face. Not too cute, not too big or small. Like her attitude, each feature of her face and body was unique.

Her breathing deepened and slowed, but she didn't snore. Didn't go completely lax, either. Hell, he doubted she ever did.

So much churning wariness probably kept her constantly on edge. He knew it affected him that way. He rarely slept soundly, but then, he didn't need much sleep.

With any luck, she'd doze right up until closing time at midnight. Since being a bartender wasn't really his vocation, he didn't keep usual hours for the bar. Most in the area were open until 2:00 a.m., but he shut down at midnight and didn't open again until 4:00 p.m. That gave him plenty of time for other pursuits, and when the two overlapped, he had reliable staff to cover for him at the bar.

They were only an hour from closing when two strangers entered. The frisson of awareness that settled in his gut told him they were about to have problems.

Instinctively, his gaze shifted to Star.

He found her sitting upright, alert, her eyes narrowed dangerously. Well, hell.

He'd never known a woman so acutely aware of her surroundings. In that, she matched him.

Didn't mean he wanted her getting elbow deep in danger, especially not when that danger just walked into his bar.

Subtly, he drifted his gaze between her and the men—hoping she'd ignore them, that she'd go back to sleep.

Should have known better.

While he watched in frustration, she pulled the tie from her hair and let it tumble down over one shoulder.

Fuck me sideways.

He'd always known the difference a woman's hair could make to her appearance. But on Star? This softer look had a near-physical impact on him. The woman had gorgeous hair. Longer than he'd realized, and a rich brown streaked with gold by the sun. He watched as she tunneled her fingers in close to her scalp and fluffed it.

He would have liked to do that for her. Hands curled loosely, he could almost feel that silky mass.

When her slender fingers flicked open three buttons on her shirt, he locked his jaw—not that she noticed. Keeping her focus on the newcomers, she parted the shirt until a fair amount of cleavage showed, then tied the shirttails at her waist.

It took her less than thirty seconds to go from plain and reserved to a total bombshell. The "hands off" signals were gone, and instead her demeanor screamed "up for grabs."

Why? What the hell was she planning?

When she stood, he cursed silently, reading her intent.

She didn't spare him a glance. No, she'd forgotten all about him, and that nettled, because she'd been his first thought when he saw the two men.

The second she stood, she caught their attention. Wearing a flirty smile, she sauntered toward them.

Cade seriously wanted to demolish them both simply for the way they looked at her.

When she reached the bigger of the two men, she asked, "Got a cigarette?"

The guy sized her up in an insultingly thorough way, then pulled the pack from his front T-shirt pocket, shook one loose and offered it to her.

Maintaining eye contact, she leaned down and slowly slipped a cigarette free.

Both men looked down her shirt.

The second guy asked, "Light?"

"I have my own outside, but thank you." She sashayed out the door, and it wasn't just the two new guys watching her. Every man in the place had his fascinated gaze glued to her ass.

Shit. Cade quickly, but casually, directed others to cover the bar. Pretending he needed a break, he went down the hall and into the private office he'd offered for her use. After relocking the door, he went to the single window in the room, opened it and hoisted himself up and out. It was an awkward fit for a man his size, but he'd practiced before, ensuring he had multiple exits if it ever became necessary.

He considered watching Star's back very necessary.

Circling around the bar on silent feet, he listened. Her boots crunched on the gravel, guiding him. She didn't go to her rig, but then, maybe she didn't want them to know which truck was hers.

Smart—except that they could ask anyone in the bar about her, and that would be one of the first things they learned.

Cade leaned around the corner, still hidden by shadows but

able to see her. She hadn't lit the cigarette, but she kept it dangling between her lips.

What are you up to?

She glanced several times at the entrance, and when the doors finally opened, she made a show of frustration.

The one who'd offered a light smiled. "Couldn't find your lighter after all?"

She shook her head, sending that wealth of thick hair to move around her breasts. Wearing a sexy pout, she asked, "Did you bring one out with you?"

He produced the lighter, then teased her with, "Say please."

Taking the cigarette from her lips, she gave him a tight smile. "Really? Because there are twenty men inside who would be glad to give me a light—without stipulations."

"Seems to me you don't like them, or you'd have gone to them for the cigarette."

Her lips curled. "You think you know what I like?"

"I know you'd like more than a smoke."

At that, she laughed, a rich, husky sound that set Cade's teeth on edge. She played a dangerous game, and he hoped like hell she didn't push too hard.

"Maybe you're right." The finger she stroked along her cleavage drew the man's heated stare. "What's your name?"

"You can call me Smith."

She laughed. "Well, Smith, how much are you willing to give?"

Not for a second did Cade believe she meant to sell herself. No, she had a bigger game in mind, and it made him scared for her.

Cade knew Smith—*what a crock*—because he and his brother had kept tabs on the man for more than a month. They knew Smith was involved in plenty of shady deals, but he was just muscle, not brains. Someone else called the shots. Someone with more power.

Cade wanted them all.

With her impetuous rush to get involved, Star jeopardized his well-made plans. Never mind that she didn't know he had plans...

"Tell you what." The guy reached to a back pocket and pulled out his wallet.

Finally, she looked a little nervous, but still, she didn't back down. Honest to God, she raised her chin.

Luckily—because Cade didn't want to blow his cover—the guy offered a card instead of cash. "You want to make a big score, come by Misfits tomorrow night. I have a buddy in need of cheering up and you'd be just the ticket."

Restoring that cocky attitude, she glanced at the card, then shoved it into her own pocket. "What time?"

"Ah, so you don't mind the idea of being his...entertainment?"

She shrugged but asked, "Is he a total pig?"

"Most of the women don't complain."

Most of the women don't complain. Meaning some did...but it didn't matter? When Smith's friend finished with them, were they even able to complain?

Breathing slow and deep kept Cade from reacting. Somehow he'd ensure Star's safety, and eventually he'd bury Smith.

For a split second, she went blank—fear? anger?—before curling her mouth in another credible smile. "I take it you've given him other *gifts*?"

"He's partial to those with long legs and big tits."

With every beat of his heart, Cade wanted her away from the bastard, but he didn't intrude. Not yet.

Toying with a long curl, Star pretended the crude language and dark insinuation didn't bother her. "How much are we talking?"

Taken by surprise, Smith reached out, wrapping his fingers in her hair. "Enough, okay? Don't push me. Just be there at nine."

She didn't flinch, didn't show any pain and didn't back down. She actually moved closer to Smith. Too damn close. "Oh, I'll be there. And I'll expect you to make it worth my while."

He leaned forward, clearly intending to kiss her, and suddenly she freed herself—minus a few dozen strands of hair. "You pay first, sugar. I don't give out freebies." Before Smith could figure out what to do, she walked away.

To her credit, she went back into the bar and relative safety. But how safe would she be when she left?

Keeping an eye on the door she went through, Smith dug out his cell phone and pressed in a number. The light from the screen emphasized his twisted smile. "Hey," Smith said, when the call was answered. "Prep the back room, okay? I have a new one coming out tomorrow." He laughed. "Yeah, you'll like her. She fits your preferences to a tee." He listened, shook his head. "No, I'm sure she's not, but I'll follow her tonight just to be safe. One thing, and it's nonnegotiable." He waited, then said, "Once you're done with her, I'm next in line."

CHAPTER TWO

Sterling didn't see Cade when she walked back in, and it left her even more rattled. He made her feel safer, and right now, with her skin crawling and her heart jumping, she needed that. Whether it made sense or not, whether he wanted to protect her or not, she wanted him near.

Ignoring all the interested stares, chin up, eyes straight ahead, she went to her table. Belatedly, she remembered the stupid cigarette in her hand.

She never had gotten that light.

Just as well. She'd never smoked and would probably have choked on the thing.

Suddenly Cade was there, brushing past her, making physical contact for a single heartbeat before he went back to the bar.

The touch shook her, and settled her. How the hell was that possible?

Sterling watched him, but then caught herself and looked away. Trying to appear casual, she pulled out her phone and pretended to check messages, just to give herself something to do. Her hands shook, but hopefully no one noticed. She worked up a smile just in case.

The two men hung around, making no bones about watching her. So…now what? If she'd thought ahead, she'd have realized she needed an exit plan. But no, she'd seen them and, knowing what they were, simply reacted. The desire to destroy them had encompassed her.

Uber. That's what she'd do. And her truck?

Damn.

Cade slid another drink in front of her. So low she barely heard him, he said, "My brother is picking you up. Dark gray newer-model Ram truck. I'll take care of your rig. Leave the keys on your chair when you're ready to go."

Sterling blinked at him, but he'd already turned away. Aware of the two goons keeping her in their sights, she caught herself. Smiling like she didn't have a care, she backed up her ruse of a fun-loving girl without caution and tossed back the drink.

Because of her life choices, choices that often put her in dive bars, she'd learned to hold her liquor. This time she didn't have to. Cade must have anticipated her cooperation because he'd watered down the shot.

Just how well did he know her?

And how the hell did he plan to take care of her truck?

So far he'd made a lot of assumptions, including that she'd accept a ride from his brother. She should refuse, but… Her gaze strayed to the scumbags watching her. Yeah, they'd be a problem.

How was Cade's plan any worse than taking a ride from a stranger in an Uber?

Keeping the frown off her face wasn't easy, not while being in such a pickle, but she'd thought fast on her feet before.

Okay, so he had a decent plan. Long as his brother didn't try anything funny, it could work.

Another glance at Cade and she saw him texting on his phone. When he finished, he murmured something to his em-

ployee—a medium-height, wiry fellow he referred to as Rob—
and then went into the kitchen area.

Because she felt safe doing so, Sterling looked at Rob again.
On her first visit she'd noticed his eyes. They were as black
as Satan's, but somehow still kind. Or maybe, considering the
overpowering presence of Cade, Rob's gaze only seemed kind
in comparison.

When he announced the last call, she realized it was nearly
midnight. Within the next few minutes, the bar began to clear.
Even the two goons headed out. Or pretended to. She didn't
trust them not to hang around outside in the hopes of catching her alone.

Cade reappeared under the guise of picking up her empty
shot glass. "My brother is out front. Go straight to his truck,
even if Smith tries to talk to you."

In the same easy tone he'd used, she replied, "Who put you
in charge? Just so we're clear, you're not my boss."

That gave him pause. Clearly he was used to issuing orders
and having them followed!

"Star—"

She ignored the use of her old name—for now. In some ways,
it was even nice to hear. Familiar from a lifetime ago, before
her whole world had upended. "I've survived on my own since
I was seventeen. I'm not an idiot, either. So I accept the help—
but if your brother tries anything, I'll kill him."

Another hesitation, and then Cade nodded. "Fair enough."

He wouldn't argue in his brother's defense? What insanity was
that? Or maybe he didn't consider her a serious threat, which
meant he didn't know her that well after all.

Less than reassured, Sterling asked, "You're sure my truck
will be safe?"

"Guaranteed. We shouldn't talk too long, though, so tell my
brother when and where you want it, and we'll get it there."

Her brows went up. "Just like that?"

Instead of explaining how he'd accomplish it, he said, "You started this. Do you have a better option?"

Sadly, no, she didn't. Standing, she scooped up her jacket—leaving her keys on the seat as he'd requested—and then pushed in her chair. "I suppose I should thank you?"

His eyes narrowed. "Not necessary. But you might consider that trust we discussed earlier."

Before she could reply, he walked away.

It was with a lot of trepidation and heightened awareness that Sterling exited the bar. Bright security lights lit the front but left murky shadows in the surrounding area. Immediately she spotted his brother. He didn't leave the driver's seat, but he did lean over and push open the passenger door.

With every crunch of her boots on the gravel, she felt eyes on her. She didn't see the goons, but she didn't doubt they were there somewhere, watching her and speculating.

Pasting on a false smile, she waved to Cade's brother as if happy to see him. She wished she at least knew his name, but Cade hadn't seen fit to tell her.

From seeing him before in the bar, she already knew his brother was a good-looking guy—not quite as tall as Cade, but close, and his body was every bit as muscular, maybe even a little more ripped. She recalled that he owned a gym and figured he'd gotten that bod as a natural result of working with customers.

"Let's go," he said when Sterling got close, as if she'd been holding him up.

Fine. She didn't want to be a nuisance, but her recklessness was over for the night. She quickly checked the door, ensuring she wouldn't get locked in, before sliding onto the seat.

She barely had the door closed when he said, "Buckle up," and put the truck in gear.

Annoyance brought her teeth together. Did he have to be as bossy as his brother? "I was planning to, so save the orders for someone else."

That made him grin. "Touchy, huh? Cade warned me, so no worries. Where we headed?"

Cade had warned him? "I'm not *touchy*, it's just—"

"Yeah, yeah. I insulted your independence. Don't chew it to death." He glanced in the rearview mirror, then back to the road. "Your place? If so, I'm going to take the long way around to lose our tail. Cool?"

Startled, she asked, "We have a tail?"

"Yeah—don't look! Damn." He scowled in annoyance. "Cade said you could handle yourself, so don't act like a rookie, 'kay?"

How infuriating! Slumping back in her seat, she snapped, "I *can* handle myself—you just caught me by surprise, that's all."

He snorted. "Sounds like a lot of shit caught you by surprise tonight. Hang on." He took a sharp turn, then accelerated until she had no choice but to grab the door handle with one hand, the dash with the other.

These were not straight, flat roads.

Even though he'd explained why, it alarmed her that he was speeding away from where she needed to go. "Look, you can drop me off at the mall—"

"Not a chance. Cade would have my head." His gaze ran over her, then returned to the road. "For whatever reason, he's decided to focus on you."

Now, that felt incredibly insulting! His "For whatever reason" made it clear he didn't see the draw.

But damn it, she was *not* going to be offended over it. She didn't want either of them to find her attractive. She really didn't.

Through her teeth, she said, "He can just un-focus."

"Yeah, right." With a snort, he replied, "Try telling him that, because he sure as hell never listens to me."

It seemed Cade had coerced his brother into this impromptu rescue, and he clearly didn't like it any more than she did. "Damn right, I'll tell him."

Judging by his grin, he found that amusing. "Yeah, you do that. Can't wait to hear how it goes. But tonight I'm dropping you at your front door—after I lose them."

She grew more irritated by the second. "If you think I'll tell you where I live—"

"You don't need to. Now shush a sec while I concentrate on driving."

Shush? *Shush!* The urge to blast him bubbled up, but she still didn't see anyone following them, and actually, a tingle of new alarm climbed her spine. What if he was just a good liar using a story to get her out of town?

She'd gut him, that's what.

Slowly, she reached for her ankle and the knife she kept strapped there, but no sooner did her fingers touch the hilt than headlights appeared behind them.

"Determined SOBs, aren't they?" He searched the road ahead of them, then the rearview mirror again. "If you want to get out of this, I'd suggest you not stab me."

Guilty heat flushed her face.

Especially when he added, "Not that I'd let you."

"You—"

In a long-suffering voice, he said, "The mall it is."

Now that she knew the threat was real, Sterling didn't much like that idea. She'd be a sitting duck until she could find a ride. Sure, she was good at hiding, but it was past midnight, the air had cooled, and at this hour the mall was deserted. How hard would it be for the goons to find her—and then what?

Except that Cade's brother pulled in to a small, recently completed outlet mall instead of the larger mall she'd referred to. Turning off his headlights, he quietly rolled away from the security lights, circled around the back and stopped, facing the main road.

So he wasn't dropping her off after all, just lying low for a few. She could handle that.

"Where do you want your truck?" he asked casually, as if they weren't hiding from danger. He half turned to face her. "I disabled the interior lights, but I can't use my phone yet. We don't want to tip our hand, right? But as soon as it's clear, I'll let Cade know. No reason he should have to stay out any later than necessary."

His ease afforded her some of her own. Getting comfortable in the corner of the door and the seat, as far from him as possible, Sterling considered him. "Cade knows how to drive a rig?"

"Big brother knows how to do a great many things. Ask him to jump out of a plane? No problem. Run five miles without breaking a sweat? Piece of cake. Swim underwater—"

"Do I detect some hero worship?"

"Hell yeah. Big-time." He turned back to the road, listened a second, then nodded in satisfaction. "There they go."

A car sped past them at an impossible speed, given the winding mountain roads. Subtly, Sterling let out a relieved breath. "We can head out now."

"We'll give it another thirty seconds. We don't want them to notice us, but neither do we want them to double back and find us, right?" He smiled at her. "Timing is everything."

Cade's brother was a little too cocky for her taste. She started to tell him so, but then he put the truck in gear and gradually moved forward again until he was at the edge of the road. From either direction, all they could see were streetlamps, but no traffic.

"So," he said, once they were on their way again, this time headed toward where she lived. "You and Cade?"

Denial rushed forward and she shook her head. "No." There wasn't a scenario of her with…anyone. Never had been and never would be.

"No?"

Did he have to sound so disbelieving? "I frequent his bar, that's it."

"Uh-huh. Cade overreacted because those were just Good Samaritans hoping to find you alone on a mountain road. Got it." He drove more leisurely now. "So where do you want your truck?"

This time the question didn't take her by surprise. "I have an office."

"Makes sense." He handed over his phone. "You can text Cade so I can keep my hands on the wheel."

He'd handed her his phone? For a few seconds there, she just stared at it with the same fascination she'd give a snake. But this could be her opportunity to learn more about Cade McKenzie. Past messages with his brother could tell her a lot.

Unfortunately, when she got around to looking at the phone, all she saw was one message: Pick her up out front.

She scrolled, but that was it. Nothing else. No other numbers in the phone, no other communication, at least none readily available. If she could dig around a little…

Glancing at Cade's brother disabused her of that notion. The jerk was grinning again.

Giving up, she texted, Take the rig to her office, and she put in the address. But her curiosity didn't wane, so she asked, "What is this exactly? Some supersecret cell phone communication?"

"Sure, let's call it that. It makes us sound cool, right?"

His good humor wore on her—then the phone dinged and she looked down to see a reply from Cade. Is she behaving?

Of all the… Without alerting Cade's brother, Sterling texted back, No. She kicked my ass n took over. Bitch is hard-core. Pretty sure she never needed our help.

To which Cade replied, Star? That you?

Damn it, her lips twitched. She curled a little more in her seat, the phone held close, and almost forgot about his insufferable brother humming beside her. Yeah, it's me. How'd you know?

Brother would never call u a bitch.

So the goofball driving had some redeeming qualities? Good to know.

She tried to figure out what to say next.

Cade beat her to it. You okay?

She wasn't but wouldn't admit it to anyone but herself. Yup, NP. That is, no problems other than his brother, but she saw no reason to go into that. It'd only make her sound petty. My truck?

Getting it there now. Be safe tonight.

Did he have to treat her like a teenager? She knew how to take care of herself, and seriously, she would have been fine on her own.

Somehow.

Narrowing her eyes, Sterling texted, You 2. She waited, hoping that might offend him, but he didn't reply back.

She refused to acknowledge the disappointment she felt. After a few more seconds, she handed the phone back to his brother. "Do you have a name?"

"Course I do. It's on my birth certificate, all legal-like."

Such a frustrating man! "Care to share it?"

"No can do. After tonight, I hope to never see you again. In fact, tonight shouldn't have happened. Cade knows better." His gaze slanted her way. "You sure you two aren't boning?"

Good God, he was so ridiculous; it almost softened her mood. Instead of smiling, she dryly replied, "Pretty sure I would have noticed if we were."

"Ha!" He had no problem grinning. "See, you're getting the hang of it now."

"Meaning?"

"All that turbulent animosity is a waste of good energy. You were over there crackling with hatred, on the edge of imploding, when snarky comebacks are easier, and more effective anyway."

"Effective?" Getting used to him and his odd insults, Sterling let her spine relax against the seat back and stretched out her legs. "When you're just laughing at me?"

"Not *at* you," he denied. "Jesus. *With* you. Lighten up, already."

"One thing—I wasn't *crackling with hatred*." What a stupid way to put it.

"Then what?"

"Confusion? You haven't exactly been forthcoming, and I'm not sure what's going on."

"I'm rescuing you, that's what—but only because Cade asked me to."

"And I can't know your name because it's top secret?"

"Exactly. Consider me an enigma." He bobbed his eyebrows. "You intrigue me, though, because Cade is a hard nut to crack."

"So he wouldn't normally have offered his help?" Did that mean he considered her special—or was she in more trouble than he could ignore? Not a good thought.

"He would have helped you without you ever knowing. That he made it personal is downright fascinating."

Yeah, she had to admit, she found it rather fascinating, too. "Will my truck truly be there when I check in the morning?"

"Yup. It'll probably be there in another twenty minutes, but I hope you'll pack away some of that prickly pride and go inside for the night. Lock everything up nice and tight and don't go anywhere alone for a while."

She'd already planned to stay in for the night, but she wouldn't share that with him. Enigmas didn't deserve full disclosure.

"Ah, you've clammed up again? I get it. I wouldn't like someone saving my ass, either."

She rolled her eyes. "You haven't saved my ass—"

"Beg to differ."

"But with every word out of your mouth, my curiosity expands. So tell me, what makes you think I'll still be in danger even after I'm home?"

"You kidding? For Cade to get involved, I'm sure it was life and death, right? Dude is usually so cool. And that means, despite my excellent driving, someone could figure out where you live."

Her place was secure, so she wasn't worried about that. "Cade is cool, but you're not?"

"I'm learning." He shrugged. "See, I used to be a hothead, but big brother has a way of tamping that shit down, ya know?"

He made it sound like he'd been a hothead in younger days, but then Cade showed up and gave him a guiding hand. Did that mean Cade hadn't always been around?

"Now, don't start speculating," he warned. "My lips are sealed."

"Is that a joke? Your lips haven't stop flapping since I got in your truck."

"Flapping? I have several lady friends who would object to that description. *Flapping*," he repeated with a snort.

Extreme exasperation had her huffing. "Might be a good idea for you to work on that sarcasm next?"

"Was I sarcastic?" He was on the verge of laughing as he turned down her street. "Guess your chipper personality just brings it out of me."

"You don't have to sound so cheerful about it."

He barely managed to bank his grin. "Look, my point is that anything you want to know about Cade you'll have to get from him, not that he'll tell you anything."

"Except that he's a bartender?"

"See, you've got it." He pulled in to her apartment complex. "Is this place protected?"

"It's safe enough." Two could play the closemouthed game. "Don't worry your pretty head about it."

Showing no reaction to the insult, he said, "Wasn't planning to." He forestalled her getting out of the truck by adding, "Here. Cade said to give you this." Opening the glove box, he pulled out a cell phone.

She didn't take it. "Have one, but thanks anyway."

"Yeah, sure, I figured that. But this one has his number already programmed in."

It could also have a tracker or something on it. She forced a snarky smile. "If I took that, I'd just ditch it."

Nonplussed, he stared at her, followed by a laugh. "You're something else—let's not speculate on what. Okay then, how about this." Pulling a small notepad and pen from the center console, he jotted down a number. "Now you have it, but it's just paper, right?" He held it up, flipping it back and forth. "Not a threat. Does that work?"

"Why not?" Quickly pocketing it, she slid out of the car. "Thanks for the ride."

"You sure you don't want me to walk you up?"

"Positive."

"Suit yourself, but I'm waiting right here until I see your kitchen light come on."

Sterling spun around to frown at him. How did he know the kitchen window was the only one facing this lot?

Still being a goof, he wiggled his fingers in the air and said, "Woo-ooo, we enigmas are so mysterious."

And damn it, there was no way she could hold in her chuckle.

Course, the humor ended the minute she entered the apartment building. She liked the place because it was spacious and open, without a lot of nooks or corners for anyone to lurk. Still, it was a nice feeling to know Cade's brother was there, waiting to ensure no one bothered her.

Keys already in her hand, she went up the carpeted stairs to the second floor and unlocked her door. Soon as she stepped inside, she pulled the knife from her boot and locked up again, not just the doorknob lock but also the dead bolt she'd installed.

Crossing the living room, she checked inside the closet, then strode through the kitchen and dining area to the bathroom, where she peeked inside, even glancing into the bathroom cabinet and the glass-enclosed shower, then into the bedroom. This was the only room where someone could adequately hide, so she looked first under the bed—easy enough because she didn't use a bed skirt. The closet here was bigger with more clothes, so she took a few seconds to move them around before heading back to the dining room to check the patio door, which was thankfully still locked, the additional bar in place.

Stepping into the kitchen, she couldn't resist peering out the window to where she saw Cade's brother leaning against the front fender of his truck, arms folded, staring up at her window.

Damn it, she smiled...and stepped back to flip on the light. Seconds later he drove away.

Huh. Actual, bona fide protection courtesy of Cade and his crazy-ass brother. She couldn't trust it—no really, she couldn't.

Enigma? He had that right. There was far too much she didn't know about Cade, and that made his concern suspect.

But...it didn't feel suspect. It felt genuine.

Blast it all, it felt *good*.

Cade waited as long as he could, then called his brother. Soon as Reyes answered, he asked, "She's settled?"

"Far as I can tell," Reyes said, and then, "What the hell have you gotten yourself into?"

"It's complicated."

"If you mean the lady, no, she's not. In fact, I thought she was pretty clear. She means to demolish someone and doesn't want our help."

True enough—with one problem. "She zeroed in on Thacker, who told her his name was Smith."

A long pause preceded Reyes's explosive *"No fucking way."*

"'Fraid so." It enraged Cade. "From what I could pick up, she's meeting him tomorrow."

"She's to be the entertainment?"

Base entertainment was the only use Thacker and his ilk had for women. "That's what it sounded like."

"You realize your girlfriend is going to fuck up a month's worth of work."

"Not my girlfriend," Cade corrected. "But yeah. Somehow we need to escalate things."

"Dad is going to blow a gasket."

"I'm aware." Cade resented that his father still tried to pull all the strings, as if they were mere puppets. "He'll get over it."

Laughing, Reyes accused, "You're not going to tell him, are you?"

"I'll tell him—a few hours before it all goes down."

With a low whistle, Reyes let him know what he thought of that plan. "And Madison? You plan to clue her in?"

Their sister, the home base of their surveillance, was absolutely necessary. "Yeah, I'll talk to her in the morning. Go get some rest. Tomorrow is going to be—"

"An unadulterated clusterfuck."

"You don't have to sound so cheerful about it."

Reyes laughed. "Funny—your girlfriend told me the same thing. Later, bro."

Girlfriend, Cade thought with a shake of his head. As if he had room in his life for anything that frivolous.

CHAPTER THREE

Hell of a position to be in, on the outside looking in, but Cade knew he had no one but himself to blame. As predicted, his father went quietly ballistic, but there was nothing new in that, at least whenever he dealt with Cade.

Reyes, of course, treated the whole thing like a lark. And his no-nonsense sister was as pragmatic as ever. For her, this was business as usual.

None of that made it easier for him to accept that Star mingled with human traffickers while he waited in the most disreputable of their vehicles, an aging, rusted white van with darkly tinted windows.

He'd parked across the street from the property in a run-down business district. Part bar, part hookup, a 100-percent members-only establishment, Misfits was, as they'd learned through meticulous research, a place for acquiring women and girls—against their will.

If Cade had his way, he'd go in, rip apart every bastard involved, then demolish the building so nothing was left but the blood of the abusers…and maybe a little dust. Unfortunately, he'd gotten voted down on that solution. He understood why, but that didn't make it any easier to bear.

Using binoculars, he watched through the front window of the squat brick building as Star was shown in. Currently the atmosphere inside the bar was all about music and dancing, but two burly guards stood just outside the door.

Not to keep people from entering, but to ensure no one left without permission.

The original plan had been to keep tabs until they could nail the one in charge, but Star's involvement changed that.

For as long as he lived, Cade would remember the horror on the faces of the five women they'd already rescued from Misfits. Kept in the back of an airless truck, ages varying from seventeen to thirty-three, they'd been to hell and back before his sister had ferreted out the transfer and they'd arranged to intercept en route.

Because they worked with anonymity, he and Reyes had merely pulverized the drivers—instead of killing them—and then left them for local authorities to pick up after a hot tip.

They'd ensured the freedom of the traumatized women. His sister had followed updates about them and knew three of them had returned to family, one moved far away and another was in the women's shelter his father funded.

He had to believe they'd recover, but still they visited him in his nightmares.

If only he could find a way to shut down these fucking enterprises *before* they abused anyone. His father, who ran the operation, had no qualms about them using deadly force when absolutely necessary. Anyone who thought to enslave another deserved nothing less than death.

Cade believed that clear down to his soul. When he killed the heartless pricks, he did the world a favor.

Just then, he spotted Star dancing in the middle of several guys. Damn, the lady had nice moves.

Had Star noticed Reyes sitting at a booth? Not much got past her, but Reyes had subterfuge down to a fine art. Without Cade's military training, Reyes could fit in with the coarsest street toughs.

His brother was there as fast backup if it became necessary. With any luck, though, this was a trial of sorts, where they only wanted to see how far they could push Star, instead of imprisoning her tonight.

For once, Cade was glad he'd joined his father's family-based enterprise, though their reasons were different. Cade had resisted as long as he could, to the point that he'd enlisted with the army at eighteen in an effort to put distance between him and his only parent.

Unlike some of the new recruits, he'd taken to basic training, liking the structure enough that he went on to airborne school, and RIP—the Ranger Indoctrination Program—and finally, he'd served with the Seventy-Fifth Ranger Regiment. Military life suited him, and he would have made it his career, but after a lot of deployments carrying heavy weight, along with hard landings from jumping out of planes, his multiple leg issues had forced him into a medical discharge.

That didn't mean his no-fail mentality had changed, or that he didn't stay in top-notch shape. In a pinch, he could even sky jump from another plane.

He just couldn't do it on a regular basis.

Teaming up with the family in their effort to combat human trafficking was the only means he had to continue using his skill set.

Star danced past the front window again. She smiled, but he could already tell she was nervous. Dressed in a black breast-hugging T-shirt with an open gray button-up shirt over that, and skinny jeans that outlined her ass and legs, she looked like a wet dream—at a time when Cade wished she was a little less noticeable. His keen interest moved down her body from her sparkling eyes to her feet—and he grinned when he saw that she wore her shit-kicker boots. He'd bet those clunky things had steel toes, perfect for causing damage.

Sterling Parson had her own unique style, and he liked it. A lot. He liked her attitude. Her perseverance. Her bravery.

All good qualities, but did she also have what it took to weather the upcoming interview?

While he watched, she danced past a booth, stumbled and practically landed in Reyes's lap.

His brother looked surprised, but Star did not. She laughingly said something to him, patted his cheek a little harder than necessary, then danced away with a different guy.

Shit.

Seconds later his phone dinged with a text message. He hated to take his gaze off her, but he already knew it would be from Reyes.

Sure enough, the message read: She said to back off.

Like hell he would. Cade returned: Stay put.

Through the binoculars, he saw Reyes laugh and stow his phone again.

For another hour, things seemed to go okay. She was handed one drink after another, though he couldn't tell whether or not she actually drank any of them. She dodged grabby hands while keeping her grin in place.

When a guard led her off down a hallway, Cade tensed.

Showtime.

They knew the layout of the building, and Cade easily guessed that they were moving her to the back room, where they could privately intimidate her.

Reyes staggered like a drunk, following after them, but he'd be forced to veer off into the john. Closer, but not close enough to shield her.

It took a precious three minutes for Cade to drive around the back, staying far enough away to remain inconspicuous. Another goon guarded the back door, but luckily side-by-side windows gave him an adequate view inside of the room.

Two women were there with her now, one laughing uncontrollably while the other, with a few bruises, looked very shell-shocked. There were also three men: the two guys she'd met at his bar and another hulk of a guy who'd just walked in.

Up to that point Star had stuck to her role of a carefree, unsuspecting party girl, not overcome with giggles like the one girl, and not fatalistic like the other.

Whatever was said just then got her tight-lipped with some strong emotion that resembled part fear, part rage. Cade couldn't tell for sure.

In fact, the only thing he knew for certain was that he had to get her out of there. *Now.*

Sterling hadn't been prepared for the double whammy. First, she was introduced to a woman who'd been clearly abused. She appeared to be in her early twenties, either drunk or doped up, with an underlying fear that kept her breathless with panic.

That smack of reality was bad enough, really driving home her precarious position, locked in with monsters and little hope for escape. It reminded her too much of another time when she'd been locked in a room.

She'd been young and helpless then.

This time, she wasn't.

Knowing the danger and hoping to spare someone else the things she'd suffered, she'd gone into this with eyes wide-open—though admittedly with no solid plan or exit strategy.

On the heels of that first surprise was the second shocker, the one that really did her in.

Mattox Symmes. Twelve years had passed since she'd had to see the cruel sneer on his wet lips. Twelve years since he'd looked at her with those dead brown eyes as if she weren't a flesh-and-blood person.

Twelve years that she'd used to grow stronger, braver, to bury the past and give purpose to her present. She'd never thought to see him again, though she'd often thought of killing him, *dreamed* of killing him.

Still built like a freezer with legs and arms, and just as brutish as she remembered. His shoulders stretched the seams of his dress shirt, his neck too thick for the collar. The receding silver hair made his forehead seem more prominent. His gut was more prominent, too.

And he still looked at her like merchandise. *But*...he didn't seem to recognize her!

Needing to know for sure, she held out a limp hand and summoned up a careless smile. "Hello, there. I'm Francis." She waited for him to correct her, to say he knew the name was a lie.

Instead, he took her hand and smiled. "Now, aren't you a nice present."

Oh. Dear. God. Mattox was the man she was supposed to cheer up?

No. *Hell* no. She couldn't do it.

Entertaining him was not on her agenda. Cutting his throat, yes. Cheering him up, not so much.

She knew she had to come up with a real plan—fast.

The effort to retrieve her hand only got her fingers crushed. He tugged her closer. "Have we met before?"

Her heart lodged in her throat, making her short laugh sound borderline hysterical. "Pretty sure we haven't. I think I would have remembered you."

"Hmm." He continued to study her, his dead eyes appraising. "How long have you been in the area?"

"My whole life." Another lie, since she'd moved here after escaping. When had *he* relocated? Or did he have contacts all over the country? A morbid thought.

Sterling told herself that she'd changed, not just emotionally, but physically, too. At seventeen she'd been skinny, with dyed purple hair, a ring in her lip and an excess of dramatic makeup.

Her rebellious stage, as her drug-addicted mother had called it when she was clearheaded enough to notice what her daughter looked like, which wasn't often.

"I think I would have remembered, as well," Mattox finally said, before towing her over to a chair so he could sit. The chair groaned under his weight. Sprawling out his tree-trunk thighs, he freed her fingers, yet she didn't dare move.

In the locked room, where could she go? The windows behind her were accessible, but too high for her to get through quickly, even if she managed to break one before getting grabbed. Smith and his crony stood there grinning by the door. The bruised girl silently wept while the other couldn't stop snickering over everything. It was almost more than Sterling could take.

Besides, if she tried to move away, he'd react as all predators did, by capturing, subduing. Devouring. He would enjoy her fear. It would probably provide the entertainment he wanted.

"Goddamn," Mattox suddenly complained. "We have one too many in here." He gestured at Smith.

Smith roughly grabbed the laughing woman and put her on the other side of the door, where a guard all but dragged her away. Only then did the woman start to protest.

Her humor wouldn't last. Not for a second did Sterling think they'd let the woman go, and eventually the drugs would wear off. Best chance of her survival? If Sterling managed to kill these three men and whoever else was involved.

As Smith again closed and locked the door, her tension coiled with familiar emotions. The sense of helplessness. The burning hatred.

"Now." Mattox sat back and laced his fingers over his gut. "You two can strip down. Make it quick, because I'm short on time."

The other girl openly sobbed as she hurriedly stripped off her sandals and pants, tripping herself twice and making the men laugh. Fucking pigs. Sterling contemplated kicking Mattox in the nuts—but that would only get her killed.

Did Cade's brother have a plan? Or was he just visiting the bar for his own hookup? He hadn't left when she'd told him to, so did he know this was a location for buying and selling women? He'd seemed sharp, and Cade was most definitely more than a mere bartender.

"Jesus, Adela. Quit that caterwauling," Smith ordered, giving her a shove that sent her into the wall.

Adela. It was the first time Sterling had heard her name. How long had she been here?

Long enough to be scared witless, obviously.

Somehow, someway, she'd get herself and the other girl out of this. Until a genius plan occurred to her, she'd just have to play along. If she could distract them, maybe they'd leave Adela alone.

"So," she said, shrugging the unbuttoned shirt off one shoulder and shimmying so her boobs bounced. "How about I do this slow, like a tease? Would you like that?" It might give her an opportunity to get the knife from her boot. If nothing else, she could straddle Mattox's lap and use her necklace blade to slit his throat.

She'd tucked the necklace inside her T-shirt, but even if he saw it, he wouldn't recognize it as a weapon. It looked like nothing more than a decorative metal medallion on a long chain, but by the push of a small button, the disk opened to reveal a curved, razor-sharp blade that when used correctly would be deadly.

She knew how to use it, and here, in this moment, she wouldn't bat an eye at ending Mattox.

The impatient bastard showed his teeth in an evil smile. "No,

I don't think I want to wait. Take off both tops." He stared into her eyes, the smile vanishing. "Now."

Well, hell. She tried to tease, but a tremor had entered her voice when she said, "Anxious for the goods, huh? Fine by me, but when do I get my money? I was told I'd be paid for this little performance, and I prefer cash up front."

Smith snorted. "Let's wait and see if you're worth it." Softer, he complained, "Adela sure as fuck wasn't, were you, doll?" He reached for the girl, who screamed. Sterling turned, prepared to attack him despite the consequences—and suddenly a chunk of concrete crashed through one of the windows, sending glass everywhere. A second later, the lights went out.

Chaos erupted with Adela shrieking and the men cursing as they lumbered around, but Sterling seized the opportunity. In a practiced move, she swiped the knife from her boot and stabbed toward the chair where Mattox had been sitting.

Her knife sank deep…into chair padding. How the hell had such a big man moved so quickly? Putting herself behind that chair, Sterling listened to the sounds of a vicious fight ensuing, trying to place bodies.

She couldn't see dick and wasn't about to use the flashlight on her phone, knowing that'd only draw attention to her. Hearing Adela's whimpers, she felt her way along the wall until she reached the girl.

Someone hit the floor in front of them, and what sounded like another body crashed into the wall where she'd just been. Whoever did the demolishing did so silently, efficiently.

Oh, she heard the grunts and groans of the men going down, but from the big shadow doing the damage? Not a peep.

Her hand closed around Adela's arm. The door behind her opened to let two more men charge in. Out in the bar, she heard pandemonium break out with panicked shouts and a lot of scrambling bodies, probably in a rush for the exit.

"Come on," Sterling said, dragging Adela with her. It surprised her that the girl didn't fight her, didn't resist in any way, and she'd stopped sobbing. Maybe because escape seemed imminent.

Someone ran into them, almost knocking Sterling over, but she managed to keep her feet. She dragged Adela along until she felt the doorknob for the men's room that she'd noted when they'd led her down the hallway. Inside, the room was dark and foul, but Sterling didn't slow. On the opposite wall, the light of a streetlamp filtered through a grungy window.

"Let's get out of here, okay?" She didn't wait for Adela to answer.

The window was narrow, and it opened out instead of up, but she'd figure it out. She released Adela, then shoved the knife back into her boot to use both hands to force the rusted knob to turn. Knowing they could be found at any moment, her heart thundered and her palms sweat.

"I can't go," Adela whispered.

"What?" The window creaked ominously, like a special effect in a horror movie, opening inch by inch. "It'll be fine. You'll see. I can hoist you up first."

"No, I can't. They'll kill me."

Why did she have to get stubborn now? "They can't kill you when we're gone," Sterling reasoned. "I promise, I'll get you someplace safe."

"Your house?"

What? Since she wasn't about to reveal her own private location, she said, "No. I know another place—"

"I can't risk it." Adela drew a breath. "I should stay. We both should."

Terror did strange things to people, sometimes paralyzing them with the worry of repercussions. Sterling understood that, but she wasn't quite sure how to overcome it.

At least Adela wasn't sobbing anymore. Wasn't hysterical, either.

Someone shouted from the hallway. A flashlight shone from beneath the door.

"We have to go *now*," Sterling whispered, reaching for the vague outline of Adela's body.

The girl backed away. "No. No, I can't."

"At least take this." Sterling fished a card from her pocket and thrust it toward Adela. "It's my number—in case you change your mind." The card had a phone number but nothing else. It wouldn't lead anyone to her, but it could be a link to freedom for a victim.

She'd handed out those cards a dozen times in recent years.

Adela took it, then opened the door and yelled, "I'm here!"

Hating herself for failing, mired in regret that she couldn't help Adela, Sterling turned and, with one boot on the edge of the sink, hoisted herself up and through the partially opened window. She scraped her spine along the edge of the casing, her hip and thigh, too, before kicking and wiggling to land hard on her side on the rough gravel drive. Something cut through her jeans. Her palm cracked on a solid surface, and one of her fingers bent unnaturally.

For a moment, in her crumpled position, her body couldn't assimilate the pain. Then feeling rushed in, and with it a welcoming wave of adrenaline.

Too bad she didn't know where Reyes had gone. She had to admit to herself she wouldn't mind some muscle right about now. Unfortunately, in the dark chaos, she couldn't attempt to find him. She was on her own, so she had to get to it.

Teeth locked, she lumbered to her feet and took off awkwardly, running as fast as she could down an alley, behind two abandoned buildings, through a parking lot and finally to the main thoroughfare. A stitch in her side kept her half doubled over—and then she noticed the blood.

Ignore that for now. Ignore the people gawking, too.

Focused only on escape, Sterling hobbled toward the lot

where she'd parked her car several blocks away from Misfits. She hadn't wanted to risk being followed, but she hadn't planned on leaving battered, either. Despite the expanding pain, she walked a wide path around the car, ensuring no one paid her undue attention, before taking the key from her boot and unlocking the driver's door.

As always, she checked the back seat, saw it remained empty and dropped behind the wheel. She hit the door locks first and then, with shaking hands, started the black Fiesta she drove when she wasn't in her rig.

What had happened with Cade's brother? Was he still in the bar? Was he the one who'd caused the ruckus?

For only a second, she considered circling back to make sure he was okay, but when she raised her hand to the steering wheel and saw her unnaturally bent finger, another slice of pain jolted her. Right now, she couldn't help anyone.

She stepped on the gas and hoped that Cade was there, watching out for his brother.

She had his number at home, and once she recovered, she'd call him. She had so many unanswered questions...

But for now, she only wanted to put distance between her and Misfits. A couple of miles out, she pulled in to a well-lit Walmart parking lot and slowly worked off her loose shirt to tie it around her bleeding thigh. God, with her mangled finger, getting it done really hurt, but even without tightening much, it'd stem some of the bleeding.

By the time she got home, she felt like one giant pulsing bruise. She still used extreme caution in going up to her place, every step a trial of determination.

As usual, the apartment building was quiet and she didn't run into anyone. Severely limping now, she forced herself to keep to her routine, checking the doors, beneath the bed and in the closets, before staggering into the bathroom.

Under the bright fluorescent lights, she freed the shirt from around her thigh and winced. A chunk of glass embedded in her skin left an inch-wide puncture. Seeing the mess she'd already made on the floor, she more or less collapsed into the bathtub.

With a harsh groan, she caught the edge of the protruding glass with blood-slick fingers and, gritting her teeth, slowly pulled it free. Swamped with self-pity, she tossed it toward the garbage can. More blood blossomed on her jeans.

Two slow, deep breaths helped, as did her lame pep talk. *You're okay. Everything will heal.*

For now, you're safe.

She needed to clean the wound or she'd be facing bigger problems, like infection or even blood poisoning. There was no one to do it for her, hadn't been anyone for too many years to count—if ever.

Stripping off her clothes caused more than a few guttural groans, as well as a light sheen of sweat. Her lace-up boots and tight jeans especially proved difficult. Stupid skinny jeans. She hadn't been skinny in a very long time, and it took a major incentive to get her to wear anything that uncomfortable.

Killing a human trafficker topped her list, but still...

It took every ounce of agonizing grit she possessed to get naked. Panting with the effort, her clothes in a heap on the other side of the tub, Sterling inspected the damage.

Black-and-blue swelling bruises marred her skin from her waist to her ankle. Christ, no wonder she hurt. If only Adela hadn't balked, if only she'd gotten that window open a little more. Failure left a bitter taste in her mouth.

She didn't want to move, but what choice did she have? It hurt like hell, but she could bend her leg, so she assumed it wasn't broken.

Slowly sitting upright, she turned on the shower and, once the water warmed, inched forward to sit under the spray, her forehead resting on her knees. At some point she must have zoned out. She didn't know how long she'd sat there, but the lack of hot water revived her. Teeth clenched, she carefully washed her thigh. When she reached to turn off the water, renewed pain seized her.

Her finger. With so many aches to choose from, she'd all but forgotten about the ring finger on her right hand. Looking at it now, she knew she'd dislocated it in her fall.

Switching to her left hand, keeping her right tucked close to her body, she shut off the shower and, leaning heavily on the wall, managed to get upright. Her thigh continued to ooze blood, so she dried it as best she could and applied several butterfly bandages, then wrapped it in gauze.

Rather than get her bed wet, she eased her injured hand through the sleeve of her big terry robe, wrapped it around her and gimped her way to the couch, where she curled up. Exhausted, she thankfully slept.

CHAPTER FOUR

Cade tried calling her. He even tried tapping quietly on her door. It was two in the morning, far from a decent hour to call on someone, but he was surprised he'd lasted this long without getting hold of her.

He and Reyes had rounded up several women, as well as Smith and his cohort, but they'd lost sight of both Star and the young woman who'd been with her. That bastard Mattox had gotten away, too, and it tortured Cade thinking he might have Star. His sister was on it, and she'd locate Mattox eventually— when it might be too late.

No, he couldn't accept that, so here he was, checking Star's apartment and praying she was safely inside.

He knocked again, hard enough that a neighbor stuck her head out and cursed him.

Somewhere between eighty and ninety, eyeglasses askew, hair frazzled, cranky and nowhere near properly dressed, the woman snapped, "What the hell are you doing?"

Great. Not what he needed right now. "My apologies, ma'am."

"Just keep it down," she barked, then slammed her door loudly enough to wake up the rest of the building.

Cade gave serious thought to breaking into Star's apartment. If she wasn't in there, he'd start scouring the area to find her—

"Who is it?" Her weak voice came through the closed door.

Fresh alarm mingled with relief, because at least he'd found her...unless she wasn't alone?

His gaze shot up to the peek hole in the door. Stepping back so she could see him, he said, "It's Cade. Let me in."

Nothing happened.

He leaned closer to the door. "Swear to God, Star, I'm about two seconds from knocking down the—"

The lock clicked and the door opened.

One look at her and uncontrollable rage returned. That was something that never happened to him. He worked best in cold deliberation, detached, proficient...but this was Star, and somehow she'd always jacked his control.

Stepping in and quietly securing the door again, he asked, "Who did this to you?" She looked like she'd been through a war.

With a pronounced limp, her face taut with pain, she went back to the couch and gingerly lowered herself. Instead of answering his question, she asked one of her own. "Why are you here?"

Several lights were on in the apartment. "Are you alone?"

She sat back. "Yes." Her robe parted and he saw her right leg.

Locking his jaw, he came to kneel in front of her. "Ah, babe, how the hell did this happen?"

Trembling, she swallowed heavily and closed her eyes. "Babe?"

Seriously, an endearment was what she wanted to talk about now? "You can gut me later. Tell me what happened."

Though she didn't actually shrug, he heard it in her tone. "I landed hard when I went out the window in the guys' john. I'm okay, though."

No, she most definitely was not. The bruising started dark

red at the top of her thigh and down the middle, but then spread outward to blue, green and black. Actually, he couldn't see how high it went because the robe didn't part any higher. He lightly touched his fingers to her skin, especially over the bandages that covered a blood-encrusted cut.

Lethargic, Sterling said, "It looks terrible, doesn't it?"

He'd seen similar bruising, just never on a woman. "My guess is a pulled hammy. I don't know how you managed to get home."

"Adrenaline, I think. *Not* getting home wasn't an option, right? But yeah, now it hurts like crazy."

He noticed she held her arm, too—which drew his gaze to her fingers. *Shit.* He winced for her, but first things first. Gesturing at her leg, he asked, "Mind if I take a look?"

Those velvety brown eyes of hers stared at him. "Actually, since I'm buck-ass under the robe, yeah, I mind."

He hadn't needed her confirmation on that. His body already knew it, and conflicting needs were bombarding him. He wanted to help her. Protect her. Touch her.

Look at her.

Stop being an asshole. He drew in a deep breath and tried to be businesslike. "You need to see a doctor."

"Nope. If that's why you came here, you can run along back to wherever you live."

"Star." He braced his hand on the couch. "You can't think I'd leave you like this."

Her eyes narrowed. "Why not? I'm not your *babe*, and I didn't ask you to—"

"Let me rephrase that." He hardened his own gaze. "I'm not leaving you like this."

They stared at each other, a battle of wills, until she relented with ill grace. Hell, she looked too spent to do otherwise.

"Fine," she groused. "Suit yourself. Not sure I could fend

off anyone if you led them here, so if nothing else, you can be backup."

"I didn't, but in case *you* did, you're right. I make excellent backup." Now with a purpose, Cade stood. "We're going to handle this step by step, okay? First, have you taken anything?"

Eyes closed, body tight with pain, she asked, "Like…?"

"Pain meds? And you should have that leg elevated, under ice packs, or you won't be able to walk tomorrow."

She gave a short laugh. "Walk? I'm not sure I could crawl." She lifted her head, and her eyes barely opened. "I probably shouldn't admit this, but just showering took it out of me. All I want to do now is sleep."

His heart softened. "You can do that soon, okay? After I get you more comfortable. So you need something for pain."

"I have aspirin in my medicine cabinet."

"And a first aid kit, apparently." She hadn't done a terrible job, but he could do better. "I'll properly clean and dress that cut, too. You know how you did it?"

"Chunk of glass." Again she put her head back as if any effort at being alert was too much. "It's in or near the trash can in my bathroom."

To know what he was dealing with, Cade went to retrieve it. Discarded clothes littered the floor, including bloodied jeans and her boots. She'd left a knife and a necklace on the counter. No, not a necklace. Though he recognized it as a hidden weapon, it took him a second to figure it out. With the press of a small mechanism built into the medallion, a claw blade opened out.

Jesus, what had she planned? Just how deep was she into her vigilante crusade?

Worrying about that would have to wait until he'd seen to her injuries. He found the chunk of glass. It appeared to be part of a broken bottle, still covered in Sterling's blood. In fact, she'd gotten blood everywhere—the floor, the tub, the edge of the sink…

The first aid kit was left open on the counter. Since the rest of her apartment was tidy, he'd pick up the mess for her once he had her better settled.

Next he detoured into the kitchen to find a bottle of water. Her fridge was almost barren, her cabinets cluttered with packaged food but nothing healthy. Figuring out something for her to eat would take a trick.

When he returned with the kit, three store-brand pain tablets and the water, she appeared to be sleeping. "Star?" he asked quietly.

"Hmm?" She sounded lethargic.

"Can you take these?" He touched her lips, and that got her more alert, her dark eyes watchful. He badly wanted to kiss that soft mouth, but all he said was, "Open."

She did, and he dropped them in, then handed her the water.

After swallowing the pills, she took several more drinks until she'd downed half the bottle. "No one's ever taken care of me."

No one? *Ever?* "Then let me show you how it's done."

Contemplative, she frowned at him, then gave up. "Fine. I'm starving, too. I don't suppose you know how to cook?"

"Better than you, apparently." He knelt down again and gently peeled away the butterfly bandages that had helped, but not enough. With the condition of her leg, it had to hurt like crazy.

"I didn't sleep at all last night," she explained, a mixture of pain and running the words together. "I haven't eaten since early this morning, either. Add in tonight's…*excitement*, and yeah, I'm shot."

"Excitement. Right." Cade let that slide to silently concentrate on the job at hand. "I'm sorry," he said, dampening a cotton ball in antiseptic. "This is going to sting."

"I know." She clutched the couch cushion with her left hand. "Go ahead."

Her breath hissed out as he worked, so he tried to distract her. "Do you often go all day without eating?"

"Do I look like I'm starving?"

Definitely not. Sterling had a strong and shapely body that had caught his attention the moment he first saw her. Broad shoulders for a woman, hefty breasts and an ass he wanted to grasp with both hands. She didn't play up her assets in any way, and Cade thought she was sexy as hell because of it.

"So you skipped food out of nervousness?"

"I don't get nervous," she denied—then caught her breath as he cleaned a spot of debris from the edge of the cut.

"So why didn't you eat?"

"I was busy prepping." She scowled at him. "Are you about done?"

He'd take her annoyance over the sight of her pain any day. "Almost. You could really use a few stitches, but since the bleeding has almost stopped, we'll stick with bandages." The robe barely preserved her modesty, not that she seemed concerned. The woman was utterly unaffected by his nearness and her own nakedness—or else she hid it well.

Whichever, he appreciated how well she handled it. Any show of shyness now would have made it that much more difficult.

When he finished, he lightly covered her again with the edges of the robe. "Now." He sat beside her.

Making it clear she didn't like his nearness, she gave him another scowl.

"That finger is dislocated." She'd either need a trip to the ER after all...or he'd need to set it for her.

Looking away from her injured hand, she whispered, "I know."

Very gently, Cade took her hand, then trailed his fingertips over the swollen knuckle. "Does anything else on this arm hurt? Your wrist, elbow?" She was guarding it pretty good.

Lips pressed together, she shook her head.

"Are you sure?" He held her wrist firmly in one hand, the dislocated finger in the other. "Have you tried moving it?"

"Yes. I was reaching for the faucet when— *Ngahhh!*"

Before she could finish, he'd tugged the finger back into place and now gently held her hand in his, trying to soothe her. "Shh, I know. It's damn painful. Take some deep breaths."

"Go to hell!" she snapped, but she curled closer to him and moaned.

Cade had trouble swallowing. He'd set fingers before, his own included, but this was different. One arm around her, his other hand still holding hers, he kept her close. "I'm sorry, babe."

Her breath shuddered in. "Don't be." Still a little shaky, she said, "You fixed it for me."

"You should really see a doctor—"

She inhaled deeply, let it out slowly and eased away from him. "I'm sure it'll be fine."

The stubbornness started to grate on him. "Does anything else hurt?"

Her choking laugh sounded with pain. "What doesn't hurt? It was a stupid idea to go out that window."

Since he'd been there to get her out, Cade agreed. But she hadn't known that. "I think it showed a lot of initiative."

She huffed a breath. "It was better than staying, I guess."

Before he could think better of it, he had his hand on her tangled hair, smoothing it down. "Can you tell me what you were doing there?"

"You first."

He looked up in surprise. "So you knew it was me?"

"I thought you might be around somewhere."

Talking seemed to help her collect herself, so Cade settled back beside her. "I was keeping an eye on you." He could tell her that much. He wanted her to know...what? That he cared, yes. That whatever she was up to, he could handle it for her. "What did you hope to accomplish, Star?"

Hand trembling, she swiped a tear off her lashes as if it offended her. "I was offered money, remember? What's your excuse?"

She had to be the most maddening person he'd ever encountered. "I can't go into it."

"Yeah? Well, ditto for me. Guess we can both keep our little secrets, okay?"

Cade tried a different tack. "You said you're hungry. Let's get the rest of the injuries looked at and then I'll see what I can put together."

"You already covered it, and I can rustle up a bowl of cereal or something."

He doubted she could rustle herself to bed, but he refrained from saying so. "Nothing else hurts on your arm? Your shoulder, back?"

"My back's a little sore, but hey, I scraped my spine on the window casing, then damn near landed on my head and shoulders, so… Guess I'm lucky I didn't break my neck."

The thought of that leveled him, made his heart thump and his lungs constrict. "Let me take a look."

Eyes narrowing, she curled a little away from him. "Don't tell me you're a doctor?"

"No, but I have some field experience—"

"Aha. Military." Pouncing on that, she said with triumph, "I knew it."

"And since you refuse to get actual medical attention, at least let me see what I can do." Seconds ticked by while she considered it.

"Yeah, all right." She struggled to sit up.

Carefully, he helped lever her more upright.

"I need panties," she said. "And maybe a button-up shirt. Then you can do all the doctoring you want."

The timing was all wrong, yet he teased, "Promise?"

"Get cute and you can get out."

Pleased to see her attitude back in full force, Cade murmured, "Sorry," and helped her to her feet. "Can I help you dress?"

"You might have to. It took all I had just to get my robe on."

He hadn't expected her agreement, but he went along without a word, letting her lean on him as they made their way to her bedroom. Once there, she settled cautiously at the foot of the bed. "Panties are in the top middle drawer."

A new experience—helping a woman *into* her panties. Reyes would find it funny as fuck, but Cade was an eon away from humor.

He opened the drawer to a jumble of colors and fabrics all stuffed in together. Most were cotton, some with lacy trim, others nylon or ultra-sheer. Such a selection. He glanced over his shoulder. "You have a preference on full coverage or barely there?"

She smirked. "If by full coverage you mean granny panties, you won't find any there. But nothing too skimpy, and preferably cotton."

"Color matter?"

"Not to me."

Meaning it could matter to him? *Hmm…*

His hand looked too big sifting through her delicate underthings. Did her bras match her panties? Somehow he didn't think so, not unless it was a special occasion for her.

Did she consider sex a special occasion?

He'd like to find out. *Don't be an asshole.*

Deciding on hot pink with little yellow flowers, he turned and found her barely awake, her shoulders slumped, her head hanging. It wasn't a look he'd ever expected to see on Sterling Parson.

It bothered him. Too much. Somehow she'd already burrowed under his skin. When had that ever happened? Never.

Kneeling in front of her, he said, "Here," and helped to get the pretty panties over her feet and up to the knees she had pressed tightly together.

Standing, her uninjured hand braced on his shoulder, she said, "Not a word."

His face was level with her stomach, his hands bracketed outside her knees, her hand warm on his shoulder. Scenarios winged through his mind, heating his blood, tensing his muscles.

If she hadn't been hurt, he would have leaned forward, pressed his face against her, breathed in her heated scent...

One day soon, he'd be back in this position—once she'd fully recovered. *Not being an asshole, remember?*

Steeling himself, Cade looked up at her face.

Her gaze avoided his. "I mean it."

"I know." Watching her expression kept him from looking at her body, at the warm, silky flesh teasing his fingers and wrists as he tugged the panties up, under her robe, and smoothed them onto her hips.

It took a lot of iron control, but Cade stood. "Shirt?"

"No, I've decided to keep the robe, but you can look at my back if you want." Turning, she opened the belt and let the shoulders droop down.

More bruises, of course. He hadn't expected anything else, but at least these weren't as bad as her leg. Lifting her thick mass of hair with one hand, he touched, lightly prodded, but she barely flinched. "I think the worst of it is your leg and that finger."

"My finger feels better already, but yeah, my leg is crazy stiff."

He had a hot tub at his place, but inviting her there would cause more problems than he wanted to deal with. That is, if she'd even accept, which he doubted.

"How about we get you comfortable on the couch with an ice pack on your leg? I'll tape your fingers, then get food together."

"Wow, this whole 'being waited on' thing is nice. I had no idea what I've been missing."

The sarcasm made it easier for her, Cade knew, so he didn't reply as he helped her back to the living room.

Maybe if she'd had a different background, having Cade see so much of her under such crummy circumstances might have been more embarrassing. Truth? Her biggest issue wasn't nudity. It was being dependent on him.

That sucked rocks big-time, though she had to admit he made it easier than it could have been. He was so blasted matter-of-fact about it, like he did this sort of thing all the time.

Did he? No, somehow she knew he wasn't anyone's toady. Nice that, for right now, he'd be hers. Besides all the pampering, the view was pretty sweet. And stirring.

Yup, even though she felt like the walking dead, her hormones took notice of him. When he'd been on his knees? Downright fantasy inspiring.

Sterling wondered if he could really cook. Probably, given he did everything else with ease. Maybe someday she'd find out for sure, but right now she didn't have any basic ingredients for him to work with. Instead they dined on pizza rolls—fresh from freezer to microwave—with colas. It was the best she had since he'd discounted cold cereal and packaged cookies.

She felt better being clean, her finger straightened and taped to the one next to it, her thigh, resting on pillows to elevate it, numb from the ice he kept rotating, and food in her belly. Not good—good was nowhere on the horizon—but definitely less annihilated.

Less alone in the world.

Not that she'd start to depend on Cade. Hell no. The man was far too secretive about every single thing.

"So." She idly rubbed an area of her leg not covered by ice. "What happened at Misfits? Was that your brother's plan, to cause pandemonium? I saw him, you know, before I got taken to that back room."

"Actually, that was all my doing, with only a short warning to my brother." He leaned forward over her injured leg to re-adjust the ice, then explained, "The other night when you left my bar to draw out Smith—who is actually Thacker, by the way—I listened in, so I knew he'd propositioned you."

What? No way. "I didn't see you."

With a shrug, he explained, "Neither did he, because I went out the office window and hung in the shadows. I knew right away you'd be walking into a trap, so I set up a hasty plan."

"You could have told me."

"So you could tell me to butt out? Not a chance."

Yeah, she probably would have. Far too often, pride overrode common sense. "I knew his name wasn't Smith."

"I figured."

So at least he credited her with some sense. "Were you in Misfits, too?"

"Outside, watching through a window. I knew what that bastard was likely expecting, and whether you were agreeable or not, I wasn't about to let you go through with it."

"Let me?" she asked quietly, with a fair amount of menace.

"Figure of speech, but accurate. I had the ability to stop it, so I did. Are you really going to protest now? Would you have handled it better on your own?"

Handle it? Ha. She'd been stuck with no way out, and he'd basically saved her. Unable to meet his direct gaze, she looked down, feeling cornered.

Damn it, she wasn't good at gratitude, at even recognizing it when she felt it, but she knew that had to be the emotion sitting heavy on her chest. "So...*surly* is generally my default mood, ya know?"

Instead of being insulted, he gave a small laugh. "I've no-ticed."

Peeking up at him, seeing the actual smile on his mouth had a strange effect on Sterling. They sat close, alone together in her apartment, and she wasn't exactly immune to his personal brand of attention. "Anyway," she said, reining in her unruly thoughts, "yeah, I appreciate the help you gave."

Trying to see her face, Cade tipped his head. "No problem."

For him, it hadn't been. In the darkness of the bar, she hadn't been able to see the ass kicker versus the ones getting their asses kicked, but somehow she knew Cade was the first. She remembered the silence from him, how he hadn't even breathed heavily while taking apart everyone in the room—except her and...

Adela! Sterling jerked her head up. "The woman who was in that room with me? Do you know what happened to her? Is she okay?"

With a small, regretful shake of his head, Cade said, "No idea, sorry."

Deflated, she decided it was past time for some truths. "Okay, enough. You were there with your brother. I was there. We don't trust each other—I get that. But I seriously need to know what happened."

Cade gave her a silent scrutiny.

Desperation wavered in her voice. "Please?"

It took him too damn long to nod, and he still didn't give in completely. "I'll share a truth, then you share. Deal?"

Dirty pool! She had reason for needing to know, but what reason could he have for not wanting to tell her?

Unaffected by her scowl, he said, "Take it or leave it, Star."

Ha! He knew she wouldn't refuse. "Fine. But you tell me what happened to Adela first."

"I can't. I told you that. But," he said before she could interrupt, "we nabbed Thacker—that is, Smith—and his buddy Jay, the two bozos who showed up at my bar. My brother also found several women locked in different rooms."

Her heart dropped hard. She grabbed his wrist. "You got them out?"

His gaze went to her hand, making her acutely aware of what she'd done. His wrist was so thick her fingers couldn't encircle it. Hot, rock-solid and dusted with soft hair—now that he'd drawn her attention to it, her palm tingled...and that tingle seemed to travel up her arm and on to places better forgotten.

"Sorry." She hastily withdrew.

"You can touch me anytime you want."

Such a thrilling offer! "I don't—"

He cut off her protest. "Those women are safe now, but we couldn't locate you, the other woman or..." He paused.

"Mattox?"

Cade's brows shot up. "He actually introduced himself?"

She understood his surprise. Mattox tended to keep a low profile, leaving it to his lackeys to do his dirty work, except for when it came to procuring women. Then the slimy bastard insisted on taking part.

Even more telling, though, was the fact that Cade obviously knew Mattox, or knew of him. So, she'd nailed it: being a sexy bartender wasn't his main vocation. Plus she now knew he had military experience. What, exactly, were he and his brother up to?

She wasn't sure how to answer him without giving away her own secrets. After considering it, she said, "No introductions were necessary."

"You already knew Mattox?"

"Yup." Knew him, despised him, badly wanted to see him suffer. "You did, too, right?"

He bypassed that to ask, "How? You'd met him before?"

"No, you don't. One question at a time. So tell me. What exactly was your plan at Misfits?"

"Keep you safe, period," he replied without hesitation. "Your turn."

"Bull! You already knew the place and the players, so don't try to tell me—"

"I've been aware of Misfits and what they do for a while. But I was there last night because that's where you went. Otherwise, I would have continued to…" He fell silent.

"Surveil?" she offered helpfully. "Investigate?" Damn it, what exactly was his role in all this?

One steely shoulder lifted.

Not good enough. Throwing caution to the wind, she looked him over. "So this is what you do? You find and expose human-trafficking rings?"

Nothing, not even a blink.

"And then what?" Were they actually on the same mission? That'd be cool. More and more, she liked Cade. She *mostly* trusted him. It'd be great to have her own personal badass around when she needed him, and the man was certainly easy on the eyes. Win-win.

"It's my turn to ask questions." He rubbed her foot through the blanket.

Almost stopping her heart.

Yeah, a foot rub was definitely not in her repertoire of experiences. Had to admit, though, it felt downright heavenly.

"So tell me, Star—"

"Sterling."

He gave a brief nod of acknowledgment. "What were you hoping to accomplish with that stunt?"

She supposed someone had to make the first move, right? Might as well be her. If she gave a little, surely he'd do the same, and maybe they could clear out the secrets between them.

Normally, she'd never consider such a thing. The less people knew her and what drove her, the safer she felt. But of all the men in all the world, she actually *liked* Cade—especially now that she realized they had a common goal: to bust up sex trafficking, free the women captured and punish the ones responsible.

With that decision made, she pondered where to start. "I hadn't figured on Thacker showing up at the bar." It was her haven...probably not anymore. "He never had before, at least not that I know of?"

Since she posed it as a question, Cade confirmed it for her. "It was his first time in."

Sterling nodded. "I've been aware of him for a while."

"How?"

"Mmm... I've talked with a few women who knew him. Yeah, vague, I know, but that's all you're getting on that." Unless he shared a few nuggets, too. This had to be an even exchange. "I kept wondering how I was going to get to him—"

"Jesus." Raking a hand over his short hair, Cade sat back and frowned.

There went her foot rub. Bummer.

"Then I saw him at the bar. Poof, he was within my reach. I saw it as an opportunity I couldn't resist."

"An opportunity for *what*? To get mauled? Raped? Sold?"

Having her worst fears thrown at her brought back her scowl. "Sheesh, what a downer. Have a little faith, why don't you?"

"*Star*," he warned.

"Sterling," she automatically corrected. When she'd started her new, empowered life, she'd changed everything—locale, appearance and nickname. "I thought I'd get a feel for Misfits, see how they ran it, you know? Getting in without an invite isn't easy, so this was the only way."

"No, it wasn't."

Right. Evidently he'd already been in there. His brother, too. They saw Misfits for what it was. Not that either of them had bothered to tell her that, even though they knew she'd planned to go.

Seeing yet another opportunity, Sterling rethought her argument. Since Cade seemed determined to keep her safe, she could use that to her advantage. It wasn't like she wanted to tackle Mattox and his perverted pals on her own. That path led to failure, as she'd already discovered.

But with Cade's help? His brother's assistance?

She just might be able to get somewhere.

Smiling with her new intent, she stared into Cade's stunning blue eyes and suggested, "If you would share with me, we could coordinate." His entire expression hardened. If she hadn't already decided not to fear him, that look alone would have set off her alarm bells. Funny that she somehow knew Cade was different.

Now she had to convince him that she was different, too.

CHAPTER FIVE

Gauging his reaction, Sterling prompted, "You could do that, right? Get in, same as your brother?"

Voice dropping to a quiet but firm whisper, he warned, "This is not a game you should be playing."

"Says you. I feel differently." For the last few years, it was the only game she played, and she called it revenge, atonement, even satisfaction.

"You still haven't told me why."

Was that worry—for *her*—putting that particular dire expression on his face? Interesting. "Why doesn't matter. You see—"

"It matters a lot."

"Anyway," she said, stressing the word to make it clear she didn't appreciate his interruption. "If all had gone well, I might've ended a few monsters and freed a few women."

Incredulous, he stared at her as if she'd grown two heads. "Things did not go well."

A reminder she didn't need. Trying to sound cavalier, she returned, "No, but you saved the day."

Too quick for her to stop him, he flipped the ice packs and

blanket aside. Indicating the deepening bruises on her leg, he said, "You call this saving the day?" Catching her wrist, he lifted her hand with the two fingers taped together. "Does this look like I'm some kind of hero?"

Whoa. That was a lot of anger, but oddly, it didn't concern her since he seemed to be angry on her behalf.

Given that Adela wasn't free and Mattox wasn't dead, Sterling considered her efforts a big old failure—and maybe, because she'd gotten injured, Cade felt the same.

Did he already feel responsible for her, just as she felt responsible for Adela? That possibility warmed her, but it also set off alarm bells. She'd been on her own too long to let anyone, especially a guy with secrets as big as her own, sidle in and take over.

Hopefully she hid her mixed reactions under sarcasm. "I'm here, alive, not mauled or raped or sold, so yeah. All in all, your diversion saved...well, at least me." She drew a breath. "That's something, right?"

Shoving to his feet, Cade paced the small area of her living room. Hers wasn't a tiny apartment, but with him prowling around it felt minuscule, as if his size and presence had shrunk the space. Looking at him was easy. All that fluid strength, tightly contained but ready when he needed it. She envied him that physical power.

He stopped to face her. "I do not want you hurt."

It fascinated Sterling, witnessing his protective instinct. Not something she was used to. "That makes two of us."

And actually, she didn't want him hurt, either, but she had a feeling he wouldn't appreciate her concern quite so much. "You said your brother got hold of Thacker and the other dude, and some women. What'd he do with them?"

He relented enough to explain, "The women were transported to a secure shelter. They'll get whatever help they need."

Nice. It's what she would have done, too. "And the scumbags?"

The look he sent her said it all.

Sterling whistled. "They're dead?"

He answered her question with one of his own. "Isn't that what you intended?"

"Yeah, but somehow I think you might have contacts that I don't."

"I have a lot of things you don't."

Was that supposed to be an insult? She laughed. "No kidding. Want me to name a few? How about big biceps and bigger fists? Muscled legs and granite shoulders. I'm tall, but you've got me on height, strength and ability." His irritation amused her. "My legs aren't short, but I know they're not as strong as yours. And while I'm not a weakling, I'm not on a par with you, either. Ability? I mean, I try. I have a lot of determination. But I'm self-taught, so I'm sure I don't have the same skill set you have."

"This is…" He turned away again, the set of his shoulders showing his tension as he paced. "I'm not sure how to handle you."

Handle her? She snorted. "You can't, so don't tax yourself. But can I make a suggestion? Try answering my questions and let's see if we find some common ground."

"We can't. Not on this."

Rolling her eyes, Sterling asked her questions anyway. "What shelter did you take them to? And how were you surveilling Misfits?"

He shook his head.

"All right, try these on for size." He had to tell her *something*, or their conversation was at an end. "How'd you know where I live? And where'd you learn to fight?"

Stubbornly silent, Cade rubbed his jaw, his gaze piercing as he stared at her. "It's almost morning. You should get some sleep."

Jerk. Extreme disappointment sharpened her anger. He didn't want to team up? Fine. She'd managed on her own so far. She didn't need him.

She didn't need anyone.

"Yeah, I am tired." She faked a widemouthed yawn. "Go on, run back to wherever you came from. Maybe I'll see you at the bar again sometime." She was just irked enough to add, "Or maybe not."

Cade went still, his nostrils flaring. Tone dark and deadly, he asked, "What's that supposed to mean?"

"It means I don't like you much anymore."

His eye twitched. "I didn't know liking had anything to do with it." Dangerously on edge, he stalked closer to her, braced one broad hand on the back of the couch, the other on the arm, and leaned down close. "You always stop at the bar after a haul."

Even showing signs of anger, his nearness fired her engines. Too bad she was out of commission. "So we're sticking with me as a trucker and you as a bartender? Fine by me." With mock innocence, she said, "I don't have deliveries for at least a week. Good thing, since I'm not sure I could manage it until my leg heals."

"Your leg is going to need more than a week, and if you're not a trucker—"

"Oh, but I am. Just like you're a bartender." Her sugary smile snapped him upright again.

"You know I am. You see me there often enough."

Sterling sighed. God, he was impossible. Also sexy and fit, and so blasted competent, how could she stay resistant? "You've seen me driving my rig. Done and done. All is as it seems."

Anger seemed to emanate off him in waves.

Oh, poor baby. Was she getting to him? More like driving him nuts, but whatever. "Did you like me better when I mostly ignored you? Well, too bad. You're the one who forced this... whatever it is. Odd friendship."

His gaze drilled into hers. "Sexual attraction."

Was he trying to shock her? Not happening. Since there was no point in ignoring him anymore, she grinned. "That, too."

His eyes narrowed. "Mutual respect."

Unwilling to give up too much ground, she looked away. "Possibly." She definitely respected his ability, but she didn't think he returned the favor.

"It's a beneficial relationship."

"How so?" Curious now, she took her own turn glaring daggers. "How do you benefit? Because I haven't agreed to anything."

"You will."

Anger stirred. "Are you talking sex?"

"I'm talking shared confidences."

"I'm the only one sharing!"

Acknowledging that with a nod, he straightened. "I need to clear a few things." He picked up her displaced ice packs and carried them back to the kitchen but continued to talk. "I don't have autonomy, so it's better if I don't act alone."

Now, that was a tidbit she could dig into. Her heart started pumping double time, and she carefully turned so her legs were off the side of the couch.

Hurt. Like. Hell.

But once he left, she'd have to get herself to the bathroom and bed, so she may as well start now. The longer she sat, the harder she knew it'd be.

She clenched her teeth and concentrated on bending her knee. Fire burned up her thigh. How was she supposed to stand or walk?

Needing a distraction and fast, she asked, "So you work with your brother?" Did he need to consult him before confiding in her?

She could hear him in the kitchen, emptying the ice packs in the sink, the clinking of ice cubes as he refilled them. The man was entirely too at ease in her apartment, but then, she imagined he took control everywhere he went.

He returned and, without answering her question, asked,

"Could we make a few agreements? I'll let you know if I find Adela or Mattox, and you don't do anything else without letting me know."

Talk about a one-sided contract. "I don't answer to you."

He took in her strained expression, then moved forward to set the ice packs on the table. Slipping an arm around her, he helped her up. "Probably better if I don't tell anything more about them anyway."

"Wait, that's not what I meant." Leaning against him, with his arm around her back to support her and her hand clutching his shoulder, really drove home the differences in their sizes. Yes, she was tall, but he stood a head taller.

For too long they just looked at each other. When her gaze dropped to his mouth, he shook his head. "You're in no shape to start anything."

Of course he was right. If he let go, she'd probably fall on her face. A kiss, though... She could handle that.

He tipped up her chin. "Where are we going?"

Guess that settled that. "You're leaving." Pretty sure that was his plan, anyway. "And I'm making my way to the bedroom. Maybe the bathroom first, but..."

He waited. "But?"

"I need to know if Adela is found, if she's safe—"

"Then agree."

If she weren't so banged up, she'd...what? Her unique set of skills wouldn't get her anywhere with a guy like Cade, and she knew it. That was part of his draw, actually. A big part. Most guys just didn't appeal to her, especially when she knew she was stronger—emotionally, mentally and sometimes physically. She was definitely more ruthless than most.

But Cade wasn't the type of guy she could dismiss on any level. He proved that with his newest tactic. "Blackmail?"

"Negotiations," he countered, never fazed, never out of control.

What could she do but agree? There, it wasn't even in her

hands. He'd removed all options for her, so she didn't have to feel guilty for the little thrill that came with her capitulation.

"All right, fine." To ensure he didn't know how she really felt, she added in a grumble, "Not like I'll be doing much for a week or two anyway."

Now that he'd gotten his way, Cade relaxed even more. It was subtle, the slight smoothing of his brows, the softening of his mouth, tension ebbing from his shoulders. He somehow felt closer, gentler...warmer.

"Bathroom first?" And then with concern, "Do you need any help?"

Not on her life. "You're pushing your luck, dude."

That earned her a small smile. "I don't count on luck anyway. I use good, sound calculation. But if you think you can handle it, I'll wait right out here. If you run into a problem, though, just let me know. I'm not squeamish."

She almost growled that she wasn't, either, but he might take that as an invitation. The day she couldn't pee on her own was the day she'd truly give up.

He left her leaning against the sink. She noticed that he'd tidied up for her. Her clothes were now in the hamper and the blood had been wiped up before it could stain. Nice. God only knew when she'd be able to get on her knees to scrub the floor.

The first aid kit was stowed under the sink, and her necklace hung over the knob of the medicine cabinet.

He'd opened it to expose the curved blade. Had he left it that way to show her he recognized it for a weapon—or because he hadn't known how to close it again? She'd bet on the first.

Cade McKenzie was a handy man to have around—in more ways than one.

While she was in there, she brushed her teeth. She gave her hair a cursory glance but didn't really care enough to mess with it. Stiff legged and limping, she opened the door and found Cade leaning against the wall, his arms folded over his chest.

He looked lost in thought, but he immediately stepped forward to put that steel band normally called an arm around her again. "Bed?"

"Yeah, but I need to lock up behind you first." She couldn't accomplish much tonight, so she might as well get some sleep. But she sort of hated to see their time together end, and she sucked at subtlety, so she asked, "When will I see you again?"

Standing there together, her more or less in his embrace, he asked, "What time do you get up?"

When she could walk? Usually by five. Now? She had no idea. "Maybe eight or so?"

"I'll have coffee ready."

He said that so casually she almost fell over. "You'll be here first thing in the morning?"

With the light of challenge in his eyes, he said, "Figured I'd stay over, actually."

"Stay over?" And she squeaked, *"Here?"*

Apparently an unheard-of occasion, if the expression on her face was any indication. That didn't surprise Cade. Everything she did screamed *loner*.

If he had his way, that would end.

"You might need me." Rather than give her too much time to think about it, Cade steered her toward the bedroom. "Don't worry about the doors. I'll lock up."

Holding his breath, he waited for her refusal, for her sharp stubbornness to kick in.

Instead she grumbled, "Fine. I suppose I wouldn't mind the help."

His eyes widened, but he kept his face averted so she wouldn't notice. On the heels of that shocker, renewed concern followed. Her quick acceptance meant she had to be in total misery. Tomorrow would be worse before things started to get better.

Getting her from the living room to the bathroom had been

the longest walk for her, but her bedroom was only a few steps away now. "Let me turn down the bed."

From what he could see, she didn't use a bedspread, but she'd smoothed the bedding into place. Leaving her to hold on to the dresser, he pulled back the sheet and quilt, then plumped her pillow.

"So." Voice strained, she asked, "Where will you sleep? Pretty sure my couch isn't long enough to accommodate a guy your size."

He'd slept in worse cramped places but didn't say so. Turning to her, he took her arm and urged her to the bed. "Where I sleep is up to you. I can crash beside you without bumping your leg—or make do on the couch. Even the floor is fine."

On her back, her dark hair fanned out on the pillow and her hands clutching the quilt, she looked younger.

And a lot more wary.

"I've never slept with anyone before."

Cade felt the bottom drop out of his stomach. "You…?"

Annoyed now, she waved away his surprise. "I don't mean that. I've had sex. I've just never spent the night with anyone."

Way to stop his heart. "The night is almost over, so it wouldn't be more than a few hours anyway."

Looking to the side of the bed, maybe judging whether or not he'd fit, she said, "You're not clingy, are you?"

"If you're asking if I'd want to hold you, yeah, I would. But that's your decision." Trying to tease the worry from her expression, he promised, "I won't cuddle you in your sleep if you'd rather I didn't."

Disgruntled for only a second more, she scoffed. "All right, let's not chew it to death." Going all brisk, she levered carefully to her side—facing away from where he'd sleep. "Get the doors locked and do whatever you have to do. I can't keep my eyes open any longer."

An hour later, enveloped by darkness, Cade silently called

her a fibber. She was faking sleep, but he wasn't fooled. Maybe being in here with her wasn't such a good idea if his nearness was going to keep her awake.

Kept him awake, too, but he knew his problem. Despite her injuries, despite her wariness, he wanted her. Didn't matter that it couldn't happen, didn't matter that he wouldn't let it happen even if she felt up for it—which she didn't.

At the very least, he wanted to curve his body around hers, but she was so stiff beside him he thought she might startle if he reached for her.

Suddenly she made a small agonizing sound, breaking the spell.

Immediately he rolled toward her. "What's wrong? Leg hurting? I can get you more aspirin."

In reply, she snapped, "Just do it already."

His turn to go perfectly still. "It?"

"This cuddle stuff you mentioned. We're both awake, so you might as well—"

Not giving her a chance to change her mind, Cade carefully scooted closer until his body molded to hers, his legs fitting behind hers, his arm curving over the dip of her waist. Placing a soft kiss to the side of her neck, he asked, "Okay?"

Audibly breathing, she croaked, "Sure."

So warm, and surprisingly soft for such an attitude. He laced his fingers with hers over her stomach. "Relax."

Turning her head toward him, she asked incredulously, "Can you?"

"Eventually." He tugged her a little closer. "Close your eyes and take slow, deep breaths. If that doesn't work, I'm moving to the couch so you *can* sleep." When she said nothing, he directed again, "Breathe slow and easy."

Nodding, she sucked in a quick breath but did blow it out slowly, then repeated it…again and again, finding a smooth rhythm that lasted until her body went lax.

Cade knew the moment she nodded off, and then finally, he dozed off, too. Expecting her to stir off and on all night with discomfort, he was disconcerted to wake with sunshine filtering in through the window. Overall, they were in the same position they'd started in. Their fingers were no longer entwined, since she now had her uninjured hand tucked under her cheek, and his hand rested over her bruised thigh. Leaning up, he checked the clock on the nightstand.

Huh. He couldn't remember the last time he'd slept after nine, but it was damn near nine thirty.

On a soft groan, Sterling shifted—and went still. She jerked her head around, then winced in pain.

"Easy. Let me disengage first. Then I can help. You're probably going to be twice as stiff now." He tried not to jar the bed as he got up and pulled on his jeans, leaving them unsnapped. He didn't bother with his shirt or shoes yet. "Can you sit up?"

"No choice," she said, teeth clenched as she let him help her upright.

Her robe had come open, so he got an eyeful, one that'd stick with him for…oh, the rest of his life, probably. Injured or not, she had a killer body. He didn't mean to, but his attention snagged on soft white breasts, tipped with rosy nipples.

Morning wood settled in real fast.

Without saying a word, he pulled the lapels together and re-tied the belt.

"You go ahead and use the bathroom," she said. "I need a minute."

"You won't move?"

She snorted. "Might as well warn you now, I'm not at my best in the morning, so mosey on while I concentrate on becoming human."

Grinning, Cade smoothed her hair. "Be right back."

A half hour later, he managed to get his unruly gonads under control, and she managed to make it to the bathroom and then the couch. They ended up positioned the same way as last night, with ice packs on her elevated leg, but now with coffee in hand.

He waited until she'd almost finished her first cup and then said, "I'll need to head out soon, but I want to make sure you're settled first."

Over the rim of her mug, those dark velvet eyes zeroed in on his face, before drifting down his body.

Several times she'd done that, her attention starting in one place and ending up on his bare chest or his stomach. Each appreciative study left him a little warmer. At one point she'd even stared at the crotch of his jeans until he worried he'd get hard again.

With the memory of her bare breasts at the forefront of his mind, it wouldn't take much.

When he cleared his throat, her gaze lifted lazily back to his. "Hey, you don't want me looking, don't show so much."

The things she said—hell, even her reactions, all of it—were entirely unexpected. "No way am I the first shirtless man you've seen."

Brows going up, she saluted him with her coffee. "No, but most don't look like you, do they? You've got some serious hotness going on. Work out often?"

Every day, but he wouldn't boast about it. "I like to stay fit."

"Because you routinely tangle with bad guys?"

Cade knew she casually slipped that in hoping he'd automatically answer, maybe tell her more than he meant to. She was slick about it, but he wasn't that easy. "Habit. Lifestyle. Discipline."

"Yup, definitely military. And I guess that explains the tats?" She waited, but he only sipped his coffee. "You don't want to share yet? Bummer. I mean, we slept together, right? That should count for something."

"You think so? Then tell me—how often have you interfered with traffickers?"

"I'd rather know what the tattoos mean."

"I'll tell you—someday."

Turning away, she finished off her coffee and plunked the mug down on the table.

Disappointed, but not surprised, Cade strode back into her bedroom to pull on his shirt and grab his shoes and socks. He returned to the living room and took the chair adjacent to the couch to finish dressing.

She was still silent when he stood, provoking his impatience.

"I started," she whispered, "by picking up a girl on the highway."

Going still, Cade took in her expression, her carefully blanked mask that said so much, surely more than she meant to. Slowly, he reseated himself. "She was trafficked?"

Sterling nodded. "I knew the signs as soon as I saw her. Or suspected, anyway, but it didn't take me long to have it confirmed." Absently, she rubbed her leg. "It was cold, dark, and there she was, without a coat, her eyes...haunted. The second I pulled over, she got in and begged me to drive. She didn't care where as long as it was away. There were bruises on her arms, a few on her neck."

Getting up, Cade moved closer, sitting by her feet on the couch and curving a hand over her calf. "You got her somewhere safe?"

"She refused the police station. Airport was out without ID. Bus station was too shady, and the hospital would be too obvious, she said, because they'd know to find her there."

"They who?"

Sterling shook her head. "She didn't want to say." Her eyes met his. "But I talked her around."

Reading the vindication in her hard gaze unsettled him. "You went after them, didn't you?"

Bypassing that, she said, "There's a woman... I knew her years ago when I relocated. I trusted her." Sterling tucked back her hair with fidgeting fingers. "I got hold of her, and she helped me figure out what to do."

"Like what?"

"The thing is, knowing I made a difference, helping some-one—it's empowering. Almost addictive." Flexing her toes, she winced, then shifted to get comfortable. "I couldn't give that up, so I've educated myself more."

Cade couldn't believe what he was hearing, but God help him, he knew this was her grand confession. It was truth, and somehow he had to bend his brain around it. "And so now you go trolling for victims?"

Insult sharpened her gaze. "There's no *trolling* involved. I'm on the most trafficked route in Colorado anyway, I'm in and out of truck stops, so yeah, I keep my eyes open, and when ap-propriate, I act."

A headache started at the base of his skull. "It's dangerous."

"Duh. But I can handle it."

He shot right back, "Like you did at Misfits?"

Pain forgotten, she sat forward and poked at his chest. "If you hadn't interfered, yeah, I'd have figured it out somehow. But you mucked it all up, didn't you? Now Adela is missing and Mattox is out there somewhere, so if anything, I'm in more danger now after your *assistance* than I'd be if I'd handled it on my own."

Cade nearly threw up his hands, but that wouldn't solve any-thing. He knew better than to let his temper take control. A man had to have a cool head to deal with most situations. Deal-ing with someone like Star? He'd let his anger fuck that royally.

Time to retrench, before she expected reciprocal confessions from him. Nothing had changed there. He still couldn't con-fide in her without implicating his family, and that was some-thing he wouldn't do.

Getting up, he headed to the kitchen and rummaged through a few junk drawers before he found a pen and piece of paper.

It gave him a second to collect himself and hopefully allowed her a minute to lose steam.

On his way back in, he preempted any angry outbursts by saying, "You're right. I'm sorry."

Mouth open—probably to blast him—Sterling paused, then clicked her teeth together. "I don't know if I accept your apology. It'll depend on what you tell me in return."

And there it was, the expectation of tit for tat. "We have a lot to discuss, but I really am running short on time, so how about giving me a list of groceries you want?"

She knew an evasion when she heard one. "Go. I don't need anything. My plan is to veg right here and watch TV."

"And what do you plan to do about food?"

That stymied her for a second. "Cereal is still in there."

"But your milk is bad."

Wrinkling her nose, she said, "Yeah, that happens a lot. Not your problem."

It bothered him that she'd seriously sit at home, hurt and without food, before she'd ask for help. Not that she had to ask, but it'd help if she didn't fight him every inch of the way. Now, of course, she had more reason than ever to be difficult.

"I do go after traffickers, with the end goal to take them out."

Eyes widening with an *aha* expression, she sat forward. "I *knew* it."

"We can compare notes soon, okay?" Maybe. Probably. Probably not.

"But right now I want to run to the store before I have to get home and then to work. If you tell me your preferences, I can get some meals figured out, stuff that you can just nuke or eat cold, like sandwiches. What do you think?"

"I think you're a real mother hen."

"My family would disagree with you, but I am realistic enough to know you aren't in any shape to go out, your cabinets are all but empty, and I doubt you'd open the door to fast-food delivery."

Without denying or confirming any of that, she narrowed her eyes. "Why does it matter to you?"

"Why do you fight me?"

Her mouth twitched to the side. "Maybe because you confuse me and I'm not sure of your motives."

Something he could sink his teeth into. Hopefully it wouldn't make her more resistant. "I like you. I'm sure you've figured out that I want you." He held up a hand. "Not that I'm trading favors—"

"I *know* that." Color, both embarrassment and irritation, warmed her face. "Give me some credit."

"Whether you and I ever get together, we're friends now, right? I'd help a stranger if I could, so of course I want to lend you a hand."

When she still didn't agree, he growled, "You like being disagreeable, don't you?"

Her mouth twitched the other way. "I don't want to be beholden."

"For food? You're telling me that once you're up and running again, you won't return the favor?"

Guarded, she asked, "Return it how?"

"Dinner? If you don't cook, we could go out."

"I cook." Touchy about it, she said, "I'm not helpless or dumb."

"Far from both," he agreed. "So we're on the same page here?"

"I'm not keen on going hungry, so feel free to play maid and chef."

God forbid she give an inch. Tamping down irritation, Cade asked, "Preferences?"

"I'll eat pretty much anything other than seafood, so get

whatever's convenient. But I want the receipt so I can pay you back."

Knowing she'd insist, he nodded. "Fine."

She countered back with her own version of "Fine," loading the word with a lot of annoyance.

He picked up her keys so he'd be able to get back in and was almost to the door when she stopped him.

"One thing, Cade, and it's nonnegotiable."

Bracing himself, he waited.

"If you don't trust me with some details, you won't be welcome back, and I won't return to the bar. Maybe keep that in mind before you insist on doing my shopping."

Driven by her inflexible tone, Cade strode back to the couch, bent down and took her mouth in a quick, warm kiss—that really got to him. Her lips were soft, parted in surprise, allowing his tongue a brief foray. She tasted good and felt even better. He wanted to learn about that mouth. About all of her.

Before he got carried away, he stepped back but took in her bemused expression. She touched her lips, her gaze seeking his. First time he'd ever seen her speechless.

Next time she started haranguing him, he'd remember what worked. "I won't be long."

This time when he left, she didn't stop him.

CHAPTER SIX

Three flippin' days of laziness and Sterling was about to climb the walls. Sure, Cade continued to spend the night, getting in late after the bar closed and leaving late the next morning. But he still hadn't told her anything substantial. He answered her questions with questions of his own, to the point they were at a stalemate. The way he dodged getting to the meat of issues, she hadn't realized how little he'd shared until she started piecing it together.

Okay, so his buff bod distracted her. He slept in his boxers and didn't bother to dress until he was ready to go. What red-blooded woman wouldn't focus on that?

A couple of times now she'd wondered if he did it on purpose, just to keep her suitably dazed and on the edge of lust. If so, she didn't want him to stop.

She enjoyed it all too much.

The way he waited on her was sweet, too, but now she realized he'd sidestepped questions by cooking, tidying up the apartment, ensuring she had everything within easy reach before he left each day.

Finally, the bruising started to fade a bit and she could bear more weight on her injured leg. No, she wouldn't be doing any deep knee bends yet, and driving her rig was still out, but she was pretty sure she could handle her car—and her own shopping.

Which meant it was time for him to fess up, or she'd have to send him packing. It didn't make sense for her to share anything more with a man who so obviously didn't trust her.

She'd just finished putting a compression wrap on her thigh when Cade asked, "How often do you actually transport or deliver?"

"Often enough to be legit," she replied, standing to test her leg. "Seldom enough that I can use my truck for other purposes."

He stood close in case she needed his help but didn't yet touch her. "Like searching for women along trucking routes?"

"Bingo." Satisfied that she could manage on her own, she took a small trip around the apartment. Her leg remained stiff and achy, but she moved on her own steam. "Mostly I pick up freight overload from bigger trucking companies, which lets me be pretty footloose with my schedule. When I have other leads to follow, I can pass on the job offer, and I never have to book myself too far in advance."

Sounding impressed, he said, "That's genius."

"I know, right?" She stopped to rest, one hand on the divider wall that separated the kitchen from the living room. "Now it's your turn, so—"

Her phone rang.

Disgusted by the interruption, she warned, "Don't go anywhere," and returned to the coffee table, grabbed up her cell and glanced at the screen. "An unlisted number." She answered, "Hello?"

"Francis?"

Oh, hell. Knees going weak, she lowered herself to sit on

the edge of the couch. Already guessing the answer, she asked, "Who's this?"

"Adela."

Her gaze shot to Cade's. As if he'd picked up on the sense of danger, he came to sit beside her.

"How are you, Adela?" Sterling used her name to let Cade know the identity of her caller. "I hope you got out okay?"

"I need help."

Not exactly a direct answer. "Okay. Where are you?"

"I'm afraid to tell you—but I thought maybe I could meet you somewhere safe? You...well, it seemed you wanted to help, right? I'm sorry I wasn't as brave as you, but you can't imagine..." Her breath shuddered. "The things they've done to me, I couldn't risk it."

"I understand." Feeling Cade's gaze burning over her, Sterling tried to think. "What happened after I left?"

"I... I thought we'd stay at the bar, but they stuffed me in a car and drove to a different place."

"Where?"

"It doesn't matter. I got away, but now I don't know what to do. Please say you'll meet me."

Stalling for time, Sterling chewed her bottom lip.

"Francis?"

"It's okay. I'm here." Some anomalous emotion squeezed her lungs. Terror, likely. But also...uncertainty? Something here felt very, very wrong.

Cade shook his head at her.

The man dared to give her orders when he wouldn't tell her a damn thing? Screw that. She could make her own plans. "I hope you're somewhere secure, Adela, because I can't meet you for a few days."

"*Please!* I can't stay here. I'll get caught again, I just know it. They use horrible drugs and...and *violence*, and it scares me so badly—"

"Shh," Sterling whispered, hoping to calm her. "We'll get it figured out, I promise. You just need to stay safe a little longer."

After some heavy breathing, Adela asked, "Then you'll come for me?"

Heart clenching, Sterling vowed, "Of course I will, just not today. I hurt my...shoulder, when I went out the window." She couldn't say what prompted the lie, except that she'd learned extreme caution whenever dealing with traffickers or victims. "I'm sorry, but I can't drive yet. Another day or two and I should be better." Not giving Adela time to start crying again, Sterling asked, "How far do I need to go to meet you?"

After a lengthy hesitation, Adela blew out a shaky breath. "I'm off I-25. That's all I can say for now."

"But that covers a lot of ground."

"I'll be more specific when I know you're on your way."

With no other choice to take, Sterling nodded. "Okay, but give me a number so I can contact you tomorrow. We'll set something up for the next evening."

"No. I'll call you back." Agonized, Adela added, "I'm counting on you, Francis. Please, don't forget about me."

Hearing the finality in that small plea, Sterling said, "Wait—" but it was too late. She'd already ended the call.

The urge to throw the phone made it extra difficult for Sterling to gently place it on the coffee table, but that's what she did.

Then she ignored Cade as she concentrated on organizing her thoughts.

"You did well."

Adela stayed silent. His moods could be unpredictable at the best of times, and this wasn't a good time. He detested having his plans upset, but she'd tried her best. It wasn't her fault the woman wouldn't cooperate.

"We'll give her a day to stew on it," he decided. "Then you'll call her in a panic to make the arrangements."

"A panic?" That suggestion didn't bode well.

Eyes full of malice pinned her to the spot. He smiled, reaching out with one hand to finger the shorter wisps of her hair over her temple.

She tried not to flinch, but she couldn't help it.

"When she sees you, she needs to know you're in trouble. She needs to be completely horrified by your condition." His meaty hand opened to cup her cheek. "Do you understand what I'm telling you?"

Unfortunately, she did. She shouldn't have been cold, but the chill of the inevitable seeped into her bones, making her shiver.

His thick hand slid down her neck and gripped tightly—seconds before his other hand made sharp contact with her jaw. Stars erupted and she would have collapsed, except that he held her by the neck.

Standing, Sterling made her way to the patio doors and stared out at the mountains in the distance. It was a sight that used to soothe her. The vastness of the Rockies meant she could hide—but now it also meant she might disappear, and who would know?

Who would *care*?

This was the first time someone had contacted her directly. Usually when she helped a young woman, it was because she'd found her on the road or in the act of being traded. Truck stops were hotbeds of trafficking, which was the main reason she'd gotten her CDL.

Promising safety, she could usually talk a woman into getting into her truck. When conditions warranted it, when sleazeballs were keeping watch, she performed hasty kidnappings.

In her seven years as a truck driver, she hadn't made as much impact as she would have liked—but for the women she'd rescued, she'd made a big difference. They'd been given a second chance.

And in doing so, she'd given herself another chance, as well. A chance to add worth to her life. A chance to—

"How'd she get your number?"

The intrusion of Cade's voice disrupted her maudlin thoughts. A good thing, really. She couldn't afford too much introspection right now or she'd chicken out of what had to be done.

Glancing at him, she said, "I gave her a card the night we were at Misfits."

Fury and disbelief brought Cade slowly to his feet. "You did *what*?"

She curled her lip in disdain. Sure, she recognized his temper as concern, but the facts remained: *he didn't trust her.*

Whatever. She was done trusting him, too.

"Don't sweat it. All the card had on it was my number, nothing else, and I don't use GPS or public Wi-Fi on my phone. No one is going to track me down."

"I did."

Her brows climbed high. "Using my cell phone? No, I don't think so." Sterling turned back to the view, but she didn't really see it. Damn it, she had hopes of her and Cade teaming up, but he'd dashed them, and now she had to accept it wouldn't happen. "More likely you followed me home—or had someone else do it. Either way, it was a breach of privacy that I don't appreciate."

She hadn't heard his approach, so it took her off guard when his hard hands settled on her shoulders. Her senses stirred, awareness spiking.

His reflection in the glass showed his resolve.

Against her back, she felt the heat of him.

Odd, but his nearness calmed her rioting thoughts. Since she couldn't rely on him, that wasn't necessarily a good thing. To put them back on track, she said, "I'll have to go after her."

Cade pulled her against his body, his arms folding over her

chest, enveloping her in his strength. "No, you won't. I can handle it for you."

"Oh, for sure, you look enough like me to fool her." Rolling her eyes, she twisted around to face him. "She'll be looking for *me*, an unassuming woman—"

Cade snorted.

"Not an imposing man. If she sees you, she'll bolt."

"You don't know that."

"I've handled it enough times that I can guarantee it. Men will not be high on her trustworthy list."

"Is that the voice of experience?" Appearing far too solemn, he cupped his hands around her neck, his thumbs keeping her chin lifted. "It'd help if you told me how you got started with all this."

It saddened her far more than it should have, but Sterling shook her head. "I don't think so. Interesting as this has been, it's going nowhere. I got that message loud and clear." She pulled away from him and hobbled toward the front door. "Time for you to go."

Cade didn't move. "I'm not going anywhere."

She spun back to face him and nearly lost her balance when her bum leg gave way. "Yes, you are."

"You can so easily dismiss this?" He gestured between them.

"I don't even know what this is. You said you needed to talk to others, to see what you could share. Well, you've had four days and still nada. I'm done. I have things to do, and they don't include dumping my past on you."

As she spoke, Cade seemed to get bigger, harder, maybe even a little menacing. In comparison, his tone was soft—and somehow more lethal because of it. "I kept putting off talking to my family because it's going to raise a lot of speculation. And I know how they'll react."

Family, meaning not just his brother? Was his sis involved, too? "Secrecy all the way, huh?"

"It's what we've lived by for many years. You know it, too. The best way to keep private info private is not to share it with anyone."

Her heart sank. Had she really held out hope that her ultimatum would change things? Stupidly, yes.

He'd done the unthinkable, dangling the carrot of shared experiences…only to yank it away. "Leave."

Instead, he scrubbed a hand over his face. "I never knew my mother."

In the process of heading to the door, Sterling froze. Afraid that he'd say no more, she kept her back to him and stayed perfectly still.

"My father raised me from birth. I'm thirty-two now and not once has my mother ever tried to contact me."

When she got light-headed, Sterling realized she was holding her breath. She let it out softly, then sucked in fresh oxygen. "Maybe she didn't know how to find you."

"No, that wouldn't have been a problem."

She heard him moving and chanced a peek back.

He now sat on the couch, legs sprawled, hands braced on his thighs. "My father never married, but he did have a life partner." He shrugged. "She was like a stepmother to me. They loved each other, and when she was taken, it leveled him in a way I've never seen before. He was…crazed."

Cautiously, Sterling approached, her heart beating double time, and eased down beside him. "She was never found?"

"Oh, she was. Dad has the kind of money that can hire the best and hire the worst."

"I don't understand."

"They turned the state upside down. He observed it all, the interrogations—and the vengeance. Finally, he found her. It's bullshit, the way Hollywood paints human trafficking as some high-style wealthy man's sport. It can be, but that's not the norm. It's what exists in our own backyards."

Unable to resist, Sterling put her hand over his. "I know."

"She was found in a shitty little hotel room, drugged to the gills and…" He swallowed heavily.

Again, with emotion making her throat feel thick, Sterling whispered, "I know."

Turning his hand, Cade clasped her fingers. "One year to the day that she returned home, she swallowed a bottle of pills."

Seeing his pain made it fresh for Sterling. Tears burned her eyes, but a crying woman wouldn't help him.

A strong woman would. "I'm sorry."

"She'd left a note, a plea for Dad to do *something* so other women wouldn't have to go through that." His gaze locked on hers. "And that's all I can tell you for now. Don't ask me names or details, because I can't give them."

She was quick to nod. This was a moment, one she could cherish, one she could build on—and God, she wanted that. She wanted more than the emptiness her life had been.

It took her a second to decide on her next step, but it was instinct that brought her forward so she could sink against his big solid chest. Wrapping her arms around his waist, she squeezed him tight. "Thank you for telling me."

"Is it enough, Star?"

Damn it, she was starting to like the way he said her name.

He nuzzled against her hair. "Will you promise me you won't go after Adela alone?"

Feeling the weight lifted from her shoulders, she nodded. "Yes. I promise."

That got her crushed against him. "Let's go over what we know."

This. This was what she'd wanted. Someone to collaborate with, to help her with her plans. A sounding board that'd give her a new perspective.

Nodding, Sterling forced herself past the satisfaction of having a cohort to address the business at hand. "Adela said she was staying off I–25, which doesn't tell us much."

"Except that it's known as a trafficking route."

Sterling knew that well. "Along the front range, drivers can easily travel from city to city and into other states. Here's the thing." With one last squeeze, Sterling straightened. "I've picked up three women along that interstate, all of them about an hour south of Colorado Springs in the same general area."

"You think it could be related?"

"Makes sense, right? It's how I knew about Misfits and— Thacker. But only if it's a widely spread organization. One of the women was from a spa that later got busted."

"Thanks to a tip from you?"

Pleased that he'd give her credit, she blushed. "Yeah, sure. I mean, I couldn't just charge in there with guns blazing, right? So I anonymously clued in some people, luckily the right people, and it turned into a big sting."

"I actually remember that. Around eighteen months ago, right?"

So *he* kept track of such things? Interesting. "That's right. Eight men were arrested and the spa was shut down."

His phone dinged with a message. Impatient, he glanced at it and didn't look pleased. "The other women you mentioned?"

Of course, now she wondered who'd sent him a message, but he'd just started opening up and she didn't want to pressure him, so she let it go.

For now.

"One had been held in a prostitution ring that operated out of this nasty little hotel. They thought they had her too intimidated to run, but she'd only been waiting for an opportunity, and that happened during a severe rainstorm that knocked out power over a wide swath. Plus the downpour made it tougher for them to search for her."

"But you found her?"

"At a truck stop, hiding behind a building. Being female, she trusted me more than the male truck drivers."

He nodded. "And the third?"

"She'd only recently been abducted. She was able to get away by jumping out of a moving car while they were transporting her, so she was pretty banged up. It was cold and she didn't have the right clothes. I think it was desperation that brought her near the road. Good thing I found her before anyone else did."

His admiring gaze moved over her face. "You're pretty remarkable, you know that, right?"

Again his words warmed her. "Just doing my part."

"Above and beyond."

"Like you?"

"There are definite similarities, and I'd love to compare notes, but that was a summons from my father and it's never a good idea to keep him waiting." As he stood, he asked, "You'll be okay until I get back after work?"

Since he'd stocked the fridge with chicken salad and pickles and left croissants and chips on the counter, canned soup in the cabinets, he didn't need to worry about her going hungry. "I'm better every day. In case you didn't notice, I can get around on my own now."

"I noticed." Intense emotion darkened his eyes. "I'm looking forward to you being one hundred percent again."

She couldn't hold back the silly smile. "Yeah? Why's that?"

For an answer, he leaned in and took her mouth again, longer, hotter this time, his tongue teasing against hers, his breath warm on her cheek. He lingered—until his phone buzzed once more.

On a low growl, he moved away, but not far, just enough to separate their lips. His hand tunneled into her hair to curve around her skull. "Make no mistake. We've come to an agreement. You'll stay in today, and tomorrow we'll make plans together?"

"Tomorrow we can discuss plans," she clarified. "But I won't go out. I'm not quite ready for that anyway. I thought instead I'd do some additional research on the area where I found the other women."

"Good thinking. I'll see you tonight after I've closed up the bar." With one last, sizzling kiss, he left her apartment.

Sterling would like to know more about his father. His brother and sister, too. Hopefully tomorrow he'd share details.

Would she share, as well? She *did* trust him, she realized, so what would be the harm? Yet caution was her constant companion, so she'd consider all the angles before making up her mind.

Crazy, but she already anticipated his return—and more than that, the day when she'd be healed enough to make him live up to the promise behind those kisses.

Dogged by his father's assistant, who also served as a butler and chef, pretty much everything, Cade went through the opulent mountain home toward the back deck, where he knew he'd find his family. "I know the way, Bernard."

"Yes, sir," he acknowledged, while continuing to be Cade's shadow.

Cade glanced back at him. "I thought we agreed you'd quit with the *sir* nonsense."

"You requested," Bernard said in his grating monotone, "and I declined."

Knowing Bernard to be as stubborn as Star, Cade let it go as he continued on through the massive great room and out to the three-tier deck that offered an amazing view of the mountains, as well as his father's man-made lake. Sitting on fifty-two acres, surrounded by wilderness, guaranteed a level of privacy not found in the skiing towns.

Cade loved the house and the surrounding land—not so much these visits.

It was cooler up here, so his sister, immersed in reading something on her laptop, had a colorful shawl around her shoulders.

Reyes sprawled in a chair, one leg over the arm, his expression pensive—until he spotted Cade.

"'Bout time you got here."

Curious over what that meant, Cade glanced at his father. Parrish McKenzie looked younger than his fifty-three years. Almost as tall as Cade, still fit thanks to the well-equipped gym on his lower level and a love of the outdoors, his father always made an imposing figure.

Sipping hot tea from a dainty cup and working a crossword puzzle, he looked nothing like a hard-core vigilante. Without looking up, he said, "You have some explaining to do."

At the same time, Bernard asked, "Something to drink, sir?"

"I'll take a beer."

"This early?" Bernard questioned, with disapproval.

"Not like I'll drink at the bar, so yeah. This early." Hell, it had to be noon. Not like he was having it for breakfast.

"Yeah," Reyes said, perking up at that suggestion. "Grab me one, too, will you, Bernard?"

His sister never stirred, but then, when she got immersed in research, she tuned out everything else.

The second Bernard left, Reyes sang, "Cade has a girlfriend."

Cutting his gaze to his brother, Cade warned, "Knock it off." He dropped into an empty chair at the table.

Reyes only grinned. "But that's why we're here. I just figured I'd throw it out there rather than keep you waiting."

Shit. It had been too much to ask that his father might not yet know about Star.

Finally Parrish put down his pencil and sent an enigmatic gaze at Cade. "This won't do, you know."

"Not up to you, so save the dictates." Cade accommodated his father whenever possible. This wasn't one of those times.

"If you want her," Parrish said baldly, "just have her and be done with it."

Reyes snorted.

Madison glanced up, brows lifted.

It struck Cade that he had to have the strangest family in God's creation. Keeping his expression bland, he asked Parrish, "Does she get a say in it?"

Hot color rushed into his father's face. As a champion of women, it was an insult that cut deep. "You know I wasn't suggesting—"

"So you just assumed she'd be on board if I'm interested? I appreciate the vote of confidence."

"Logical conclusion." Shifting his gaze to Reyes, Parrish asked, "What's so special about this woman?"

"No freaking idea."

Cade thought about tossing his brother over the railing. He could roll downhill until he hit the lake.

"Is she beautiful?" Expounding on that, Parrish said, "Describe her."

Uneasy now, Reyes glanced at Cade, then shrugged. "Tall, strong figure, average face. Nice hair. Definite lack of fashion sense."

Frowning in confusion, Parrish turned back to Cade for enlightenment.

It was almost laughable. Almost. "Looks aren't everything, Dad." And then to Reyes, "Though you have to admit there's something about her."

"She's sexy," Reyes agreed. "But that's not what Dad asked."

"It's the attitude." Cade didn't mean to offer up details, but the words came out anyway. "If you got to know her, you'd understand what I mean."

"Yeah, uh… I got a small taste of that attitude, enough to neuter me, so no thanks." To their dad, he said, "It'd take someone like Cade to go toe-to-toe with her. She's what you'd call *challenging*."

"Challenging how?"

"Let's just say she's not a 'polished nails and styled hair' kind of gal—more like 'I'll gut you and walk away smiling if you get in my way' type."

Appalled, Parrish asked Cade, "Is that something you want?"

Even Madison put aside her work to hear the answer to that.

Their reactions left him grinning. Was it so unheard of for him to be interested? All right, so he never let his personal life cross paths with his work—until now.

It wasn't like he set out to find a balls-to-the-walls woman. Nope. Had he been looking for someone to match his strength? Not likely, since he usually was attracted to ultrafeminine women. Actually, he hadn't been looking for anything.

Then Sterling Parson had walked into his bar one night and he hadn't been able to put her from his mind since then.

That was his business, though, no one else's, and he wouldn't sit here while they dissected her. "Maybe you all missed it, but I'm thirty-two, too old to explain myself, so leave it alone."

"But you need our help," Madison said, then fell silent as Bernard returned with beers, little sandwiches and some type of individual cakes on a round tray.

"Bernard!" she exclaimed, already snatching up two of the small cakes. "You know these are my favorites."

"Yes, I do. That's why I made them." He handed her a napkin, then refilled her tea before offering the contents of the tray to Cade and Reyes.

Glad for the reprieve, Cade took two sandwiches, popping one into his mouth right away. Good. Some kind of specialty bread, with a tangy sauce, sliced roast beef and fresh tomatoes. "Not bad, Bernard."

"You'll make me blush with that type of praise."

Laughing, Reyes grabbed a few sandwiches for himself. "We all know you're invaluable, Bernard, so don't go fishing for compliments."

"Can't imagine what I was thinking." After setting the half-empty tray on the table, he turned to Parrish. "If you need anything else, let me know."

Parrish waved him off. "Go take a break. Maybe grab a swim. Put one of the pools to use."

"The indoor pool is heated just right," Reyes said, "but fair warning, the outside pool is cold enough to shrivel your…"

"Ahem." Bernard censured Reyes with a single withering look, then said to Parrish, "Thank you, but I need to start preparations for dinner." With a sniff, he added, "The meat must marinate. Perhaps I'll indulge a swim later this evening."

After the French doors closed behind him, Reyes burst out laughing. "I do love shocking him."

Parrish shook his head. "For twenty years I've been telling that man not to be so formal."

"He enjoys the pomp," Madison said. "Let him have his fun." Her eyes, the same bright hazel color as Reyes's, narrowed on Cade. "Now, as I was saying—"

"I don't want your help."

She smiled. "Sorry, but you're getting it anyway."

CHAPTER SEVEN

Cade turned his ire on Reyes. "Felt like you had to confess all, huh?"

Unfazed, Reyes shook his head. "Wrong tree you're barking up, there. I didn't say jackola." He gestured toward Madison. "Did you really think *she* wouldn't find out?"

No, it would have been more surprising if she hadn't. His baby sister didn't miss much. By accessing street cameras and security cameras on businesses, and with the help of good old-fashioned bugs, she had surveillance everywhere.

No problem when it came to work, but apparently she knew he hadn't been home the last few days, either.

Because he'd been staying with Star.

Cade shifted his attention to his sister.

Defiant, Madison elevated her chin. "Of course I told Dad. When you risk yourself, you risk the rest of us."

An insult he couldn't ignore. "You think I'd let harm come to you?"

She winced in apology. "No, not really. I didn't mean that."

"So you think what? That Star will hold me hostage until I tell her all about you?"

Parrish scowled at Cade. "Don't put your sister in an untenable position with divided loyalties. We work as a family. You know that." Admonishing, he added, "And she wouldn't have had to tell me if you'd done so instead."

"I planned to tell you soon."

"Why wait?"

Reyes started to speak up, likely with another joke.

He shut down when Cade turned on him. "I wouldn't if I was you."

Hands up, Reyes said, "Take it easy. Here on the balcony isn't the right place, but if you want a go at me, the gym is available downstairs."

Parrish slammed a fist to the table. "I didn't teach you to fight so you could maul each other."

For too many years, Parrish had been fanatical about his children learning both defensive and offensive moves. While he trained with one expert after another, always with the intent of one day getting the men who'd kidnapped his companion, he included his children so that they were trained, as well.

From the day his stepmother committed suicide, Cade was told his purpose in life was to seek justice for those who couldn't defend themselves. He, Reyes and Madison couldn't just be good—they had to be the best.

Once Reyes had stopped grieving his mother, he'd loved the discipline and had embraced the vigilante purpose with enthusiasm.

Madison, too, accepted her role as tech genius, falling into place from the age of nine.

Cade was different. He'd balked at having his purpose predestined by his overbearing father. Oh, he'd learned what he could. Training was a satisfying outlet for his sorrow at losing the only mother he knew, and having siblings he'd wanted to protect.

Fifteen at the time and already rebellious, he'd butted heads with his father at every opportunity—right up until he'd joined the military in defiance of his father's dictates.

"If you want to spar," Parrish said, "you'll do so when neither of you is angry."

Smirking, Reyes asked, "When is he *not* angry?"

Cade rolled his eyes. True, he used to stay at some level of rage day in and day out. But that was a decade ago, before the military had helped him tamp down the emotion under firm control. Reyes knew that, but Bernard wasn't the only one he liked to heckle.

"I'm not angry now," Cade said, "but I'd still be happy to kick your ass."

"Nah. I think I'll wait and take you by surprise." He grinned. "Ups my odds, ya know?"

Getting back to the matter at hand, Madison shared one of her gentlest smiles. "For what it's worth, I admire Sterling a great deal." She turned her laptop so Cade could see the screen...where she'd expanded her research to include a history of Star's life.

He didn't want to read it here, under his family's scrutiny, but he knew how proprietary Madison could be about her investigations. She preferred to keep everything in-house—literally—and under her own impenetrable security protocols.

If he wanted to learn about Star, he needed to read everything now. And there was the rub. "This feels like a huge invasion of her privacy."

Madison's smile quirked. "You don't think she'd read everything she could about you if she had access?"

Actually...he knew she would, if for no other reason than that she didn't fully trust him.

Aware of Parrish, Reyes and Madison all watching him, Cade

pulled the laptop closer. At first he merely skimmed the details. Abducted at seventeen from her high school. Escaped at some point between then and her eighteenth birthday, because new photos of her emerged after that—driver's license, concealed carry permit (now, why wasn't he surprised that she'd carry a gun?), her CDL for driving. She'd used different names, lied about her age a few times and moved around a lot, all the way from Ohio to Colorado.

"Last page," Madison said. "Child protection services had been to her home multiple times before she was abducted. That probably explains why she didn't return for her mother's funeral, even though she was apparently free by then."

Various photos from different ages, some of them grainy, others clear, filled the file. Damn, she'd changed.

At one point she'd been more colorful, more dramatic, likely outgoing. Now she was usually so contained she was like a different person. Quiet, intense, focused on a single purpose...

No wonder she didn't want him to call her Star anymore. She'd reshaped her life, her appearance, her entire persona. She'd made herself into a different person altogether.

The reach of his sister's abilities never failed to amaze him. "How did you do all this?"

"Facial recognition software, mostly. It's easy once you have access to various databases. Biometrics map out features and match them up. I wasn't sure about a few of the photos, so I had to do some cross-referencing to be positive they were really her."

Parrish sat back, his hands laced over his stomach. "In case you didn't realize, she's a vigilante, same as us."

"But without our connections," Reyes said.

"Or our financial means," Madison added.

Were they championing her now? Cade didn't know what to think of that. Until Parrish wrapped it up for him.

"All of which means she could bring us down with her blunders." Parrish watched him closely. "You understand that?"

They all waited, while Cade's calm chipped away. He met his father's gaze. "You may as well save your breath, because I'll do whatever I can to keep her safe."

"I'd like to know how." Parrish picked up his tea. "It seems keeping her out of trouble is going to be a full-time job."

"Put our stuff away."

She would, but… "It's cold." Arms wrapped around herself, Adela listened to the hollowness of her footsteps on the warped wooden floorboards. Drafts circled her legs. Cobwebs hung in every corner. It smelled damp, as if moisture had seeped in.

The mountain cabin—more like a shack—offered only minimum comfort. A rickety cot, a small generator to run the coffee machine and the mini refrigerator, and a private cell tower so making a call wouldn't be a problem.

Nervousness sank into every pore of her body. Already the cabin looked dark. How bad would it be when the sun set behind the mountains?

She swallowed hard. "What if someone finds us here?"

"We'll claim we were lost and needed shelter." Mattox rolled a massive shoulder. "If that doesn't work, offer yourself up." He went to a dirty window to look out. "No matter what, don't leave the cabin tonight."

As if she would.

When she didn't answer, he turned to face her, his gaze piercing enough to make her tremble. "You heard me?"

"Yes." She looked around again, dreading the next few days. Hopefully Francis wouldn't make her wait long.

"You wouldn't make it to the road, not in the dark," he warned, "and you could run into a snake, a mountain lion or a black bear—"

"I won't step outside." God no, she wouldn't. The mention of snakes made other threats unnecessary.

She shouldn't ask. She knew better, but she heard herself say, "I don't see why we have to stay here."

His gaze went icy. "Don't you?" Stalking toward her, he growled, "You fucked up, Adela. That's why Misfits is temporarily shut down. That's why fucking Francis got away. That's why we're losing money as we speak, and that, my little idiot, is why we're stuck in this fucking cabin."

A spark of anger ignited, but she kept it under control. "I played my part. How was I to know someone would kill the lights or launch an attack, or that she'd be so quick at finding a way out?"

Disgusted, he said, "You didn't stop her, did you?"

"I called out!" God, she hated getting blamed—even if what he said was true. She should have found a way to stop Francis, but she'd drawn a blank at the woman's lack of fear and her daring, plus it had been so damn dark she couldn't see her hand in front of her face. "You'll get her back."

For the longest time he studied her, his expression unreadable. Then he touched the bruise on her face as if fascinated. "Yes, I will—although I'm starting to wonder if she's worth the trouble."

Her eyes widened. "You think she'll stop now? That she'll just go away?"

"No, but it might be better, easier, to put a bullet in her skull and be done with it."

Adela was sure he didn't mean that. "So you've given up on making her pay?"

"No. We'll stick with the set plan." With a shrug, he added, "It'll work—if you play your part."

Glad that he'd relented, Adela promised, "I will."

Mattox tipped her face one way, then the other. "You look very much like a battered woman."

Which was the point, the very reason he'd struck her like he did. She held his gaze.

As if she stumped him, Mattox shook his head, then looked around the cabin. "For this insult alone, I'll make her beg for death. You can count on that."

Now that he was back to normal, Adela went about fixing them a light meal. Silence settled in, other than the occasional creak of an evergreen swaying or the whistle of wind.

Soon she'd contact Francis again—and then hopefully this would all be over.

Cade's brooding silence was starting to get on Sterling's nerves.

They sat at the small dinette table sharing the country breakfast they'd prepared together. He'd handled the bacon, eggs and toast. Mostly one-handed, she'd done the fried potatoes.

Impossible to remember the last time she'd cooked so much food for the start of her day. Her normal practice was to grab a protein bar and a cup of coffee. Because she didn't have it often, the food tasted extra delicious.

It felt good to be functioning again, to be off the couch and properly dressed. Okay, so she wore only a big T-shirt and yoga pants—her typical at-home clothes. She'd even gotten her hair into a ponytail, no small feat with her fingers still taped together.

An hour ago she'd awakened with his arm around her, his breath warm on her neck, excited by the possibilities of their new relationship.

Shortly after that he'd gone all silent and introspective. He hadn't even commented on her getting dressed, the jerk.

Tired of waiting for him to perk up, she demanded, "What's wrong?"

That got his gaze up from his plate. "Nothing."

So he'd make her drag it out of him? Fine. Not like she had anything more pressing this morning. "Couldn't sleep?"

"I slept fine. You?"

She ignored the question to ask another of her own. "Trouble at the bar last night?"

"No." Frowning, he set aside his fork. "Why?"

Well, that left only one other possibility. "Daddy get on your nerves? Or was it that annoying brother of yours? Don't tell me you got a cease and desist on sharing, because we already agreed."

His mouth quirked at her wording.

She did love his mouth, the shape of his lips, the crooked way he smiled…how he'd tasted. And that strong jaw, now covered in dark, sexy stubble.

Oh, and those electric-blue eyes—which were now trying to peer into her soul. "Uh-uh, no you don't." She pointed a crispy piece of bacon at him. "I see what you're doing, but you have some explaining to do first."

"As I recall, I did all the explaining last night—and today was to be your turn."

"Actually…" She thought about it, but if she told him a few select details, would he further reciprocate? She'd never been this curious about a guy, so the lure of learning more tempted her into agreement. "Okay."

"Okay?"

Ha. She'd caught him off guard. Always a good thing. Spreading out her arms, she said, "What do you want to know?"

Taking that question far too seriously, he pushed aside his empty plate and folded his arms on the table. "You're too passionate about helping others, so I assume you have personal reasons?"

Something in his tone… Why did this feel like a test? Did he already know the answers and he wanted to see if she'd be up-front? Irritation sharpened her tone. "Why can't I just be a Good Samaritan?"

"You can. You *are*. The way you tried to help Adela, how you're worried about her still, is commendable."

"Yeah, someone should pin a medal to my T-shirt. At least give me a gold star sticker, right?"

His shoulders flexed—and he ignored her sarcasm. "But it's more than that, isn't it?"

So. Much. More.

She'd never really had a chance to talk about that awful time. Her mother...no, she hadn't been clearheaded enough to listen, and there'd been no guarantees she wouldn't blab to the wrong person.

With Cade sitting there waiting, his expression warm, open and caring, the timing felt right to get it off her chest.

Sterling stared at the remains of egg yolk on her plate. "So... I killed a dude."

She waited for a gasp, for questions, maybe even accusations.

Nothing. No reaction, definitely no outrage or shock.

When she worked up the nerve to look at his face, all she found was honest empathy etched there. It almost choked her up.

Screw that. Making her tone as dispassionate as she could, she quipped, "He had it coming, though, you know?"

"Then I'm glad he's gone." Reaching across the table, his hand palm up, he offered her something new.

Understanding.

Theirs needed to be a business relationship...preferably with benefits. Getting emotionally involved with him could pose a problem.

But even knowing that, she couldn't resist lacing the fingers of her left hand with his. Unlike any other man she'd known, Cade made her feel delicate in comparison to his strength.

With him, it wasn't an unpleasant feeling.

Brushing his thumb over her knuckles, he asked, "Will you tell me about it?"

Telling him would be better than getting all maudlin. "Yeah, sure. Not much to tell, really. I got snatched during my junior year, right after I left school. Two guys. They were flirting and I stupidly fell for it."

"Got too close to them?"

"Yup. I made it so damn easy." She blew out a breath. Self-recriminations got her nowhere. She'd lived through it, learned from it and would never again make that mistake. "I was in a van going…somewhere, before I could even figure out what had happened. For the rest of the day they transferred me around from one place to another, moving me farther from home each time. Then I killed the dick who paid to use me, and got away."

His hand tightened around hers, not painfully but in reaction to that stark recounting. "How did you kill him?"

"I'm not sure I want to talk about this." But when she tried to pull her hand away, he held on.

"I told you about my stepmother."

True, he had. "You didn't force the pills on her, though."

Both his hands held hers now. His nails were short and clean, his fingers long. Slightly calloused. Very warm.

Very masculine, and they made her think of things that involved his hands and long fingers—

"I'm not going to judge you, Star, and I swear to you, your secrets are safe with me."

Jostled from her inappropriately timed sexual thoughts, she used her bandaged fingers to trace along his knuckles, up to his thick wrist and then over the downy hair on his forearms. "You know, it's the oddest damn thing. I was aware of you all that time at the bar, and then we started talking and I felt like I could trust you."

"Because you, lady, have good instincts. Same as me."

Sterling eyed him. "You saying you trust me?"

"I wouldn't be here if I didn't."

Hell of a compliment there. He did that a lot, heaping little bits of praise on her and making her almost glow with it. Could she do this? Could she repay his understanding with a brief, glossed-over version of what had happened that night?

Sensing her uncertainty, he asked, "Have you ever told anyone?"

No, she hadn't. "Never seemed like a good idea."

"But now? With me?"

Would it make her feel better? She sort of figured it might. "All right, fine. I got put with several other girls. Some of them had already been…" She swallowed hard. "It was awful, Cade. Seeing them, knowing what they'd been through, made it all the more real. They hadn't gotten away, so how could I?" The guilt swamped her again, strong enough to choke a horse, because she *had* escaped.

And in doing so, she'd left others behind.

Cade said nothing, but he held her hand steady in his and somehow it felt protective. If only she'd had someone like him back when she'd needed him most.

All she'd had was an addict for a mother, and a society that barely knew she existed.

"Like I said, they shuffled us from one place to another, as if we were cattle. Or even…boxed goods, you know? Not people. Not humans with a heartbeat, or girls who felt fear and pain. They didn't acknowledge any of that. They didn't care." This detailed stuff was for the birds. It made her tremble like that long-ago girl who'd been so terrorized. "So anyway," she said, more brisk now, "we ended up at this big old house that was mostly bedrooms, with a small sitting room, one upstairs john and a tiny kitchen. Each bedroom had a lock on the outside of the door. They somehow advertised us and people put in orders, like…pizza. Except instead of thick crust, they wanted a

heavier girl. Red hair, black, like pepperoni or sausage. Fresh…"
She swallowed hard. "Or a little more seasoned."

Cade briefly closed his eyes. Yeah, if he thought it was hard
to hear, he should have tried going through it— No. No, she
wouldn't wish that hell on anyone. She'd gladly kill those who
instigated or added to the misery, but she wouldn't make them
suffer the same humiliations and abuse that she had.

"Guess I got ordered up. Gullible teen with purple hair and
a pierced lip who cried a lot. Sounds delicious, right?"

"Don't." His voice turned to rough, broken gravel. "Please
don't downplay what you suffered."

Suffered, an apt word. Looking away, Sterling nodded. He
didn't need to know that downplaying it was the only way she
kept it from taking over her life. "The guy was disgusting, old
with a beer gut and jowls, and he literally savored every second of my shock. But he showed up half-drunk, and after that
door was locked on the outside, he locked it on the inside, too.
Just to intimidate me more, I think, but turned out that was
his biggest mistake."

Cade's eyes turned steely. "With the door locked, no one
else could get in?"

"I figured it would slow them down, at least—if they even
heard the scuffle and bothered to investigate. They were used
to hearing screams and cries and…rough stuff, so they played
loud music in the hall."

Mouth tightening, he growled, "I wish they were all dead."

"You and me both." And if she had her way, eventually they
would be. "So like I said, he had a bottle with him and I offered to pour him another drink. Just desperate to buy some
time at first, but the idiot agreed, and when I got close to him,
I smashed the bottle in his face." Bile seemed to clog her throat,
cutting off her air.

Cade waited, gently stroking her palm…letting her know
she wasn't alone.

It helped, enough for her to continue.

"It stunned him, but he was still upright, looking at me like he couldn't believe my audacity. That really set me off—that he'd be surprised because I fought back, that I wouldn't just meekly be raped—and since I had the broken neck of the bottle in my hand, I… I jammed it into his throat and twisted it deep."

Without hesitation, Cade said, "Good for you."

Trying a smile that felt a little sick, Sterling skipped past the massive amount of blood that had gone everywhere, the god-awful gurgling sounds the man had made. "That was the start of my great window caper. It was a hell of a drop, and I was afraid I'd break my legs, or maybe my neck, but I figured it was worth the risk."

"Jesus. You were on the second floor?"

"Yeah, but the ground broke my fall." This smile was a little more genuine. She'd gotten past the worst of it and Cade hadn't rained down judgments, so she guessed he was okay with it. Or at least he got it, that she'd done what she had to. "Knocked the wind out of me, and you should have seen the bruises I got then."

As if he couldn't quite believe it, Cade slowly shook his head. "That was exceptionally brave and resourceful."

She wrinkled her nose. "I should be honest and say I had second thoughts once I was hanging out the window, but my grip slipped and I didn't really have any choice. Luckily that room faced the back, not far from an alley. I had no idea where I was, but I knew where I didn't want to be."

"So you ran."

"Down alleys, through buildings, across backyards. I think I ran that entire day, weaving my way as far from them as I could get." She shrugged. "In fact, I pretty much ran for a whole year."

"You didn't go home?"

"Mom wasn't really into helping anyone but herself, and most times she couldn't even manage that."

"How did you survive?"

"Halfway houses, soup kitchens. A little thievery. There was a woman at one halfway house who worked with battered women. I've contacted her since, when I first helped another woman. She's the one who told me what to do."

"I'm glad you could trust her."

"Trust her? No. But I liked her, and she was good for info." It seemed one memory churned up another, until it felt like she was living it again. "This elderly guy busted me stealing some of his laundry." That particular memory lightened her mood. "Know what he did?"

"I'm guessing he didn't call the cops?"

"He gave me more clothes, including some that had belonged to his deceased wife. He fed me, too, and didn't complain when I insisted on staying outside so he couldn't trap me. He told me I was smart for being cautious, but that if I was going to hang around, I might as well earn some money."

Cade stiffened.

She quickly said, "He offered me a job working on his lawn."

Relaxing again, Cade asked, "Cutting grass and stuff?"

"And trimming bushes, edging the lawn, picking up old tree branches. He kept that place pristine."

Cade actually smiled. "I like him."

"One day after this big storm had made a mess of things, he came out and started helping me work. We didn't talk or anything, we were just there together, getting the job done. After a while he insisted I take a break, and we sat together on a bench drinking colas." At the time, it had seemed the most normal, most domestic thing she'd ever done. "Finally he asked where I went when I left his place. At that time, I used to crash in the park, or I'd catch a snooze in an all-night diner."

"Not safe."

"Eh, it feels fine when you don't have any other options. But then he showed me his garage. Said he had a sleeping bag and I could lock the doors so at least I could rest without worrying. He didn't ask me to sleep in his house, but I think it's because he knew I wouldn't." Remembering brought a sense of melancholy that left her eyes glazed with tears. "He was so brusque about everything, real no-nonsense attitude, but he showed me that as bad as those bastards were who'd tried to use me, there were equally good, kindhearted people in the world."

Lifting her uninjured hand to his mouth, Cade kissed her knuckles. "Was he a truck driver?"

"Retired, but he had been, so yeah, the trucking company was his idea once he knew what I wanted to do. I stayed with him for years. We cleaned out the garage, and he put an actual room in there for me, with my own toilet and tiny shower. I had a chair and a TV, a cot to sleep on." She realized how lame that sounded, but for her, it had been a real home.

"It sounds comfortable."

"I swear," she whispered, "he was like my grandpa."

"Did neighbors assume that relationship?"

"Not likely, with him being Black." She grinned. "But he didn't have any close neighbors anyway. Didn't have any family left, either, since he and his wife had never had kids."

"You loved him."

The tears spilled over, so all she could do was nod.

Cade reached out to gently brush her cheeks. "I'm so glad you found him."

It took her a minute to regain her composure. Normally she would have been more embarrassed for the pitiful show of emotion, but as he'd said, Cade was different. With a sniffle and a clearing of her throat, she whispered, "When I was twenty-two, he helped me get my CDL, even gave me a reference for Brown Transportation. I worked there until I was twenty-six."

"Why didn't you stay there?"

"Gus passed away in his sleep. I knew we'd gotten close, but it stunned me to find out he'd left me his house. Isn't that crazy?"

"Sounds like you were as important to him as he was to you."

"Not even close, but God love that man, he made me feel... valued." More tears fell, and this time she angrily swiped them away. "There was a note with the will. He kept it vague, I guess in case anyone else read it, but he said to sell the house and use the money, with what he had in his accounts, to do what I needed to do."

Cade still held her left hand, but now he gripped it as if he couldn't let go. "You didn't want to stay in his house? Find a regular job?"

"Me? No way. I'm not cut out for that, you know? Gus had provided a lifeline and I grabbed it. When he said he knew what I needed to do, he was right. I *need* to do this." That god-awful guilt shortened her breath and compressed her lungs, but she admitted her greatest sin. "When I escaped, I left other girls behind."

"You alone couldn't have helped them."

No, she wouldn't accept that, wouldn't take the easy out. She'd let her fear run her. All she could do now was own the truth. "I could have led police there. I did try calling it in once, but it was a week later before I thought of it, and I'm guessing after what happened, they'd moved on."

Cade sat quiet for far too long. He kissed her knuckles again, started to speak but didn't. Finally he said, "Hearing all this... it occurs to me that I might have been too pushy."

"No denying that." He'd pushed his way right into her life, but she enjoyed having him there. More than she'd ever thought possible. "Too late to take it back now."

As if magnetized, his gaze caught hers. "I'm guessing some things might be...difficult for you."

Not liking the way he verbally danced around it, she said, "A lot of stuff is difficult, so what? If you mean something specific, spit it out already."

"Sex."

"Oh." He was concerned that she was traumatized still? Well, yeah, in some ways she was—but that wasn't one of them. "You know me now, right?"

"I hope so. I'd like to know you even better, but yes, we're getting there."

"So do you *really* think I wouldn't have fixed that?"

Skeptical, and obviously a bit confused by her wording, he repeated, "*Fixed* it?"

"With what I do, I knew I had to overcome some things. Getting caught would be bad enough, but if the thought of regular sex with a non-psychopathic guy left me paralyzed, how would I deal with a freaking monster who treated women like trained dogs?"

Finally he released her hand. He looked steady enough, but she saw the fire in his eyes and the acceleration of his breathing. "And you fixed that…how?"

He looked so intense right now that she could guess how he'd looked when he broke into Misfits. "Cool your jets. It's nothing bad."

"Define *bad*."

"I had sex," she said with a shrug. "Few different guys, few different occasions. Until it wasn't so scary anymore."

Sitting back hard, Cade studied her. "Did you like it?"

"I didn't hate it." Not the last few times. "That was the important part. Now I'm in the camp of take it or leave it."

Seconds ticked by. "Except with me."

The man did not lack confidence. "Yup. There you go again, standing out from the pack. I liked kissing you, so I'm guessing the rest will be fun."

Slowly, he pushed back his chair and stood.

Sterling held her breath, but when he reached for her, he only stroked her ponytail, down and over her shoulder, until his fingers cupped her chin. "When we get together, it'll be more than fun. I'm going to make damn sure you love every second."

Wow, now she could hardly wait.

CHAPTER EIGHT

Cade was patient, always, but two additional days passed without a word from Adela. He knew the waiting wore on Star. He understood that. With a woman in need, every day—hell, every hour—could mean life or death.

Using the time to get closer to Star, he'd kissed her a few more times, each a little longer, a little hotter, easing into her life. She was so open about what she liked, and she clearly liked intimate contact. It astounded him that she hadn't been more sexually active, but it made sense, given what she'd been through.

He wanted to be the one to show her just how hot sex could be—with the right person. So far she was on board with that plan.

She was recovering quickly but still had a limp to her walk, and she couldn't yet make a fist with her injured finger. Until she was 100 percent, he wouldn't let it go beyond kissing. For now, it worked as extended foreplay, wearing her down, softening her attitude. Not that he wanted to change her.

It was the hard-core woman who'd drawn him.

But when they came together, he wanted her totally involved, as ready as he was, maybe even more anxious for the ultimate release he'd give her, though how that was possible when he wanted her nonstop, he didn't know.

For now, sleeping with her each night was enough. Torture, yes, but he wouldn't be giving it up anytime soon.

He knew eventually he'd have all of her.

And then what?

His life wasn't set up for a significant other. Any day now his father could send him off on a mission. Reyes might hear something at his gym that required follow-up. Madison might uncover a lead.

He hadn't yet told Star that the main reason he ran a bar, besides fitting into the neighborhood, was because conversations from seedy characters could be overheard. More than a few times he'd gotten information he needed because too many drinks lowered caution. He could subtly ask the right questions and get good information that he then followed up on.

There'd been a man who bragged about the internet arrangements that had gotten him a few hours of pleasure. Another who'd laughed about how cheaply he'd bought time with a girl.

Keeping his hands off them was difficult, but when it led to bigger stings, Cade could hold it together.

Same with Reyes and his gym. All different types came in to bulk up. Even if they didn't talk about personal involvement, word from the street was usually sound. Reyes would hear enough to know when a new crew moved into an abandoned house or if a different guy was suddenly offering services from the corner.

Parrish had planned it all well. He'd purchased the bar and gym at opposite ends of the same downtrodden area, instructed each of them on what they'd do—and then he'd fully expected to be obeyed.

That part of the equation still annoyed Cade, but he couldn't deny they were effective. Not just in Ridge Trail, Colorado, but all over the US, since many of the roads here were used to transport women, kids and sometimes men in and out of various states. A local lead often branched out to different headquarters. Not all traffickers were on a grand scale, but some were—and they all deserved to be eliminated.

"I need to get back to work soon." Star didn't look up to make that announcement. At the dining table, her laptop open, she said, "I've had a few requests for deliveries."

Cade understood, but he didn't like it. When he had to take off to follow a lead, would Star understand? He might not see her for a day or two, or more. Would she demand answers that he couldn't give?

Unwilling to borrow trouble, he joined her at the table. "Local drives?"

"One is for an overnight, but two others are local." Brows scrunched up, she studied the screen.

"Problem?"

"I keep thinking about Adela." She rubbed her temple wearily. "She was supposed to have called by now. If my stupid leg hadn't been hurt—"

"You still needed time to plan."

"I know. But it's been too long now. What if I'm gone on a job and she needs me?"

Knowing he had to be careful here, Cade tried for an offhand tone. "If you're away, you could call me with the details. I could follow up for you."

She slanted him a look. "We've been over that, right? You're a guy, so not trustworthy. She probably wouldn't let you get anywhere near her."

"She might if you told her that *you* trust me."

Slumping into her seat, she sighed. "I don't know. There are some things I prefer to do myself."

Right—like *most* things. That prickly attitude was a part of her personality, like her sarcasm and her inner strength. Altogether, they were…sometimes annoying, yes. But he also saw them as tools she'd used to survive, and for that he was profoundly grateful.

For now, she was safely ensconced at home, she slept with him every night, and each day a little more of her reserve melted away.

She had a strong will—but so did he. In the end, he'd convince her to see things his way.

When her phone buzzed, they both turned to look where she'd left it plugged in on the end table next to the couch.

"You rarely get calls," Cade noted.

"Rarely, as in never." She bolted out of the chair, limped hurriedly across the room and frowned at the screen. "Unlisted number again."

"Put it on speaker."

"Magic word?" she asked, but then did as he requested without making him say "please," answering on the fourth ring. "Hello?"

"Francis?"

Star gripped the phone tighter. "Adela? Hey. I thought you'd call before now. I'd about given up on you."

Voice choked, Adela said, "Please don't. Please don't give up on me."

Gently, Star said, "No, I won't."

"I'd have called sooner, but I couldn't."

Cade didn't move.

Star didn't appear to be breathing. "Why not?"

"I think he's found me, Francis." Softly weeping, she said, "I was in a cabin without cell service, and when I went into town, I saw him there. If I don't get away soon, I'm afraid he'll kill me."

Carefully sitting on the couch, Star said, "Tell me exactly where you are."

"I want to," she said in a small voice. "But you can't call the police. One of the cops is a regular. He'd lead Mattox right to me."

Eyes narrowing at that info, Star promised, "I won't tell the police, but I can't help you if I don't know where to find you."

"You'll come alone? You swear?"

Star's gaze met and held Cade's as she answered. "Yes, I swear."

Closing his eyes, Cade vowed that wouldn't happen. He wouldn't *let* it happen. If he had to dog her day and night to ensure she didn't try this on her own, that's what he'd do.

"All right." Adela sniffled. "I trust you."

"When should I come for you?" Star asked. "Right now?"

Like hell. Already Cade was reconfiguring his schedule, who he'd get to cover for him at the bar, how quickly he could arrange for Reyes to be backup.

He didn't doubt that his brother would do it. Come to that, Parrish would also extend all the protections he could. But that shit took time, and if she left right now—

"No!" Panic sharpened the single word. Then Adela immediately tried to explain. "Tonight. When it's dark. That way he...he won't be able to see us leaving."

"All right." Standing again, Star went into the kitchen and retrieved the pen and paper, then carried them back to hand to Cade. "Give me a number to reach you."

"No, it's too risky."

"I need *something*, Adela. At least an address or directions."

"Right." She breathed audibly, then asked, "You really won't say anything to anyone?"

Star rolled her eyes over the continued—frustrating—worry, but replied in a soothing tone, "I already gave you my word."

"You tried to save me that night. At Misfits."

"Yes, but I understand why you were too frightened to go then."

"He would have killed me," Adela claimed. "Right there on the spot. I didn't think you'd actually get away, but you did."

"We'll both get away this time, okay? Now quickly, tell me where to find you."

With only the briefest hesitation, Adela said, "There's a small town. Coalville. It's only five or six miles off I-25. As you enter the town, there's a stone church. Right after that, take the dirt road. It'll lead you up to the cabin where I'm staying. In case Mattox is watching the roads in that area, turn your headlights off."

It all sounded majorly fucked to Cade, even as he jotted it all down.

Star must've agreed, because she suggested, "Why don't you just meet me at the church? That'll be easier, right?"

"But if you don't show up, I'll be too exposed."

"I'll be there, and being close to the road will give us a better chance to escape." Not giving Adela a moment to change that plan, Star asked, "What time?"

"I guess…ten?"

"I'll be there. Adela? Try not to worry. I won't let you down."

"I can't thank you enough, really, but I should go." Nervously, she whispered, "I never know if Mattox has men watching the town looking for me. I'll go back to the cabin for now and wait."

"Until ten."

"Thank you, Francis. You're a lifesaver."

Deflated, Star returned the phone to the table, then just stood there.

It would be easier to have her cooperation, so Cade came up behind her, drew her back against his body and kissed her temple. "I'm going to help."

As if he hadn't spoken, she said, "Good thing my leg is so much better. I have a lot to get done now."

"Like what?"

Looking at him as if he were nuts, she said, "Like I need to rent a car. No way am I letting anyone track me down by my ride. And of course I want to go scope out that area. It could be a trap. Could be Mattox forced her to make the call."

He found no fault with her deductive reasoning. "It does seem a little too pat."

"She did agree to switch locations, and hopefully the church is more in the town than the cabin would've been. But... I don't know. Something doesn't feel right."

Turning her, Cade cupped her face in his hands. "You have incredible instincts, honey, so trust them."

"Yeah, I do." She frowned. "Those instincts are telling me something isn't right." She looked up at him. "But I still have to go."

"I know." Only she didn't need to go alone. "Will you trust me?"

Head cocked in challenge, she asked, "Trust you how?"

"I have...resources."

Her mouth twisted. "That you can't discuss."

A reality he couldn't get around. "Let me have the area checked. We'll be discreet. I can get you the alternate car, too. No need to use a dealer."

"Huh." Sounding impressed, she said, "No kidding? Just like that?"

"Yeah, just like that."

For several seconds, Star considered it. "The thing is..." She moistened her lips while carefully selecting her words. "I do trust you, because I know you. These other obscure peeps you talk about—they're big unknowns, and I just don't go there. So how about *you* trust *me* to get this job done without your interference?"

He didn't like having his assistance labeled as interference, but he got where she was coming from. He wouldn't trust the unknown, either. Still, he couldn't let her do this alone.

Looking past her, he checked the clock on the wall. He had only a few hours left if he wanted to accomplish all that needed to be done—with or without her approval.

He needed to accelerate their relationship—but would she see that as underhanded? Find it difficult to forgive—or insanely satisfying? Hard to say, and unfortunately, it was the only thing he could think of. His time to slowly win her over had abruptly run out.

"Is your leg healed enough?"

"I won't be running any races yet, but yeah, it's fine. Hardly sore anymore."

Yet she still limped—and he couldn't let that matter. Not now. "Good to know," he whispered as he bent to her mouth, kissing her softly at first, just moving his lips over hers until she leaned into him—which he took as a sign of agreement.

One hand at the back of her head, the other sliding down to her backside, he aligned her body with his. Hell if he wasn't already hard, but he'd wanted her for so long that giving himself permission was like flipping a switch. He was now *on* and only hoped he could get her there, too.

With all she'd suffered in her past, he planned to take it slow, to make use of the entire two hours he had. He could scramble last-minute with plans, but he wouldn't rush this.

He wouldn't rush her.

Her lips opened to the touch of his tongue, and the kiss quickly became hot. He turned his head for a better fit. She did the same. Her fingertips curled against his chest. Her hips nudged his.

Open mouths, lots of tongue play, heavy breathing. Now petting, too… Christ, she'd escalated things fast, but then, she was like that, a lit fuse waiting to explode.

He'd take a sexual explosion over her temper any day.

Urging her head back, he trailed his lips to the velvet skin of her neck, her warm throat, that sensitive spot beneath her ear. Tilting to give him better access, she gave a soft groan.

"Wow, I like that."

Had no one ever…? No, he didn't want to think about her healing brand of sex, meant only to help her over an emotional hurdle, with no thought for pleasure.

He'd drown her in pleasure, and she'd never forget him.

The comfortable clothes she wore made touching her oh so easy. Liking the feel of her beneath the stretchy yoga pants, he opened his hand wide to enclose an entire cheek, then trailed his fingers down the cleft—then under, to touch her more intimately.

Gasping, she went to her tiptoes but didn't pull away.

Her tightened nipples, covered only by the soft cotton of her loose T-shirt, pressed against his chest. With a love bite, Cade encouraged another gasp…one that faded into a vibrating groan.

"Mmm," she whispered. "Do that again."

"Which part?"

"All of it?"

Even now, when he'd launched to the ragged edge, she made him smile. Star had substance, both emotionally and intellectually.

And in her curves. God yes, those curves.

She was as soft as a woman should be, but with core strength. She was bold enough to speak her mind, as she'd just done, and brave enough to travel to a remote area alone, without backup, to save a woman in need.

How the hell was he supposed to resist that enticing mix of attributes?

He couldn't.

With her active participation so obvious, he stroked her waist, then slipped his hand under her shirt and up to one heavy breast. He held back his own groan, but the warmth of her, the silkiness of her bare breast, made him forget his resolve.

"Cade?"

He came back to her mouth for another deep kiss. She tangled the fingers of her left hand into his hair, and with the right, she cupped his face. He felt the roughness of the bandage on her fingers and turned to gently kiss those, too. "Hmm?"

"Is this your way of coercing me?"

Stark reality crashed onto his head. Had his motives been that base? That cold? Not with the way he'd always wanted her. Hell, he'd been looking for an excuse to rush his own self-imposed timeline.

Since he hadn't heard anger or accusation in her tone, just curiosity, he straightened to look into her eyes.

She gave him a smug, knowing smile.

Nothing got by her. He wouldn't have lied anyway, but now he knew she wouldn't have fallen for it no matter his reasons.

Before he could say anything, she grinned and cuddled close again. "Understand, I'm not complaining." Her uninjured hand traveled to his ass. "And if you live up to your promise, I might even be swayed to take you along."

Now, why that outrageous comment fired his lust, he couldn't say, but he crushed his mouth down on hers again. Full participation, that's what he got from her.

No reserve. No remnants of bad memories.

Such a remarkable woman in every way.

"So much enthusiasm."

God, she pushed his buttons. And humbled him. "Thank you for understanding."

"That you're not a user? No problem."

Her faith meant more than she knew, prompting him to another kiss, this one full of tenderness. And yeah, lust.

No way to dodge the lust.

"Bedroom?" she suggested, when he came up for air.

Cade smoothed her hair and cupped her cheek. Unique in so many ways. "No argument from me."

Smiling in satisfaction, she took his hand and led him through the kitchen–dining area, past the bathroom and into her room with the still–rumpled bed.

His conscience decided he needed one more confirmation, so he started to say, "Are you sure—"

But she pulled the T-shirt up and off, and he forgot he had a conscience. Shoulders back, spine straight, chin elevated. Her breasts were a handful, yet somehow she'd always downplayed that asset with her wardrobe choices. Her rib cage tapered into a smaller waist, then flared out for her shapely hips. His gaze lingered on the slight curve of her belly, exposed by the low-fitting yoga pants. Every inch of her fascinated him and made him want more.

"You're staring."

Without lifting his gaze from her body, Cade shrugged. "How could I not? You're perfect."

"Ha. I'm still bruised some, you know. It's all these hideous shades of green and yellow now. Really nasty."

Insecurity, from Star? That, more than anything, helped him gain a measure of control even though she stood there half-naked, tempting every basic instinct known to man. "I've seen bruises before, and I saw part of yours today before you dressed."

Wrinkling her nose, she tugged the band out of her hair so that it fell free. "Then you know what I mean."

Reyes was right. She did have incredible hair. Having it loose and tousled around her naked breasts added to the sensuality of the moment. "They're just bruises, babe, and they don't keep me from wanting you."

"Good thing, I guess, since I want you, too." She nodded at him. "Shirt off."

All too happy to oblige, Cade reached back for a handful of material and stripped it over his head.

"You still haven't told me about these tats." She moved closer, first trailing her fingers through his chest hair, then tracing the edges of one tattoo, a waving American flag that twined from his right shoulder to his elbow. Eyes dark with interest, she teased that soft touch to the eagle on his right pec.

He had another on the back of his left shoulder of a soldier drifting from a battlefield into heaven. All in all, pretty self-explanatory. "How about after?"

"After we do the nasty?"

She wanted to make it less than it was—but he wouldn't let her. "Nothing nasty about it. Not between us." He gathered a thick hank of hair in his fist, resisting her breasts for the moment. It felt cool in comparison to her hot skin. "Okay?"

"Another promise. You've got a lot to live up to."

"I'll do my best." And with that he cupped a breast, kneaded gently, then bent to circle the nipple with his tongue.

"Okay." Shakily, she drew in a breath. "Let me just get my pants off."

"Soon." He drew her in, sucking softly—then not so softly—while she moved her hands all over him. "Easy. Don't hurt your fingers."

"Worry about what you're doing."

The order amused him, especially since he understood it. "All right." He shifted his attention to her other breast, but at the same time he worked his hand inside the loose waistband of her pants, his hand cupping over her heat.

"You're a tease," she complained, her head tipped back, eyes closed. "Men aren't supposed to tease."

"Me and you, Star. I told you, we're different." He kissed her slightly parted lips. "Quit trying to put us in a category."

Her heavy eyes opened. "Fine. But I've been waiting for this for too long, maybe even before I admitted I wanted you. So now is *not* the time for teasing."

God, he loved her forthright way of speaking. "You need to come?"

Her eyes flared, and a wash of color tinged her cheeks. "Well… I need *something*, okay? So stop playing around."

"All right." He went to his knees and reached for the waist-band of her pants. "But one of these days you're going to like the way I play."

"One of these days—meaning you plan to stick around?"

Digging for future plans? What could he say? He wouldn't make promises until he knew he could keep them, so without answering, he tugged the pants and her panties down to her ankles. "Step out."

At first the only thing she did was breathe deeply.

He took his time looking at her body. And a hell of a body it was. Gorgeous legs, despite the bruising that drew his lips. He skimmed them over her skin as if he could heal the last remnants of her injury. The cut had closed nicely, but she'd have a small scar. He pressed a soft kiss to that, too.

The rest of her…so beautiful. He'd admired the length of her legs plenty of times, but seeing her like this, totally bared, ramped up the churning need. Sliding his hands to her hips, he leaned in—

"Wait." Sleek with muscle, her long thighs flexed as she balanced with a hand to his shoulder. Hastily, awkwardly, given the lingering stiffness of her injured leg, she kicked away her pants. Free of clothes, she straightened, nodded down at him and said, "Go ahead."

Cade actually laughed. Physical need consumed him, yet he'd never known anyone quite like her. In every way imaginable, she was incredibly special.

She was *his*.

She might not know that yet, but somehow he'd make it so, starting right now. "Anything you don't like—"

"Yeah, you'll hear about it." Again she threaded her fingers through his hair. "You curl my toes, Cade. I never knew that was a real thing."

He smiled again. "Let's see what else I can curl."

★ ★ ★

Oh. My. God. Over and over again, Sterling repeated that in her mind. She had Cade McKenzie, all six feet, five gorgeous inches of him, kneeling in front of her, touching her in incendiary ways while kissing her belly and thighs.

Now that she could play with it—and basically use it as an anchor—she found that his hair was thick and soft on top and in front, and she liked the way the shorter sides and back felt against her fingertips, like velvet almost.

Soon as he finished what he was doing—because she wasn't about to interrupt again—she planned to glut herself on his bod.

With his lips nibbling at her hip bone, he stroked over her sex. Yeah, she had to lock her knees for that—and then he pressed a finger into her, growling at finding her so wet. What did he expect? From the moment he started seducing her, she'd wanted to melt.

Didn't matter that he might have started this to get his way. It was as good a reason as any, right? Especially when it got her what she wanted most.

Him. Naked. With *her* naked. Full-body contact—and a big payoff in the way of pleasure.

Besides, he'd find she wasn't easily manipulated, awesome sex or not. If she invited Cade along, it'd be on her own terms, for her own reasons.

She had a feeling he'd meet her halfway, and until then, why not enjoy herself?

As he slowly fingered her, she not only heard but felt his groan. The pleasure built, coiling, heating… She wanted it bad. This, now, and more.

So much more.

She whispered that, *"More,"* aloud and got a second finger because of it. Much as she enjoyed watching the flex and roll of his broad shoulders, sensation compelled her eyes to close.

Her head tipped back of its own accord, as if her neck offered no support.

Her knees were getting to the same point, especially when he used his other fingers to open her...and she felt his mouth.

Biting her lip to hold back the groan, she tightened. His tongue...yeah, that velvet tongue performed some magic, touching her just right, exactly *there*, over and over again, leisurely at first while he made sounds of enjoyment, then with more deliberate purpose.

She couldn't stay quiet any longer. Her nipples throbbed, needing him, but not enough to ask him to stop. The sweetest, almost painful ache curled in her lower belly. Despite the way she'd been pampering her leg, her thigh muscles tensed, a necessary adjustment to keep her upright so he could continue.

Shifting, he opened his hand on her behind and pressed her closer—then drew in her clit for a soft suckle and, good God, she cried out. Without restraint.

Who cared?

An incredibly powerful orgasm raged through her, leaving her one giant pulsing beat of sizzling sensation. Panting, a little sweaty, she realized she'd curled over him when he finally let up. Yup, that had pretty much wiped out her backbone. Maybe all her bones.

He shifted her so he could stand.

"Don't let go," she warned, unwilling to open her eyes. "I'll fall flat on my face."

Against her ear, he whispered, "Never," in a way that sounded like he meant more than this single moment. Her heart seized at the thought, but then in some crazy, gallant, straight-out-of-a-film move, he lifted her into his arms and placed her on the bed.

"Oh," she mumbled, stretching a little, snuggling into the bedding. "Well done. Very romantic."

Grinning, he opened his jeans. "You think so?"

"Yup." No way was she going to miss this. She managed to

keep her eyes wide-open, didn't even blink. "Promises made, promises kept. I'm now a believer."

"And just think," he said, shoving down his jeans to stand there buck-ass and incredibly stunning, "we're not done, yet."

Wow, he was put together fine. Better than fine. It was as if someone had taken all things she considered masculine and expertly pieced them together. Dark chest hair, roped muscles over arms and legs, long bones and obvious power.

A big cock.

Sterling cleared her throat. "Looks like I won the lottery."

His smile went crooked. Pulling his wallet from his jeans, he dug out a condom. While she watched in fascination, he rolled it over a very rigid, pulsing erection.

Her mouth went dry. "What if I'd wanted to touch that?" When he glanced at her, she nodded at his crotch. Honestly, every inch of him fascinated her. She wanted to explore him— without a rubber in the way. In fact, she wouldn't mind stroking that firm butt, too, and those muscular, hair-dusted thighs, his flat abdomen with that sexy happy trail.

"It'd be over too quick," he said, stretching out atop her and pecking her mouth. "Next time, I promise, you can touch all you want."

"Hardly seems fair, considering."

Using his knee, he opened her legs and settled between her tingling thighs. "Complaining?"

On principle alone, she considered it, but he was already stroking her breasts, thumbing her nipples, and she felt that hard cock against her... "Nope. No complaints from me."

"Good." He sealed his mouth over hers—and thrust into her.

Holy cow. In sheer reaction, her hips lifted off the bed. He filled her up, the fit snug, the glide smooth, wet, pure pleasure, but it was so much more than that, too.

It was Cade's scent making her light-headed, the sleek feel

of his taut skin under her hands, the provoking sound he made deep in his throat—a sound of pure, unadulterated lust.

Yes, she'd gotten used to sex.

Yes, there'd been times when she'd somewhat enjoyed it.

None of those times had anything in common with this.

She wrapped one leg around him, keeping him close, and lifted her other along his hip.

"Easy," Cade whispered against her throat. "I don't want to hurt you. Your leg—"

"Shut up, Cade." She grasped his butt in her uninjured hand and urged him to move, at the same time *she* was moving, rocking against him, twisting…exciting herself on the hard length of him.

He laughed roughly and took over.

It was a hard ride, one she encouraged however she could. Keeping him locked to her, she bit his shoulder, licked the spot, then sucked on his hot skin as another climax rocked her.

Grinding into her, Cade put his face to her neck and growled out a long, harsh release.

Huh. Hearing other guys come hadn't moved her at all. But Cade? She wanted to cuddle him—and how nuts was that? You didn't cuddle a tiger, right? But she couldn't let him go, couldn't stop putting soft kisses along his shoulder, couldn't stop stroking his hot skin.

It was a good ten minutes before she moved, and even then, her limbs felt sluggish and uncooperative. Yes, her leg throbbed like a son of a bitch, but it was worth it.

"Good going," she whispered in a teasing grumble as she tried to adjust. "How am I supposed to deal with Adela or Mattox when my muscles have turned to noodles?"

An utter stillness settled over him, replaced seconds later by determination as he levered up, bracing his arms on either side of her shoulders. "You let me help."

He surrounded her with his size, his scent, his iron will. Didn't bother her at all. "Your muscles aren't limp?"

"I'll recover. Quickly." He pressed a firm kiss to her mouth. "This, what we just did, was a commitment."

What? No way. "Who says so?"

"I say so." Far too serious, his intense gaze drilled into her. "You're strong, Star. Strong enough to share the burden without worrying that I'll take over. I won't, you know."

She snorted at that. "You already are."

"No, babe. I want to share the plans, the setup and the risk. I'm guessing you don't know this yet, but it's easier that way."

"What's easier?"

His expression softened. "Everything." With extreme gentleness he smoothed back her hair. "Everything is easier when you're not alone."

"So…" Knowing she was out of her depth, Sterling tried to think, but it wasn't possible, not right now with his body all over her body, his gaze catching her every thought. Full honesty, then. "This wasn't a one-off?"

His smile was so tender that it turned her soft, too. "Once isn't near enough for me. Don't tell me it was for you."

"I want more." More of him, more of this. Maybe the sharing he mentioned, too.

"Good." He released a pent-up breath. "Difficult as it'll be, we have to get out of bed, shower—"

"Together?"

"*Alone*, because I have calls to make."

She pretended to pout, but seriously, showering with him would have been nice.

"We need to coordinate plans. I need to prove to you that having me along will be a good thing. But if we shower together…?" He shook his head. "All my good intentions will go right out the window, because now that I've had you, I won't be able to keep from touching you." He cupped her breast. "Kissing you." He nuzzled her neck. Near her ear, he whispered, "Tasting you—again."

Sterling shivered. "You're promising a lot."

"Don't let it scare you." Laughing, he dodged her smack, caught her hand and pressed it down beside her head.

"I'm not *scared*."

"Wary, then." He pushed off the bed but took the time to look her over as he picked up his boxers and jeans. "Take a few minutes more if you want. I'll shower first."

She watched him walk away with a sense of…peace? That, or something equally serene, invaded her very soul. It was a new, unfamiliar feeling, one of many thanks to Cade.

He was right, of course. He did scare her, mostly because she hadn't relied on anyone in a very long time. Maybe because she liked Cade so much, because she really wanted to rely on him, it made it somehow worse. More alarming.

But she wasn't a wimp, so she got out of bed and went for her laptop. She had a lot of research to do. Maybe that'd get her mind off the naked hunk currently in her shower.

Doubtful, but she'd give it a try.

CHAPTER NINE

After the explosive sex, Star finally agreed to let him take part in retrieving Adela. He would have assisted her anyway, but having her agreement simplified things.

He'd known they would be good together. After all, the chemistry was through the roof.

Yet the depth of what he'd felt, the extreme connection, had surprised him. He'd like nothing more than to spend an entire day in bed with her, exploring her incredible curves and enjoying her blunt, uninhibited way of responding.

Impossible when they had so much to do.

They'd already picked up the alternate vehicle from his family's private lot, a reinforced van with darkened windows that he and Reyes used when they expected gunplay. The black matte paint helped hide it in low light, plus it had incredible speed for a van.

He'd spent an hour trying to convince Star to let his family take part. Her protestations—that she didn't know his family, so how could he expect her to trust them?—made sense.

He understood and offered a compromise, suggesting, "Just

my brother, then." Reyes made one hell of an ally. If there were ten men waiting to ambush Star, Cade could handle them. He had no doubts on his own ability. But a sniper bullet? Mattox was the type of cowardly abuser who might do anything, including lure her in for a fast death.

Making a woman suffer was more his speed, though, but Cade wouldn't take chances either way.

"You've already met him," he reminded Star. "He'll stay out of the way, but he'll be an extra set of eyes just in case something goes wrong."

"He's annoying," she announced, as if that settled it.

Laughing, Cade couldn't deny that she'd nailed Reyes. "It's true, my brother takes extreme pleasure in pushing people over the edge. But he's reliable, capable and loyal."

With ill grace, she growled, "Fine. So he's a sterling example of humanity."

"Let's don't go overboard." He knew and accepted his brother's faults—same as Reyes did for him.

With a frustrated growl, she said, "Involve him if you want." She gave him a hard glare. "But he's *your* responsibility."

Cade could just imagine Reyes's reaction if he heard that insult. Struggling not to smile, he said, "I appreciate the vote of confidence."

"Is that what it was? Felt more like me giving up because you wouldn't let it go."

That had been hours ago, and she was still bristling about it as they prepped to take off.

In the back of the van, Cade reached out to touch her cheek. "I have to do what's necessary to keep you safe."

Mouth firming, she slid the Glock she'd just checked into a holster at her hip and stared up at him. "Long as you know I feel the same about you."

That declaration deserved a kiss, but he kept it soft and quick to say, "I assume you've practiced shooting left-handed?" Her injured finger wasn't taped now, but it was still swollen and no doubt painful.

"You're asking me now?" Grinning, she indicated the small arsenal they'd amassed by combining their weapons. She reached for a Smith & Wesson .38 revolver to put in her ankle holster. "I plan for all contingencies, including an injured right hand, so yeah, I've had plenty of practice. I'm more accurate right-handed, but I can make do with my left, especially if it's a target as big as Mattox."

As she tugged the leg of her jeans over the gun, Cade asked deadpan, "Packing anything else?"

"My knife," she said, turning to shake her booty at him so he'd notice the sheathed knife at the small of her back. "But I'd only use it if I got caught up close."

No way would he let that happen. Cade drew a breath.

Seeing her so heavily armed had a dual effect on him. He believed she was proficient at protecting herself; her ease with all the weapons reassured him of that. At the same time, he wished he could insist she hang behind and let him handle things. He'd get Adela, and kill Mattox if possible, but he knew Star well enough to know she'd never go for that.

If he suggested she sit this out, she'd not only refuse, she'd revert to handling things on her own.

"Let me help," he said when she lifted the bulletproof vest he'd brought for her. It was the one thing she seemed unfamiliar with. He dropped it over her head, then adjusted the Velcro straps so it properly fit her.

While she pulled on her button-up shirt, which was a tight fit now, he put on his own vest, and then the tactical belt that held more ammo, nylon cuffs, a Taser, knife, strobing flashlight, flash bang and two Glocks.

Brows up, Star nodded at the flash bang. "A grenade? Really?"

"Nonlethal, but good at disorienting people—in the case of a mob. There's no telling how Mattox might set this up."

"*If* he set it up," Star said, then asked, "You don't believe Adela?"

He stashed the first aid kit into a panel of the van, along with other emergency items. "I don't think I do," Cade admitted, "but mostly because I don't think you do, either. Want to tell me why?"

She appeared to like his answer. "There's something about her, right? I've dealt with traumatized women before. I *was* a traumatized woman. But this just feels a little…off. Not enough that I won't help her, but yeah, I've got my guard up, big-time."

"Do you know what triggered that feeling?"

"She knows Mattox. I know him, too." Casual as you please, she tossed out, "He's the bastard who had me kidnapped all those years ago. The one who was in charge, who ordered me into that room with a drunken rapist, who employed the goons who stood guard."

Completely floored with that last-minute disclosure, Cade stared at her in disbelief. Pretending it was nothing, Star pulled the cargo door closed and locked it. Gaze averted, she started past him for the driver's seat, but he caught her arm.

At first, no words came to mind. She looked at him in mild inquiry, but he wasn't buying it. She knew she'd just dropped a bombshell on him, and now she waited to see what he'd do.

Sensing there was a lot riding on his reaction, he forcibly tamped down the extreme annoyance trying to take precedence. "You have a history with Mattox?"

"Yeah, but the big lummox didn't recognize me. Remember, I looked way different back then."

That she'd kept this from him left him seething. "Is there a reason you didn't tell me before now?"

"Couple of reasons, actually. One, I figured you'd freak out."

Cade took a step closer to her. "I do not *freak out*."

"No?" She pointedly looked over his rigid posture. "What do you call this?"

"Furious?" He caught her shoulder before she could spin away. "Damn it, Star. You know you should have told me."

"Because we had sex? Get real." She pointed a finger at his chest. "That's one reason why I didn't. You're acting all territorial and stuff."

"How do you figure that?" Hell, he felt that way, sure. But he'd kept from showing it.

Or had he?

No, he definitely had. If he'd had his way, she wouldn't be in the back of a bulletproof van strapping weapons all over her lean, sexy body, making plans to charge into danger.

"It's the way you look at me now," she explained, as if it surprised her that he didn't know.

He pulled his chin back. "How do I look at you?"

Mouth turning down, she quipped, "Like you think you have me all wrapped up."

Yeah, right. "I'm not deluded." She was a loose cannon. God, he wished he had a little control over her… No, he didn't.

Part of what he admired most about Star were her guts and fortitude. She might bend, but she would never break.

He found that confidence sexy as hell.

And deep down, a small part of him thought she might be strong enough to handle the life he'd chosen.

Most weren't.

Tell other women that he eliminated human traffickers at any cost? They'd bail real fast.

Only Star saw it as an opportunity to team up.

"Maybe not deluded, but if I'd told you earlier, you'd have wanted me to stay behind—which isn't happening, so don't even go there."

He let his own anger show. "Don't assume my thoughts."

"I don't have to. It's right there on your face."

"Regardless of what you think you see, I know this is important to you. And you're important to me."

Her belligerent expression faltered. "I am?"

New irritation surfaced. "How the hell can you be surprised over that?" He cut her off when she started to speak. "I care enough that I'd like to stand with you, but I wouldn't stand in your way."

"Wow. Okay." A small smile formed, then went crooked. "Do I owe you an apology?"

"Damn right. You withheld info that I need to share with Reyes."

That took care of her softened mood. "I don't see why."

Cade already had his phone out. "Your past relationship with Mattox ups the chance that this is all a ruse to get to you."

Scoffing, she said, "I told you, he didn't recognize me."

"You can't be sure of that."

She threw up her hands. "Aren't you the one who said I have good instincts?"

The text he sent Reyes was brief and to the point. "You're giving me second thoughts on that." Given her gasp, Cade assumed the insult hit home.

"Well, too bad." Suddenly she moved against him, hugging him as tight as she could while they wore bulletproof vests.

Definitely not the reaction he'd expected. Automatically, his arms went around her. Without thinking about it, he rested his face against the top of her head, breathed in the warm musk of her skin and hair, and relished the feel of her.

How had she become so important to him so quickly?

Voice lower now, a little confused and a little worried, she said, "I watched Mattox's face at Misfits. It leveled me, seeing him again after so long. I don't mind telling you I was struck with a sort of blindsided panic."

Cade wished he could have spared her that. It had to be rough, having her past just show up like that.

To reassure him, she pressed back to make eye contact. "There wasn't a speck of recognition. I swear, he had no idea who I am." Biting her lip, she added, "He didn't know that he'd ruined my life so long ago."

"Listen to me, babe, okay?" Here she stood, armed to the teeth, ready to take on the world—and her abuser. She'd suffered that recognition alone. She would have done this alone, too, if he hadn't found a way to talk her around. "You need to be ready to shoot. Shit goes sideways, don't think about it. Just protect yourself." Abusive assholes were expendable. She was not. "If anything at all sets off a warning, promise me you'll get out of there, okay?"

She nodded. "You betcha."

A returning text from Reyes dinged into the silence. Are you sure there won't be any other surprises?

No, he wasn't, but he replied: Just be ready for anything.

Reyes sent a thumbs-up emoji.

Putting the phone on vibrate and pocketing it, Cade said, "Time for us to go."

She nodded and got behind the wheel. He disabled the interior lights and then sat behind the passenger seat, where he'd have a view out the windshield and could also easily see Star. There was no more talking as she drove out to the meeting place.

Coalville was a minuscule town, a population of around one hundred, give or take any recent deaths or births, with most of the residents being elderly. The quick research they'd done claimed it was a ghost town—a story that started back in the early 1900s when a mine explosion caused over fifty deaths and effectively destroyed the growing mining industry.

"If anyone lives here," Star murmured, "they must be up in the hills somewhere." She drove slowly over railroad tracks onto broken pavement that turned to gravel…that led to a dirt road.

The van's headlights bounced over scrubby bushes and boulders along the narrow sides of the road. They passed a couple of shacks that appeared abandoned, two mobile homes nearly rusted through and a small store with most of the windows boarded up.

"Should I kill the lights?"

"No." That's what Adela wanted them to do, and he wasn't in an accommodating mood. At the end of the bumpy, uneven road, Cade spotted the church. "Nice and slow. Reyes is already in place. If he's spotted anything shady, he hasn't said so."

"Where exactly is he?"

"Up in the hills somewhere, well hidden but with a good view."

"Wouldn't he have been noticed getting there?"

"Nah, he's good."

The van bounced roughly over deep ruts. Brittle branches from pinyon pines and junipers scraped against the roof. There were no streetlights and the moon wasn't bright this night, so heavy shadows lurked right outside the headlight beams.

Grime-darkened windows and dirty clapboard indicated the church had lost its congregation. It was the last building before the road climbed up the mountain.

"I don't like it," Cade muttered.

"Shh," she said in return. Without looking at him, she stopped the van several yards away. After a moment, a woman stepped out on the front stoop. "That's her."

"Let her come to you," Cade insisted.

"She's not. She's probably worried that I might be Mattox." Drawing a deep breath, Star opened the door and stepped out.

Cade swallowed his curse and did the same, sliding silently out the cargo door and hunkering down low, in a better position to defend her if necessary.

In a hushed voice, Star called, "Adela?"

"Who is it?" Adela gripped the railing and peered toward the van. "Francis?"

Star stepped out farther, moving to the front of the van so the lights hit her. "Quickly. Let's go."

Taking one step toward her, Adela asked, "Are you alone?"

"Yes," Star lied. "C'mon."

And suddenly Adela had company.

Sterling wasn't all that surprised when two men, dressed all in black, came out of the church around Adela, each of them armed, each of them aiming at her. Worse, she spotted movement in the scrub bushes to the right, and more to the left.

Surrounded? No, she wouldn't accept that.

They were all in the darkened shadows, but she stood in the light—an easy target. That got her feet moving.

Knowing she'd never get back in the van before they were on her, she ducked behind the open driver's door and glanced back for Cade.

The van was empty. How had he moved without her hearing it? He was like a damn wraith! A sound snapped her back around. In the three seconds she'd used to look for Cade, the dude had gotten far too close.

She smiled as she pointed her Glock. "Move and I'll put one in your forehead."

Laughing, he continued edging casually toward her. "You're lucky he wants you alive."

Screw that. She shot at his leg, but the bullet hit the dirt near his feet. Damn lousy left-handed aim—not that she'd wanted to kill him. Yet. And at least it made him dive off to the side for cover.

Since that had worked, she fired left and right, too. No one cried out, but she definitely heard some fast rustling.

Take cover, you goons. I won't go easy. She wouldn't go at all... not until she got what she'd come for. "Adela!"

"I'm so sorry," Adela wailed.

Sterling searched the darkness. Voices seemed to echo here,

with the mountains around them, the night so still. Narrowing her eyes, she detected movement far ahead on the road.

It appeared someone—maybe Mattox?—was dragging Adela away.

How many men were there? So far she'd noticed four—if the men trying to close in around her were alone. There could be more. If they worked in pairs...insurmountable odds.

Mattox wasn't taking any chances, but then, he never did.

Was Adela in on it?

When a bullet zinged over her head, Sterling ducked—then looked back at the loud groan. A man was on the ground, clutching his leg and cursing a blue streak. Clearly he'd tried to sneak up behind her, but Cade's brother, wherever he was, must have spotted him.

Night-vision goggles? Seemed probable.

Just then, she saw Cade disable a different man with one vicious punch to the face. The man stiffened, then fell hard. Another launched at him, but in a very smooth move, he pivoted and elbowed the guy in the throat, sending him gagging and gasping to join his buddy on the dirt road. While he was down, Cade planted a boot in his face and the gagging stopped.

Huh.

She searched the immediate area but didn't see anyone else. "Is that it?"

His incredulous glare burned her. "There are now four bodies down around us, but a few of them might not stay that way, and I counted at least two more, so get in the van." With practiced ease, he disarmed the downed men. One of them groaned, but Cade ruthlessly punched him silent again.

"Wow." He had incredibly effective fists.

As he gathered up the weapons to dump in the cargo area, he repeated, "Get. In the. Van."

"Then what?" Before she took orders, she needed to know the plan. "More of them might be waiting on the road ahead."

She should have already figured out a way to retreat, but instead she'd been focused on all the wrong things.

Like an unlikely alliance between Adela and Mattox.

And what Cade had said to her.

Could he really care that much? Given the way he'd protected her, he might.

She heard Adela scream again, but she couldn't see anything.

"Don't even think it," Cade ordered as he put nylon cuffs on the men. "You're staying here with me."

She knew that taking charge probably came naturally to him, and now wasn't the time to argue, especially since it was a good thing he'd come along.

If he hadn't, Mattox would already have her again, and her odds of getting away from him a second time wouldn't be favorable.

No, she wouldn't argue, but she did grumble, "I'm not an idiot." She wouldn't chase after Adela into unknown circumstances, but what to do about her?

It was only a small sound that alerted her, a soft-soled shoe crunching on the loose dirt and gravel road.

Swinging around, she managed to get off one shot before a big bruiser knotted a hand in her hair and jerked her around the door toward him.

"I'm done fucking around with you," he growled.

She nutted him as hard as she could. Using her injured leg for balance, she lacked some of her usual power, but she still connected solidly.

Groaning, he loosened his hold, just not enough, and with the way he pinned down her arms, she was as likely to shoot her own foot as his if she dared to fire.

So instead she headbutted him. Her aim was off because she nailed him right in the nose. Blood sprayed.

"You little bitch—" he spit...just before a fist flew over her shoulder and knocked him out cold.

With his arms around her, she suddenly found herself crashing toward the ground.

Cade caught her, drawing her upright and pressing her back against the van. Face twisted with fury, he stomped the downed man, once, twice.

"He's out," Sterling whispered, awed by his violence. "Cade, he's out." She caught his arm. "Let's go while we can."

His jaw locked, but he did stop pulverizing the guy. Muscles pumped and expression deadly, he turned to her. "You're all right?"

She had that dude's blood on her face, but she nodded. "Fine."

"Stay put," he said, already moving away. "I'll be right back."

What the hell was that supposed to mean?

She got her answer a second later as the battle erupted behind her. Two men against Cade? Clearly not a problem for him.

How many more? A freaking army? She stayed alert, constantly looking around in case anyone else joined in, but she didn't see any others.

The man nearest her, the one Cade had stomped, stirred. Following Cade's cue, she kicked him in the face and put him out again.

She knew the dirt road continued on and then curved back to meet the paved street that would lead to an interstate on-ramp. Far ahead she saw the sudden glow of red taillights.

Whoever had Adela was getting away.

What to do? She couldn't give chase, not now.

Cade rejoined her, and together they watched the taillights fade away.

The eerie silence left behind seemed almost threatening. Neither of them spoke until his phone beeped.

"Your brother?" she whispered.

He ignored the question, saying, "In the van and lock the door," while half lifting her to do just that.

She quickly secured the lock but then stepped into the back

to help him inside. He was already there, slamming the door and locking it.

"Stay down." He read the text. "My brother is giving chase on the car that took off."

They heard the roar of a motorcycle and briefly saw the lights flash over the road, and then he was gone. "That was him?"

"Yeah." He sent off a message, then shoved the phone in his pocket. "Are you hurt?"

A few hairs missing, but... "Not a scratch, thanks to you."

"Your leg? Your finger—"

"I'm fine, Cade." Just trembling from an adrenaline dump. "I heard Adela scream. Do you think your brother will be able to catch up?"

"He'll be in touch soon. Get behind the wheel, okay? Let's get out of here."

Through the windshield, she saw the long expanse of darkness. "It's safe?"

"Yes, as long as we don't linger." Gingerly he removed his vest.

That's when she realized...he'd been shot! Her legs seemed to give out and she dropped into a seat. "Oh my God."

"I'm fine," he said absently, lightly touching a wound near his collarbone. "Just a ricochet."

"But...you're bleeding!" Regaining her feet, she started toward him.

He caught her hand and kept her from touching his chest. "I need you to drive, babe. Can you do that?"

Filled with new purpose, she nodded fast and rushed to the driver's seat, putting the van in gear. "Hospital?"

For three seconds, he considered it, then growled out a breath. "No. I need to go to my dad's place."

"But..." She glanced back at him. "You could be seriously hurt."

"Dad is a surgeon. Or was, anyway. He's still the best option." Cade joined her in the passenger seat, not really moving like a mortally wounded man. With the first aid kit in his hand, he gave her directions.

Panicked fear tried to take over. "That's at least forty minutes from here."

"I know." Using a cotton pad, he covered the injury. "It'll be okay." His mouth tightened. "The bullet didn't go deep."

She started forward in the darkness, her gun in her lap. Actually, he had his with him, too. He was far too alert, one hand holding that makeshift bandage in place, the other holding his weapon as he constantly scanned the area.

They got to the highway without any trouble. Still...

Longest. Drive. Of her *life*.

She kept glancing at Cade. "How you holding up?"

His mouth quirked. "Worried about me?"

"Well...yeah." Her tone plainly conveyed what she thought of that stupid question. "I didn't know... When did it happen?"

His expression went dark and deadly again. "Right before that bastard grabbed you."

Reaching over, she patted his tensed thigh. "Down, boy. I told you, he didn't hurt me."

"It'd be a different story if I hadn't been there with you."

Yeah, he couldn't resist making that point. "Maybe." Most definitely. She'd been far outnumbered, and outmaneuvered, too. "I'm not one hundred percent yet. Usually when I nut a guy, he's out. That dude had brass balls or something." She smirked. "I did smash his nose, though—I mean, before you completely rearranged his face. Pretty sure he's never going to look the same again."

Cade continually checked the mirrors. "It's not a joking matter." His glare burned over her. "I want another promise from you."

She almost groaned. She did give a quick roll of her eyes. "What now?"

"Whether Mattox recognized you or not, he's out to get you. That much is clear, yes?"

"He sent a small army, so yeah, not like I can deny it."

"Swear to me, until we have him locked away, or preferably dead, you won't try to deal with him or Adela on your own."

Her heart tripped, then settled into a fast, steady drumming. "You signing on for an extended period? Because there's no way to know how soon something like this could be wrapped up."

With no hesitation at all, he stated, "That's exactly what I'm doing. I don't care if it's a month, six months or a year." Tension poured off his big body, and he added in a hard, don't-argue voice, "We work together."

The warm glow started down deep in Sterling's jaded soul and fanned out until she couldn't keep the smile at bay. They were pretty crazy circumstances, and she was incredibly worried for Cade—despite his macho posturing—and still she couldn't repress a smile. "All right, you have my word." Urgency rushed back in on her. "Now no more talking. And don't you dare bleed to death!"

CHAPTER TEN

Getting shot was never a good thing. Cade didn't say it to Star, but it was his distraction with her that caused the mishap. The bastard had just grabbed her, and the man he'd been binding had managed to pull away. He didn't get in a clean shot, not with the way Cade broke his arm for the attempt, but the gun had discharged, the bullet ricocheted off the ground…and he got nicked.

Luckily below his face, but unluckily right above his vest. It hadn't slowed him down, not with Star being manhandled, but it sure as hell hadn't felt good, either.

His dad and Reyes would be worried. Then once they knew he'd be okay, Reyes would find it hilarious, and his dad…would have a fit. Not that Parrish McKenzie had ordinary fits. No, he'd condemn and harass and overall be a pain in Cade's ass.

He should have killed that prick who'd dared to lay hands on Star. Knowing what they had intended, he'd wanted to kill them all. If Star hadn't been involved, he probably would have, but that type of cleanup, with a witness around, would have really sent his father through the roof.

He'd have enough explaining to do already.

Chewing her bottom lip, Star's gaze repeatedly darted to him. It was almost endearing, seeing her fret, because he hadn't figured her for the type. If anything, he'd thought she'd take the same tack as his dad and bitch him out for it.

She needed a distraction, so he said, "I didn't see Mattox."

"Neither did I, unless he's the one who dragged Adela away."

Every bump in the road sent an echo of pain through him. "Might have been." A text dinged on his phone. Getting the damn thing out of his pocket wasn't easy this time. Knowing it would be Reyes, he locked his teeth, twisted, and finally pulled it free of his back pocket. He glanced at the screen.

"What?" she asked. "Is that your brother?"

"Yeah. He's caught up with them. It was definitely Mattox who took Adela."

Hands tightening on the wheel, Star asked, "Is she okay?"

"He says she is and that he'll explain soon." Reyes wanted to know where they could meet up. Given his injury, Cade had no choice but to text back: Home base.

The return text came fast. You shitting me?

Of course, his brother wouldn't just accept that when he knew home was the last place Cade wanted to be. He had to explain, but he kept it simple. I'm fine, but caught a ricochet.

On my way.

Damn. A full house. He glanced at Star. "Would it be pushing my luck to make one more request?"

"What's wrong?" Her gaze swept over him before returning to the road. "You won't pass out, will you?"

Cade snorted. "No, I won't fucking pass out. I told you, it's not that bad."

"You're still bleeding," she accused, her voice going a little high with stress. "And here we are, taking the long way to help."

He wished he could take her hand, but his were now smeared with blood. "Stay with me."

"I'm not budging."

That quick answer didn't reassure him one bit. "I mean it. No matter what."

Her brows climbed high. "Just what the hell does that mean? What are you expecting to happen?"

No help for it. He had to be up-front, if for no other reason than to prepare her. "I'm expecting you'll want to run once you meet my family. But don't."

"Bunch of scary ogres, huh?"

He wasn't about to go into detail. "Let's just say they can be overwhelming."

Softer now, more sincere, she vowed, "A pack of wild dogs couldn't chase me off, okay? We're sort of like partners now. And partners stick together."

They were a hell of a sight more than that, whether she wanted to admit it or not. But for now, partners would do. "I'm going to hold you to that." He indicated the next exit. "Get off here."

When the road quickly narrowed and climbed the mountainside, she asked, "Where are you leading me?"

"I told you, my father's place. It's home base for what I— we—do. And FYI, he's not going to be pleased."

She frowned. "With me or you?"

"Both—but mostly me."

Her neck stiffened. "Then why are we going there?"

For an answer, Cade lifted the pad and saw that the bleeding had almost stopped. "He can handle this—quietly." Taking in her profile with her brows now set in an obstinate line, he said, "Hospitals report gunshots, and that would bring up too many questions that we don't want to answer." She started to speak, probably to say something grouchy, judging by her frown, but he said, "Veer to the right."

"This isn't much of a road."

"That's the point."

Craning her neck, she looked up through the windshield. "Are those security cameras?"

"Two of the twenty scattered around the property."

Star fell silent. Awe? Intimidation? Or wariness?

They ascended a few more miles, and there in the distance, lights glowed. Day or night, the mountain retreat made quite an impressive sight. Stone columns climbed high to support a curved roof over a sprawling deck, backlit by floor-to-ceiling windows that overlooked the mountains.

Eyes rounded, Star pulled up to the gated entry.

"You need to enter the code to get through the gate." He shared the series of numbers and letters with her, and the wide iron gates opened.

Star paused. She looked as though she wanted to turn around and leave.

"It'll be fine," Cade told her. "If anyone can handle my family, it's you." At least, he hoped that was true. Before her, he'd never considered putting it to the test.

Incredulous, she blinked at him, then frowned at whatever she saw on his face. "You're ready to keel over, when you promised you wouldn't!" Misgivings gone, or buried under her worry for him, she stepped on the gas.

There'd be no keeling. It'd take more than the paltry injury he had to make him do that. But if it propelled her past her nervousness, he didn't mind the misconception.

And in fact, he did feel wretched. Loss of blood, maybe.

Well, that and the fact that he was about to break a cardinal rule. He'd meant what he said, though. He didn't know another woman who could deal with what lay ahead. Star was the exception. Always. In everything.

With her, he believed it'd work out.

Driving past tall aspens and magnificent boulders, Sterling pulled up to…a freaking lodge. "That's not a house."

"It is."

"No." She shook her head and pointed at a different home off to the side. "That smaller place over there, *that's* a house." The place in front of her…she'd never seen anything like it, not even in a magazine.

"That's my sister's private cottage. Drive right up to the front door there and help me inside before I lose more blood."

That silenced her. But God, she was caught in conflicting emotions. Cade took precedence, most definitely, but this, all this grandeur and wealth? Not her cup of tea.

She put the van in Park, turned it off and rushed around to his side. He'd gotten out on his own steam, thankfully, because Cade was a huge guy and she wasn't sure she could bear his weight on her own, especially not with a bum leg. At the door, she leaned on a buzzer. "Didn't they see us driving up? What good are security cameras if you don't—"

A tall man jerked the door open, already glaring in fury. "What in God's name…!"

The only way to brazen through a situation was to really brazen it through. "Out of the way, man," she barked. "He's been shot."

Immediately the man tucked his own shoulder under Cade's other arm. "I'll take care of him. You may leave."

Leaning heavily on them both, Cade stated, "If she leaves, I leave."

That caused a visual standoff between the two men—until Sterling slugged the stranger in the ear. "He. Is. *Bleeding.*"

Impotent fury darkened the man's face. He looked like he wanted to say or do something—to her—but instead he bellowed, "Bernard!"

The sound echoed around a grand sky-high foyer.

"She follows us," Cade warned.

The man said nothing, but he didn't try to stop her. Another man—she assumed poor Bernard—came to a halt before them.

"What in the world."

"Get the door," the man said, but before Bernard could do that, Cade's brother came to a screeching halt on his motor-cycle and bounded in.

"Run every red light?" Cade asked.

"And drove ninety," his brother said, moving her out of the way so he could take Cade's other arm. "But I'm here, so don't complain."

Securing the door, Bernard said, "I'll get things prepped," and then he rushed off.

"Can you walk?" his brother asked Cade.

"I'm fine—but I'd like to see you try to carry me."

The older man snapped, "Don't you two start."

They all ignored *her*. If she'd wanted to leave, now would be her chance.

Of course she didn't. She'd promised Cade, and besides that, she wanted to see with her own two peepers that he was okay.

So she meekly followed along.

A pretty young woman came out of a room, took in the scene before her and immediately set aside a laptop on a pol-ished table to rush ahead of them. She now led the pack, while Sterling pulled up the rear.

They went across the great room, which really was great, before they veered off to the left and through the wide expanse of the kitchen, around a powder room, down a small flight of stairs, where the woman opened doors...into a lab?

Disbelief rounded Sterling's eyes and turned her in a circle as she took it all in. It looked like an honest-to-God operating room. Just what had she stepped into?

The men helped Cade to a white-sheeted bed that the handy Bernard had just finished making up with sheets from a metal cabinet.

Cade's brother neatly ripped open his shirt.

Blood was…everywhere, and Sterling felt her knees going weak. She reached out until her hand flattened on a wall, offering needed support.

Bernard set out a tray of stuff that looked too ominous for her peace of mind.

The older man, not Bernard, was busy scrubbing his hands and muttering, "You are the most stubborn, difficult—"

"Son. I know," Cade said, not really sounding like a man with a bullet in his chest. In fact, he was staring at Sterling, so she tried not to look so worried. "Reyes is the constant joker and Madison is the most obedient."

Reyes and Madison? Difficult *son*?

Her gaze slowly traveled to the sink where he washed. So that fire-breathing dragon was Cade's father? Yes, she saw the resemblance now, but…

Madison took offense at what he'd said. "Obedient? That's a lie."

Cade snorted. His brother did, too.

Madison folded her arms. "Don't take your temper out on me because you were foolish enough to get shot." Then to their father, who was now pulling on surgical gloves, Madison asked, "Is it serious, Dad?"

Sterling gaped at her. Serious? He'd caught a bullet! In his *chest*.

"No, it's not," Cade said, still not sounding all that wounded. "Damn bullet deflected off a rock and came back on me."

"You coulda shot your eye out," Reyes mused.

Madison reached out to swat him, but he ducked away.

They were all certifiably insane. From one to the other, Sterling stared—until she got snared again by Cade's gaze.

His father leaned over him, pressed…and announced, "It stopped at his collarbone, but luckily it doesn't appear to have broken anything."

Good news? At the moment, Sterling would take any she could get.

Utilizing scary surgical-type pincer thingies, his father poked and prodded while Cade gritted his teeth.

Madison stood stoic and Reyes was thankfully silent as he paced.

Bernard held a metal bowl…which clinked when the man dropped something into it. "Bullet's out. Let me make sure there's no other damage."

"X-ray?" Bernard asked.

Cade's father peered down at him. "Are you hurt anywhere else? And don't hold back."

Sounding disgusted, Cade said, "No."

"A few stitches, then." He turned to Sterling. "You're not sterile, so please remove yourself."

Of all the…! That sounded like a truly terrible insult. Reyes and Madison—were *they* sterile? Or Bernard?

But he must have meant them all because Reyes went to Madison and, with an arm around her shoulders, led her to the door. Bernard stepped away.

And that left only her.

"Bernard?" Cade called out, still looking at her.

"Yes?"

"Don't let her leave."

His father rolled his eyes, dismissed them all and began a thorough cleaning that, to Sterling, looked worse than what had come before it.

Feeling a little sick, she told Cade, "I'll be right outside the door."

"You'll wait in the kitchen," his father said without looking up. "Since my son has quite a bit of explaining to do, you may as well get something to drink."

"Come along," Bernard said gently. "I'll get you settled."

She didn't want to. But damn. These people were daunting, far more so than Mattox with a gun.

The second they were alone, his father gave up even the slightest pretense of politeness. "What the hell were you thinking?"

"That I make my own decisions? That I want her with me? That you don't run my life?"

A deep growl crawled up his throat, but his hands were steady and competent as he numbed the area. "You could have been killed."

Without Star to focus on, Cade stared up at his father. "No more so than on any other job."

He paused. "We cover every possible scenario."

"Best we can, I know. I did the same tonight. That's why I convinced Reyes to tag along." He felt the tug of the first stitch going in, but no pain. "When you explode, don't include him. Against his better judgment, he did it for me."

Instead of doing some of that exploding that Cade expected, his father sighed. "Is the girl truly that important to you?"

Cade didn't doubt that his father had already surmised much of what had happened. Pesky details were only finer points of an overall view. "You already know the answer to that."

He finished stitching in silence. Once he was done, he treated the area with something and applied a light bandage. "You'll stay here tonight and tomorrow so I can keep an eye on this."

"Not without Star."

Moving away to wash his hands, his father remarked, "You shouldn't call her that. I've read your sister's report, you realize. Sterling Parson has good reason for having shed that name, and you endanger her by using it."

Cautiously, Cade sat up. His head swam a little, but he'd suffered worse injuries and he had a good grasp on what his body could and couldn't do. He took stock, flexed each arm and surmised that he'd walk out of the lab on his own. "I won't let anything happen to her."

With a sound of exasperation, Parrish turned back to him. His face was pinched. His eyes were narrowed. He looked pissed, but he said, "I suppose we should get to know her."

It was that concession more than anything else that allowed the residual aches and pains to swamp back in on Cade. Until he'd known if he had to fight his own family, which had been his presumption, he hadn't allowed himself to feel much of the discomfort.

The others would follow Parrish's lead, and he'd just offered an olive branch. Surprising, and very much appreciated.

Resigned, his father said, "I'll take you to your room so you can wash up and change clothes. Then we'll have a little talk with our guest."

Each of them had their own living quarters in the main house, for situations of this type. They were used when necessary, kept prepped otherwise.

Cade had his own house nearer to his bar, Reyes lived nearer to his gym and Madison had insisted on the separate cottage.

It was times like this that made having the quarters so convenient. He hated to admit to his own limitations, and he *could* make it back to Star's place if he needed to, but he didn't relish the idea of bouncing along the rough roads again.

Nodding, he carefully let his feet touch the floor. His head spun, but not too badly. "It was Mattox," he admitted. "And he had Star once before. He's the one who started her on this path of vengeance."

"You don't say? Hmm." Again with his arm around Cade, Parrish started them forward.

His father was not known for an excess of sympathy, and he definitely didn't indulge coddling. Cade had never wanted or needed either, and Reyes pretended he didn't care. But Madison? He and Reyes tried to make up for his father's lacks, but

Cade wasn't sure if they'd succeeded or not. He understood Reyes, but his sister was often a mystery to him.

Right now, though, Cade was glad his father didn't fuss with him, trying to insist that he rest. Not yet. Not until he convinced Star that she needed to spend a few days with him.

Here, where it would be safer.

Where they could come up with a better plan—to end Mattox, once and for all.

Sterling had left that home surgery center feeling pretty numb. Passing the powder room reminded her of the blood, and she detoured in there to wash her hands and face but couldn't do anything about her shirt. She still wore the bulletproof vest, but with Cade hurt, she hadn't even thought about it.

A knock at the door got her moving again. "Hold on." She smoothed back her hair, made a face at herself and stepped out.

Bernard smiled gently. "Come to the kitchen and rest. I'll get you something to drink while I prepare food."

She didn't need rest; she needed Cade.

No, she didn't *need* anything. Certainly not a guy. But she would stick around for a bit just to talk to him again.

It wasn't until she sat down at the kitchen table that Sterling realized how badly her leg thumped and her finger throbbed. Even her scalp hurt now, from where the goon had pulled her hair. And that damn vest nearly suffocated her. With Cade safe in the bosom of his lunatic family, all the discomforts settled in and made themselves known.

She wasn't sure what to think about these people yet. Cade's father was obviously wealthy. His sister tall, slim and beautiful. His brother still a raging pain in the butt.

But anyone could see that they loved one another.

Even the stuffy Bernard, who was trying so hard to look unconcerned as he prepared food, couldn't adequately hide how much he cared.

They were a family in every way that mattered. Blood related. Loyal to one another. Comfortable with heckling—and confident in assistance when needed.

And here she was, stuck in the middle of them, feeling like a mutt Cade had dragged home.

It didn't help that Reyes hadn't stopped staring at her with the same fascination he'd give a cockroach.

She tried to ignore him, she really did, but waiting to know how Cade had fared sent her temper spiraling and she couldn't grapple it back under control. Glaring at Reyes, she snapped, *"What?"*

Lifting his chin, Reyes said, "Just trying to figure it out."

Honestly confused by that answer, Sterling asked again, this time with less animus, "What?"

"You got my brother shot."

Hands fisting, Sterling bolted to her feet and leaned over the table. "I've had just about enough of you."

He eyed her up and down without concern, still showing only curiosity.

It unnerved her, damn it. "In case you failed to notice, Cade is a big boy and he makes his own damn decisions. Do you honestly think I could've stopped him from going along? For your information, I tried."

"And failed," Reyes said.

"But don't you see?" Madison said. "That's the lure."

They planned to verbally dissect her? Screw that.

Sterling pivoted to Madison. At least this sibling was calm and apparently not that interested in provoking her. "What's that supposed to mean?"

It was Reyes who answered, "All that." He gestured at her rigid posture. "Apparently Cade likes them fiery."

Madison gave him a quelling look, saving Sterling the trouble. "I think Cade likes her because she's as strong as he is."

One side of Reyes's mouth quirked in a way that was so familiar to Cade's smile that Sterling's heart clenched.

Then he ruined it by saying, "Since she's standing while he's on a table bleeding, maybe she's even stronger?"

"You're an asshole," Sterling accused, choking out the words around the lump in her throat. She strode away before she did something truly appalling. Like cry.

Silence throbbed behind her, until Reyes ordered, "You can't leave. You heard what big brother said."

Like she would without first seeing that Cade was okay? She wouldn't, but she replied, "Don't plan to, but I don't have to stay in the same room with a jackass!"

She'd take a turn around this mausoleum and hopefully get herself in check before returning to the kitchen.

But first...she headed out the front door and to the van.

Madison came trotting behind her, then just fell into step with her. Pretending she wasn't there, Sterling opened the door of the van, yanked off her shirts, then ripped open the fastenings on the vest and tossed the heavy thing inside.

Madison said not a single word while Sterling stripped down to her bra. In fact, she got comfortable against the side of the van, watching as Sterling pulled back on her T-shirt. Madison held out her button-up shirt, her expression enigmatic.

Shrugging it on, Sterling slammed the van door and walked away without thanking her. She went back inside the open front door of the house, aware of Madison trailing her.

The silence dragged out until Sterling wanted to scream, but she clamped her lips together and managed to keep quiet. Where to go? She couldn't imagine traipsing through the house without an invite. Besides, it was so damn immense she might get lost. From the great room she spotted doors that led to a deck and darted that way.

Naturally, Madison followed.

Outside, gulping in the damp evening air, Sterling leaned on the railing. Being here like this, in the quiet night, the majestic mountains barely discernible in the moonlight, she felt incredibly small. Insignificant.

Then Madison shoulder-bumped her. "This is better than leaving, right? You had me concerned for a minute there. I wasn't keen on tackling you."

Tackling her? Though her eyes narrowed, Sterling kept her gaze trained ahead, doing her utmost not to react.

"By the way, you shouldn't let Reyes rile you. He does it on purpose, you know, but if he doesn't get a reaction, he loses interest."

Damn it, that deserved a response, and she heard herself say, "What if I reacted with a fist to his face?"

Madison went still—then burst out laughing. "Oh, I'd love to see that. But you should be forewarned, we're all excellent at fighting. Dad made sure we studied a wide variety of disciplines. The only one I know who can best Reyes is Cade. My guess is that if you tried to punch him, you'd probably end up in some ridiculously undignified hold that would only infuriate you more, and then Cade would be angry with him and he'd pulverize Reyes, and then Dad would be upset. Me, too, I guess. I love my brothers, even though they're far too alpha and bossy. It's always distressing when they go at each other."

Very slowly, Sterling turned her head to stare in amazement at this particularly chatty sibling. "Maybe I should shoot him instead?"

"Well, as to that…" Grinning, Madison caught her hair in a fist to keep it from blowing in her face. "We're all pretty good at anticipating that sort of thing, too. Which makes it really curious that Cade allowed himself to be shot. Did you see how it happened?"

Sterling snapped her mouth shut and looked away. If Cade wanted to explain to his sister, then he could. Right now, she wanted to concentrate on ignoring the girl so she'd go away.

Turning to lean her back on the rail, Madison wrapped her arms around herself. "It's chilly out here."

"Feels good." Damn it, she hadn't meant to reply.

"Cade will be fine, you know. He's probably busy trying to order Dad around, and that never goes well. Neither of them seems to realize it, but they're just too much alike to always get along. Dad isn't a dummy, though. He'll see the situation for what it is and then it'll be fine."

Sterling wondered if her eyes had crossed yet. Had she really thought this sibling wasn't provoking? Unable to ignore everything Madison had just said, she gave up. "What, exactly, is that supposed to mean?"

"Dad knows when to cut his losses. He won't like it, but Cade brought you home, so he's obviously going to get his way."

"He didn't *bring me home*." Did Madison consider her a stray mutt, too? "He needed me to drive him here because he had a bullet in his chest."

"Oh, please. Cade could have driven—or even removed the bullet himself. He defines *tough guy*, you know."

Yeah, she did kind of know it.

Madison leaned closer, as if in confidence. "Personally, I think he saw it as a good excuse to push his own agenda."

"His agenda?"

Madison nudged her again. "You."

Bernard tapped at the doors, then stuck his head out. "I have food prepared, if you'd like to return to the kitchen now."

Before Sterling could decide what she wanted to do, Madison linked her arm through hers and pulled her along. "Thank you, Bernard. I'm suddenly famished."

Indulging her own whisper, Sterling asked, "Is he a butler?"

"Bernard? Oh, he's pretty much everything." Then louder, Madison added, "You take excellent care of us, don't you, Bernard?"

"I try."

And…that told Sterling nothing.

The only upside was finding Cade in the kitchen when she got there. His hair was wet and finger-combed back, he wore a clean dark T-shirt and fresh jeans, socks but no shoes, and in no way did he look like an injured man.

His gaze searched hers as she strode in, then moved to his sister with silent question.

Madison released her, saying, "We were just enjoying the view."

"Can't see much at night," Reyes pointed out.

Sterling shot back, "A black void is still more pleasant than you."

His mouth twitched. Then he said to Cade, "I like her."

Throwing up her hands, Sterling decided to stop wasting her time on that particular annoying brother so she could concentrate on Cade. Stopping before him, she took in the visible edges of a square white bandage at the base of his throat.

Maybe that's why her voice emerged all soft and feminine when she asked, "Are you okay?"

Enfolding her in his arms, Cade drew her close and asked, "Were you worrying about me? I told you I was fine."

Carefully, Sterling rested her cheek against his shoulder. Knowing for a fact that he was okay, seeing him hale and hearty, left her legs weak with relief. "I've never had to worry about anyone before."

"Baloney," he replied. "You worry about everyone."

Interrupting their moment, Reyes said, "You can stop worrying about Adela. That conniver is not a victim. In fact, from what I saw, she might be helping to run the show."

CHAPTER ELEVEN

Cade wanted to hear all about Adela and his brother's impressions, but a few other things took priority. Giving Star one last hug, he urged her to a chair.

Bernard had "thrown together" one of his incredible pasta dishes, and Cade wanted her to eat before she got more distracted.

Taking the seat next to her, he asked, "What do you want to drink?"

She stared at the angel-hair pasta smothered in a cream sauce that Bernard had pulled from his private stash for just such an occasion.

Bernard said, "I suggest sauvignon blanc—"

"Got a cola?" she asked instead, interrupting him. "Anything from a can is fine."

Smiling, Cade glanced at his family, daring them to say anything derogatory. "I'll have the same."

"I, as well," Madison said.

God bless his sister. Cade gave her a grateful smile.

Parrish said, "Pour me a glass, please," and took his seat at the head of the table.

Grinning, Reyes looked from one to the other. "Damn, this is fun. Guess as long as we're going with variety, I'll take a beer."

Appalled, Bernard stared at him. "With my pasta?"

"Yeah, but you're not the one driving me to drink, so don't sweat it."

Cade gave him a warning look, but Star smiled sweetly.

Once everyone was served, Bernard fixed his own plate and sat to Parrish's right. It was unusual for him to do so, but being unaware of the family dynamics, Star didn't seem to think anything of it.

No doubt about it, Bernard was curious about Star, and with good reason. Cade had never brought a woman home before. There were rules against such things, and he'd just crashed through them all.

Taking a bite of the pasta, Star gave a low groan that had each man staring at her. "Oh, Bernard." Another groan. "This is amazing."

Bernard actually flushed. "Thank you."

Pointing her fork at Reyes, she said, "So spill it. What do you know about Adela?"

That sounded so much like an order that Reyes took his time replying, and not with an answer but another question. "You're not surprised that she might be in cahoots with Mattox?"

"Nope, but I'd like details."

"We already suspected her," Cade explained.

"But naturally you rushed ahead anyway." Parrish made no bones about his disapproval.

"Hey, that was my fault." While twirling more pasta around her fork, Star said, "She contacted me, so I felt I had to be certain. Even tonight, it wasn't one hundred percent clear if she was a victim or helping to set a trap. And it *was* a trap, bigtime. Dudes swarmed out of everywhere. I lost count. Six, maybe seven."

"Eight total," Reyes said, and Cade could see he was starting to relax. How could he not with Star being so casual?

"Night-vision goggles?" she asked. "Awesome. I need some of those."

"They come in handy," Reyes agreed. "I take it you couldn't see much?"

"Not in that darkness. Anything away from the headlight beam was more shadow than anything else."

"Yet you seemed to know when someone was moving in."

She shrugged. "Just sensed the movement, you know? Or heard a small sound."

"So astute," Madison enthused. "Dad, isn't she amazing?"

"Don't answer that," Star dared to order Parrish, then said to Madison, "I'm as far from amazing as a person can get, so don't fool yourself. I completely dicked up tonight. If it weren't for Cade—and actually, you, too, Reyes—I'd have been toast."

"You'd have been in Mattox's capture," Parrish stated with blunt insistence.

"Yup." She gave an exaggerated shudder. "Not a place I want to be, so gratitude all around, guys. Thanks for saving my bacon. And, Cade, seriously, I am so damn sorry you got hurt."

Everyone fell silent again. Cade knew she wasn't what any of them had expected.

She was better. More refreshing.

Pride, that's what he felt. Star handled his family with more ease than he'd expected, mostly by just being her usual candid self.

Reyes raised a brow at Cade. "She must have been hangry before. She's much more agreeable now that she's fed her face."

"Food is always good," Star agreed with a wink at Bernard. "Especially when it's this delicious."

Heat crawled up Bernard's neck. "Again, thank you."

"And you," she said, playfully growling at Reyes. "You do like to push those buttons, don't you? I considered punching you in your face, but your sister warned me against it." She smirked. "Considered just shooting you, too, but Cade might not like that. For some reason I can't figure out, he seems fond of you."

Reyes burst out laughing, earning a look of censure from Parrish, which he pretended not to see. "You want to spar sometime, lady, just let me know. You're welcome to my gym any day."

"I might take you up on that." Plate empty, Star pushed it back. "But I'll wait until my leg and finger have completely healed. Now, enough of the pleasantries. Tell me what you saw with Adela before she decides to call me again. I need to know how to handle things."

Slumping comfortably into his seat, Reyes held his beer loosely in one hand. "Adela and some other guy got out at an empty lot. Mattox was there. I assumed they were going to meet up with anyone else who'd been able to crawl away."

"I left them bound," Cade said. "Unless someone releases them, they'll be there awhile."

Parrish looked up from his plate. "You didn't kill them?"

Deadpan, Cade said, "You tend to frown over random murders that you haven't sanctioned. And at that point, I didn't know I'd be bringing Star back here."

"He was trying to tiptoe around the rules," Reyes offered. "Not all in, but not out, either."

Eyes wide, Star looked from father to son and back again. "Wish someone had told me the options. I wouldn't have had a problem sending a few of them to hell."

Realizing that he'd said so much, Parrish scowled. "This conversation didn't happen."

Star pretended to lock her lips and toss away a key.

Her antics had Reyes chuckling again. "No worries about anyone left behind. Mattox used the phone, so I assume he sent a lackey or two back for his men. If someone else finds them, it's not a worry. They won't say anything about us being there because that'd just expose their own agenda." He turned his attention to Star. "Your little victim gave Mattox hell."

"Seriously?" Star leaned forward, her arms crossed on the table. "You couldn't have misunderstood?"

"I know a female temper when I see it," he assured her. "Adela jabbed him in the chest, her mouth going the whole time. Mattox argued back, but she didn't look afraid. Mostly it looked like a lovers' quarrel."

"Euewww." Revulsion twisted Star's mouth. "Knowing what a disgusting ape Mattox is, I don't want to imagine that. It's too gross, but I suppose anything is possible. She did seem determined to hang back at Misfits, even though I could have gotten her out of there. And after that, when she claimed to want help escaping, she insisted that I come alone. You'd think she'd welcome an army, right? More rescuers would up her chances of getting away."

"If you knew all that," Parrish said, "then why did you go?"

"Because Mattox could have been forcing her." She shrugged. "You know he controls women, and most would do whatever he said to avoid the consequences."

"True enough." Reyes turned to Cade. "I followed them to another house. We can fetch her easily enough if that's what you want to do."

"Just like that?" Star asked.

"When we formulate an actual plan together, we're more successful than not," Reyes said.

Cade stroked her arm. "One of us could grab her while the other gives cover."

"And I can figure out the best time for it," Madison offered. "If Adela isn't under lock and key, it could be even easier. I'll sort that out."

"Not saying it'd be a piece of cake," Cade clarified, "but we can do it."

"With proper surveillance followed by careful planning,"

Parrish insisted. "Not this…" He flagged a hand at her. "Running off half-cocked business, like what happened tonight."

"Got it, but I don't think we should do that," Star said, thinking out loud. "With the extra info Reyes got, this could be a good opportunity to get all the players. Adela still thinks I consider her a victim, so it should be easy enough to set her up."

Overruling that idea, Cade shook his head. "Once we have her, we can question her."

"And she may or may not confide in us, right?" Star argued. "But if we use me as bait—"

Every muscle on his body clenched. "No."

Reyes, Parrish, Madison and Bernard all went still at his uncompromising tone.

Undaunted, Star continued as if he hadn't refused. "I can pretend to let her capture me, with you guys all keeping track."

The hairs on Cade's nape stood on end. *"No."*

"You were all just boasting about your skill. Well, just think, we could uncover Mattox's whole operation."

Shoving back his chair, Cade rose to his feet to tower over her. "I said no."

Parrish sent him a look of disapproval for the outburst. "It's actually a sound plan."

"The hell it is," Cade shot back. "You know what could happen to her."

Slowly, Star stood to face him. "I'm aware of the risks. I'm also aware of the rewards."

"We'll come up with a different plan," Cade said with finality.

Trying to break the tension, Madison smiled. "And this time, we'll all work on it together."

Sterling looked around the suite of rooms with dread. Even this, Cade's private section of the mansion, was nicer than anything she'd ever known. Way more upscale than her cheap apartment—an apartment she actually liked and, until now, had thought was pretty spiffy. She should have headed home after dinner instead of letting them all bulldoze her into staying over.

Madison had acted like it was a done deal.

Reyes had told her not to be dumb.

Parrish had insisted, with a stiff smile, that she was welcome.

Even Bernard had promised an amazing breakfast in the morning.

But Cade was the deciding factor, saying it was her decision—and if she left, he'd go with her.

Tough as he might be, getting jostled along mountain roads wouldn't be good for him. How could she put him through that with her stubbornness? So here she was, looking around in amazement at his sitting room, kitchenette and bedroom.

The ceilings were high, tall windows everywhere, and it all looked like a designer's dream, like something she'd see in a magazine of the rich and famous.

"Bathroom is right through here," Cade prompted, opening a door to an opulently decorated retreat.

Smooth stone covered the floor and the walls of the shower, a vessel sink topped a carved but masculine cabinet, and a lit mirror and heated towel shelves polished off the decor.

"Wow."

He came to her, looping his arms around her waist. "Why don't you shower? I'll give those bloody clothes to Bernard to wash."

Appalled with that idea, she pushed him back. "Not happening."

"Bernard wouldn't mind."

"I mind." She looked around again. "I'll wash my shirt in the sink and hang it in the shower to dry."

A quiet knock on the entry door had them both looking that way. Madison stuck her head in and searched the couch and kitchenette before spotting them in the bedroom, then smiled. "Oh, good, I was afraid I might be…interrupting."

"And you opened the door anyway?" Cade teased. He released Sterling from his embrace but kept his arm around her waist as he led her into the sitting room. "We were just discussing Star's clothes."

"Then I have perfect timing." Madison held out a stack of shirts, a pair of loose cotton pants, a blow-dryer, a round brush and a bottle of lotion. "I noticed when she got rid of the vest that she could use a change of clothes."

Looking down at her shirt, Sterling groaned. "I'd forgotten about that jerk bleeding all over me or I'd have…figured out something before dinner." No idea what she could have done, but she scowled up at Cade anyway. "You let me sit at that table with your family looking like this. Why didn't you remind me?"

"Because no one cared."

"But…at dinner?" She wasn't stupid. She knew his family understood decorum better than she did, but even she knew you didn't share a meal with polite company while wearing some cretin's nose blood on your shirt. Her cheeks actually went hot with embarrassment.

Cade ran a hand over her head. "Bloody shirt or not, I wanted you to eat, relax and get to know everyone."

"And that's what we did," Madison said happily. "So mission accomplished."

Yeah, she'd tried. For the most part, she'd managed to get along, too. That is, until Cade blew up about her excellent plan—a plan she hadn't yet given up on. It would work; she believed that.

And the important thing was to stop Mattox once and for all.

"The shirts are stretchy," Madison was saying, "so they should fit okay. We're both tall, but I'm skinnier than you, so I grabbed cotton drawstring pants instead of jeans."

There was nothing skinny about Madison McKenzie. Cade's

sister had a tall, willowy body with gentle curves that Sterling thought was far more appealing than her own sturdy figure.

"I figured you could sleep in one of Cade's shirts." Grinning at him, Madison added, "Didn't think you would mind."

"Thanks, hon." Cade drew his sister in for a one-armed hug, then took the stack from her.

"Yeah," Sterling said, a little overwhelmed with the generosity. "Appreciate it."

"We'll talk more at breakfast, okay? Bernard usually has everything ready by eight, but since we're up so late, I asked him to make it nine. Will that work for you?"

Sterling looked at Cade. His house, his schedule.

He nodded. "That's fine. We'll see you then." He followed Madison to the door.

Sterling saw them whispering but couldn't hear what was said. Probably something she wouldn't like anyway. This time when Cade closed the door, he locked it, then came past her in the bedroom to ensure the French doors leading to a patio were also locked. With that done, he set his sister's offerings in the bathroom.

"No more interruptions." Opening a dresser drawer, he pulled out a snowy white T-shirt and handed it to her. "Want some boxers, too? Or how about you go without?" He gathered her close, one large hand caressing her behind. "I won't mind."

Concerned for his injury, Sterling gently rested a hand to his shoulder. "Let me shower first, okay? You don't want to hug this mess."

He treated her to that crooked smile and, leaning in, kissed her without drawing her close. "Use whatever you need in the bathroom. Toothbrush, lotion, shampoo and conditioner. Make yourself at home, okay? I'll fold down the bed."

Standing there, Sterling looked past him at the king-size bed, then stupidly whispered, "We're sleeping together? In your dad's house, I mean?"

He actually laughed. "No one will know."

"Bull."

"Okay, so they'll all assume. We're adults, babe." His grin faded into a tender smile. "And I want to hold you."

She wanted that, too. "But you were shot. What if I bump you?"

"I'll keep you too close for that." He kissed her again, this time lingering until her toes curled in her boots.

It took her a second to regain her wits. Then she breathed, "All right." It had been an exhausting and disappointing day, and she was still worried about Cade. Snuggling close, reassuring herself that he was fine, sounded too nice to resist. "Be forewarned, though, if Reyes says anything tomorrow, I can't be held responsible for what I do."

"Whatever you do, I'll help." He steered her into the bathroom, leaving after a smack on her behind. "Let me know if you can't find something you need." He closed the door before she could come up with more objections.

Of course she knew her reservations were absurd. As he'd said, they were adults.

But she'd never before stayed over with a guy in his father's house. Cade had probably sneaked in a lot of girls, but their formative years were vastly different. Overall, there'd been no fathers for her to deal with, not even her own. A grandfatherly figure, yes, but that was different, since she'd lived in the garage and never, not once, had she considered inviting a guy to share that precious space with her.

She pampered herself for a bit, but not as much as she'd have liked with only Cade's masculine products at hand. At least the lotion Madison had brought smelled more feminine. She slathered it on, occasionally lifting her wrist to sniff it again. Lavender, maybe. Or something more exotic. Whatever the scent, she liked it.

Her hair was thick, and by the time she'd dried it, nearly an hour had passed.

Sterling glanced at herself in the mirror. If she weren't so tall, Cade's T-shirt would have covered more of her. Instead, it barely reached below her backside. Of course, that made her think of the affectionate smack he'd left there, and his comment...

He's injured, she reminded herself. *No sex, not tonight. Maybe not for a while.* Still, as she opened the door and stepped out, her nipples pulled tight.

Already stretched out in the bed, his big, gorgeous body bare except for snug boxers, his shoulders propped against the headboard, he looked relaxed, maybe even asleep.

Until his eyes opened.

"Sorry I took so long." She stood there, framed in the light from the bathroom.

His slumberous gaze traveled over her. "Feel better?"

"I didn't feel bad." Not really. Tired, frazzled, achy...but not bad. Feeling like a feast he wanted to devour, she tugged at the hem of the shirt.

A morbid thought occurred to her—how awful it would be if...*when*...they went their separate ways. No other man would be like Cade. And no other man could make her feel the way he did.

Standing here now, in this moment, seeing the naked desire on his face, it was easy to think they could carve out a real relationship, yet all she had to do was look around to be reminded that they came from very different worlds.

Because of the circumstances, his father and brother were tolerating her, and Madison was kind. If he hadn't gotten shot, he would never have brought her here. This was a one-off, because Cade's family loved him.

"What are you thinking?" He left the bed to stalk toward her. "I think you just wrote a book in your head, didn't you? Will you tell me about it?"

Not being a dummy, Sterling determined to enjoy it all while it lasted. She wouldn't waste a single second by moping about an uncertain future. Heck, there was a chance Mattox would kill her, so what did the future matter?

When Cade got close, she touched the bruising she could see around his bandage. "I was thinking that, even wounded, you are seriously sexy." Tilting into him, she lightly brushed her lips over the heated skin of his chest. His chest hair tickled, and he smelled indescribably good. "I hate that you got hurt because of me." He frowned, and she quickly corrected, "I mean, I hate that you got hurt, period. It's just extra sucky that it happened while you were helping me."

Taking her hand, he lifted it to cover the bandage. "I know better than to get distracted. That's not on you, okay? I was where I wanted to be."

"Because I was there. If I hadn't involved you—"

"Then I wouldn't have you here now." He stroked an open hand down her spine and over her rump to cup a bare cheek. Grinning, he bent to nuzzle her neck and whispered, "With your sweet ass available."

Sterling laughed. It was that sort of thing, the playful compliments and sexual teasing, that she enjoyed so much. "I'm putting my sweet ass in the bed. The bathroom is all yours."

"Give me five minutes. And don't you dare fall asleep."

The second the door closed behind him, Sterling hurried to the bed and got under the covers.

In only three minutes, Cade emerged. He'd showered earlier but hadn't shaved. She liked him like this, his hair a little messy, not as precisely groomed, the beard shadow adding a rugged edge to his appeal.

It wasn't until he reached his side of the bed that she noticed the condoms on the nightstand. Her eyes flared, but he didn't notice as he clicked off the light and slid in beside her. In one smooth move he drew her against him and his mouth covered hers, stalling any protests she might have made over her concern for his injury.

Those large, rough hands slowly roamed everywhere, along her back, her shoulders, her thighs, yet they returned again and again to her behind. If she could have caught her breath, she might have laughed. He really did like her backside, when she'd never thought much about it.

He wasn't taking any chances on her using his wound as a reason to turn him down. How could he want her so much? It had to be magic, because no one else ever had.

Finally getting her mouth free, she whispered, "Slow down."

"Say yes, and then I will." He kissed a searing path along her throat to her ear.

He teased with his tongue, making her squirm. "Yes," she agreed. "With one condition."

"No conditions in bed, babe."

"I insist." Gently pushing him to his back, she crawled over him and sat on his abdomen. Her leg protested, but not enough to change her mind.

Staring up at her in the darkness, he held her waist and bent his knees so his thighs supported her back. "Lose the T-shirt."

It seemed second nature for Cade to give orders, but here in bed, she liked it. After whisking off her top, she said, "Now."

"Now," he agreed, shifting his hands to her breasts, lightly tugging at her nipples and obliterating her thoughts in the process. "Did I tell you how much I love these?"

She was starting to think he loved everything about her body. Dropping her head back, she let him have his way.

"So damn sweet."

He toyed with her nipples so long that she knew she was wet and beyond ready. "Cade…"

Leaning up while urging her down, he strongly sucked one nipple into the wet heat of his mouth.

Holy smokes. His tongue rasped over her, and she felt it in

other places, especially between her legs. "That's enough." If he didn't ease up, she'd come before he ever got inside her.

He closed his teeth gently around her—and tugged insistently. Her breath shuddered in and released as a broken groan. She didn't mean to, but she rocked against his hard abs.

Humming his approval, he switched to the other breast.

"Whoa," she gasped, struggling for air.

"No."

Oh, what he did with mouth, lips, tongue and teeth... But he'd been shot, and she couldn't let this get out of control. *Yes.*

With a last leisurely lick, he rested back on the bed. Her harsh breathing filled the air. His hands continued to stroke all over her.

Trying to regain control—as if she'd ever had it—Sterling braced her hands over his pecs, but that was a mistake. His skin burned, his muscles all knotted tight. He was closer to the ragged edge than he wanted to admit, and that turned her on even more.

"You're rushing it," she accused softly.

"You liked it."

"Yeah, course." She wasn't dead yet! One more cleansing breath helped to calm her racing heartbeat. "But seriously, Cade, you're hurt, regardless of how you want to minimize it." Getting words out wasn't easy, not with her nipples wet and aching. "To make this work—"

His fingers contracted on her hips. "It was working just fine."

"You need to let me take care of you."

He was silent a moment, just thinking. "Take care of me how?"

"You'll be still, and I'll do all the moving."

He snorted, and yeah, she got that. During sex, it was pretty damn hard to not move. "I mean it, Cade."

Lowering his arms to his sides, he said, "Go for it."

"I need you to relax."

"I'm relaxed."

She tsked. He felt like steel under her thighs. "Will you promise to tell me if I hurt you?"

"Hell no."

Such a *guy*. "Then I'll just have to be extra careful." Stretching out over him, she lightly teased her lips over his, dodging him when he tried to deepen the kiss. "Behave."

He choked on a laugh.

She trailed her tongue along his bristly jaw…to his ear. Closing her lips around his earlobe, she waited to see if he'd react the same as she had.

He did. Arms closing around her, he gave a vibrating groan and even turned his head a little for her.

Sterling ran her fingertips over the shorter hair at his temples, around to the back of his head to hold him still as she opened her mouth on his throat, grazed him with her teeth and sucked to give him a love bite.

His long fingers tangled in her hair, fisting gently.

Careful to keep pressure off his bandaged area, she rocked against him, deliberately teasing the hard cock straining beneath the material of his boxers.

A little roughly, he steered her mouth to his and took over the kiss. She didn't mind that…but then, she couldn't think straight. In fact, she wanted him too much to think.

Right *now*.

Maybe it was the chaos of the day, the resulting fear from him being hurt, but she felt totally out of control—a novel thing for her. She'd never had a craving like this, but she craved Cade.

The kiss went on and on while she touched him everywhere, moved against him, drove them both to the brink.

Pulling her mouth away, she sat up and away from him, then began wrestling off his boxers. He lifted his hips to help…and there he was. Long, hard, throbbing.

Sterling didn't think about it, didn't plan it; she just gave in to her desires.

Taking him in her fist, she kissed his erection, tentatively at first, just brushing her lips over his velvety length. The heated, musky scent of him encouraged her. His choppy breathing did, too.

Wanting more of him, she licked—from the base up to the head—and felt him go rigid. She liked that enough that she growled low and drew him in for a soft, wet suck.

CHAPTER TWELVE

Cade had to grip the sheets to keep from taking over. He couldn't stop his hips from lifting. Or quiet the groan that rumbled from his chest. Her tongue...damn, her tongue kept lapping over the sensitive head of his cock, and he thought he might explode.

Star wasn't skilled, but she was damn sure enthusiastic, and that seemed to be all that mattered.

Her hot little mouth slid down his length, back up again, over and over while her hand squeezed and her wet tongue tasted him—no, he wouldn't last.

"Condom," he nearly gasped, reaching to the nightstand as he said it. "Babe, put the condom on me."

With a small, hungry sound, she took him deep again.

"Star... God." He squeezed his eyes shut and thought of everything under the sun except what she made him feel. That lasted five minutes, maybe, and then he knew he had to end the torture.

Tangling a hand in her hair, he gently tugged. "Let up, babe, or it's over for me."

Slowly, as if she hated to stop, she released him. Breathing deeply, eyelids heavy, she licked her lips. "I liked that."

His eyes had adjusted and he could see her well enough to know she was every bit as stoked as he was. "I more than liked it." He decided to do the condom himself. Keeping his gaze locked with hers, he used his teeth to open the packet, then rolled it on. Even touching himself pushed his control.

"Stay on your back," she whispered, already climbing over him. "I like being able to see so much of you."

So her eyes had adjusted, as well? "No complaints from me." He held her waist as she positioned herself, rubbing her wet heat against him—before sliding down, taking all of him, in one steady move.

Christ, she was wet. And so hot. They both groaned.

Everything became fast and furious at that point.

Star had strong legs and she rode him hard, moving how she wanted, needed. With her hands braced on his biceps, he couldn't touch her as much as he'd like, but her breasts were right there, bouncing with each hard thrust, each roll of her hips. Her fingertips dug into him, and she tipped her head back on a low, throaty cry.

Lifting into her, Cade kept up the rhythm until she slumped forward, replete enough that she forgot about his wound and collapsed against him. Hell, he barely felt it with so much sensation pulsing in his erection.

Holding her hips tight to his, he easily rolled her to her back and hammered out his own mind-blowing release. Damn, she pleased him. Wrung him out, too.

In no hurry to move, he relaxed over her.

Long minutes passed like that, him resting on her warm, giving body, her sprawled legs around him.

Her choppy breathing had evened out, her thundering heartbeat slowed, and she lazily toyed with the hair at the back of his neck.

Soft and warm, she complained, "You ruined my plans."

Smiling, Cade lifted up to see her. And yeah, he felt it in his chest, around the bruised wound. But hell, it had totally been worth it. "How's that?"

"I didn't want you to exert yourself." She kissed his shoulder. "How are you? Okay?"

"Actually, I feel terrific." Tired, but also oddly satisfied. He turned to his back to take the pressure off his collarbone but gathered her close to his side.

To his surprise, she got out of the bed. "Hey." Catching her hand, he asked, "Where are you going?"

"I want to take care of you. Don't budge." She pulled free, warning, "I mean it," before disappearing into the bathroom.

The sounds of running water reached him. Then she stepped from the bathroom, beautifully naked, not in the least shy. Because she left on the bathroom light, he saw that she held a tissue box and a damp cloth.

As she reached the bed, she said, "I'm getting rid of the condom and washing you."

What? Cade started to sit up, but she already had hold of his now flaccid dick. Leave it to Star to do something totally different. With every other woman, he'd had the honor of cleanup. Choking on an odd mix of embarrassment and tenderness, he said, "You don't need to—"

"Shush." She dropped the spent rubber into a tissue and then smoothed the damp rag over him. He twitched.

So maybe he wasn't so spent after all. How could he be when she concentrated on him like that?

Grinning, she glanced up at his face. "This is all so interesting."

"This, meaning my junk?"

"Yeah." Leaning forward, she pressed another kiss to him, then said, "Be right back," and strode off again, all sassy and without a care.

Of course, Cade watched her. She had *such* a fine ass.

He didn't know how he'd gotten so lucky, but he knew she was worth fighting for, whether that meant fighting his family, fighting traffickers or fighting the lady herself.

Everyone looked up the second they stepped into the breakfast room. Surprised, Cade realized they'd kept them waiting. From the stove, where Bernard had been keeping the dishes warm, he began serving.

Star had assumed they'd eat in the kitchen again, but Cade explained that wasn't the norm, just something that seemed to happen during unusual occurrences.

The breakfast room was large and airy with windows that faced the mountains and the man-made lake below. There was no end of incredible views in his father's home.

Sipping from his coffee, Reyes glanced up, caught Star yawning and lifted a taunting brow. "Cade didn't let you sleep, huh?"

"Don't start," Cade ordered, unsure how she'd react. This morning she dragged a little, and yes, she kept yawning, but then, they'd had a trying day yesterday, and a satisfying night… that hadn't allowed for much sleep.

Today, he felt the activity in his collarbone but he wouldn't complain. No way did he want Star having any regrets, not when it was his own fault for waking her once in the middle of the night by nibbling on her shoulder. He hadn't been able to resist, but then, she'd come awake with her own intentions, completely on board in a nanosecond.

"What?" Reyes asked with mock innocence. "She looks… exhausted."

Taking a seat across from Reyes, Star picked up the silver knife at her place setting and studied it quietly. When she glanced at Reyes, Cade had to stifle a grin. He knew exactly what she was thinking.

Even sluggish, Star didn't disappoint, saying to his brother,

"On top of all your other skills, are you good at dodging knives?"

Smile banked, Reyes sat back. "Depends. You planning to use it up close or throw it?"

"I'm thinking...throw it."

Reyes's amusement grew. "It's not really a throwing knife."

And, Cade recalled, Star had said she kept her knife for close contact.

"True," she agreed, placing the knife beside her plate—and reaching to the small of her back, where she kept a real blade strapped in a clip-on holster. She lifted it for Reyes to see and asked sweetly, "What about this one?"

Bursting out a big laugh, Reyes said, "Should I be ducking?"

"Not right now." She returned the lethal weapon to the sheath. "If I decide you deserve it, I'll wait until you least expect it."

Grinning ear to ear, Reyes flagged his napkin in the air. "Then maybe I should call a truce. What do you think?"

"If you stop needling me...maybe."

Bernard handed her a glass of orange juice. "A hearty breakfast will improve dispositions all around."

Star inhaled the scents of breakfast meats, scrambled eggs, muffins and potatoes. "It certainly smells good enough to cause miracles."

Laughing, Madison loaded her plate. "This is fun, isn't it?"

That earned her a quelling frown from Parrish. "We have plans to make."

"I know, but usually we're all deadpan other than Reyes and Cade sniping at each other." She turned her smile on Star. "You're shaking things up, and I, for one, love it."

Bernard set fresh-cut fruit on the table. "I, as well."

Everyone looked at Reyes, but with one hand he just waved his napkin again while forking two sausage links with the other.

The ease with which Star dealt with his more bothersome sibling amazed Cade. Reyes didn't warm up to many people. Most never really knew him. He excelled at showing only what he wanted others to see, but with Star, he'd relaxed and opened up.

That may or may not be a good thing, considering Reyes's brand of humor could wear thin quickly, but so far Star didn't seem bothered.

Putting a hand to her back between her shoulder blades, Cade stroked her. He loved touching her, and he enjoyed the way she got up on his brother, how she didn't let Parrish intimidate her.

The urge to kiss her again nearly had him skipping breakfast, except that she was obviously hungry.

Parrish gave him a frown, making it clear he didn't condone the familiarity. Too bad. With Star near, keeping his hands to himself wasn't possible. Smiling, he let his father know what he could do with his judgment.

While helping himself to a slice of cantaloupe, Parrish said, "I assume Adela called you from an unlisted number."

"You assume correctly," Star said. "She's been very cagey about any details. It took some coaxing—or she wanted me to think I had to coax her—just to get a location on where to meet."

"She doesn't live in Coalville," Madison said. "I already checked. My guess would be that she's in another area altogether, that she chose Coalville because, one, it'd be easy to set a trap. Two, not many witnesses, since the town is so tiny. And three, it gave quick access to I-25, meaning she could make a hasty exit once she had you under wraps."

"Any idea why she wants you?" Reyes asked.

"I don't know her." Star shrugged while dishing up a bite of fresh pineapple. "I assume it's Mattox who wants me, and he's either forcing her to help, or she's a willing accomplice."

That careless attitude rubbed Cade the wrong way. "It occurs to me that you're in more danger now."

Brows lifting, Star asked, "How do you figure that?"

"They probably don't know where you live, but they do know that you frequent the bar. It'd be easy enough to ask around there and find out about your truck. You travel that way often. Some of the roads are long, lonely stretches."

"Perfect to shanghai me? You could be right." Star sipped her juice. "But you're in the same shape, right?"

Cade conceded the point. "If anyone at that church recognized me, then yes, they'll trace me back to the bar."

"And you travel back and forth, too," Madison pointed out.

Yes, and Cade hoped they'd come after him instead of Star. He could handle himself, but if they overwhelmed her...

No, he wouldn't consider the possibility of her being taken again. He'd kill them all before he let that happen.

Parrish held silent, watching, listening, allowing them to work it out. It was his way—not that he hesitated to interject whenever he chose to, but he considered discussion a learning opportunity. That he didn't object over Star's participation in what would normally be a family matter meant that he trusted Star, at least in part.

"Your trucking business is an issue," Reyes said. "It's too hard to monitor you if you go far."

Cade waited for her reaction to being monitored, but she skipped right past that.

"Thing is, it gives me legitimacy for what I do. No one questions a truck at a truck stop, right? And I have a reason to repeatedly hit the east-west expressway where long-haul trucks pass through."

Chiming in, Madison said, "That's why that area is ideal for human trafficking."

Glancing around the table, Star asked, "So you guys set up a bar and a gym for legit businesses, huh? Makes sense. I imagine both of you hear all the nitty-gritty, right?"

Reyes didn't answer, so Cade said, "That's the idea."

"You've rescued a lot of women?"

"Quite a few, yes." Parrish fidgeted with his napkin, then crumpled it in his fist. He asked Cade, "You completely trust her?"

Shocked, Cade knew exactly what his father was ready to do. It was unheard of, yet they'd all seen how concerned she'd been for him. And Reyes had probably explained to Parrish just how hard Star had fought against those men trying to take her. Anyone could tell she had the right edge, a sharp intuition and a core strength that couldn't be faked.

Aware of Star looking at him, wanting clarification for what was happening, he nodded. "Yes, I do."

Bernard quickly pulled up a chair, expectant anticipation in his eyes as he took in each person at the table.

"Whoa," Star said, growing wary as tension thickened the air. "You're not planning to put me through a blood rite or anything, are you?"

Clasping her thigh beneath the table, Cade said, "I believe my dad is ready to tell you more about the task force he funds."

"A task force? No kidding?" Fascinated, Star folded her arms on the table. "That sounds pretty awesome."

"It is," Madison enthused. "It's at the heart of everything we do."

"But we keep our involvement quiet," Parrish explained. "It's always best to avoid obvious links to your private life."

"Probably easier to do if you have a lot of dough, right?"

"Yes," he allowed. "Wealth has its advantages."

"Benevolence being one of them?"

Parrish gave a slight nod.

Since no one else was jumping in to explain, Cade did the honors. "The task force is possible because of Dad's funds. It ensures victims get counseling, plus legal representation when needed."

Bernard took over. It wasn't often he got to brag on Parrish.

"They also get financial assistance to start over, and guidance so that all legal avenues are used to convict the ones responsible."

"We make sure we have it all zipped up," Reyes said. "Dates, names, addresses, witnesses—the whole shebang."

"Wow." Impressed, Star asked, "I take it that's for the perps who don't die in the process?"

Bernard put his nose in the air. "There are, necessarily, a few who do."

She grinned at the way he said that with proper gravity. "You won't see me crying about it. I'd wipe them all out if I could."

"But you're just one woman," Reyes pointed out. "Unless you join us."

Eyes flaring, Star blinked at Reyes. Her gaze shifted to Parrish and Bernard, then to Madison, before she slowly pivoted to face Cade. "Is that a joke?"

"No." Cade squeezed her knee. "It'd be safer for you, and you'd have more effect."

As if they couldn't hear her, she leaned closer. "But I work alone."

"You work with me."

"Just that once!"

Cade considered her attitude, but he couldn't convince her here with his family all riveted. "I think maybe we need to talk privately. Are you done eating?"

"What? Oh, yeah." Standing, she picked up her plate and started for the kitchen.

"I'll do that." Bernard rushed around the table.

She kept going. So did Bernard.

Madison fretted. "She needs a minute, doesn't she?"

"She's been alone a very long time," Cade explained. He'd sway her, but he didn't delude himself that it'd be easy. Star was one of the most independent people he'd ever met, and with good reason, she didn't trust easily. Yes, she'd taken to him fast enough, once he'd introduced the idea, but he was one person, not a family unit.

And his family... Cade glanced at each of them. His father had initiated this, but he still didn't speak up. Cade pushed back his chair. "I'll convince her."

"I hope so." Rubbing his mouth, Reyes stated the obvious. "It's going to be a problem if she wants to walk away at this point."

"She won't." Cade picked up his own plate and went after her.

He stalled when he didn't find her in the kitchen, but Bernard said, "She went out the side door to the deck," as he took the plate from Cade. "I had to wrestle the dishes from her. She's a very determined young lady, and she was most insistent that she 'pull her own weight,' even though I explained that this is part of *my* job." He made a rude sound. "But she's wonderful and I like her—as long as she understands the parameters of my domain."

Sounded about right. "I'll talk to her," he promised again and almost laughed. He had a growing list of things that required his skill at convincing. Usually not a daunting task, but with Star? She could be very bullheaded.

She wasn't in back, which would have put her in line with the windows where his family dined. Instead she'd taken up a corner of the wraparound deck, facing the side yard with tree-covered hills.

The second he stepped out behind her, she said, "Don't start," without turning to face him.

"Come on."

That got her attention. She glanced back with suspicion. "Where are we going?"

"I thought we'd take the trail down to the lake. One day we can fish there, if you'd like. Or take out kayaks. It's a private lake, so pretty damn peaceful."

Bracing her back on the railing, she smiled at him. "That sounds nice."

"Today, we'll just walk." And talk. He held out his hand.

She didn't take it right away. "Are we going to have a fight? You want to get me alone so your family won't hear me yelling?"

So damn astute. He snagged her hand and pulled her forward into his arms. "I want you alone so you can speak freely."

She snuggled close. "Wasn't I already doing that?"

He couldn't help but laugh. "Do you need to be a hard-ass to the bitter end?" Pressing a kiss to the top of her head, he suggested, "Meet me halfway here, okay?"

"You're right," she said, surprising him. "Sorry."

Disbelief had him levering her back. "Do you ever say the expected?"

Her mouth opened, then snapped closed as she gave it thought. "I have no idea what the expected might be, so I don't know if I do or not. Other than brief exchanges with clients who want to hire me to carry a load, or when shopping or requesting food, I don't really have conversations with anyone."

"What about the women you've helped?"

Uncertainty darkened her eyes. "More like a question-and-answer deal. Like if they had a specific place to go, if they wanted cops involved or not, or if they needed a trip to the ER. Stuff like that."

He imagined she was a lot more compassionate than she made it sound, but he got her point. "Come on. We'll go this way." With her smaller hand held securely in his, Cade tugged her to the spiral stairs that led down to the lawn. From there they circled around for the worn footpath to the lake.

"It's a long walk?" she asked.

Depended on the perspective. "It'll take us ten or fifteen minutes to get down there, but with a lot of nature to see along the way."

"I wasn't complaining, just curious." Tipping her head back, she peered up at the bright blue sky. "It smells different here."

"Fresh," he agreed. "All the trees and earth and the scents from the mountain…"

Smiling, she bumped him with her hip. "You love it here, don't you?"

"The land, yeah. Who wouldn't? There's something about being surrounded by the mountains, all the peace and quiet, immersed in nature. The scrub oak brush is something to see in the fall." Would he be able to show her? He hoped so, and that brought him around to the reason for their walk. "It was a huge concession for Dad to include you."

"I figured." Distracted by a boulder, she said, "Look at the size of that rock," and proceeded to climb atop it.

As agile as a mountain goat, she clambered up to the highest spot about six feet off the ground, then spread her arms wide. Cade moved around to the side of the boulder so he could catch her if she fell.

"I declare myself king of the mountain."

God, he loved seeing her like this. Playful. Relaxed. Mostly unguarded. "You might have to take that up with Bernard, since he claims he holds that title."

Laughter bubbled out. "No way! Stuffy Bernard does? Are you pulling my leg?"

"He loves it here, says it calls to his soul."

"I can believe it." She inhaled deeply. "It's awesome, for sure." Putting her head back and closing her eyes, she breathed deeply, but then abruptly looked down at him again. "What's up with Bernard? Does he live here? He's like a butler, right?"

"He and Dad have been best friends a long time, back before Reyes and Madison were born. As Dad's wealth grew, Bernard came along, working various jobs, though Dad swears he wasn't helping Bernard, that Bernard made his life easier because he could trust him. He moved in after Marian died—"

"Marian was his love? Mom to Reyes and Madison?"

Cade nodded. "Dad was a mess, and he was so consumed with grief, Bernard picked up the slack where he could. He loves to cook, though, and he's an organizational whiz, so that's mostly what he does."

"Huh. So he's part of the family?"

"Very much so." Tired of the distanced chatting, Cade held out his arms. "Jump."

"Ha! Not on your life." She looked around for an easy way down.

Cade knew she'd find that getting down was the hard part. "Chicken."

Her gaze clashed with his. "Take that back or I might just launch at you, and we both know I'm not a lightweight."

Cade mimicked her "Ha!" and left his arms up for her. No, she wasn't a delicate woman, but compared to him, she was still very female, smaller boned, curvy where he was straight, soft where he was hard. She needed to stop underestimating his strength. "Trust me."

Her brows pinched together. "Have you forgotten you were injured?"

No, but he wished she would. "I'm fine." If he said it often enough, maybe she'd finally believe him.

Softer, with worry, she explained, "I don't want to hurt you."

"I promise you won't." He waited and knew the second she planned to prove him wrong. Using her strong legs to propel her forward, she did indeed launch at him.

He was grinning before she landed against his chest and was grinning still as he swung her around, going with the momentum until they stopped, body to body, her feet off the ground. Yes, that impact jarred him, but the pain was minimal and the reward made it worthwhile when she fit him so perfectly.

Not just physically, but in so many other ways, too.

Against her lips, he whispered, "Told you so."

Her laughter made it tough to kiss her, but he persisted until she slumped against him, her arms tight around his neck, her mouth open, her tongue greeting his.

It would be so easy to get carried away, but he didn't think she wanted to get naked on the mountainside. Plus, yeah, he wouldn't put it past his brother to break out the binoculars.

When Cade moved to kiss her throat, she whispered, "You are a certified stud."

"Don't forget it."

She laughed a little too hard over that, so he set her down and again got them walking toward the lake. It was ten minutes of peaceful quiet before they reached the edge of the water.

They had a dozen things to discuss, but Star's awe kept him quiet. Her eyes went soft and wide as she took in the reflection of junipers and fluffy clouds on the placid surface of the lake.

This early in the day, you could see to the rocky bottom. Rough boulders bordered one whole side of the large lake, with thick evergreens behind that. It was only this section that offered easy access to the water. Cleared per his father's instructions, a pebble-covered shoreline made it easy to fish.

Random wildflowers grew from between rocks, drawing hummingbirds that flitted here and there. Overhead, red-tailed hawks soared.

Silently, Star went to the water's edge and reached down to trail her fingers over the glassy surface, sending ripples to feather out. "Do you ever swim?"

"The water is always freezing."

She glanced back. "Is that a yes or no?"

"I have, yes. So has Reyes."

"But Madison has more sense?"

He grinned. "A nice way to put it."

"Women don't feel the need to prove things the way guys do."

"Oh, really?" He climbed up to sit on a flat sun-warmed

rock, his arms resting over one bent leg as he stared out at the lake. "So that wasn't you who felt it necessary to challenge my brother?"

Joining him, she accepted the hand he offered to help her up. "Totally different," she said as she got settled. "Your brother needs to be knocked down a peg or two."

"I do that on a regular basis."

Leaning against him, she said, "I can't challenge your dad."

"No?" Cade had been wondering how to bring it up, but he should have known Star would beat him to it. She wasn't one to shy away—from a subject, danger or anything else. "Why not?"

Her shoulder lifted. "He's your dad. I don't know what to do with dads, but I do know I won't like being under his thumb. He's a dictator, isn't he?" Wrinkling her nose, she specified, "Super bossy, I bet. And if I go along with this whole…alliance, he'll expect me to toe the line. But that's not me."

As Reyes had said, there wasn't much choice at this point. That was Cade's doing. He'd brought her here, forcing the issue and putting his father in an untenable position.

But he didn't regret it.

After drawing her between his legs so he could wrap his arms around her, Cade propped his chin on top of her head. He relished the light breeze that blew over his face, and the way she rested her hands over his forearms. "You think I toe the line, babe?"

A sudden stillness settled over her. "Did I insult you?"

A little late for her to worry about that now, but he didn't want her to change, not when he already admired so much about her. "I butt heads with my dad plenty often enough."

"So how do you deal with him?"

"By listening when what he says makes sense." Which, much as it annoyed Cade, was most of the time. "When I disagree, I say so."

"Does he ever listen to you?"

Only when Cade wouldn't relent, but he didn't want to scare her off. "How about we put it this way—if you work with us, what's the worst that could happen?"

"I could lose my cool and…"

"What?"

"I don't know. I might make an ass of myself."

That candid confession had him barking a laugh, which had her turning on him. He kissed her before she could blast him.

"So what?" She looked like such a thundercloud that he kissed her again. "You're allowed to be human, honey. I am. Reyes and Madison are. My dad…well, he's more distant, very driven, but he's not bad. You *can* deal with him." One more kiss, this time teasing. "You know the best things that could happen? You'd be safer—and I'd know you were safer, so I wouldn't worry about you. You'd be able to help a lot more women."

"In more meaningful ways."

"Not what I said. I'm sure for any woman you've helped, it made a life-altering difference."

She stared out over the lake. "You think I can do this?"

Insecurity? From Sterling Parson? He hugged her. "I have faith in you."

Her scowl hadn't lightened up, but she grudgingly said, "Okay—on a trial basis."

That wouldn't do, but for now he'd accept it. If nothing else, it'd give him time to talk her around.

And then what?

He didn't know for sure, but she fit so well into his life, he wasn't ready to let her go. Not today, not next week.

Not for the foreseeable future.

CHAPTER THIRTEEN

Cade would have been happier if he could have convinced Star to stay at his father's house, but he'd known that wouldn't happen, not without him there, and he had to go to work.

At least he'd talked her into coming to the bar with him instead of going to the apartment alone. Nothing unusual in her being at the bar. During deliveries, she'd often stopped in and stayed for hours. He doubted anyone would pay any attention.

She'd had to turn down two jobs for now, but for how long would she do that? If Adela didn't call back, then what?

He'd go after her, that's what. One way or another, this had to end. It was the only way to be fair to Star.

Tonight they'd go back to his father's—he'd used the excuse of Parrish checking his wound in the morning—but after that? Star made her own decisions, and she wasn't big on concessions. But then, she was also smart and she'd understand the need for extra security until Mattox was locked up or dead.

"I should check on my truck tomorrow. I never leave it to sit this long."

"We can do that, no problem." Cade pulled in to the parking

lot of the Tipsy Wolverine. His tendency was to park around the back and go in through that door, so when they left, it was likely no one would notice that they were together.

"Now that we're a thing…" She let that hang out there for a bit before continuing, maybe waiting for him to object.

Of course he didn't. Putting his SUV in Park, he asked, "What?"

Relief brought a brief smile to her mouth. "How did you come up with the name of this place?"

"Don't put that on me." He turned off the car. "The name was already on it when Dad bought the place. I came out of the military and got dropped into the Tipsy Wolverine practically in the same week." Pretty sure his dad had wanted to lock him down while he had the opportunity. "The name was already known, and I don't really care, so I never bothered to change it."

"What a disappointing answer." She opened her seat belt. "I was all set for a good story."

Laughing, Cade got out and started around to her side of the SUV. She didn't often let him open her door for her, but the instinct was there anyway.

Luckily he had amazing peripheral vision. He caught the rush of movement and automatically reacted, turning and kicking out at the same time.

He caught the tallest guy in the knee, watched it buckle awkwardly, but didn't have time to follow up as two more men charged him.

Dodging a short pipe aimed at his head, he buried a heavy fist into that fool's gut, followed by a head-snapping pop to the chin.

Something broke over Cade's back, almost taking him down as he staggered forward, but he caught himself and spun with another kick. He missed the man's face and only hit his shoulder. It was still effective enough to knock the guy on his ass, only he didn't stay down.

With only a quick glimpse, Cade realized all three men were

young, probably no older than midtwenties. Had Mattox run out of muscle, or did he consider these boys expendable?

Willing Star to lock the car doors, he concentrated on ending the attack quickly.

They were definitely injured, but other than the one with a busted knee, they weren't yet out of the fight.

Handling that swiftly, Cade grabbed one by the throat, lifted and slammed him hard to the ground. Stunned, the breath knocked out of him, he didn't fight as Cade flipped him over to pin him down with a knee pressed between his shoulder blades. The rough gravel would cut into his face.

No more than he deserved.

The third fellow thought that'd be a good time to press his advantage, but Cade was using only one knee on the guy he held down, leaving both arms and a foot free.

"You're a dead man," the third guy said, then dived at him.

Cade flipped him, too—did they not learn? In a finishing blow, Cade punched him in the nuts.

An inhuman sound squeaked out of his gaping mouth, and pain curled him tight.

"Someone better start answering questions fast," Cade said. He got to his feet, pulled up the guy he'd been holding down and slammed his face into the wall of the bar. He crumpled backward without a sound.

Gaze locked on the goon with the badly mangled knee, Cade smiled. "Looks like you're it." Knowing the man he'd just nutted wouldn't function again anytime soon, he started forward.

The guy tried to crawl back but couldn't get more than a few inches before Cade hauled him up with a fist in his hair. "I'm going to ask questions, and you're going to give me answers. Got it?"

Face contorted in pain, he gasped, "Yeah, man, let up."

"Name."

"My name?" he asked, confused.

Tightening his hold, Cade lightly kicked his knee, earning a groan. "I'm only asking each question once."

"Right, yeah. I'm Paulie Wells."

"And the other two?"

"Brothers."

The one with crushed gonads growled, "Shut up, Paulie."

"You want another?" Cade asked him.

Wincing at the threat, he curled tighter to protect his jewels.

"That's...that's Ward Manton. You knocked out his bro, Kelly."

Cade dug a hand into Paulie's pocket and found a wallet but no cell phone. He checked for ID, saw Paulie had told the truth, then searched him for weapons before letting him fall into a whimpering heap.

He turned to Ward. "You like wielding pipes, my man?" Cade strode over to where it had fallen and picked it up, hefting it in his hand.

Ward amused him by looking both defiant and terrorized. "Just business, dude. Nothin' personal, I swear."

"Whose business is it?"

Shifty eyes darted around. "We, ah, we were just robbin' you, that's all. It's cool."

Cade spun the pipe in his hand, then rested it against Ward's temple. "That's your one and only lie. Tell me another and you won't be able to talk for a very long time." He paused to tell Paulie, "If you don't sit your ass down, I'll break the other knee."

Paulie promptly stopped looking for an avenue of escape and instead put both hands to his head, his expression lost.

Back to Ward, Cade tapped the pipe none too gently to his temple. "Do we understand each other?"

He heard *"Euewww"* and glanced back to see Star standing behind the open car door watching. Damn it, he would have preferred she stay hidden.

But of course, she did the opposite and stepped out. "If you're going to splatter what little brains he has, will you warn me first? I'd rather look away."

"Better yet," Cade said calmly, "why don't you get back in the car and—"

"Nope." She sauntered forward. "I'm not missing all the fun. In fact, I'll check this one while you do your brain splattering."

Ward eyed her warily, his gaze going from his still-unconscious brother to Star, then to Cade.

Kneeling down by Kelly, Star efficiently went through his pockets, tossing out a wallet, then a knife, brass knuckles and nylon hand ties. "Looks like they had a party planned." With the small collection in front of her, a look of icy rage on her face, Star said, "Maybe I want to watch you cave in his skull after all."

Kelly groaned, and without a blink, Star brought her elbow hard to his temple, knocking him out again. To Ward, she said, "You better start talking fast or neither of you will have any brains left."

Cade wasn't happy with her interference—the less low-life thugs knew about her, the better. Couldn't tell her that right now, though, not with their audience.

Glaring down at Ward, he whispered with tight control, "Were the brass knuckles for her or me?"

Properly terrified, Ward stammered, "For...for you, dude. You're big. We weren't gonna hurt her none. Mattox wants her in one piece."

"That answer is the only thing saving your ass." Cade shoved him over to his face. "Give me the cuffs."

Star lifted a brow at the order, then shrugged and carried everything to him. While he bound Ward's hands, she slipped on the brass knuckles. "I like these." Her feral gaze dropped to Ward. "Let's see how well they work."

Cade had to jump up to keep her from breaking Ward's jaw.

Quietly wrestling her into submission, he said, "Not now. I have more questions for them."

"He was going to use these on *you*," she practically yelled in his face, the brass-enhanced fist almost touching his chin.

"Was never going to happen. They're children. You can see that."

"What I see is that they're a bunch of cowardly goons." She kicked past Cade's restraint, landing that steel-toed boot to Ward's shin.

Howling, Ward tried to scuttle away from her.

Fighting amusement as well as frustration, Cade urged her back more. "Hey," he whispered, "you're giving away too much. No need for them to know you care."

Nostrils flaring and expression red with antagonism, she said, "Well, I *do*."

Cade couldn't help it. He laughed. Leave it to Star to growl that declaration at him with murder in her eyes during a violent altercation. "Good to know."

She blinked, then shoved away from him. "You have a warped sense of humor."

"Maybe." He put his mouth to her ear so the downed goons wouldn't hear. "Now get it together, *Francis*."

It took her a second. Then she gave a stiff nod. Just as low, she said, "I want credit for letting you handle things."

His eyes flared.

Unconcerned, she pointed out, "I didn't jump to your defense right off since I saw you had it handled. You can thank me."

"Thank you."

She nodded and moved on. "No phones?"

"Let me check Ward. I have a feeling he's the head of this comic trio." Sure enough, once he'd roughly gone through Ward's pockets, he found an old burner phone, a slip of paper with the bar's name scrawled on it and a nearly empty wallet.

There were only three numbers saved in the phone, none

with contact info. He toed Ward with his boot. "Who's going to answer if I call these numbers?"

"Those two," Ward said, giving a slight nod toward his brother and Paulie. He didn't have much range of motion with his face in the gravel.

"And the third?"

Ward's face tightened.

"Need some incentive?" Cade asked. "I suppose I could turn her loose on you. Let her bloody up your face a bit, but I should warn you, she's damn strong and has a solid punch—"

"Mattox," he snapped. "It goes to Mattox." Then in a whine, "Dude, he's going to kill us."

"Mattox is the least of your worries right now." Cade wanted to ask about Adela, but the bar would open soon and customers would start showing up. He still had to clean up this mess. Besides, the clowns on the ground around him didn't look like the type to have any real info.

"What are we going to do with them?" Before he could answer, Star said, "FYI, I called for backup. Should be here any minute."

Renewed anger rushed through Cade. He said one word. "Who?" If she'd called the cops, that'd be a huge problem.

Cocking her head, she listened, then looked out at the road. "That's probably him now. Yup, it is."

Reyes pulled up and without a word joined them, his gaze going over each man. "From Mattox?"

"Yeah." Relieved that Star hadn't brought authorities in on things, Cade still said, "I could have handled it."

"Women," Reyes commiserated, just to rile her. "Guess she was worried about you."

And of course it worked. Star gave him a killing glare. "I still have my knife."

Hands in his back pockets, Reyes pursed his mouth, then shifted his gaze to Cade. "Gunning for her?"

"It's what they said."

Star jammed her fist at Reyes, showing off the brass knuckles. "They were going to use these on him."

His mouth twitched. "Pisses you off, huh? Well, no worries, doll. I'll handle them."

Her eyes narrowed. "By *handle them*, you better mean beating them to a bloody pulp!"

"If that's what it takes," Reyes promised, taking a pack of nylon cuffs from his pocket.

Snorting, Star said, "You're a little overprepared, aren't you?"

Shrugging, Reyes said, "You were all hysterical—"

"I was not!"

"So I thought there might be a mob or something." He grinned at her blustering indignation. "Now, why don't you wait in the bar? I'll handle this."

"*Ugh.*" Face flushed, she snatched ties from him and stomped over to Kelly to deftly bind his hands behind his back. It roused him, but Star was already working on his ankles, pushing up his jeans, dragging down his socks so the nylon was tight against his skin. He wasn't going anywhere.

"Ward?" Kelly struggled, twisting his head to try to see his brother. "What's going on?"

"We're done," Ward groaned. "Done."

"So much drama." Reyes was quick, and a little brutal, in how he bound Ward. Then he quickly gagged all three of them. Hoisting Ward over his shoulder, Reyes carried him to his truck and dumped him in the bed none too gently.

It took a little time to get them secured to grommets and concealed with a tonneau cover. It was a tight fit in the short bed, but bound and gagged as they were, no one would discover them.

Appearing a little worried, Star asked, "Where are you taking them?"

"Someplace private, where I can do a proper interrogation."

She bit her lip. "Will you kill them?"

Reyes slowly grinned. "Now you're worried about that? Just minutes ago you wanted them annihilated."

"Forget it." She started to stomp away.

Reyes caught her arm—then shocked her by pulling her into a hug. "Rest easy, hon. Once I've found out what I can, I'll hand them over to someone else."

"Who?"

Arms folded, Cade leaned back against the truck and explained, "We have contacts who'll make sure they're off the street and that they're legally punished for their part in Mattox's plans." Interesting that Star allowed Reyes to hold her. Was it possible she didn't dislike his brother as much as she pretended? If they got along, it'd make things easier.

For Star.

"They won't die, though," Reyes assured her.

Shoulders relaxing, she glanced at Cade. "You said it yourself, they're boys. If anyone's going to die, I'd rather it be Mattox."

With another hug, Reyes said softly, "I'm glad you're not quite as bloodthirsty as you pretend." Not giving her a chance to blow up on him, he released her and headed around to the driver's side.

Cade put a hand to Star's back and together they followed. Lower, so the men wouldn't hear, he said to Reyes, "I took a cheap phone off one of them. I'll give you time to get well away from here before I call the three numbers."

"If you call now," Star mused, piecing it together, "they might realize their plan backfired. They could set a trap to at-tack—"

"Me on the road," Reyes finished. "I'd almost like them to try." He looked back at the truck bed. "That is, if I didn't have cargo."

Nodding, Cade explained what he'd learned from Ward. "I

think he's telling the truth about those numbers, that one will lead to Mattox, but I'll let you know."

Reyes nodded at Star's hand. "Plan to keep that little decoration?"

She curled her fingers around the thick brass knuckles. "Yup."

Shaking his head in a laughing way, Reyes got in the truck and drove off.

"Come on." Cade drew Star around to the bar door. He wanted her safe inside before he got more distracted with details. "We'll give it fifteen minutes so Reyes is off the worst of the winding roads. Then we'll call."

"We?" she repeated, as he relocked the door behind him. Strolling to a barstool, she took a seat, her long legs stretched out, one elbow resting on the counter.

She looked sexy as hell sitting there. Part of it was that she took the attack in stride. Star was unlike most people; she didn't fall apart under pressure, and in fact seemed to gain an edge.

Except when she'd lost it a little over those brass knuckles. He didn't want her worried about him, but he also enjoyed the show of concern.

Sidetracked for a moment, he asked, "What did you say to Reyes when you called him?"

Rolling her eyes, she gave a soft laugh. "He's a damn doofus—and a giant liar. I was *not* hysterical. Can you even imagine?"

No, he couldn't.

"I gave him the facts—maybe I gave them a little quickly, you know? I told him we'd pulled up to the bar and three guys tried to jump you."

"Just like that, huh?"

"Mostly like that. But yeah, I didn't know if there was a fourth or fifth around somewhere, or if Mattox was hiding nearby with a gun. So I told your brother to get his butt over there in case the tide turned." She rolled a shoulder. "Didn't take me long to realize you had it under control—which is kind of astounding, I have to say. Wimpy guys or not, it was three to one, with a pipe and a chunk of wood, but in no time, you had it all well in hand."

So it was a chunk of wood they'd broken over his back? He hadn't been sure. In the long run, it hadn't mattered. "Appreciate the vote of confidence." He went behind the bar to start prepping. Workers would show up shortly. They wouldn't have long alone.

"It's earned." She turned on the stool to keep him in her sights. "So the number we're going to call?"

"I assumed you'd want to be a part of it."

"Part of it? You do realize I'm the one who should call, right? I mean, in case Adela answers. She'd hang up on you, but there's a chance she'll talk to me. And if she does, she might give something away. I might even be able to goad her into losing her pretense of being a victim. It's worth a shot."

Actually... "You're right." After he finished the bar prep, he checked the time, poured them each a cola over ice and set the cell phone on the counter between them. "On speaker."

"You betcha." Almost rubbing her hands together, she opened the screen, went to the first number and pressed to dial it.

"If any employees show up early, we can step into the office."

"Got it." With Cade leaning close, Sterling listened as the phone rang and rang... No answer.

"One down," she said, aware that her palms were a little sweaty. "Probably went to his brother or Paulie, as Ward said."

Cade lifted her chin. "You have great instinct, babe. I've told you that enough times. If anyone answers, just go with your gut. You've got this."

His confidence helped shore up her own. Yes, she could do this. If it was Adela, she'd play her part depending on what the other woman said or did.

Drawing a breath, Sterling moved on to the next number. Each ring caused her tension to notch up.

Again, no answer. Crazy that this was making her so nervous. They were away from the danger for now, and even better, she had the dynamic McKenzie family as backup. Whatever rolled out, it'd be fine.

But she knew, of course. Her frazzled nerves were based directly on one particular McKenzie. A specimen of the first order, impossibly strong, remarkably fast, unshakable and... He hadn't denied that they were "a thing." That made the risk about more than just her, because now it was about *them*.

That made it so much worse.

She'd already discovered firsthand that seeing him hurt sent her into a tailspin.

"Two strikes," Cade said, and he brushed his thumb over her cheek. "Third has to be a charm."

Sterling nodded and pressed the last button.

Immediately following the first ring, a deep voice growled, "Tell me you have her."

Ah. Mattox. Amazingly enough, her nervousness left and she settled in with a smile. This she could handle—as Cade predicted, her instincts kicked in with a vengeance.

"Hello, Mattox."

Silence, then a snarled, "You fucking bitch."

Sterling actually laughed. "What? You figured I'd be stuffed in a trunk by now or something?" That thought struck her, and she glanced up at Cade to mouth, "Car?" How had those three hoodlums arrived at the bar? In the middle of the chaos, she hadn't even considered that.

Cade shook his head and whispered, "Later."

Unaware of her sudden distraction, Mattox said, "I thought I'd have my hands on you any minute. It would have been such a pleasure—for me."

"So those boys you sent after me were planning to meet you

somewhere?" She sat up a little straighter, all teasing gone from her tone. "Tell me where and I'll come to you right now, you miserable pig."

"I don't think so," he said with a laugh. "I'll get you soon enough."

"Really? How do you think to do that? You must be running out of lackeys by now. How many have I already brought down?"

Mattox snorted. "I doubt you've done any real damage, sweetheart. More likely your hulking bodyguard—but he won't be around forever."

The thought of him getting hold of Cade sent a wash of ice through her veins. Cade wouldn't appreciate her fear, and Mattox would try to use it against her, so she purred, "Oh, please. Please, underestimate me. It'll make gutting you so much more satisfying."

Cade shook his head. Apparently he didn't want her goading Mattox quite that much, but hey, too late to pull back now.

"So where's Adela?" Sterling asked. "Is she standing right there, listening to our conversation?"

"Is that what this is?" Mattox replied. "A conversation? I thought it was me telling you how fucking bad you're going to suffer before I cut your throat and watch you bleed out. You want to hear details?"

Aware of Cade's hands curling into fists, she said, "Not particularly."

Of course, that didn't stop Mattox. "I have plenty of men left—and they'll each get a turn with you. Might have to make them draw straws to see who goes last, because by the end there won't be much of you left."

Though her stomach turned, Sterling laughed. "That's a lot of bold talk for a dead man." She hesitated, but the timing felt right, so she added, "Especially since you tried handing me out once already, and all you got for your troubles was a corpse."

Like the ticking of a bomb, the tension stretched taut—until it detonated. *"You fucking whore!"* Mattox roared. "You're the one who got away!"

"Ding-ding-ding!" All pretense of calm shredded away as she got to her feet and smirked down at the phone. "I recognized you right off, big disgusting ape that you are. But you had no idea, did you?"

He snarled something low, but then snapped, "That was years ago, when I was still starting out. After all this time, the meat starts to look the same."

God, she wished she could kill him right now.

Cade took her hand and held it. Strong, steady, sexy Cade. He was counting on her, and she wouldn't let him down.

When she didn't reply, Mattox asked, "Do you have any idea of the trouble you caused me?"

Ah, it bothered him that he hadn't made her lose her temper. Good. Sterling smiled. "The upside is that when you're dead, your troubles will be over."

"You think you're smart?"

"Smart enough to get to you when you least expect it. There's not a hole deep enough for you to crawl in, not enough men to watch your back, to keep you safe. You better sleep with one eye open, because the second they both close, I'll end you."

He hung up and Sterling wanted to pitch the phone. Instead she peeked at Cade and asked, "Did I go overboard?"

Eyes like the center of a flame and jaw clenched tight, he drew her forward to lean over the bar. "I will never let him touch you."

Wow. She hadn't even realized his temper had risen. He'd seemed so cool during the call. He tried to act cool now, too, but yeah, she saw all that fierce rage in his eyes. "Er...thanks?"

Not amused, he put his mouth to hers. And proceeded to devour her. Holy smokes, possessiveness had really gotten his engine revving.

To soothe him, Sterling stroked the side of his face.

He let up but kept her close, his forehead to hers. "Sorry."

"No worries. Kind of turned me on."

He looked into her eyes—and laughed. "There can't be another woman like you in the entire universe."

And just like that, he lightened her mood. Unfortunately, a knock at the back door interrupted them, and shortly they were joined by employees, and then customers, too.

They had a lot of plans to make. Mattox would be coming for her—or rather, he'd send more men after her. Odds were, he'd try to take out Cade first. Obviously Mattox knew Cade, maybe even recognized him from the church.

She bit her lip, thinking about that. It was time to follow through on that trap, and if it required using her as bait, Cade would just have to get over it.

Talking him around wouldn't be easy, but she figured Parrish, Reyes and Madison would agree. They'd vote on it or something, she'd win, and finally she'd get the chance for her revenge. Now that Mattox had crossed her path again, she had to end him or die trying.

Once that was done, what would happen with her and Cade? She didn't know. For now she'd have to take their relationship one day at a time.

She glanced over at Cade as he served two pretty women sitting at the bar. The women flirted, their expressions showing awe, but then, Cade was such a big dude he had that effect on a lot of people.

He smiled at them, but it was his patented polite smile, not the kind he gave to her—the kind full of secrets and shared lust and so much more.

Over the next few hours, in between customers, Cade used the phone. Each time he held her gaze while quietly talking.

Strangers came in, putting her on guard, but no one that acted suspicious. They drank, talked and left.

She was starting to think it'd be a quiet night, and she even considered dozing like old times.

And then the call from Adela came in.

CHAPTER FOURTEEN

"Francis?"

She blinked, for once unsure what to say. "Yeah... Adela?"

"Oh, God, I was so afraid you'd be dead." Voice shaking, Adela whispered, "I knew he was trying to get you, and I'm so sorry. I couldn't figure out how to warn you."

Sterling caught Cade's eye to let him know what was happening, but he was stuck in a crowd. It'd take him a few seconds to get away, so she moved out of the main room of the bar and into the hallway where she could better hear.

"Are you still there?" Adela asked frantically.

"Yeah. So..." What to say? "I'm surprised to hear from you."

"I'm sorry, Francis, but listen to me. He's hiring men. A *lot* of men. He said he knows where to find you."

Sterling really didn't trust the woman. Not that she ever had completely, but now? She accepted Reyes's take on things, yet the thinnest doubt remained. Having been in captivity once herself, Sterling understood better than some how you said and did things that normally you would never consider.

Doing those things had allowed her to escape.

They'd allowed her to survive.

Was Adela trying to escape—or trying to entrap her? Sterling didn't want to believe that another woman would be so cruel, but too many things didn't add up. "How do you know all that?"

"I don't have much time. He'll be back in a minute, but I was able to listen through the door. He's...*enraged*. Francis, God, the things he's planning to do to you..." She started to cry.

Damn it, that sounded real enough.

"It's all my fault," Adela sobbed. "I shouldn't have involved you."

Twisting her mouth, Sterling considered things. It'd probably be best if she didn't question Adela's motives, so instead she asked, "How does he plan to get me?"

"He said he knows where you live. Or will know. I'm not sure. He plans to follow you, I think. Oh, Francis, you have to be careful. You should just go away—" Suddenly Adela screamed.

It sounded like the phone crashed to the floor. Sterling heard a man's voice. *"Stupid bitch."* Loud thumps. Slaps.

Worse.

With her heart caught in her throat, Sterling heard Mattox snarl, "When the hell will you learn?"

Frozen in horror, Sterling listened to Adela's hysterical, babbling voice, pleading, crying out... She winced at a louder crash, and then—deafening silence.

Her heart hammered in her chest.

There was rustling, and then, "Is that you, Francis?"

Sterling didn't reply. Anger roiled inside her, helping to settle the fear and upset.

"She's bleeding," he said, his tone taunting. "If she dies now, it's your fault."

The call ended.

Blindly, Sterling stared at the floor, trying to assimilate what she'd heard and what she knew.

"Hey." Joining her, Cade slipped both hands around her neck. "What's happened?"

"I don't know." She shook her head. "Something. Or maybe nothing." She gazed into his stunning blue eyes. "Either Mattox just beat Adela badly, or they're working together and want me to… I don't know. Act hastily? Or just feel bad, maybe."

"If you're mired in guilt, you can't think clearly." He drew her into his arms. "Whatever happened, none of it is in your control."

"But what if Adela is innocent? What if she really was trying to escape?"

"Reyes didn't think so."

She pushed him back. "Reyes could be wrong!"

"Could be, but probably isn't."

For once his calm, in-charge tone annoyed her. She was ready to lose it, and Cade was unaffected. "I still want to know for sure."

"I have some news that might help." He kissed her forehead, then took her hand and led her to the office. Once inside, he closed the door and leaned back on it, his arms folded over his chest. "The three stooges gave up a few locations before Reyes handed them off."

"Locations for Mattox?" Finally, some good news! "Why are we still standing here? We should check them out."

"Reyes is doing that right now."

"He's one man! He can't be in three places at once."

"No, but my sister can. Remotely, that is. She's able to tell which buildings are occupied, which ones have activity."

Sterling didn't ask how. So far as she could tell, Madison had scary tech ability that'd be well over her head. "And?"

"An old house seems more likely than the other two. Mattox hasn't survived this long by being careless, so odds are he'll be relocating real fast. If Reyes gets lucky, he might be able to follow him, find out where he holes up."

That sounded beyond perilous. "What if he gets caught?"

"Worried about Reyes now, too?"

"You aren't?"

Taking mercy on her emotions, Cade admitted, "A little. He'll check back in soon."

How long was *soon*? Pacing, Sterling absently took in the room. Neat, of course. A solid but plain desk, comfortable chair—and the short sofa he'd offered her for napping. "We need to find out how the men got here today. There weren't any cars in the lot. Did they park somewhere close by?"

"Actually, they told Reyes they were dropped off so we wouldn't see a car and be alerted. They were to use my own SUV to bring you in."

Her mouth went dry. "You mean us, don't you? Bring *us* in?"

He looked away. "They don't want me, honey. I'd only be in the way."

No. Charging up to him, Sterling went on tiptoe to say, "Don't you dare act indifferent about someone trying to kill you."

For the longest time Cade just stared at her. "You understand the situation. You don't need me to tell you anything."

No and no again! Fear pushed her away from him. She needed distance to think, a way to lessen the awfulness of that possibility.

Cade caught her before she got far, pulling her into his arms and holding her when she tried to get away. "Why is it you can handle it if someone threatens you, but this is a problem?"

Her laugh sounded almost hysterical. "You, dead? No, I can't handle that at all."

His expression softened. "Did I look in danger of dying?"

No, he hadn't. He'd dealt with those men as easily as he

would have children. *But they won't all be that way.* "You're not invincible, you know."

She felt his smile against her temple. "I know. But I am highly trained for all situations, so the odds will always be in my favor."

Right up until they weren't. God, she felt sick.

"We need to stop and think now, okay?" He led her to the couch and sat down with her. "While I have Rob covering for me out front, tell me everything Adela said. We'll sort it out."

Because she wasn't sure what else to do, Sterling started at the beginning of the call and gave every grisly detail until she finished with what Mattox had said.

The calm retelling aided her, giving her a new perspective. "They might have wanted to panic me."

"If Adela is working with him."

She nodded and met his gaze. "I have to know for sure."

"We all do, okay? None of us takes chances with the lives of innocent people. That's first and foremost."

Yes, she'd realized that right off. Cade and his family were the good guys—and they were far better organized than she could ever hope to be on her own.

Calming even more, Sterling asked, "So do you have a plan?"

"I do, and it involves luring them in. Letting them think they have the upper hand, when in fact we're the ones in control."

"Awesome." It sounded like they were thinking along the same lines. "It's like I said, right? Use me as bait, but I'll be safe because you guys will be on it."

His expression went blank. Then a second later he scowled. "Close, but I'll be the bait instead of you."

"What? *No.*" If he'd thought it through, he'd already know why that wouldn't work. "They want to *capture* me, but you they want *dead.*"

"They'll take me alive, hoping it'll help them get to you."

"You can't know that!"

He kissed her fast before she lost her cool all over again. "I have to get back out to the bar, but I promise you, Star. We'll go over every detail, and we'll all be in agreement before anything is put in motion. Does that work for you?"

What could she say? It worked for her only because she'd never agree to anything that dumb. But damn it, she had joined their little group, and what if she got outvoted, instead of the other way around?

Hand to her churning stomach, she gave a grudging nod, but deep in her heart, she had a very big problem.

She'd already fallen in love with Cade McKenzie—and nothing dicked up clear thought like an overblown emotional attachment. Well, hell.

Knocked to the floor, her jaw aching, her lip split, Adela scooted to sit against the wall. Thacker entered the room quietly, keeping a wide berth around Mattox, and handed her a cloth filled with ice.

Busy watching Mattox, she didn't thank Thacker. He looked nervously at Mattox, then sidled out of the room again, closing the door softly behind him. The cell phone, probably busted, lay on the floor between them.

Mattox was out of control in a big way. She hadn't lied about that. The floor shook beneath his stomping stride.

He'd made two turns around the room, knocking furniture out of his way, before he paused in front of her. "You okay?"

"Yes." Quickly, not trusting his feet, she stood but stayed against the wall.

"That shouldn't have happened."

"It was her fault, not yours." She tried to smile, but the swelling in her cheek made it difficult, and with him glowering at her… "She infuriates you. I understand."

Taking her wrist, Mattox lowered her hand to see her face. Whatever he saw tightened his mouth in disgust. "She's going to pay. For everything."

He said it like a promise, so she replied, "I… I know."

"We have to relocate, the sooner the better. Be ready in five minutes."

Adela watched him storm out. He had a mercurial temper, but his rages didn't last long, thank God. She'd probably be dead already if they did.

When she knew he was far enough away, she picked up the phone. The screen was cracked, but it seemed to work still. Not that she had anyone else to call.

"Sorry, sugar. My plans got changed." Sitting in yet another car, one of ten that Parrish had purchased for different occasions, Reyes stared through the windshield at the front of the old house. Patience might be his weak link. He detested downtime. If he had his druthers, he'd just plow into the house, find Mattox and beat the prick to death.

Unfortunately, no one wanted him to do that, least of all his father. The plan was to bring down the whole shebang, not just one man, but damn. Stakeouts were boring as shit.

"Reyes," she complained. "I already had dinner planned."

Seeing movement behind the front window, Reyes narrowed his eyes and said in distraction, "Sorry, Annette. I'd be there if I could."

"You could come over when you get done with…whatever you're doing."

"Family stuff." He lifted the binoculars and looked at those windows more closely. Yup, that was definitely shadows shifting. "I'll have to eat on the fly."

"So we won't do dinner first." Her voice went low and throaty. "I'll still be here all night."

"You're tempting me, doll." Unfortunately, he couldn't afford a distraction. "It could be late."

"So wake me when you get here." She added in a singsong voice, "I'll be naked."

A quick visual flitted through his mind. Annette's curly blond hair and sexy smiles, big boobs and shapely legs... "Sold." Yes, he was that easy when it came to sex. "If I can wrap it up before midnight, I'll be there. But if I'm a no-show, it won't be lack of interest for that intriguing offer, okay?"

"I'll make it worth your while."

The front door opened, and Reyes rushed to say, "I do enjoy how you tease. Gotta roll now, but keep the motor revving for me." He disconnected the call before Annette could say anything else.

Four people came out of the house. First was Thacker, the slimy worm, and he didn't even try for subtlety as he searched the area, a gun already in his hand.

Behind him was Mattox...*dragging* Adela along with a bruising grip on her wrist.

Well, hell. The binoculars gave him a very clear view of Adela's battered face. Someone had socked the lady, and none too gently. Head down, short brown hair tangled and shoulders slumped, she followed meekly to a clichéd black sedan, where Mattox shoved her into the back seat.

Frowning, Reyes wondered what had changed. Did he need to reevaluate the situation?

He rubbed his chin, sorting through it all as he'd been taught.

No, he wouldn't make up his mind, not yet. Not until he had more to go on.

With that thought, he tailed the car from a safe distance, checking constantly to ensure he hadn't picked up a tail himself. That's what he and Cade would have done. Switched it up. Let someone think they were following along, while they were actually being followed.

A short time later, he called Cade. Soon as his brother answered, Reyes said, "Best as I can tell, they're heading back to that cabin in the woods, near Coalville."

"Ballsy," Cade said, "since we're already aware of that area."

"Yeah, but it was a good hideout, and situated where it's easy to spot anyone coming or going. If it came to that, they could hide in the mountains, or in one of the old coal mines, plus I can't follow them there. They'd be onto me in no time."

"For now you're safe?"

"Yeah, just rode past. I'll circle around a few times, just so they don't catch on to me. Then I'll hang out an hour or so to make sure they're not moving again."

"I want you to be extra careful," Cade said. He explained about the call Sterling had gotten. "Mattox is unhinged, and I have no idea what's going on with him and Adela."

"Yeah, as to that… Someone knocked her around. The scene was total opposite of the other day. Fucker dragged her out of there and she looked cowed."

"Shit."

"Yeah, hard to read them, but I retract my earlier conclusions, at least until I can see more—which might be difficult with them hiding away. Doubt there's any electronic eyes there for Madison to pick up. Hell, might not be Wi-Fi, either."

Cade didn't answer, but Reyes knew the silence meant he was thinking. Cade was like that. Quietly methodical in all he did, whether it was plotting or kicking ass. Impressive stuff. He'd always admired his big brother, but no, he wasn't much like him.

Cade could handle a stakeout all day and never lose his edge. Sometimes it was eerie. He didn't know what the military had done to his brother—but then, Cade had always been somewhat remote. Deep. A loner.

Sad part was, he dealt with women the same way—or at least he had until Sterling charged in. He grinned, just thinking about it.

She was one hell of a surprise.

Not that his brother avoided female company. Hell no. But a relationship? That was the shocker. Anyone who knew Cade could see he'd staked a claim. The amusing part was that Sterling seemed every bit as possessive.

"Star is worried," Cade said, interrupting Reyes's thoughts. "Mostly because she's not sure of things, either. I trust her impressions on this, so I think it's more complicated than we first considered."

"I agree she's sharp." Reyes took an exit to circle back and make another loop. "I just got an idea. If Madison could come up with an eye of some sort, I could sneak in later tonight and hook it up. Maybe at the main entrance to the town. It's one dusty road, right? Should be easy enough to do, and then we'd at least get a heads-up if Mattox leaves there. If Madison has anything super high-tech, we might even be able to tell if he leaves alone or with Adela."

"Good idea, the sooner the better. You want me to get hold of her to ask?"

"Just so you can relay to me? No, I'm already bored to tears. I'll make the call."

Without comment on his complaint, Cade said, "Then keep me posted. And I mean, posted as in every hour or less. Star isn't used to worrying, but she's worried about you."

His brows shot up. "No shit?" The grin came slowly. "Now, ain't that sweet?"

"Check in," Cade ordered again, "and let me know what Madison has to say."

"You got it." As he drove past, he did see Thacker just departing, but Reyes was close enough to see he was alone. So he'd dumped Mattox and Adela somewhere inside the town or up in the mountain? Without transportation? Or was Thacker just running an errand?

He called his sister and explained the situation, adding with concern, "There's not a lot of light in this section—"

"I know just the thing," Madison said, and it sounded like she was on the go.

"I'm guessing we'll probably need three of them."

"Perfect," she enthused. "I've got it covered."

"It needs to be something I can install superfast."

"Won't take me more than a few minutes to get them each going."

"What— *Whoa.*" No way in hell did he want Madison getting physically involved. "You won't be installing them."

"Course I will. You can keep watch. I think you're forty-five minutes from me, but I'll leave within five. I'll call you when I'm close so we can meet up. No reason we can't sneak in there together."

Talking tech always excited Madison, but Reyes wasn't at all keen on her being in the same vicinity as Mattox. "We'll meet and you can talk me through how to do it."

"Byeeee," she said, and the call ended.

"Son of a…" Reyes cut short his discontent, knowing it wouldn't do him any good. If he could figure out exactly where the three cameras should go, he and Madison could get out of there quickly. Thinking of what they needed to know, and what would be least dangerous for his kid sister, he chose a post next to the railroad tracks—it would catch anyone attempting to arrive or exit that way. The second could go on a telephone pole but would require him standing on his car to get it high enough so it wouldn't be noticeable. That'd exclude Madison.

Under the overhang of the shabby church would be the perfect spot for the third camera because it would also catch anyone coming down the mountain on the narrower trail. But did he dare let Madison do that? Could he stop her?

Probably not.

He wouldn't let anything happen to her, though. They'd use extra care, which meant it'd take a little longer, but he'd deal with it, and Annette would just have to deal, too.

Once he had that worked out in his mind, he drove south

to the next exit, found a gas station a mile down on the right and called his sister.

"I'm on my way," she assured him. "Where do we meet?"

He gave her directions, then tried insisting again, "I'll put up the cameras."

"Reyes." Exasperated, she stretched out his name. "I have to be there anyway to ensure they're properly connected and that I can access them. The three I have are motion activated, but that could still mean an animal, a bird or even a tree branch moved by the wind would kick them on. I'll be able to remotely clear recordings, which will be on my server and impenetrable from outside, so that we don't have a cluttered feed."

Making a winding motion with his finger, Reyes said, "That's all over my head. I'm talking about actually getting them mounted—"

"I want them done a certain way. You can ensure no one sees me."

"You realize you sound as stubborn as Cade."

"Thank you." With laughter in her tone, she said, "Love you, brother. See you shortly." Again, she disconnected him.

Sisters, he grumbled to himself. Yes, he knew he was sexist—most especially when it came to a baby sister he loved. Did he know she was capable? Yup, he did. Was he confident she could do it with or without his help? No doubts.

But that didn't mean he wanted his sis in the line of fire. Not if he could help it.

Couldn't stop her, though. Madison was sweet, but she didn't put up with any macho crap. So he slumped in his seat, drummed his fingers on the steering wheel and waited.

She arrived sooner than he'd expected, which was good, since he'd already been away from the site too long. Typical of Madison, she immediately took charge, but at least she allowed him to drive. They rode to the site together, all the while with her chatting about the cameras and what they could do.

For the most part, Reyes tuned her out, uninterested in the technical details that fascinated her when he'd rather work out the logistics of getting her safely in and out of the area.

He just knew Cade was going to have his head, being he was ten times more protective than Reyes.

Fortunately for him, he was able to park down the tracks away from the small main road, close enough that they could sneak into Coalville on foot, unnoticed. Since she insisted on installing each one, he had to hoist Madison onto his shoulders to get two of the cameras in place, but she was incredibly efficient, as well as silent, in getting that completed. After only a few brief adjustments, she wrapped it up.

As he lowered her back to the ground, she whispered, "Now I just need to connect them to my device so I can transfer it all back home and voilà—I'll have eyes here."

"You're so clever," Reyes murmured absently, while constantly scanning their darkened surroundings. So quiet, not even a rodent stirred.

Sort of electrified the small hairs on the back of his neck.

If he didn't have Madison with him, he'd creep around a little, see if he could figure out exactly where Mattox had hunkered down, maybe discover if Adela was okay.

But not with her along for the adventure. "Let's go." Reyes nudged her forward, considerate of her slower pace while she picked her way over the rocks and rubble.

When they reached the car, they both did a quick check around it, ensuring they hadn't been discovered. Madison flipped on her phone light just long enough to see that no one had hidden in the back seat. Then they went dark again.

Reyes drove slowly without headlights until they merged onto the interstate. He flipped them on and released a tight breath at the same time. "I'll take you to your car." And he'd follow her home, just to be extra safe.

Annette would keep, or not. He wouldn't leave his sister's safety to chance.

He checked in with Cade a few times, and yeah, big brother was all PO'd over Madison being involved at the site. Reyes listened, and since he didn't disagree, what could he say? "It wasn't *my* idea."

Cade still chewed his ass, but in that controlled way that sounded more like a disappointed father—as if he needed two of those. "Next time, I'll call you and you can try your hand at talking her around."

Cade exhaled sharply, but said, "Be safe tonight."

Rolling his eyes, Reyes said, "Yeah, same to you."

It was two long, grueling hours later before he got to Annette's front door. She'd left the outside lights on for him, making him smile. Since he had a key, he let himself in without a sound.

Unlike him, Annette was far too trusting.

Not in a million years would he give a key to anyone other than family.

Inside, he flipped on the foyer lamp. The house was quiet, and he didn't sense any threats—something he always checked—so he slipped off his shoes and started down the hall.

Her bedroom door was open, and with the light from the foyer barely filtering in, he saw her slender form in the bed, stretched out on her stomach...and naked as she'd promised.

Already getting hard, Reyes caught the edge of the sheet and slowly pulled it to the foot of the bed. Annette shifted to her side, curling her luscious bod to keep warm.

Yeah, he'd help her with that.

Without taking his gaze off her body, he removed his wallet and placed it on the nightstand. Quietly, he set his gun beside it. Then his knife. Annette knew not to touch his weapons, but he always put himself between her and them anyway.

He peeled off his shirt and tossed it to a chair, then opened his jeans and tugged down the zipper.

Annette opened her eyes, purring sleepily, "Reyes?"

"You expecting anyone else?" If so, he wouldn't stay.

Going to her back, she whispered, "Come here."

"Yes, ma'am." He finished stripping and climbed in beside her.

Out of the three women he currently visited, Annette was the most affectionate. Cathy, an exec in the business world, wanted her booty calls scheduled in advance, and he had to be prompt. Unlike Annette, Cathy wouldn't tell him to come by whenever.

Lili loved to call him when the mood struck her. If he was available, fine; if not, she moved on to the next guy.

Annette would do the same, but she always swore he was the best. And after sex, she wanted to laze around together. She wasn't clingy—none of them were, or he wouldn't visit them—but she did enjoy an extra closeness.

Tonight, he wouldn't mind that, either.

Her hand snaked down his chest and went straight to his dick. "Mmm, already ready for me?"

"I was ready the second I stepped in the door."

Laughing softly, she kissed his chest, his ribs…and slowly worked her way down.

Annette had an *amazing* mouth, meaning his night would definitely be more rewarding than his day had been.

CHAPTER FIFTEEN

Sterling was excited about seeing Reyes's gym this morning. It was yet another facet of the whole McKenzie operation, and she wanted to learn as much as she could.

It might give her a leg up in dealing with Parrish, because she was pretty sure their relationship would take some adjustment.

Relationship. With Cade. With his siblings and father. With the awesome Bernard. She wanted to hug it all to her chest and cherish it for however long it lasted.

She was always cautious when she went out, but Cade took it to a whole new level. Getting jumped last night hadn't helped. He'd been extra attentive in delicious ways, but she knew he'd also strained his injury. His father hadn't been pleased this morning when he insisted on checking things, but he wasn't really the doting sort, either. More like a sour general.

Getting from the bar to her apartment so she could get some things last night, and then back to his father's house, had taken twice as long as it should have just so Cade could backtrack twice, his way of guaranteeing no one followed them. By the time they'd actually gotten to bed, she'd been exhausted.

Not *too* exhausted, not when Cade had stripped down and curved around her, all hot and hard and keenly interested. She'd taken quick advantage of that and the incredible pleasure he offered.

But she felt the lack of sleep catching up with her today.

Good thing they were doing something fun.

A massive front window showed the interior of the gym where Reyes stood on a mat instructing two men. He wore only shorts and wrestling shoes, and she had to admit he was a good-looking guy.

"What's he teaching them?"

Cade shrugged. "I'm guessing basic defense."

Through the window, she watched as the guys went into a stance. Reyes continued to instruct, right up until both men charged him.

Her brows climbed up in delight as Reyes lowered a shoulder and tossed the heavier of the two men. Just as quickly, he tripped the other. While Cade's brother still stood there instructing, the other two men sucked wind from their backs.

Sterling laughed.

"Amusing, right?" Cade put an arm around her and steered her to the door. "We can watch for a while, or you're welcome to try out the equipment."

More interested in seeing than doing, Sterling shook her head. "I'm not dressed for it."

"There's not a dress code, babe." As he often did, he stroked along her spine down to the small of her back over the soft cotton T-shirt she wore, then down to the seat of her faded jeans, where he lightly copped a feel of her backside. "Other than your boots, you're fine. You'd just need to remove them before you stepped on a mat."

One of these days she'd get used to all the familiar touching, but it was going to take a while. Trying not to show how deeply he affected her, Sterling asked, "You know all this stuff, too?"

"I do."

She leaned into him. "Then I'd rather you teach me."

His slow smile did crazy things to her. "It'll be my pleasure."

It was nice to know that his brain stayed centered on sex as often as hers did.

A sign on the door read "Walk-ins welcome, but we can't guarantee all equipment will be open."

Once she stepped inside, she knew why: the place was packed.

The interior was more spacious than she'd realized. Every inch utilized in one way or another by sweat-damp people ranging in age from late teens to early sixties, male and female alike.

In the back section, heavy bags hung from reinforced beams and, beyond that, speed bags. It appeared to be mostly younger males using those. Stationary bikes lined one wall, occupied by women and elders. Various racks of weights and bars, with a few benches, took up the opposite. One of the men doing bench presses had grotesquely huge arms…especially in comparison to his thin legs.

Cade whispered, "No balance. Reyes has tried to tell him, but he focuses on that one exercise and won't do anything else."

Sterling snorted, then glanced around at the women. A few of them seemed mostly concerned with looking stylish, standing around in their cute clothes and chatting. Others were clearly there to work out, their hair in ponytails or clips, sweat dampening T-shirts or sports bras.

One gal in baggy sweatpants, an oversize T-shirt, shoulder-length blond hair held back with a wide band and earbuds in her ears, popped her neck as she walked to a heavy bag. She wore fingerless gloves and shin guards.

She looked absurd in her getup but didn't seem to care—and that impressed Sterling.

"I'm going to talk to Reyes a few minutes," Cade said. "Want to join us?"

"I'd rather look around." Whatever they discussed, Cade

would tell her later. Why risk letting Reyes provoke her temper when she didn't need to?

With a long look, Cade said, "Stay where I can see you." He touched her cheek. "Everyone in here is probably fine, but Reyes can't know each person, and I'm not willing to take chances right now."

"You don't think you'd notice someone dragging me out the front door?"

His fingers spread, threading into her hair and cupping her head. "There are two back doors, one out of a break room and another at the end of the hall near the bathrooms."

Ah, yeah. If she went to the bathroom, and someone was waiting… "I'll stay within range if you will, too," she promised, then sauntered off.

Something about that other lady drew her. As Cade had noted, she had good instincts. Something inside her screamed that the woman had trouble on her heels and could use a friendly face.

Often Sterling felt that way with the women she helped. She was good at reading them, at knowing what to say and when, whether to push or just wait.

Odd, but she hadn't quite felt that connection with Adela, or at least not consistently.

Finding one heavy bag unoccupied, she gave it a tentative push. The woman stood next to her, giving the bag hell—and ignoring Sterling. She seemed intent on abusing her legs. Even though she wore shin guards, Sterling winced.

With the earbuds in, she couldn't really give a friendly "Hey" to break the ice, so she moseyed on. But her gaze repeatedly went back to glimpse the woman working. She was so intense, so focused that Sterling couldn't help but be impressed.

And worried.

Fifteen minutes later, while she idly examined a weird contraption that looked too complicated for her to figure out, Cade and Reyes joined her.

So much for avoiding the annoying brother.

And with him stripped down so much, ignoring his presence wouldn't be easy.

As if he'd read her thoughts, he said in a singsong voice, "Hi, Sterling."

With a roll of her eyes and a sigh, she turned to him. "What's up, troublemaker?"

Reyes grinned. "Let's head to the break room. I could use a cold drink."

"First…" Damn, Sterling really hated to involve him, but if he knew the woman, maybe he could put her worries to rest. "So, don't stare, but the lady back there, kicking the stuffing out of the heavy bag?"

Curious, both men glanced that way.

"You guys suck, you know that?" Hands on her hips, Sterling scowled at them. "I said don't stare, but you both did."

"There's staring, and then there's *staring*," Cade said. "Besides, you didn't specify it was anything like that."

She rolled her eyes.

With his gaze still on the woman, Reyes asked, "What about her?"

Already frowning, Cade gave her a longer look, too. "Something's off."

Sterling nodded. "Fear is working her hard."

After a lengthy perusal, Reyes cursed softly. "You're right."

It reassured Sterling that she wasn't imagining things. "Do you know her?"

Reyes shrugged. "She's been coming in for about a month but keeps to herself."

"So no?"

His mouth flattened. "No."

"Huh." She'd expected Reyes to have some snappy comeback, but instead he looked displeased. With her? No, with himself. Digging a little, she said, "Haven't hit on her, huh?"

That got his eyes narrowed. "This is my gym. Think what you want of me, but I take my pleasure elsewhere."

His sincerity made Sterling feel a little bad for deliberately provoking him—but *only* a little. "Scruples. Bravo." Aware of Cade grinning and Reyes growling, she turned to keep the woman in sight. "She's not here to stay in shape, or to bulk up or trim down. She wants to know how to hurt people."

Cade slanted a look at Reyes. "Told you she was astute."

"I never denied it." Propping his hands on his hips, Reyes asked, "If she wants to learn offensive moves, why didn't she ask for instruction?"

"Maybe because you look like that?" Sterling nodded at his body, and when she did so, she couldn't help eyeballing his sweaty, naked torso. Not out of interest, but because he really was a specimen.

She noticed him the same way she might a really nice pair of stilettos. She appreciated the style, but you'd never catch her wearing a pair.

Rocking back on his heels, Reyes asked, "What the hell is that supposed to mean?"

"You're intimidating." Much like Cade, Reyes had muscles everywhere. Not overblown, but very defined. His eyes were hazel, like Madison's, instead of electric blue like Cade's, but they were still nice.

He was almost as tall as Cade, too, but he wore his dark hair a little longer, and his attitude was a lot less restrained.

"I've never intimidated you," Reyes pointed out.

She grinned. "I'm not the average woman."

"True enough." Laughing, Cade drew her into his side. "You're above average."

Reyes groaned. "It's almost nauseating the way you two fawn all over each other."

"Oh?" Feeling devilish, Sterling asked, "So I know how to bug you, while getting awesome benefits at the same time? Sweet." Even as she spoke, she cuddled closer to Cade and walked her fingers up his chest.

"Hey, I run a reputable business, you know," Reyes mock-complained. "Take that foreplay elsewhere."

Cade reached for him, but he ducked away, then asked, "So you think my size has put her off?"

Sterling wasn't sure if he threw that out there because of real interest or just to get her off molesting Cade. But whatever, she'd save the good stuff for when she had Cade alone.

"You are big," she admitted.

He and Cade both grinned, and she knew exactly what they were thinking.

Willing herself not to blush, she spoke before Reyes could. "But it's not just because you're tall and fit. You're…sexual?" Considering that, Sterling shook her head. "Yeah, not a great word, but you know what I mean."

Both brothers now stared at her, prompting her to roll her eyes again. "A woman who's unsure of men wouldn't want to approach someone as cocky as you."

More disgruntled by the minute, Reyes said, "I'll have you know, plenty of women like me just fine the way I am."

"I bet they do." She snickered. "The thing is, the same reason why those other women like you is probably why that one prefers to watch a video or something on her phone. At least, I think that's what she's doing. See how she keeps looking at the screen and repositioning her stance?"

Cade nodded. "Trying to mimic the moves…but not really doing them correctly. It's tough to figure out without in-person instruction."

While Reyes was distracted watching the woman, Sterling sent her elbow into his stomach. "You need to offer."

"Ow, damn." Scowling, he rubbed his side. "Maybe, but not now. She's heading out."

Without being obvious about it, they watched the woman walk to a duffel bag she'd left in the corner near a wooden bench. She dug out a bottle of water and took a long drink. After storing it away again, she located a small blue towel, which she used to dry the sweat from her face and arms. Then she removed her earbuds and unplugged them from her phone, stripped off the protective gear and stuffed everything into the bag, located keys in the front pocket, and started for the door.

Judging by the frowns the brothers wore, they didn't like having to wait any more than Sterling did, but Reyes was right— stopping her would seem too presumptuous, especially when she already seemed...well, not exactly skittish, but more like reserved. "You're sure she'll be back?"

"She's been here every day for a month," Reyes said. "So unless you scared her off with all that staring—" This time he dodged her elbow. Laughing, he predicted, "She'll be back. And yes, I'll see if I can figure out a way to offer."

"Thanks." Looking up at Cade, she asked, "You two finished your talk?"

With a nod, Cade took her hand. "You want a tour around the place, or would you rather head out?"

"A tour." She added to Reyes, "I'm impressed, by the way. Nice place you run here."

Grabbing his chest, Reyes pretended to stagger, but the second Sterling turned away, he mussed her hair and took the lead. Anxious to show her around? It seemed so. Little by little, she was starting to like Cade's brother—or at least she was learning to tolerate him.

Reyes strode ahead of them, and yup, the back view of him was impressive, too. Nowhere near as nice as Cade's, but she glanced around and saw many of the women looking their way.

Sterling they didn't even see, because Cade and Reyes held all their attention.

And here she was, right in the middle of them.

Overall, not a bad place to be.

The next morning, wearing snug shorts, a clingy tank top and battered sneakers, Star looked entirely different—and downright edible. Cade watched as she twisted her long hair up onto her head. He couldn't take his eyes off her. No matter what she did, or how she dressed, he found her irresistible.

But like this? Her body clearly outlined under the close-fitting clothes, those long, toned legs on display… He wasn't a saint. Far from it. And right now, he'd rather take her back to his room, where they could both get naked.

The more he had her, the more he wanted her.

It was like an addiction—Cade's first, since he avoided vices. This vice, though, sating himself on Star's unique brand of sex appeal, he didn't mind at all.

The plan was to spar here in the privacy of his father's private gym so he could assess her ability, fine-tune what she already knew and teach her a few new tricks.

Most important, she had to be able to defend herself. If anything should happen to him, which was unlikely but still possible given his vocation, he needed to know Star would be okay.

"Quit primping," he finally said, knowing it would rile her. "If someone attacks, you won't have time to put up your hair."

She snorted and strode out to the middle of the mat. "You might have to pay for that."

Banking a grin, Cade joined her, then easily ducked the swing she threw and followed it by tripping her to her back.

Instead of being annoyed, she stared up at him with a smile and a droll "That was slick."

Little by little, he got used to her attitude. She got angry when someone tried to take over, him included, but she was always up to learn something new and didn't mind being instructed.

Or tripped to her back.

Cade held out a hand. "Your turn to try it." He showed her the moves, when to pull, how to use her feet in combination with her hands and body, and by the third try, she nailed it.

"Good job," he praised as he rolled back to his feet. "Especially since I'm a lot bigger."

Her mouth twisted to the side. "You *let* me do that."

"To see if you could, yes. While I'm coaching, that's the best way. We'll get to the hard-core stuff soon, I promise. One step at a time. Okay?"

"If you say so." She got into her stance. "Ready when you are."

For the next hour they practiced hard, and by the end, Star was a lot smoother. No matter how many times she hit the mat, she didn't get frustrated or angry.

She brushed herself off, asked pertinent questions and tried again.

She had so much moxie it made him want her even more. How was that possible?

Groaning, she rolled to her back. "I think I finally understand it. Thanks for not losing your patience."

Amazing. How many women—or men, for that matter—would thank him for repeatedly tossing them to their backs? Star was unique because her motives were unique, and they aligned with his in a way he hadn't expected to find. Definitely not with a woman he desired.

She wanted to be highly trained to successfully attack, defend and rescue those in need, even against the most insurmountable odds. Her mettle impressed him, as did her dogged attitude.

"Hello," she teased. "Yoo-hoo, Cade. You still with me? You're just staring."

Shaking his head, he squatted down beside her and got back

to the business at hand. "That's one move," he explained. "We'll work every day until you have a cache of ingrained responses. The idea is for it to be automatic. What one person does triggers what you do, preferably without you having to think about it."

"That's what you do, huh? The other night at the bar, it amazed me how easy you made it look."

Drawn by the way her sweat-dampened shirt stuck to her breasts, how the waistband of her shorts rode low to reveal a strip of her flat, damp stomach, he felt himself stirring.

"Bad example, because they weren't much challenge at all. With trained men, it'd be a little tougher."

Her lips quirked. Still breathless, she pushed a hank of hair off her temple and asked, "Tougher, but not impossible?"

Cade couldn't claim an ounce of modesty, not when it came to his ability. "I'm good."

Her voice dropped as she purred, "At many things."

That did it. He started to reach for her, but she utilized the move he'd taught her and lunged for him instead.

Laughing, he countered it by catching her to him, then rolling her to her back to come down over her, pelvis to pelvis, his hands holding her breasts but his elbows catching some of his weight.

Eyes gone heavy, she asked, "Is this a legit move?"

"Damn right," he said, devouring her mouth with a kiss that made him forget about further lessons. Star always tasted so good, and now her exertion had intensified her scent. As he breathed her in, it added to the sudden onslaught of lust.

When he moved to kiss her throat, she whispered, "Then I'm glad it's you teaching me instead of your brother."

Reyes? Jealousy slammed into Cade, and he reared back to scowl at her—only to see her barely repressed grin. He should tell her that joking like that wasn't allowed. He opened his mouth—

Taking swift advantage of his distraction, she bucked him to the side and straddled his hips.

Laughing in triumph, she said, "That was a joke, for crying out loud."

"I'm not sure it's funny."

She only laughed harder. "All's fair in love and war."

Thoughtful, Cade caught her waist to keep her still and asked, "Which are we?"

Her expression shut down at the question. "Um…"

Yeah, maybe he shouldn't have asked that. Star was still skittish about any references to their relationship. He knew he had to go slow, to give her plenty of room.

Every day that got a little harder.

For now, he slowly grinned, then flipped her again and said, "You're too easy."

"Jerk." She smacked his shoulder, then blanched and carefully pulled aside the neckline of his shirt. "I keep forgetting you're wounded. Maybe because you don't act like you are."

"I forget myself. It doesn't hurt anymore." When he was this close to Star, his physical need blunted everything else.

He started to kiss her again, but she protested. "No. I'm gross with sweat. Let's go shower first."

Clearly she was getting used to being in his father's house. One of these days he'd have to tell her that he had a place of his own. He hadn't yet because he didn't want her to insist on leaving.

If Star weren't with him, he'd be home alone right now, but Mattox's last threats had been extreme and they didn't yet know what was going on with Adela. He hadn't said it to Star, but they'd take care of that soon. Another reason to stay here. Being in his father's fortress during a sting was not only the safest place to be, but it also provided the quickest way to get info.

While they were still sprawled together on the floor, the door opened and Reyes and Madison stepped in.

Seeing them entwined, Reyes quipped, "Not sure that form of defense will be effective."

Maybe he needed to teach his brother a new lesson, Cade thought as he moved away from Star. She sat up but didn't yet say anything.

"Got any gas left in the tank?" Reyes asked her.

She rolled her shoulder. "Could be. Why?"

"I want to give it a go."

"Nope."

"Chicken?" Reyes asked.

Slowly, Star looked up. "If you persist, I'll agree. But I strongly advise you wear a cup, because I'll go after your vulnerable spots full force."

Scowling, Reyes tucked his hips back, his hands protectively folded over his junk. "That's not how you spar."

"That's how *I* spar—with you." Her smile looked evil. "I have wicked knees." She clenched a hand. "And my fist isn't too bad, either."

"Damn." Reyes turned his accusing gaze on Cade. "What the hell are you teaching her?"

Already grinning, Cade held up his hands. "I'd say the animosity was taught by *you*."

"Men and their precious jewels," Madison complained. She kicked off her shoes and stalked closer. "Come on. I'll go a round or two with you, and the boys can observe."

Star's smile slipped. "I don't think—"

"I'm trained," Madison promised. "But I'd prefer not to get my lady parts wounded, so how about we make this a teaching moment? Cade and Reyes can then offer suggestions. They are good at this sort of thing, you know."

Brows up, Star looked at him for confirmation. Cade nodded. "Madison knows what she's doing, and she is good, so why not?" He gave Reyes a shove that nearly took him off his feet. "Even my brother occasionally has valuable input."

Under her breath, Star grumbled, "It's the audience I object to," but she got to her feet and quickly tucked loose hairs into her topknot. With a glare at Reyes, she said, "No color commentary, got that? Just pertinent facts."

"Yes, ma'am." Then he said to Madison, "Go easy on her."

Star drew a big breath, got in a stance—and barely stopped Madison when she shot in on her.

Standing next to Reyes, Cade watched Star deflect one move after another. To his brother, he said, "She's actually better than I realized now that she's with someone closer to her own size."

"She's fast," Reyes agreed. Then with a sideways glance at Cade, he added, "But how often will she get attacked by someone smaller?"

True enough. Madison was shorter than Star, though both were tall, but she was probably thirty pounds lighter. Where Star was sturdy, Madison was delicate.

His sister compensated for that with speed and agility, and a refined skill in technique. He could see that both women had forgotten about the men watching while they enjoyed the combat.

Star, especially, looked invigorated. She even laughed a few times, either when she missed Madison, or when she caught a hit or kick.

Reyes stepped closer, calling out to their sister, "Wrong leg. Left...*now* the right."

"Block it," Cade countered to Star. "That's it. You have to immediately move."

"When she reaches for you, grab... Yeah, that's it."

Star had tried grabbing Madison's wrist, but Madison knew that move and how to counter it. She locked her own hand over Star's and pivoted, and Star ended up with her arm twisted behind her, forced to her knees.

Cade briefly stepped in to show Star how to avoid that trick.

He encouraged them to go through the same scenario three more times before he was satisfied that Star had it down.

Once she'd nailed it, he had them reverse so that Star knew how to use the move to subdue an attacker.

"She's a quick learner," Reyes said.

Without taking his eyes off the women, Cade nodded. "A natural survivor. Always has been."

"Didn't have a choice?" Reyes asked without his usual caustic humor.

"No, she didn't." Distracted, Cade said, "You're being defensive, Star, instead of offensive. Don't try to escape until you have control."

This time Reyes demonstrated, and with him in teacher mode, Star didn't seem to mind.

Life would be easier if those two got along. Ignoring him wouldn't do her much good, would in fact only encourage Reyes to ramp up the taunts. So far, Star had managed by giving as good as she got, and Cade had a feeling she'd earned Reyes's respect because of it.

More kicks were thrown, punches blocked.

"How about another lesson?" Cade asked. "That is, if you're both up for it?"

"Sure," Star immediately said, rolling her head to work out a kink in her neck, shaking her hands to loosen them up again. "I'm game."

"Fine by me," Madison agreed.

"This one might work better if Reyes takes part." He beckoned his brother to the mat.

Reyes stepped in with a grin, rubbing his hands together. "Which one is my victim?"

For that comment, Madison kicked his feet out from under him. Since Reyes wasn't expecting the attack, he went down, but he shot right back up with a laugh, pointing at his sister and saying, "Sneaky. And you already know payback is hell."

While he shared that silly threat with Madison, Star got an impish look in her dark eyes—and copied his sister's move so that Reyes went down again. This time he sprawled out with a chuckling groan. "They're ganging up on me, Cade! Get control of this lesson already."

"You're a good sport," Star said, her wide smile proof that she was having fun.

As if requesting help, Reyes raised a hand to her, but she backed away shaking her head.

"We're not both fools," she laughed.

Loving the way Star fit right in, Cade drew her close for a quick kiss, then explained what he wanted them to do. "Reyes is going to behave himself for this demonstration, isn't that right, brother?"

"Me? Maybe you failed to notice that I'm the one on my back?" Saying that, he rolled to his feet and gave both women a *try me* look. They snickered but didn't engage.

"Reyes is going to invade your space."

"You got it," Reyes said, knowing the lesson and stepping in close to Star—at least until she leaped back. "Hey, I can't show you if you don't let me get hold of you."

Rife with suspicion, Star asked Cade, "Why can't you demonstrate?"

"You're too comfortable with me." He thought of the expression on her face after she'd joked that all's fair in love and war. And without thinking, he'd replied, *Which are we?*

She'd looked ready to bolt, and it bothered him, because Star didn't run from anyone or anything. Love? Yeah, he was there, but clearly she wasn't.

Not yet, anyway.

He'd sway her eventually by building on their shared inclinations and showing her how great they'd be together.

With that goal in mind, he gestured for Reyes to continue.

This time, Star went stiff, but she allowed him to put his

arm around her and crush her close into his side—just like a creep would do.

"Now," Cade said, walking her through the process of freeing herself. It took a few tries, especially since Reyes wasn't making it easy for her. Then she nailed it, getting a firm grip on his brother's wrist, ducking under his arm and, in the process, twisting his hand up behind him. Immediately, she put her foot to Reyes's ass and shoved him forward, giving her the opportunity to flee…if she'd been in real danger.

Madison applauded.

Reyes did, too, actually, but Cade tried to keep it on point by saying, "If you try that move, be ready to race away as fast as you can, but keep in mind that it'd only work if you're in a congested area where you can quickly find help."

"Or if your attacker is severely out of shape," Madison added. "It's a disgusting reality that *just* fleeing isn't usually the best option."

"So let's give me a weapon," Reyes suggested, "and you can show her how to take it from me."

Intrigued by that, Star held up a hand while breathing hard. "Give me five. Then we can try that."

That's how they ended up working an hour more, with all of them involved in one way or another. Twice she'd successfully taken the dummy knife from Reyes. The concept was the same with a gun, and eventually they'd practice that, too.

But for now, before Star completely collapsed, Cade called a halt. He and Reyes were fine, but then, they took physical training to an extreme. The women, however, looked completely spent.

Hands on her knees, sucking in air, Star said, "That was invigorating."

"Right?" Madison agreed, gulping her own breaths. "I got more of a workout with you than I ever do with my brothers."

"You two are more evenly matched," Cade said. "That's a good thing, but also problematic."

Reyes stepped forward to offer them each water. "You did great, Sterling. You have a natural ability, but Cade's right. Next time we need to wear protective gear so we can really push it. You were both holding back. Cade and I sometimes do the same for simple sparring, but the best way to learn is to go full force."

"Sweet," Star said, accepting the water and chugging it down. "What kind of gear?"

"Headgear and face protector, for starters," Cade offered. "It'll ensure against broken noses or cracked jaws while you practice face strikes. Mouthpiece to protect teeth. Some pads would help, too." His family always took self-defense seriously.

"Sounds good." Star finally straightened, still breathing hard, yet smiling. "The better prepared I am, the more I like it."

Madison grinned, too. "My sentiments exactly." She tossed a towel to Star. "Give it a few days, and then we can work on marksmanship, as well."

And speaking of that... Cade took Star's hand. "You can shower in a minute, but first I want to show you one more thing."

As they crossed the length of the lower level, all the way to the other side, Reyes and Madison followed along. It made Cade wonder if Parrish knew they were congregated downstairs. No doubt he did, because not much slipped past his dad, but he wouldn't take part in giving Star the tour of their armory. Later, perhaps over lunch, Parrish would weigh in with his thoughts—and no doubt judgments.

Didn't matter. Star would be working with Reyes and Madison, and that's what he'd wanted.

Things with Mattox would come to a head very soon. Madison kept a log of movement. They wouldn't stay hidden long, and they all needed to be prepared.

CHAPTER SIXTEEN

Never in a million years would Sterling have guessed that she'd one day be in a freaking mansion practicing lethal skills with three totally badass people. Talk about unbelievable things to happen… This one would top her list.

Reyes had actually been fun, and Cade was such an amazing teacher. Everything he did fascinated her even more.

Plus, she loved it that Madison was *so* incredibly proficient—which meant that, one day, Sterling could be that good, too. It gave her a rush, made her blood sing and had her eyeballing Cade hungrily, wondering when she might be able to get him alone.

How working herself into a sweaty mess and turning her limbs to noodles could make her hungry for sex, she didn't know, but then again, there'd been a lot of close contact with that big hunk she currently got to call her own. What red-blooded woman wouldn't react to all those warm, straining muscles, the incredible scent of his heated skin, his sexy take-charge attitude and bone-deep confidence? Cade was the whole, delicious package, and she wanted to gobble him up.

Reyes and Madison were still following along, and Sterling knew she needed a shower, but she figured if he wanted to show her one more thing, she may as well indulge him. He'd certainly indulged her long enough, teaching her so many valuable moves.

He led them all to a back room that appeared to be mostly empty, with a few crates and storage boxes stacked around. There was no drywall on the walls, only exposed studs.

Sterling wondered if there was something in one of the boxes that Cade wanted to show her—until he pressed a concealed lever on the floor and a section of wall swung open, exposing another room behind the insulation.

Eyes flaring wide, she slowly stepped inside to take it all in. Holy smokes. The hidden room was smallish, maybe eight by eight, and it was utilitarian in design—linoleum floor, concrete walls…and an astounding display of weaponry. "You have an arsenal."

"We're prepared," Cade countered.

"For your own private war?" She didn't say it as a criticism, more in awe. Strolling along the back wall, Sterling took in rifles, revolvers, handguns of every make and model. Grenades, smoke bombs, flash bombs. Long knives and switchblades. Tasers and batons. She also noted helmets, body armor, camo and utility belts. "This is remarkable." On another wall, ammo filled multiple shelves, surely enough to last them for a good long while.

Madison and Reyes stood aside, silent and watchful, apparently leaving this introduction to Cade.

That worked for her. In fact, she'd like it even better if they gave her some privacy with Cade, but she knew that wasn't going to happen. They might quibble with one another, but the siblings were close. Probably came from protecting one another.

"I'm fascinated," she said, to put them all at ease. "Impressed, too, and I'd love to try every one of them." She ended her circuit of the room in front of Cade. "Got some specific reason for showing me this?"

He put his hands on her shoulders. "We don't leave things to chance, so if Mattox doesn't make a move very soon, we'll go after Adela. I want to know that you can protect yourself—when I'm not available to do it."

Aw. That was sweet. Surprisingly, it didn't insult her. Facts were facts, and although she'd already known it, today's practice reinforced that Cade was far better trained for combat. Being military, that made sense. But of course, he'd taken it well beyond that. She'd never met another person so wholly equipped to handle danger of any sort.

He and his siblings were trained pros, and she was not.

Sterling accepted that she had a lot to learn. One day she'd love to be on a par with them. Until then, she liked that Cade would look out for her—if it became necessary. Knowing he wouldn't let her be hurt made her feel better about being bait to lure in Mattox. Sure, Cade still thought he'd do the honors, but she'd talk him around somehow.

Her plan made more sense.

She smiled. "Thank you." *For so many things.* Getting close, she hugged him tight. "*Now* do you think we can get that shower? I'm ready to melt in my own sweat."

Reyes laughed, and a definite note of relief resonated in the sound.

Had they expected her to be shocked—in a bad way?

She wasn't. If anything, she loved that they were so well prepared to care for others. It was what she'd always wanted to do, had tried to do, but obviously they did it better.

"That's my cue to head out," Reyes announced. "I'm already running late for the gym."

"And I need my own quick shower before I get back to monitoring things," Madison added. "Bernard will only cover for me so long before he loses interest."

Once they were alone, Cade closed up the room and led the way to his suite.

Taking his hand, Sterling pulled him into the bathroom and clasped the hem of his clinging T-shirt, tugging it up and over those scrumptious abs, broad chest and rock-hard shoulders. She paused at the sight of his injury. It didn't seem to bother him, but the skin around the stitches was now more discolored. "I hope you didn't overdo it."

Without replying, Cade finished tugging off his shirt, then returned the favor by removing hers and her sports bra, as well.

Breasts bared, Sterling trailed a finger over one of his tattoos. She wanted to trace the design with her tongue, and thinking about it sent a curl of desire through her. "I've been worrying about Adela. I'm glad we won't wait to save her."

"If she needs saving."

Yeah, there weren't any certainties yet. "Reyes said she was hurt. That's enough for me."

"I know." He opened his hand on her cheek. "As long as you don't try anything on your own, we can push it whenever you want."

Nice, so he'd leave it up to her instead of Parrish? That was an unsettling idea. After all, they had a smooth-running out-fit. She ran more on emotion.

But thinking logically, she got the idea of throwing a wider net. That method would ultimately save more women...but could she sacrifice Adela for a possibility that may not pay off? "How do you feel about it all?"

Without hesitation, Cade said, "I don't like it when things don't add up. Something is going on between them, I just don't know what."

And that made it riskier. If she had to worry only about her-self...

"What?" he asked, his thumb brushing the corner of her mouth.

Guessing how he'd react to her thoughts, she smiled. "Every time I see you, I'm struck by how lucky I am."

That got him refocused real fast. "You think I'm any different?" In rapid order, he removed the rest of her clothes, even kneeling down to tug off her sneakers. "Every part of you, Star, this—" he ran his hands up her bare legs, around to her backside to draw her in for a kiss to her stomach "—but also the way you smile, your core strength, your occasional insecurity and your bold attitude—"

"Hey," she protested shakily. "I'm not insecure." *Liar.* She knew she sometimes was, and apparently he knew it, too. But he didn't disagree. Strong and bold, those were attributes she didn't mind.

"The way you argue," he added, with a nibble to her hip bone. "God, how you smell, how you feel—I love all of it, everything about you, inside and out."

Her lips parted. *Love.* Earlier, when he'd teased about love and war, she'd at first gone blank…and then accepted it as a joke, nothing more. But this? The way he looked at her now?

Honest to God, Sterling didn't know what to do, what to say. She knew how *she* felt, but him? She didn't have a clue. "You confuse me."

Smiling, Cade rose back to his feet. So tall. So damn strong. So freaking impressive in every way.

As he finished stripping, he said, "I don't know why you'd be confused. You're sexy, smart, quick-witted, strong, compassionate—"

Embarrassed heat flushed her face. "That's enough."

"Not even close." Taking her shoulders, Cade turned her away from him so he could free her hair. His fingers were gentle as he loosened the band and slid it free. "You're a remarkable person in so many ways. Do you honestly think I can be around you without wanting you?"

Wanting, sure. She wanted him nonstop, too. But he'd mentioned *love* again. Frowning, she turned to face him. "Instead of standing around talking, how about we make use of that warm shower? Together."

Cade pressed a soft kiss to her mouth. "Love the way you think."

Her eyes widened. Did he use that damn word on purpose now?

With a lazy smile, he turned on the water and got out two towels. A little numb, Sterling stepped under the spray to soak her face and hair. She needed to stop gawking over the things he said. She also needed to know if he meant anything substantial by it, but she was too cowardly to ask.

Getting in behind her, Cade took the shampoo bottle from her. "Let me."

Why not? If she was going to stand there feeling stupid, she may as well let him take over.

And take over he did. In diabolical ways.

Massaging the shampoo through her hair was somehow very erotic, especially when she felt his powerful body behind her. Cade made her feel small—and very feminine. It was unique for her, and her hormones loved it.

After she'd rinsed her hair, he picked up the soap and, keeping her back to his chest, proceeded to clean her.

All over.

Slick fingers worked her nipples until she couldn't breathe. Her breasts felt heavy, so sensitive that she trembled all over. "Cade…"

"Shh." He kissed the side of her throat. "I love touching you."

She groaned at his insistent use of *love*, but she couldn't muster up a real protest. Trying to distract him, she moved her backside against his erection, but being the man he was, he lightly sank his teeth into her shoulder.

Delicious sensation prickled all over her body, every nerve ending electrified. Good God, she felt close to coming, and all

he did was play with her breasts. "Let's go to bed," she pleaded.
Pleaded. It was both appalling and exciting that he'd reduced
her to that needy voice.

"Not yet." He licked the spot where he'd given her a love
bite, and those broad, slightly rough hands coasted down, over
her stomach, her thighs, between them…

Pressing back against him, Sterling tipped her head to his
strong shoulder.

"That's it, babe. Don't fight me."

Fight him? What a joke. He was bigger, stronger and currently far more in control.

"Feel how slick you are?"

Very aware of her body's response, she gave another small
groan. He pressed a finger into her, worked her carefully, then
pulled out only to add a second finger.

She clenched around him. It felt so good—but she wanted
more than his fingers. Reaching back, she clamped a hand
onto his thigh to ground herself. With her other hand, she
covered his and pressed his fingers deeper, then moved sinu-
ously against him.

She was close, so close, if he'd only—

Cade pulled away, then repositioned her. "Lean against the
wall. That's it. Now open your legs."

Eyelashes spiked with the shower spray, Sterling looked at
him through a haze of lust—and did as ordered.

Lowering to his knees, Cade touched her again. Her breasts,
down to her belly, lower, exploring, and pressing his fingers in
again. Nuzzling against her, he found her clit and licked.

"Oh, God." Sterling locked her knees, her eyes squeezed
shut, her head back…

He drew her in, sucking, teasing rhythmically with his
tongue while keeping those long fingers thrust deep—on and
on it went until an incredible climax crashed through her. Like,

literally *crashed*, stealing the strength from her limbs, wringing a harsh cry from her throat, putting tears in her eyes even.

Luckily the shower would hide that, but wow. She tunneled her fingers into his close-cropped hair and rode out the pleasure until she felt herself slipping down the wall.

Cade caught her hips and stood in a rush. His mouth on hers, his tongue delving, that solid erection pulsing against her belly.

She reached for it, but he caught her hand, lifted it to his mouth for a tender kiss and said, "Not this time, babe. I'm too close to acting stupid."

Gulping breaths, Sterling managed to get her eyes open. A tiny bit, but enough to see that the blue of his eyes had turned incendiary. Curious, she whispered, "Stupid...how?"

"Forgoing protection."

"Oh." He turned away before she admitted that she wouldn't mind. Actually, the idea of feeling him and only him sparked a new stirring deep inside her.

In extreme haste Cade washed and rinsed, then turned off the water, grabbed the towels and pressed one against Sterling's chest.

"I would do the honors, but I need you too damn much. Get dry, or close to it, and let's go to the bedroom where I can grab a rubber."

Her mouth twitched with a secret little smile of happiness. She'd never seen Cade so frazzled.

She'd never been wanted that much.

Her heart expanded, making her chest feel tight with emotion. Lazily, while watching him, she dried off, then flipped her hair forward and wrapped it in the towel.

She was still bent forward when Cade hoisted her over his shoulder, making her laugh.

"I like the way you lust for me," she admitted. "Especially since I lust for you so much."

"Good to know." He put her on the foot of the bed so that

her legs hung off the end, then strode to the nightstand to grab a condom and quickly rolled it on. "Turn over."

Since she was already on her back, she blinked. "Do what?"

Without waiting for her to understand, he flipped her to her stomach and kneed her legs apart.

Curious, she lifted up on her arms to look back but went flat again as he gripped her hips and drove into her.

He filled her completely and was already thrusting, lifting her up to meet him each time he sank deep. His thighs met the back of hers, his firm abdomen slapping against her softer backside. Another climax started to build, and she knotted her fingers in the bedding.

"Star," Cade growled low, the sound almost tortured. "Can't wait." Reaching around and under her, he found her clit again, did no more than lightly pinch, holding her like that as he continued the hard rhythm, and far too quickly they were both coming.

It was so deep this way, his thrusts more powerful, and she loved it. Every second of it.

Because she loved him.

This time the knowledge didn't frighten her. Heck, she was now too exhausted to be frightened. Her thoughts were blessedly free of any angst. Even long-buried fears seemed to have evaporated, leaving her utterly replete.

Resting over her, still in her, Cade murmured, "Every time."

"Hmm?"

"Every time...is somehow better."

In total agreement with that, she sighed. "Mmm."

She felt his smile on her shoulder, then the tender kiss he pressed there before he pulled away.

Sterling wasn't sure she could move, not even for an earthquake, but Cade took care of it, cleaning her with his towel, then scooping her up and placing her in the bed, even tucking her in. He kissed her forehead and whispered, "Be right back."

It was the last thing she heard…until he woke her sometime later.

After arriving at the gym an hour ago, Reyes had repeatedly lost his concentration.

It was her fault. That cute little mystery woman.

Even while listening in on a trio of knuckleheads talking about some underhanded business—one that could pertain to his family's pursuits—Reyes couldn't keep his eyes off her.

She appeared to be close to his age of thirty—maybe a little younger. Honey-blond hair swung loose to her shoulders, dipping and swaying each time she landed a kick or threw a punch.

Improperly.

He chewed his upper lip. She did okay, and she put plenty of effort into it, but her stance was off. To get the best impact with her strikes, and to avoid getting thrown off balance, she needed to lead off with the other leg. She also let her hands drop each time…

Why the hell was he still dwelling on her?

He heard one of the guys say, "Seriously, man, easy cash. Just gotta be ready to pull the trigger."

Ears perking up, Reyes listened more closely.

"I traded my hardware a month ago," another complained.

"Damn, G, they'll give ya the firepower to protect the deal."

"What kind of deal?"

"The fuck does that matter?"

Reyes silently sighed. *G?* As in *gangster?* What a misnomer for the strung-out, scrawny fool sporting very amateurish tattoos all up and down his skinny arms.

"I don't know, man. I got that bum beef already. Don't wanna be messin' around."

"There'll be four of us," the recruiter continued. "Meetin' out at some farm. I was gonna catch a ride with you."

While listening, Reyes studied the woman.

What curves she lacked up top, she made up for with a really stellar ass.

Suddenly her attention snagged on him with a nasty glare.

Oops. Busted.

Busted looking at her *butt*. Definitely not cool.

Even all narrowed with annoyance, her blue eyes were nice— a soft color, thickly lashed.

Dismissing him, she turned away, which made his gaze return to that premium part of her anatomy. She didn't get back to work, though; instead she stood there with her hands on her hips, her shoulders set in annoyance.

He hadn't meant to interrupt her workout…but he also hated to miss anything else the knuckleheads said.

He heard "Aspen Creek," but the rest was indistinct, and now they were heading out, spines bowed, feet shuffling.

One of them glanced toward him. Reyes met his gaze. "Can I help you?"

"You seen Mort?"

Having no idea who Mort might be, Reyes lied, "He usually shows up later in the day."

"Tell him I was lookin' for him, yeah?"

"And you are…?" For certain, they hadn't come to his gym to work out, but then again, it's why he had the place, so cretins like that could pass along info.

"Hoop."

Novel name. "You got it, Hoop. You want to leave a number?"

"He has it."

Reyes looked back at Will, who manned the desk. "You see Mort come in, tell him to call Hoop." Then he walked away from Will's confusion, because Will had no idea who Mort was, either.

Satisfied, the two-bit thugs left.

Reyes waited until they were out of sight before he went to Will. "If you see anyone named Mort, let me know."

Will had learned not to ask questions, so he just nodded. He was a good worker, always showed up, and because Reyes paid him extra, he knew to keep his mouth shut and his eyes open.

The mystery woman regained his attention.

Guessing that she wouldn't linger much longer, Reyes moved toward her through the crowd. Occasionally he answered a quick question for a patron, all the while keeping his gaze on her.

He was pretty sure she felt his attention, but she didn't look at him again, not until he reached her.

Lips tight—very plump lips, he couldn't help noticing—she pulled out her earbuds and draped the cord around her neck.

Damn it, he never hesitated to speak his mind with women, but with her being so unapproachable, he floundered.

With a resigned sigh, she looked up at him and asked politely, "What?"

"I'm Reyes McKenzie, owner of the gym—"

"I know who you are."

She did, huh? But he noticed she didn't introduce herself. He rubbed his neck, shifted his feet like a friggin' schoolboy and waited.

This time she rolled her eyes before saying, "Kennedy Brooks. I've signed up for a year, but if there's a problem with my membership—"

"There's no problem." Surprised him, though. Most didn't choose the yearly option. In this part of town, people sometimes didn't know from one week to the next if they'd have money or time. Most of his clientele was fluid, which was how his father had planned it. Lots of people coming and going made it easier to catch information from the street.

He'd tell Will to let him know from now on whenever they sold a big membership.

"Kennedy." Somehow the name fit her. She probably stood five feet five, making her damn near a foot shorter than him. "You need any help?"

She shook her head. "No, thank you."

He should have walked away, but he didn't. With Sterling's certainty in his mind, Reyes said, "If you want to defend your-self—"

"Just getting in shape."

Complete BS. She'd said it too quickly, and she didn't meet his gaze. "I don't think so."

She'd just been ready to punch again but paused at his reply. Slowly, she turned to face him. Crossing her arms and cocking out a hip, she looked him over with mere curiosity.

No interest. Nope. Just like...she wondered why he was still bothering her.

Reyes sighed.

She half smiled. "Why do you say that?"

"I've been watching you," he explained, hoping that'd lead into more.

"I noticed you watching," she replied, with no invitation to extend the conversation.

Well, too bad for her.

"I was watching because I see the difference between getting in shape and learning how to fend off attackers."

"Huh." Very sexy lips curled. "Well, that confirms some-thing for me."

For whatever reason, he found himself stepping a little closer to her. "What's that?"

Her chin lifted. "You're not a mere instructor."

Her insight nearly blew him over, but he quickly recovered. "I already told you, I own the gym."

"So?" She rolled a shoulder. "You're more than a mere gym owner, too."

He opened his mouth, then closed it. Her lips were *really* distracting, especially when curved in a superior smile.

"You think you're the only observant one here? No, Mr. McKenzie, I notice things, too."

"Reyes." Mr. McKenzie was his father, for Christ's sake.

"Like you listening in to those young toughs. I noticed that, as well. Did you hear anything insightful?"

Well, hell, this lady was dangerous. "I give my attention to everyone who comes in."

"Yes, there's attention, and then there's listening in on a conversation to ferret out info." She gave his own words back to him. "I see the difference. So, Mr. McKenzie, how about you mind your business and I'll mind mine, and we'll get along just fine."

Well… He really had no idea how to react to that, so he merely saluted, said, "Carry on," and stalked away. He wasn't running, but it did feel like a strategic retreat.

This time he felt her gaze drilling into his back.

Later, he'd give Sterling hell. For now, though… Kennedy intrigued him even more. He couldn't get her off his mind—and the fact that she didn't pack up and leave immediately, that she stuck around, glancing at him every so often, felt almost like a dare.

Or an invitation? Not likely.

He wouldn't act on it anyway, not yet. He didn't want to be a creeper who bothered the clients. But he wondered if she reconsidered her stance, maybe she'd approach him next time.

It was a nice little fantasy, one that included him getting his hands on that plump backside… Shaking his head, he retrieved his cell phone and sent Cade a message about what he'd heard.

Four guys probably didn't mean anything, but a farm in Aspen Creek might. Never hurt to share the tidbits he heard.

He'd just finished when Will called out to him. "Hey, Reyes, you have a call."

As he headed to the desk, he decided it was time to get his mind off a certain prickly-but-somehow-sexy woman. He wasn't a glutton for punishment like his brother.

Yet even as he made that vow, his attention wandered back to her. He needed things with Adela and Mattox to blow; that'd give him something else to focus on.

While speaking with the head of a youth group about sponsoring a field trip, he deliberately turned his back on Kennedy. When he heard the front door open, he jerked around and saw her walking through it, her gym bag in hand.

Even while keeping up with the phone conversation, Reyes tracked her movements through the big front window. She scanned the parked cars, up and down the street, her gaze watchful. Made sense for the neighborhood, but he sensed it was more with her, like an ingrained wariness.

Most people took safety for granted; clearly Kennedy did not.

Reyes saw the moment her attention snagged on something out of range of the front window. Frowning, she tossed her bag into a little red compact, relocked the car and headed slowly, cautiously along the sidewalk and out of view.

What the hell?

Too curious to ignore it, he wrapped up the call so quickly he bordered on rudeness, ending with, "Sorry, something's come up, but sure, I'd be glad to sponsor. Just give the details to Will. Thanks." He handed the phone to Will, then hurried out the door just in time to see Kennedy walk between the two buildings.

All kinds of shady shit happened in the alleys. Never mind that it was the middle of the day, or that he wore only shorts.

Reyes went after her, his stride long and fast—until he spotted her kneeling next to some garbage cans. Behind a broken-down cardboard box was…a very mangy cat.

"Careful," he said softly, already moving forward to join her.

"Shh," she replied without looking up, as if she'd already known it was him. "He's scared."

Reyes could imagine. The cat, who had probably once been white but was now too messy to tell for sure, had very strange eyes, one pale gray, the other mustard yellow, and a little… googly. Mud and filth streaked his face, and part of his tail was missing.

He hunkered back, eyeing Reyes.

"Do you think we can catch him?"

Staring at her, Reyes asked stupidly, "Catch him?"

"He's hungry," she cooed.

Cooed.

For him, she'd been all snippy and smug, but for a mangy cat— And then he heard a softer, squeakier little sound. Ah, hell. Resigned, he let out a groan.

"Shh," Kennedy said again.

Her bossiness made him grin. "That's not a tomcat."

She didn't look at him, only asked, "No?"

"You don't hear it?"

"What?"

"Kittens." The tiny meows came again—very nearby, in fact.

Her eyes went wide, her mouth forming a soft O. Then she breathed, *"Kittens."*

Yeah, he knew exactly what that expression meant. Either way, he'd have helped the cat, but kittens changed the manner he would have used.

When she started to stand, he said, "No. Don't start looking for them yet. They're close by, but we might spook the mama if we disturb them before we've won her over."

Trusting him, at least on that, Kennedy nodded. "Right."

Reyes considered the situation. "If she's nursing, she needs to eat."

"I was trying to figure out how I'd sneak in a cat, but a cat with kittens?" Kennedy turned to him. "Where I'm staying, pets aren't allowed. What are we going to do?"

We? Minutes ago she'd told him to buzz off, but now they were working together? Okay, he'd take it. "If I can corral her, I can put her and the babies in my office for now." Responsibility for the cats would give them a neutral link, one that might bridge the divide so she'd tell him what she was up to, and whose ass he needed to kick for her.

"Would you really?" Excited now, she smiled at him, a genuine smile that made him want to lick her mouth.

Down, he ordered himself. "Keep an eye on her while I go find a box. I packed food for later today—we might be able to use it to lure her in." *We.* He used that word, reinforcing it for her.

And she didn't object.

But that was a little too easy, so he wanted it confirmed. As he stood, he asked, "You *will* be back to help me figure this out, right?"

"You know I come to the gym nearly every day. Of course I'll be back." Just then, the cat crept out enough to butt her head into Kennedy's extended hand. "Aw."

The lady looked very different when she was being all gentle and sweet. She looked a little too appealing, in fact.

Maybe seeing all that overblown chemistry between Sterling and Cade was starting to wear on him. Not that he wanted anything that substantial...but it did have him looking at Kennedy differently.

Before he said or did something stupid, he went inside to get what he needed. He returned with a nice-sized cardboard box, a plush towel in the bottom of it and half of his chicken salad croissant.

Kennedy had the cat nearly in her lap at that point. "After this, I'll pay for her food and whatever else she needs."

No way would he commit to that. "Let's just see how far we get today, okay?" He held out the sandwich.

Kennedy gave him an incredulous look over his bait. "Croissant? You?"

What did she think, that he sustained himself on Cheez Whiz and beer? "It's delicious—but I didn't make it."

Her brows leveled out. "Ah, girlfriend?" Then on the heels of that, with a darkening frown, she asked, "Wife?"

That particular acerbic tone caused a laugh that startled the cat.

While she won the scraggly thing over again, Reyes said around a big grin, "No girlfriend, definitely not a *wife*."

Her jaw flexed over the way he stressed the word, but she said nothing. It took only seconds to locate the kittens in a torn bag of trash. Reyes carefully transferred them into the box. There were only three, thank God. He double-checked, looking everywhere. The mama, still on Kennedy's lap, went alert and immediately started fretting...until she found the food.

Making a sound somewhere between a purr and a growl, she devoured it but still kept her eyes on Reyes. She ate the entire sandwich, croissant roll and all, which made him realize just how hungry the poor thing had been.

When she finished, she went into the box with her kittens, circled once, then lay on her side to lick her paw while the kittens nursed.

Yeah, that melted even his own heart a little.

Standing close to his side, Kennedy whispered, "She was starving."

He glanced down at her, then had to look away again. He'd never seen a woman with quite that particular mix of tenderness and sympathy.

"She'll be fine now," he assured her, slowly closing the box so she couldn't leap out the minute he moved her. He was about to suggest that Kennedy walk with him, one hand on the cardboard flaps, until he got the animals inside, but his phone beeped, and when he checked the message, he saw it was go time.

CHAPTER SEVENTEEN

Watching Star stir awake from her nap was a distinct pleasure, one that Cade wanted to enjoy every day for the rest of his life.

She still had a towel, now lopsided, on her head, and a hickey on her shoulder. He lightly brushed his fingertips over the mark.

The core of his basic nature was to protect his own, and she *was* his now, whether she'd accepted that as fact or not. Eventually she would. He'd see to it. "Hey, sleepyhead."

On a sinuous stretch, she murmured…and settled again.

Knowing he'd caused her exhaustion with sexual excess left him aching with renewed lust—and love. The urge was to cradle her close, coddle her, spar with her, train her, make love to her and then start all over again. Conversations, meals, showers, danger, sex… Sharing with her made everything better.

It struck him that he needed a lifetime of that, a lifetime with her.

The emotional overload left him combustible, agitated and needing her again. He curved his hand around her shoulder, absorbing the satiny feel of her skin, the warmth.

Her lashes barely lifted. "Cade?"

Smiling at her, he said, "You taste so good I'd prefer to have *you* for lunch. But since everyone will wait on us…"

Eyes popping open wide, she stared at him in blank surprise. "Lunch?"

Damn, she was a sweetheart with that comical confusion on her face. "Bernard has outdone himself, and he's waiting for your praise."

"Bernard," she repeated, before coming up to one elbow and groaning. "It's time for lunch already?"

"You've been asleep awhile."

She reached up to keep the towel on her head. "But I *never* nap."

Leaning in, Cade whispered, "Guess the awesome sex tuckered you out. I gave you two big Os, if you recall."

The fog left her gaze and she grinned. "Of course I recall. Sex with you makes up my favorite memories."

Severely disliking how she worded that, he clarified, "Reality."

"What?"

"Us, together. That's reality, not a memory."

She softened, her lips curving. "You do like to say confusing things, but if everyone is waiting, I need to make myself presentable instead of trying to figure you out."

She made to get out of the bed, but with a kiss, Cade took her down to the mattress again, his chest against the soft cushion of her breasts, one leg thrown over hers to keep her still. He searched her gaze, determined to gain an admission. "Tell me you understand, babe. Say that you like our relationship."

"You kidding?" She ran her fingers along his jaw, around his ear to his nape. "Course I do. I'm not dumb."

That answer didn't really satisfy, either, but then, short of her telling him how much she cared, no answer would. Cade gave her a firm kiss. "Dad checked my stitches, bitched because

I'd pulled one, and redressed it. If he says anything in front of you, ignore him."

Blanching, she whispered, "Your dad knows what we were doing?"

Cade almost choked on his humor. Because teasing her was so much fun, he used the same hushed tone she'd had. "Yes." Scorching heat rushed into her face, leaving her cheeks blotchy. The grin broke through. "He knows we were *sparring*."

Relief took away her starch. "Not nice, you butthead. You knew what I was thinking."

"I couldn't resist. Seems to happen a lot where you're concerned." With a last firm kiss to her mouth, he rolled out of the bed, then hauled her up. "Bernard has hot roast beef sandwiches with caramelized onions on crusty bread—that's the description he insisted I share, along with the warning that you'll want to enjoy it while it's hot, so hustle up. Lunch is in fifteen minutes."

"Ack." Beautifully naked, she darted around him, already whipping away the towel. "You should have told me all that five minutes ago!"

Sitting on the side of the bed, Cade listened to the blow-dryer and smiled with bone-deep satisfaction. Had he done this much smiling before Star? He didn't think so. For most of his life he'd been driven. Driven to buck his father's dictates, then to succeed in the army, and now to right wrongs for women and children exploited by traffickers.

Singular focus kept him on track, or at least it did before Star. Now he enjoyed thinking of her, seeing her, touching her. He'd always do the best he could, but responsibilities had moved aside to make room for pleasure.

To make room for Star.

When the noise quit, he found himself saying, "I have a decent place of my own."

The door jerked open and Star stood there, still naked but now with her hair loose the way he liked it. She stared at him a moment, then stalked forward to get clothes. "A place other than this apartment?"

He'd never really thought of these rooms as his apartment, but then, he knew he had a small home to call his own. Star didn't. "I bought it after I was medically discharged from the army while serving as a Ranger."

Pausing with her panties halfway up her legs, Star's gaze clashed with his. After a second, she pulled them up and came to sit by him. Breasts bared, eyes watchful.

Cade said nothing, leaving it to her to ask any questions she had.

"You were a Ranger?"

"Once a Ranger, always a Ranger, so I'm a Ranger still, medically retired."

Uncertainty trembled in her fingers as she tucked back her hair. "Medically retired, why?"

It felt good to share with her, to finally, completely open up. He laced his fingers with hers, moving her hand to his thigh. When with her, he couldn't touch her enough. "After a lot of deployments and hard landings when jumping from planes, I had multiple leg issues."

"You jumped from planes?" Surprise was immediately followed by concern. "You're hurt?"

"I'm in prime physical shape for the average man."

The concern shifted to amused interest. "Heck yeah, you are."

"But for a Ranger?" Keeping his attention off her breasts wasn't easy. "Not so much."

That statement left her disgruntled. "Who says so?"

His mouth twitched. "Don't act like you're sorry I'm here."

"What? No, course not." She stood again and reached for her bra. "So tell me about your house—and how come we're not there instead of here?"

He'd known that would be her response. "Like I said, it's

small. Two bedrooms, one I use for storage. Family room, eat-in kitchen, bathroom. A single-car garage. There's a nice big basement, though, so I have my workout gear down there. Nothing like Dad's downstairs setup, just bare concrete walls and floor, exposed pipes and all that."

She pulled up straight-leg jeans, tugging a little to get them over her perfect ass, and then pulled on a loose shirt. "And we're here because?"

"It's the safest place to be right now."

Brows pinching in thought, she sat beside him again to get on her socks and those shit-kicker boots of hers. "If I wasn't with you, would you feel the same?"

"You are with me." He trailed his fingers through her hair. "And you matter to me, Star. A lot."

Some turbulent emotion brought her gaze snapping to his. He saw her slender throat work, watched her lick her lips. Shooting for cockiness, she said, "Ditto."

He wasn't buying it. Her attitude was mostly uncertainty, not disinterest. What would she do if he said that he loved her? With everyone waiting, he decided not to put it to the test.

Bent at the waist to tie her boots, she said with nonchalance, "You're the only one who calls me that now."

"Star? It suits you."

"I thought Star had disappeared years ago."

Very softly, he said, "I found her again."

Denials hung in the air, but she didn't give them voice. Instead she stood and held out a hand. "Come on. I'm starved."

Knowing this was difficult for her, Cade let her lead him out. "Before I got to know you, I called you something else."

"Yeah? You called me Sterling?"

"No." They started up the steps.

"Then what?"

"Trouble." Catching her at the top of the stairwell, he pinned her to the wall. "Massive trouble—especially to my libido."

Her laugh sounded almost like a giggle, and damn, that pleased him. "Your libido is fine."

"It's in hyperdrive around you."

Dodging his mouth, she said, "Lunch is waiting."

"Then give me a kiss to carry me through the next hour or two."

Challenge sparked in her dark eyes and she focused on his mouth. Small but capable hands slid around his neck. "All right."

Damn. She leaned forward—and singed him.

He shouldn't have started this when he knew the others were waiting, but he wasn't about to end it, either. She nibbled on his bottom lip, licked the upper, sealed her lips to his and dueled with his tongue.

He had his hips pinned to hers, grinding against her, when he heard the door open.

Star freed her mouth and immediately used his shoulder as a shield. Cade concentrated on breathing.

Behind them, stunned silence reigned, and then Bernard stated, "Lunch will not keep, so I hope this will." He slammed the door again.

Shoulders shaking, Star held on to him.

"I have a boner."

The snickers turned into full-blown howls.

It was nice, hearing her laugh so freely. He wanted to hear it more often. "It's not that funny."

She tried to catch her breath, took one look at him and fell into another fit.

To get even, Cade moved his open palm over her breast, whispering against her ear, "Your nipples are also telling a tale."

That earned him a groan and a tight squeeze. "If I wasn't so hungry, I'd say to hell with lunch, but after all that exercise this morning, I think I need to eat."

"We have the rest of our lives," he said and tugged her through the doorway before she could stop sputtering.

Getting past her reserve was a challenge, but also strangely satisfying. And fun.

Especially since she liked the physical side of their relationship as much as he did. The rest? He didn't know yet, but he refused to believe he was the only one falling hard.

"Bernard, you outdid yourself." Sitting back, one hand to her full stomach, Sterling sighed. Much as she wanted to see Cade's home, she would definitely miss Bernard's cooking.

For the moment, she refused to dwell on why Cade hadn't yet shown her his place. There'd been opportunity, before the danger ramped up, so why hadn't he? Did he want to keep his personal life separate?

Even to her skeptical mind, that didn't make much sense, not with the careless way he threw around the *L* word. And what was that comment in the stairwell? *The rest of our lives.*

Like maybe he expected them to spend that life together?

Hoping for too much could lead to the biggest disappointment she'd ever known—and God knew, she'd known plenty. But she couldn't help herself. Her heart had already launched on a gleeful path of "what if?"

Was it possible?

If he had something to say, why didn't he just come out and say it already? All those verbal clues that she didn't know how to decipher were making her a little nuts.

"Oh, hey," Madison said, sitting forward to stare at her laptop. "We have movement."

Cade's sister had alternated between eating, joining in the casual conversation and scanning her screen. No one had commented on the laptop set on the table before her.

"What is it?" Out of his seat, Cade went behind Madison's chair, one hand braced on the back of it, to see for himself.

The expression on his face warned Sterling, apprehension instantly filling her.

Why? She wanted to get Mattox, so she needed to know the truth about Adela. It's what they'd been working for, what she wanted.

But she'd just been contemplating her future and now reality came crashing down around her.

"It's go time." Already with his cell out, Cade keyed in a message.

"Getting hold of Reyes?" Parrish asked.

"He'd messaged me earlier about some guys hanging out, talking about a job tonight. No idea if they're connected, but it's possible."

"My instincts are telling me this is it." Madison glanced up. "Tell Reyes to make arrangements to leave the gym."

Getting her gumption back—sort of—Sterling asked, "He has someone to cover for him?"

"Every eventuality has been prearranged," Parrish explained.

Of course it had. Clearing the sudden lump of nervousness from her throat, Sterling asked, "Do you see Mattox? Is Adela with him?"

Already shaking her head, Madison used her mouse to take a few screenshots. "It's a ten-foot box truck and I'm willing to bet there are women inside. Here comes a car."

"Reyes said he'll be ready in five, just waiting for directions." Returning his phone to his pocket, Cade went back to looking at the screen with his sister. "That's Mattox getting out of the back seat. I can't see if Adela is in there."

Sterling sat still, listening as they coordinated around her. She felt like a useless lump, but she was out of her element and didn't want to slow anyone down.

"He's opening the back of the truck—I wish one of the cameras showed that view!"

Cade rested a hand on his sister's shoulder. "The three cameras are helping, hon. Will you be able to follow them?"

"Probably, or at least enough to get a fix on where they're

going. Tell Reyes to get over to I-25 near there. He needs to be closer to pick up the tail once we know."

Almost at the same time, Sterling's phone rang. Startled, she gave an inelegant jump.

All eyes turned to her.

The lump in her throat expanded, but she managed a cavalier smile that carried over to a neutral tone. "Hello?"

"Francis?"

That panicked voice had her sitting forward. Was Adela not with Mattox?

Quickly, she put the phone on speaker and said, "Adela. I haven't heard from you in a—"

"You have to help. *Please.* He has new women, Francis. They'll be in the same shape as me, but if you can figure out a way to stop him... I didn't know who else to call!"

Knowing how the others would react, but wanting to gauge Adela's reaction, Sterling suggested, "The police?"

Parrish shook his head at her. Alarm raised Madison's brows.

Cade just held up a placating hand, indicating they should wait and let her do her thing.

So what was her thing? Somehow, while falling in love with Cade, she'd forgotten.

"Not a good idea. I told you, he's bought off some of the cops."

So Sterling hadn't tripped her up on that. Did Mattox have a few cops in his pocket? It'd be worth finding out. "How do you know?" It wasn't unheard of for a cop to be complicit, but it was rare, and she figured Cade and his family would have forewarned her if the problem was around here.

"I don't have much time! He could be back to the cabin any minute."

"What cabin?" Sterling asked, playing along—just in case. "Where?"

"It's a shack in the mountain, near Coalville."

Brows shot up everywhere. Adela admitted it? She was either truly desperate or riding out with Mattox right now.

"But that doesn't matter," Adela rushed on. "He has eight new girls. I overheard him talking about north on I-25, something about meeting at an abandoned farm near Aspen Creek."

Cade's entire demeanor changed. It was amazing to witness as he started texting Reyes again.

Gently, with understanding and sympathy, Sterling asked, "If you don't want cops, how do you expect me to handle it?"

All she heard was heavy breathing. "I thought... I thought you had that big guy with you. Mattox has been furious that he was able to fight off all the men he sent after him. He even said some of his guys are still missing."

Huh. Adela had managed to hear a lot. "He's one man, Adela. And I assume Mattox won't be alone."

"No. He doesn't go anywhere without personal protection, plus I think he hired on a few more."

Sterling waited.

"I'm sorry. You seemed so resourceful..." Adela caught her breath. "Guess I was wrong, so maybe you could go ahead and try the police? Just, please, don't tell anyone I tipped you off. He'd kill me if he ever found out."

"I can come get you from the cabin—"

"No, he's leaving people here to watch me. It'd be too dangerous. Besides, I don't matter right now. I just don't want those other women..." She drew a shaky breath. "I want them to have a chance, okay? But I have to go now. If I don't hide this phone, he'll know." The call died.

Just like her nerve. Just like her backbone.

Sterling looked up at Cade. Dear God, she wasn't sure what to do.

"I've got this," Cade said, his voice firm. "Did I tell you that Rangers are critical thinkers? We are, so let me handle things."

Relieved that this time she didn't have to sort it out alone,

Sterling swallowed back her misgivings and came to her feet. "Okay. Right." She'd made her voice firm. She wasn't a wimp and she wouldn't start acting like one. "So what do we do first?"

Parrish's discerning gaze missed nothing. He turned to Cade. "You're good to go?"

"Glad things are finally in motion," he said. "The men Reyes overheard at the gym also mentioned Aspen Creek."

Madison frowned. "What else?"

"Four men, and Mattox is ensuring they're all strapped."

"You've devastated his organization," Parrish mused as he pushed back his chair and began to pace. "First getting Misfits shut down, then going through his men. He's afraid to operate until you're out of the picture. This is his Hail Mary, a last desperate attempt to try to regain his footing."

Desperate? Sterling wondered if Parrish was delusional. "Four men," she emphasized. "All armed."

Cade shook his head. "Bozos, Reyes said. Nothing to worry about."

Incredulity tensed her body. "You can't know that."

Perturbed by her tone, Parrish zeroed in on Cade. "Do we need to wait, to investigate more?"

"Forget the number of men. There may be eight women. Eight innocents."

"If she wasn't lying," Madison pointed out.

Resolute, Cade said, "I'm not willing to chance it."

Parrish's eyes narrowed, but he nodded.

Not good enough, not for Sterling. "If they're armed..."

"I'll disarm them."

Of all the idiotic— She couldn't believe he was that arrogant.

Cade held out a hand to her. "Come on. We'll need to leave quickly so we can rendezvous with Reyes on the way."

Knowing she had to find her own arrogance and fast, Sterling nodded.

"Bernard, would you please keep an eye on things here while I help them get ready?"

"I'll be diligent," Bernard announced while taking her seat. "If anyone moves, I'll alert you."

"Thank you." Madison jogged around and ahead of Cade.

Getting ready, Sterling found, meant donning body armor, strapping on guns, and stowing a sniper rifle and plenty of ammo. Much better stuff than the knife necklace she'd worn to Misfits. God, that felt like a lifetime ago.

When she'd been all alone in the world.

Shaking off those maudlin thoughts, Sterling put her knife in her boot, the brass knuckles in her rear pocket. With Madison's assistance, it was such seamless prep that within minutes she was seated in the passenger side of Cade's SUV while he had a few quiet words with his father. Madison had returned to the kitchen as command central.

Through the window, Sterling watched as Parrish put a fatherly hand on Cade's shoulder. Seeing that touched her heart. Cade's father was nearly as tall as him, still very fit, and for once she detected concern in his gaze. This, she realized, was how Cade would look as he aged. Distinguished, impressive and in control.

Maybe Cade had inherited his attitude from Parrish, too. With their cool command, the two of them were very different from Madison's joyful persona and Reyes's maddening personality.

The more she looked at Cade, the harder her heart pounded.

This could be it. She could die—worse, *Cade could get hurt*—and all her newfound happiness would mean absolutely nothing.

This caring stuff was awful. How simple her life used to be when she had no one, when even *she* didn't matter that much. Now she was crazy in love and worried sick because of it.

It changed everything.

Cade slid into the driver's seat and started the SUV.

Looking back at Parrish, she found him still standing there, his hands clasped behind his back, watching as they drove away.

Sterling lifted her hand in a wave. He returned the gesture. Parrish might be a dictator, but he obviously loved his kids.

How stressful must it be for him, having his sons in the field?

Facing forward again, she glanced at Cade. His hands rested on the steering wheel, his posture relaxed. It all felt surreal.

"Everything okay, honey?"

"Yes." *No.* She wasn't sure anything would ever again be okay.

"You're staring."

"Because you are devastating to my senses." *And I need to absorb more of you while I can.*

Smiling, Cade handed her his phone. "Here, Madison will send updates, in case they get too far ahead of us."

Her palms felt sweaty when she accepted the cell. Why? She'd done stuff like this before… Okay, *that* was a big lie. She'd never done *anything* this complex.

But she'd wanted to, right?

Apparently sensing her turmoil, Cade put a hand on her knee. "We'll pick up Reyes shortly."

Knowing Cade's brother was also effective in this crazy stuff, that he'd be good backup for Cade, made her feel a tiny bit better.

Again, anticipating her reaction, Cade drew a bottle of water from the door and handed it to her. "Hydrate."

Hydrate, she mocked silently, even as she took a quick drink. His "business as usual" attitude was really starting to irk. "What about you? Don't you need to drink some?"

"If I do, I have another bottle."

So calm, so matter-of-fact.

Get it together, Sterling ordered herself. Cade was smart enough to know if he couldn't handle the situation. She should take comfort in his confidence, not get annoyed by it.

Scenery passed in a blur, much like her thoughts. Madison texted once to say that she'd confirmed two men in the truck, and one in the front seat of the car chauffeuring Mattox.

Sterling read the message to Cade and sent back his simple acknowledgment, but her mind scrambled on the math. Four men hired, three accompanying Mattox, and Mattox himself... That was *eight* men.

Against the three of them.

And they still didn't know if Adela was along for the ride, complicit in everything, or cowering, possibly injured, back in an isolated cabin.

Not long after that, they turned down a narrow road off the highway and picked up Reyes. He'd parked his truck behind some trees and strode out with the same insouciance as Cade.

She was ready to chew her nails, and they acted like it was nothing.

Cade got out and walked around to meet his brother at the back of the SUV.

Twisting in her seat, Sterling watched as Reyes suited up, starting with a back holster that held two handguns. Unlike Cade, Reyes adjusted his bulletproof vest right over his T-shirt.

Too antsy to sit still, Sterling got out to join them.

Reyes glanced up with a smile. "Hey, girl. How's it hanging?"

"Hey."

Far too perceptive, Reyes did a double take, but wisely chose not to comment on the visible tension in her frame.

Instead, he picked up the semiauto precision rifle. "It's going to rain."

Cade shrugged. "Every afternoon, this time of year. You won't melt."

"I'd rather not calculate wind, though."

When Sterling frowned, Cade explained, "Reyes will cover us from farther away."

That was news to her. "He won't be with us?"

"I'll ensure no one sneaks up behind you."

Well…that was reassuring. "You're a crack shot, huh?"

Tugging on a lock of her hair, Reyes said, "Even with wind and rain." He closed the back of the car. "Let's go. I'll drive."

So that Cade could ride shotgun, Sterling took the back seat. Heavy clouds moved in and around the sun, one minute making it gloomy, the next leaving the day bright. She knew they were right. Rain was inevitable, and it fit her mood.

If they all got through this day unscathed, she'd reevaluate how she lived her life. Cade mattered. His family mattered.

And by God, that meant she mattered, too.

CHAPTER EIGHTEEN

They came into the farm from the side, skirting around scraggly woods, making their way over a neglected field. Given that dried stalks remained scattered about, she guessed someone had once grown corn.

Age and neglect had ravaged the farmhouse, the windows all broken, the roof half gone. Farther back, and to the right, an old weathered barn remained standing.

If not for the box truck and black sedan parked behind it, Sterling would have thought they had the wrong place. But no, the evidence was there. Had they come in through the front, they wouldn't have seen either vehicle parked in back.

Both men were quietly focused as they took in a big gnarled tree near a fence line, a massive boulder and an old trestle bridge over a creek.

"There," Reyes decided, nodding at the bridge. "I'll have a better line of sight from there."

Cade nodded. "I'll circle around and come in on that side of the barn. I'll be able to see what I'm up against and you'll be able to cover me."

"Should I pick a few off right away?"

"That would just announce us and might not be necessary anyway. Wait and see how it goes."

Sterling frowned at them as they went over plans. There were eight men out there, waiting, anxious to kill Cade and probably Reyes, too.

Anxious to get hold of her.

In no way did she feel equipped for this—but how could she say that when they were so freakishly calm?

Reyes lowered the binoculars. "I only counted five inside the barn. Think they're planning to stash the women there?"

"How secure could it be? Wouldn't take much to have the whole structure falling down around them."

"What if it's a trap?" When both men turned to her, Sterling curled her fingers until she felt her nails digging into her palms. "What if one of them has a sniper rifle of his own? He could pick us off as we close in."

"Not likely," Reyes said. "I'm not sure these buffoons can manage that much planning. The punks at the gym definitely don't have any talents beyond finding their way into trouble."

"Mattox is not a punk," she insisted. "He's a bloodthirsty, heartless bastard who would take pleasure in killing all of us."

Slowly, Reyes lowered the binoculars. Seconds passed before he spoke, and again he chose to overlook her trepidation. "A few of them have gone to the back of the truck. They don't appear to be aware of us."

"Mattox?" Sterling leaned forward, staring hard, but without binoculars of her own, she couldn't make out any people. "Did you see him?"

"Neither of them look thick enough. Besides, I can't imagine Mattox doing the grunt work."

"We've stripped him of his resources." Cade took another look. "He's here. I sense it."

Sterling whispered, "Me, too." Somehow she knew Mattox was there...and she knew everything about this was wrong.

Cade glanced back at her in sharpened awareness. Dissecting her. Analyzing her. Coming to conclusions.

How could eyes so cool be so scorching?

In defensive belligerence, she asked, "What?"

"Now isn't the time to hold back. If you have suspicions—"

"It feels *wrong*," she blurted. "All of it. In my gut, I know we're being set up." Sitting back, she waited for their derision. She waited for their doubt.

The brothers shared a look.

Reyes surprised her by saying, "Gut feelings have kept me alive more than once."

Cade nodded. "So this might not be the cakewalk I anticipated."

Now that she had their attention, Sterling started to relax.

Until Cade caught her hand. "I don't want to piss you off, babe, but I have a favor to ask."

Reyes hummed a little, drummed his fingertips on the steering wheel and went back to surveying the barn.

With a terrible foreboding, Sterling lifted her chin.

"I think you're right. I think it's a setup of some sort—but it's nothing I can't handle."

Tension burrowed into her every muscle. "You've gotten through things like this before?"

"Many times."

Clearly he wasn't retrenching—and she wasn't willing to hold him up. "Okay, so let's go. The waiting is worse than the doing."

Cade didn't budge. His hold on her hand tightened. "Since it likely is a trap, we need someone at the wheel, ready to go, in case we have to bounce in a hurry."

Of course she knew where this was going. "You mean me?"

"You're good. I'd never say otherwise." His low voice seemed to brush over her skin like a reassuring caress. "Put to the test, I know you'd handle any situation. No doubts at all, I swear. But the truth is—"

"You and Reyes are better at this." A blatant truth.

"We're bigger. Stronger." His thumb rubbed over her clenched knuckles. "And yes, better trained for this."

It galled, knowing that Cade was giving her an out.

He must have known that, too, because he tacked on, "It's either you or Reyes—"

Reyes snorted but continued studying the barn. "Still only see five. No women."

Sterling knew she should have been gracious, should have accepted the excuse with gratitude, but instead she said, "I'm agreeing under duress."

His shoulders relaxed, telling her that her decision had mattered to him.

Before Cade, the concept of the future had no real meaning. Now she wanted to see what happened between them. She wanted to know what tomorrow, the next month, an entire year would bring. "You need to understand, Cade. I'm going to be very worried for you. *Very.*" It horrified her that her voice wavered with emotion. "Damn it, you've stolen my edge!"

"I'll go get in position." Taking the rifle from the floor near Cade's feet, Reyes left the SUV, then kept low as he cut across the field. He'd have to wade out into the creek to climb the trestle, but she didn't have a doubt he could do it.

With terrible timing, Sterling realized she liked Reyes now. Heck, in such a short time, the entire McKenzie family had become dear to her.

When Cade got out and circled around, she stepped out to meet him, oblivious to the light rain that immediately dampened her clothes and hair. Without missing a beat, he pressed her to the side of the SUV. His rough hand cradled her cheek. "The timing is fucked, but I need you to know something."

"Wha—"

"I love you."

Her heart shot into her throat and stuck there, feeling as big as a grapefruit. Unfair! *Now* he decided to make it all crystal clear, with her rowdy emotions flying out of control?

At her stunned silence, his mouth quirked. "I *love* you, Star."

It took a second, but she found herself smiling, as well. "Cade—"

"There's no way in hell I won't come back to you." He punctuated that with the briefest of kisses to her slightly parted lips but then wasted no more time talking. "Get behind the wheel, keep the doors locked and stay alert."

He took it one step further, practically putting her in the seat himself, locking the door and quietly closing it.

He hadn't given her a chance to tell him how she felt, and now she desperately wanted to. Did he not trust what she'd say? Was he uncertain of her?

A laughable idea. She was a complete nobody, without special talent, no family, nothing to recommend her, and he was…

He was everything to her.

Cade loves me. She hugged his confession to her heart, and in that moment, she believed it would be all right.

Had he known her misgivings? Course he had. Cade missed nothing. He'd deliberately saved her by saying they needed a driver. That hadn't been discussed in their prior plans, so she knew he'd come up with it on the fly.

Somehow, he truly knew her, well enough to understand her even when she had trouble understanding herself. Without the excuse he'd given her, she *would* have gone along. And she likely would have been up to the task.

She knew it. Cade knew it, too. And that's what mattered.

He'd been considerate…because he loved her.

More focused because of that, she stared ahead, already losing sight of Cade, still unable to spot Reyes. She picked up Cade's discarded binoculars. If it became necessary, she'd lend a hand.

Otherwise, she'd be right here—waiting.

Spotting Reyes on the bridge, positioned behind a beam, Cade stole low through the high weeds and cornstalks until he was on the other side of the barn, then crept forward. Once he got close enough, he could hear men talking. Not Mattox, not yet, but he sensed the bastard was near.

"Think they'll show?" someone asked. "Should have been here by now, right?"

"Have a look around. Take someone with you."

Cade flattened his back to the rough, weather-bleached boards and waited. The men murmured low, mostly complaints about the rain. Then one said, "You check around back. I'll go this way."

Perfect. He could take them on two at a time, but individually would be quieter, ensuring he didn't alert the others.

The first started around the corner. Slouched, one hand shoved in his pocket, the other hand holding a revolver at his side, he spotted Cade a second too late.

Snagging the much smaller man into a tight choke hold that both kept him silent and immobilized him, Cade torqued up the pressure until the man's skinny legs gave out and he slumped. Lowering him to the ground, Cade quickly wrapped his mouth with duct tape, then secured his hands and feet with nylon cuffs.

He stuck the guy's weapon into his waistband and in less than thirty seconds was at the back of the barn—where he caught the startled surprise of the second guy as he stepped into view. Hair in a ponytail and missing two front teeth made the sight pretty comical.

When the thug opened his mouth to scream, Cade slammed his fist into his face, putting him down, dazed, but not yet out.

Easy enough. Straddling him, Cade gripped his throat tight. "Make a sound, and you're dead."

Blinking fast in panic, the idiot went still. Cade released him but only to land another hard punch, and this time it put him to sleep. He trussed up that guy much like the first.

Reyes had spotted five, so he had three to go.

A twig snapped, and Cade looked back to see two more men standing there, and if their wild-eyed expressions meant anything, they were scared spitless. They each held guns but hadn't yet aimed them.

Even more reckless, they were within reach.

Slowly, Cade smiled—then spun, leg out, taking them off their feet. They crashed into each other.

Either Mattox was getting really desperate by using wannabe street toughs with no training, or he didn't care if they all died.

Not that Cade committed random murder, but still, he took them apart pretty easily, even while preparing for another threat to show. He bound their hands and feet, and when he heard the shot, he knew it was Reyes.

On the other side of the barn, someone howled in pain. The last man? Or maybe Mattox.

Back on his feet, Cade peered into the barn, saw it was empty and felt fury expand. Where the fuck was Mattox?

He had a few prisoners who might be able to tell him.

Turning back, he met the gaze of one of the punks.

Face bloodied and eyes wild, he watched as Cade strode toward him.

Trying to scuttle back, the panicked guy asked, "Who the fuck are you?"

Cade kicked him in the ribs. With his hands bound, he couldn't block the strike at all. "Where's Mattox?"

"*Goddammit!*" he yelled, trying to curl in on himself. "Fucking asshole!"

The outpouring of profanity didn't faze Cade. He aimed his Glock. "You have two seconds. One, t—"

"He's in the farmhouse!"

"Shut up, Mort," the other man growled. "Mattox'll cut your fuckin' throat."

"And this one will shoot me, man! Either way, I'm dead."

In the house... "Why?"

"Don't want his biz told, that's why."

Idiot. Ignoring Mort, Cade stepped on the other one's nuts, hard enough to make him scream. "*Why* is he in the house?" With the house barely standing, the barn would have been a better choice.

Urgency beat in Cade's brain. He needed to see Star, needed to touch her. Needed to know—

Mort stammered, "Some sort of setup, dude. We don't get details. Now let up 'fore you kill him."

Blinding rage coalesced. *Star.* It all became a blur at that point. He quickly gagged Mort and the other idiot. Then in a flat-out run, he headed for the house.

The gunshot scared Sterling, making it impossible for her to stay in the car. Heart rapping, she got out with the binoculars and stared, but everything must have been happening on the other side of the barn.

Had Reyes fired, or had one of Mattox's men?

Caught in indecision, she chewed her lip—and suddenly Adela slammed up to the fender of the SUV. Swinging around to face her, the gun already in her hand, Sterling gaped in shock.

Adela's mouth was swollen, crusted over with dried blood, and one of her eyes was blackened. A purpling bruise spread out on her jaw. "What in the world—"

"Francis..." Now half draped over the hood of the car, her legs unable to hold her, Adela groped her way around. "Please. Help me."

Empathy took over, sharpened by rage, and Sterling snapped to attention. "What happened?" After holstering the gun, she hurried over to put an arm around Adela. "Mattox did this to you?"

"Yes." Slumping against her, Adela held on for dear life. Her clothes were torn, a dirty T-shirt ripped from the hem halfway up her midriff. Jeans ragged and dirty. Hair tangled.

Struggling with the deadweight, Sterling tried to steer her to the side of the SUV so she could open the door and get her inside. "Easy. Take a few breaths." She reached for the handle...

Adela laughed as she pushed her back, taking her off guard. She had Sterling's gun in her hand.

Things clicked into place easy enough. "Huh. So I was right. You're part of the setup."

"Don't lie!" Adela raged. "You had no idea."

Curling her lip, Sterling said, "I suspected you all along."

Stymied, Adela's mouth firmed, her eyes narrowed and she looked ready for murder.

Sterling immediately considered how to react, what she'd do, when she'd do it. It'd be dicey, but she wouldn't go down without a fight.

Then Adela surprised her by smiling. "Did you know I arranged it all? Ah, I see that you didn't."

All? No, she wouldn't buy that. "Mattox doesn't take orders from a woman."

"Of course not. He's all man. He's all *mine*." As if gloating, Adela said, "I suggested how to get you, and he liked the idea. It's worked before."

Worked before? What the ever-loving hell.

"I don't want to kill you out here. Mattox would be disappointed, so turn around and walk."

At the moment all Sterling felt was stark anger and firm resolve. Cade was near, but she'd handle this without distracting him. He already had his hands full.

"Move!"

Smirking, Sterling asked, "And if I don't?"

Adela limped closer. "Mattox will shoot your boyfriend right in the face." Glee twisted her abused features. "He has him, you know."

Cade told her to trust him, so that's what she'd do. Keeping her expression impassive wasn't easy, but Sterling gave it her best shot. "You've already proven yourself to be a liar, so why should I believe you? If anything, Mattox is already dead."

"No!" Closer still, Adela's breath rasped harshly. "Mattox has him, and if you don't come along, I'll shoot you in the leg and drag you there."

If Adela got near enough, Sterling felt certain she could disarm her. But no, she stopped with too much distance still between them.

To goad her, Sterling snorted. "You can barely keep yourself upright."

"Fine. I'll shoot you in both legs and tell Mattox where to find you."

On the off chance Cade had been outmaneuvered, Sterling wanted to be near him to help, so going along suited her. "Fine. To the barn, then."

"No, not the barn." Adela stayed behind her. "The house."

The house? "You're kidding, right? There is no house."

"Two inner rooms are intact." Breathing heavily, probably in pain, Adela snapped, "Hurry up. It's going to rain again."

Sure enough, lightning flickered in the distance, and the sky grew dark and menacing.

Outlined by the coming storm, the house looked like a specter of bad things to come.

It seemed a good idea to keep Adela talking. "Was taking a beating part of your grand plan? You look like you've been through hell and back."

"That's *your* fault! He can be more tempered, except when

you've enraged him. You forced us into hiding, forced him to lose business." Adela laughed brokenly. "Now he's going to make you pay."

"Looks like you already did."

"Mattox can be very gentle. Once he's finished with you, he'll be gentle again."

It twisted Sterling's stomach to witness such madness. "You forgive his abuse that easily?"

With a shrug in her tone, Adela said, "It was necessary to reel you in. No, I didn't like it, but there's a lot of necessary things I don't like—especially the way Mattox obsesses about you." She made a giggling sound. "He'll be so thrilled to see you again."

"Somehow I don't think *thrilled* is the right word."

"Oh, but it is. He doesn't like hurting me, but you? He's going to take great pleasure in hearing you cry."

Sterling steeled her resolve. If she let it, fear would weaken her. She couldn't think about Mattox, about what he might do to her if things went wrong. She'd never again be a victim.

She wouldn't.

Adela prodded her hard in the spine, probably leaving bruises behind, before scuttling out of reach again. Perverse bitch. But even as Sterling thought it, she felt pity. It seemed pretty clear that Adela wasn't well. Whatever she'd gone through in her life had left her damaged enough to see Mattox as a hero.

She glanced back, but already Adela had put enough space between them to be out of reach. She might be insane, but she wasn't taking any chances on Sterling getting her hands on her.

"See the light in the house?" Adela gloated. "They're in there. Who knows? Your man might already be dead...or dying. So hurry it up if you want a chance to say goodbye."

Yes, she did hurry, going so fast that Adela had difficulty keeping up with her. Whatever motivation Mattox had for beating Adela, he'd overdone it, leaving her weakened and hurt.

Sterling went up the broken front steps, alert to any opportunity to turn the tables. So far there'd been none.

Missing boards in the porch forced her to pick her way cautiously before she stepped over the threshold. Rainwater puddled on the floor beneath an entirely collapsed section of roof.

Up ahead, in one contained room, Mattox stood, gun in hand, massive shoulder propped on a mold-covered wall, face twisted with cruel satisfaction. "Well, well, well. You actually did it, Adela."

"I told you I would." She shoved Sterling forward, almost making her fall.

Senses keenly attuned to the danger, Sterling noticed the eerie silence.

Mattox didn't have Cade.

Relieved, she breathed easy again. Cade was still out there with Reyes, and that meant she had a chance. They all did.

"Ah, I see the hope in your eyes," Mattox crooned. "It's lovely, truly it is."

"I told her there were women in the truck," Adela said with a sneer. "She doesn't yet know that you actually brought more men."

"Four more," Mattox explained. "They're already out there scouring the farm for your hulking friend."

Sterling leveled an unimpressed stare on Mattox. "You sent more sacrifices to be slaughtered?"

"I sent them fully armed."

"And you think that'll help them?" She scoffed. "So far no one you sent has even been a challenge."

Mattox didn't seem bothered by that. "It's true, I've been forced to use the dregs of society. They're not exactly reliable backup, but there's strength in numbers, so I'm confident they'll be dragging in his body any minute."

Sterling allowed a slow, smug smile. "Amazing. You really don't realize that you've sent them all to their deaths, do you?"

The relaxed posture left Mattox and he shoved upright. "Bullshit."

"They were in the barn, right? Well, they're useless now. Hear that silence? Think hard and you'll know what that means. Better still, you'll know that you're next." The words no sooner left her mouth than blinding pain exploded in her skull and she dropped to her knees. Jesus. Fighting off a rush of nausea, Sterling watched stars dance before her eyes.

Tsking, Mattox said, "Don't say things that set her off. Adela is unpredictable in her dedication to me." He smiled at the other woman, his expression bordering on tender. "What if you'd accidentally killed her?"

Heaving, Adela snarled, "She had it coming."

"Sick fucks." Sterling had the forethought to withdraw the knife from her boot before struggling awkwardly to her feet. Keeping it hidden was a challenge, but she pretended to stumble into the wall so she could slip it into the back of her waistband. To distract them both, she said to Adela, "You'll pay for that."

Enraged, Adela started to lunge forward.

Sterling braced for impact. At the moment, with her temples pounding, she wouldn't mind breaking Adela's neck.

Unfortunately, Mattox interfered, snatching Adela away none too gently, then cupping her bruised cheek in his meaty mitt. "I don't have a quick death in mind for her. You don't want to rob me of my pleasure, do you?"

Faced with so much hatred, it wasn't easy to keep a cool facade, but Sterling gave it her best shot.

It didn't help that Adela snuggled against his wide frame with complete adoration. "I'll behave."

Worse, Mattox coasted fat fingers over her swollen cheek and bloodied mouth, frowning a little, then pressing a tender kiss to her forehead. "I know you will."

"Gawd," Sterling groused. "If you two don't knock it off, I'm going to puke up my guts."

He glared at her for that remark but said to Adela, "Give me your gun so you aren't tempted to shoot her too soon."

Uncertain, Adela offered it up, then flinched when he roughly snatched it away. He shoved it into his pocket, meaning he now had two guns.

Wincing inside, Sterling again took in Adela's battered face. Mattox definitely had to die—but could Adela be saved? Didn't seem likely.

To be sure, Sterling asked, "So you don't have new women held captive?"

"Oh, he does," Adela bragged, regaining her attitude. "They'll replenish some of the profits *you* cost him."

Nope. Not a chance in hell of saving her. At that point, knowing other women were terrorized because of her, Sterling no longer cared.

Instead of speaking to Adela, she asked Mattox, "If they're not here, then where?"

"You think I'd tell you?" He evaluated her new posture against the wall but didn't seem to notice anything amiss. "No, I'll keep that information to myself, but I will tell you that they'll be transported soon." He eyed her distress with interest. "That bothers you? Well, it's partially your fault. I need cash, and they'll each earn a fair price. No daily rentals, as I had planned for you way back then. These women will be pets... Perhaps you'd like to be one, as well? Maybe even my own personal pet."

"Seriously, dude, I'm going to puke."

Mattox grinned. "When I'm done with you, you won't have such a smart mouth."

Adela scowled. "I thought we were going to kill her?"

Licking his thick lips, Mattox murmured, "Yes—*after* I've gotten my fill."

Trepidation kept her guts churning, but Sterling eyed him up and down with disdain. "You won't live long enough to make those threats a reality."

Fury brought Mattox forward. Stopping a few feet from her, he demanded, "Call out to him."

"Him?" Sterling asked, pretending confusion.

"If she plays dumb again," Adela shouted, "shoot her in the leg!"

Mattox raised his brows at her ruthless suggestion.

Stalling for time, Sterling asked, "What do you want me to say?"

"Yell his name." Mattox grinned with satisfaction. "That should do it."

Drawing a slow, deep breath, Sterling called out, "Cade?"

No answer—not that she'd expected one. Cade wasn't stupid. She had no doubt that he already had a grasp of the situation and all the players. He had a plan, and he would come for her. She only prayed he didn't get hurt in the process.

"I think I need to make you scream." Adela started to move forward.

Again, Mattox pulled her back, this time with keen impatience. "Call him again, and you better make it good."

Trying to determine which way Cade would enter, Sterling quickly scanned the open areas of the half-demolished house. Mattox had his back protected by a wall, so Cade couldn't come in behind him. That probably meant he'd enter through the side of the house where much of the structure was missing, or the front doorway that Sterling had used.

Either way, they'd see him coming, and that would make him an easy target for Mattox.

Just then, three rapid shots rang out. They echoed over the barren fields, making it impossible to pinpoint a direction.

In her heart, Sterling knew it was Cade, doing what he did best—kicking ass.

Adela blanched. Equally rattled, Mattox swung his heavy

Glock around and took aim at her chest. "Call him! Make sure he knows I have you."

If Mattox thought that would save him, he'd find out otherwise.

"Call him, call him," Adela sang, her eyes going vague with excitement. *Call him.*

By the second, she became more unhinged.

Sterling filled her lungs. "Cade!" To appease Mattox, she added, "I'm in here, Cade."

Eyes glittering, Adela held her breath.

The silence dragged out while Mattox's flinty gaze bounced back and forth between the two entrances—and suddenly Cade dropped through the hole in the ceiling, landing on his feet right before them.

A sort of blindsided panic held them both enthralled, but not Cade. Incandescent rage seemed to emanate from him. He appeared bigger, as invincible as he claimed. Turning fast, he violently kicked the gun away from Mattox, likely breaking his forearm in the process. While Mattox flailed, Cade grabbed him by the throat, lifted him from the floor and slammed him into a crumbling wall. His boulder-sized fist connected with Mattox's crotch. Then a forearm to his face cut off the scream of pain. Last, a punch to his throat.

Mattox was done for, a heavy deadweight hanging limp from Cade's grip.

It all happened so fast that Sterling stood there staring, riveted by the fluid ease of his attack.

Adela's shrill, earsplitting scream of rage jolted her back into action. She watched Adela scrabble for the gun.

She's going to shoot Cade?

Like hell! Throwing everything she had into a tackle, Sterling took them both down hard. She was bigger than Adela, surely stronger…and yet she wasn't fast enough.

The gun discharged with a deafening explosion.

Fighting a rush of suffocating fear, Sterling managed to glance up. But no, Cade hadn't slowed at all. His heavy fist repeatedly hammered Mattox's face.

"No!" Insanity made Adela stronger. Despite Sterling's efforts, she forced the gun around again, snarling like an animal, consumed with hatred.

Sterling tried, but she couldn't wrest the gun from her. *No, no, no.*

She would not let Cade be shot.

Savage protective instincts surged up…and her lessons kicked in. She reacted, fast, harsh. Brutal.

Just as Cade had taught her.

Her elbow slammed into Adela's already injured nose, crunching it and sending out a thick spray of blood. It dazed her long enough for Sterling to grab her knife and, without pause, drive the blade deep, once, twice, a third time.

Just as quickly, Sterling withdrew, moving back in horror.

Mouth going slack, eyes wide and sightless with shock, the gun slipped from Adela's hand. Blood pulsed and oozed from the wounds in her midriff.

Trembling with the aftereffects, Sterling saw her try to speak, then slump flat to the floor. Lifeless.

They weren't yet safe. Tamping down the horror of what she'd just done, she snatched up the gun and got back to her feet in time to see Cade release Mattox.

The floor shook as his body landed.

A big blackened hole gaped in his side. Adela had killed him. Somehow that seemed fitting.

The queasiness returned in a rush, but before Sterling could assimilate all the sights and scents of death, Cade had her, crushing her close, his face in her hair.

God, he felt good. Warm, safe…*alive.*

"Are you hurt?" He thrust her back, his gaze searching over her, his hands examining her arms, her waist, down to her hips.

Sterling rested a trembling hand against his steeled shoulder. "I'm okay."

"You don't look it."

Maybe because her head was splitting now that the adrenaline waned. She made a lame gesture toward Adela's body. "She cracked me in the back of the head with the gun."

Immediately, Cade turned her. "Aw, babe, let me see."

"It's all right." It annoyed her that she'd gotten caught like that while he stood there without a scratch other than his knuckles.

Tenderly, Cade sifted his fingers through her hair, lightly prodding her skull. "Damn. You have a massive goose egg." He turned her again to look into her eyes.

"I'm fine, Cade. I promise." Shock settled in, making her shiver and shake. "You?"

For an answer, he pressed his mouth to hers. The kiss wasn't sexual but reassuring. Soft, lingering, comforting.

From behind them, Reyes asked, "Some new form of resuscitation? Because I *know* you're not making out when we have shit to do."

Cade ended the kiss but didn't step away. He gathered her to his chest and said to his brother, "Madison called it in?"

"Ambulance and cops will be here any minute." Looking past Sterling to the bodies, he asked, "Dead?"

Sterling didn't have an answer to that.

Stepping around them, bypassing Mattox, Reyes went to one knee and pressed his fingers to Adela's throat. "Light pulse. She might make it."

In a truly gallant move, Cade lifted Sterling into his arms and turned to leave the destruction behind. Once outside, he moved a good distance from the house—and didn't put her down.

"Do you think Adela will—"

"Either way," he said, "that's not on you."

Understanding that and accepting it were two different things. "I couldn't let her shoot you."

Jaw flexing, arms tightening, Cade struggled with himself, all while his vivid blue eyes held hers captive. "Just so you know," he rasped in a growl, "I'm never letting you out of my sight."

Liking the sound of that, Sterling rested her head against his shoulder and whispered, "Good."

CHAPTER NINETEEN

As soon as they'd gotten home, his dad checked Star, going over all the signs of a concussion. She did have a slight headache but otherwise seemed fine. Introspective, but not lethargic. Quiet, but responsive to questions asked. No blurry vision, and hungry enough to eat a few cookies.

Though she grumbled about it, Cade stayed with her while she showered and changed clothes. There were many things he wanted to say, but he could wait. He had her with him, she was safe and that's what mattered.

When she'd finished dressing warmly, they moved outside to the deck, where the cool mountain air revived her. She hadn't complained when he'd sat down and pulled her onto his lap. In fact, she'd been so silent it worried him.

With her attention on the mountain view, Star said, "It's a good thing that Mattox is gone."

"A very good thing."

"Even though she didn't mean to, I'm glad that it was Adela who killed him."

They knew that an ambulance had taken Adela away, but no

one really thought she'd make it. Previous injuries from the sick games she'd played with Mattox had already worn her down.

Cade didn't know how many beatings she'd taken, but Adela participated in hurting women and she'd wanted to hurt Star, too. She'd done her best to lure them into a trap.

If she died, he wouldn't lose sleep over it.

"Have you heard from Reyes yet?"

His brother had gone after the captive women, using the details Cade had gotten from one of the men hired to kill him. "He checked in."

"And?" Twisting around, Star faced him. "Were they there? Those men hadn't lied?"

Their loyalty to Mattox ended as soon as Cade had started wiping them out. "Once Reyes found the women, he allowed the task force to take over." Not everyone realized that his father founded the task force, and that they were, ultimately, answerable to him—which meant they could keep tabs on the women to know, without a doubt, that they were helped.

That, more than anything, was important to his father. To him, Reyes and Madison, too.

And now, obviously, to Star, as well.

She searched his gaze, and as understanding dawned, she again relaxed against him. "We need to know where Mattox got them."

"Working on it." In fact, that was the next step, and his sister was already chasing down leads. The thugs hadn't known much about the operation, but Mattox's driver, and the bastards who'd brought the truck, proved to be better informed—once they'd been persuaded to talk.

Luckily his father had great contacts in both law enforcement and politics. Within a few hours, Parrish had learned that the police had rounded up all the fucks involved. There were a few unavoidable fatalities beyond Mattox—and maybe Adela—but with any luck, there'd be nothing to trace the incident back to

them. Not that they couldn't handle it, but it offered unnecessary complications.

If anyone did sniff in that direction, Parrish would handle it.

Star's small hand opened over his chest. "I want to be a part
of that, okay?"

She could be a part of everything, as far as he was concerned.
"That's a given, babe." But he added, "You can be involved as
much, or as little, as you like."

"Good. They all need to be destroyed."

"Agreed." Cade knew she was working things out in her
mind. Yes, she'd done some awesome work on her own, but
the violence today was at a new level.

For him, it was routine. For her...not so much.

"Everything that happened today..."

Her voice trailed off, so Cade didn't push it. He just held her,
his hand coasting up and down her arm, over her hip and back.

"When I was taken all those years ago, I was nothing but a
victim."

A victim who had used her wits and bravery to escape. Sadly,
not every person in her position had a chance to do the same.
"No, babe, you were a survivor."

She turned her face to kiss his throat. "I got away, but I was
still...still a casualty. Helping other women helped *me*, too, because I felt useful, like I was making a difference."

"I understand."

"Today, leading up to things, I got so nervous I couldn't
think straight. It was terrible."

Again Cade said nothing. He'd picked up on her growing
anxiety and had tried to spare her. In that, he'd failed.

She drew in an audible breath, rubbed at her eyes and shivered again. "I learned that I can handle it, you know? I did
okay today."

"You did amazing. I keep telling you, you have incredible

instincts and you're a fighter. But it's more than that. You're a natural defender."

She kissed his throat again. "Why do you say that?"

A fresh wave of fury ran through his veins. Knowing Mattox had been *that close* to her, knowing that Adela had hoped to witness her murder, kept him teetering on the edge of rage. He wanted to secure her safety, he wanted her to let him care for her the way he wanted to—the way she deserved.

He wanted to spend his life with her. To share everything. Especially commitment.

He wanted marriage.

Tilting up her chin, Cade looked into her eyes, hoping she'd see everything he felt. "You protected me today."

A wry smile twisted her mouth. "Well, I tried, but I'm not sure it was necessary."

"If Adela's aim had been better?"

Wincing, she said, "Well, she did get off a shot."

"Just one, because you acted fast, ensuring she didn't get another. You were there, and I trust you, so I was able to focus solely on Mattox." But he'd lost his control, and that never happened. "Because of what he did to you in the past, because he dared to come after you again, I wanted to kill him with my bare hands. If Adela hadn't shot him, I would have beat him to death."

She swallowed heavily. "You almost did. I was…impressed. You moved like a very agile wrecking ball."

Cade wanted to give her time, but it wasn't easy, not when she looked at him with her heart in her eyes.

He wanted it all. Did she?

Just then, Parrish opened the door and stuck his head out. "You two might want to come see this."

They each looked up, but Parrish was smiling, so Cade wasn't concerned. "In a bit."

"You'll be sorry if you miss it."

"Well, now I'm intrigued." Scooting that sweet rump over his lap, Star got to her feet. Looking a little desperate for a change of topic, she took his hand and tugged. "Come on. I need a distraction."

Cade didn't, but he let her pull him to his feet, then held her back until his father went inside ahead of them. She might not have a concussion, thank God, but Cade could see that her head hurt. It was there in her pinched expression, the shadows under her eyes.

"Before we go in, I want you to know that I'm incredibly proud of you."

Her bottom lip trembled before she caught it in her teeth.

Not exactly the romantic declaration he wanted to make, but definitely something she needed to know.

"I don't think anyone's ever said that to me before."

No, probably not. Her life hadn't been an easy one. She'd conquered more hardships than any person should have to, and was still beautiful inside and out, strong and independent, caring and sexy. "What you did, how you handled yourself, was nothing short of remarkable."

Leaning into him, her forehead against his chest, she shivered. "I was afraid if I showed my fear, they'd just feed off it. That's what happened when Mattox first had me. They all loved fear, like it was a big joke." Her hands fisted in his shirt and she confessed, "But I was afraid, Cade. So afraid."

"God, me, too."

That got her gaze up to his real fast. "You?"

"Don't you dare be surprised by that." Tears filled her eyes, shredding his heart. "Please don't cry."

"I'm not," she denied, sniffling.

He brushed her cheeks, catching the tears on his fingertips before cupping her face. "I've never in my life been that afraid. If I'd lost you..." He couldn't finish that thought. Putting his arms around her, he gathered her close. "I *can't* lose you."

Swiping her eyes on his shirt, she swallowed, nodded. "I don't want to lose you, either."

Cade started to remark on that, but they heard the laughter from the great room and it drew Star's attention. She gave a tremulous smile. "Are they having a party?" Curiosity took her to the door, and since he wasn't about to leave her side, Cade followed along.

In the great room, they found the usually stuffy Bernard on the floor, long legs crossed, with a very grungy cat rubbing against his chest.

Star stalled. Cade stared.

"Yes, precious," Bernard crooned in a ridiculous voice while stroking the cat's back. "You're a beauty, aren't you, darling? Such a sweet little mama."

"Little?" Cade eyed the long, gangly cat currently getting white fur all over Bernard's dark slacks.

"Mama?" Star asked at the same time.

"Kittens." Sitting opposite Bernard, Madison gazed down into a cardboard box. "Three of them."

Star made a beeline for the box, dropped to her knees, and seconds later a beautiful smile bloomed on her face. Emotion bubbling over, she lifted a tiny ball of fur to her cheek.

God, he loved her. So goddamn much it was killing him. He thought of how she'd stood strong, how despite her fear she hadn't buckled. And now seeing this, that soft, tender side of her...

She smiled toward him. "Cade, isn't it adorable?"

Still holding her gaze, he whispered, "Very."

Arms folded, Parrish stood by the fireplace, watching it all with a slightly dazed expression. Reyes was there beside him, his stance aggressive.

Amused by that, Cade joined them. "Where did—"

"It's my cat," Reyes stated, his muscles bunching and his chin jutting.

Holding up his hands, Cade fought a grin. "Okay. No problem. So you got a cat. Makes perfect sense. Can't imagine a better time for it."

The blatant nonsense stole Reyes's angry edge, and with a roll of his eyes, he said, "It's not like I planned it. She was in the alley next to the gym. Starving, trying to care for those three little fur balls. What could I do?"

"You had to take her in," Cade agreed, clapping his brother on the shoulder. "I'd have done the same."

"That's all understandable," Parrish said. "You wouldn't be my sons if you could turn a blind eye to any suffering. The shocker is Bernard." Smiling in disbelief at his old friend, he said, "Just look at him. Have you ever seen anything like it?"

Now on his back, unconcerned with his usually impeccable clothes or his gawking audience, Bernard laughed as the cat walked over his chest to butt into his chin.

Cade shook his head. No, most definitely he hadn't. "I didn't know he liked animals."

"Neither did I," Parrish admitted. "I knew he was a loyal friend, that he loves you all like his own, that cooking is his passion and that he's a ladies' man—"

"He *what*?" Reyes asked.

Yeah, that was news to Cade, too. From what he'd observed, Bernard cared about many things—his appearance, his job… all of them. But sex? "Where the hell does he find the time?"

"Where there's a will, there's a way" was all Parrish said. "But in all the time he's worked for us, he's never mentioned having a soft spot for animals."

Reyes stared in disgust as the older man sat up again, hugging the cat to his cheek, much as Star had hugged the kitten. The difference was that the cat hung from his arms, her crooked, mismatched eyes half-closed in bliss, her broken tail twined around Bernard's forearm.

"I didn't bring her home as a gift to him. I just…" Reyes ran a hand over his head. "I couldn't leave her alone at the gym, right? I mean, that was my intention at first. But I got the call to get moving, so I didn't have time to set her up as nicely as I meant to. After I wrapped up things today, I kept thinking about her, and it bothered me."

"Understandable," Cade said, while fighting a grin at his brother's discomfort.

"I stopped by the gym on my return. She was in the box with the kittens, but it was a tight fit. She needs a real bed, cat food, too, and—"

"A litter box," Star added as she joined them. She'd put the kitten back in the box, but that sweet little smile remained on her face. "You're keeping the cat?"

Reyes stared at Bernard. "Hell, I don't know if he'll give her back." Slanting his gaze at Star, he said, "And that's going to be a problem, because Kennedy will want to know where the cat went."

"Kennedy?" Parrish asked.

"Sterling pointed her out to me at the gym." Then to Cade, Reyes added, "The hedgehog teaching herself defense techniques?"

"You talked with her?" Star asked.

"I offered her help, but she wasn't receptive. In fact, she was downright insulting about it." Gaining steam, Reyes glared at Star again. "She'd already figured out that I'm more than a gym owner. Said if I didn't want her snooping in my life, I shouldn't butt into hers."

"Huh." Star fought a grin. "So she's not only cute, and maybe in danger, she's also shrewd. I like her already."

Aggrieved, Reyes rolled his eyes.

Madison stepped up. "Want me to look into her background? What's her last name?"

Succinct, Reyes said, "No."

"Why not?" Star asked. "You guys didn't hesitate to check up on me."

"Cade was interested in you." Denying it a little too strongly, Reyes said, "Totally different story with Kennedy."

"Uh-huh." Madison nudged Star, making it clear she wasn't buying Reyes's declarations. "I want her last name—just in case."

"*Anyway*," Reyes said with irritation, "she's the one who found the cat. I just followed her when she started down the alley."

Brows up, Star said, "You followed her?"

On the spot, Reyes flung a hand toward Bernard, then rounded on their father. "What am I supposed to do now? She expects to see the cat at the gym."

Parrish always had an answer. "Tell her you took it home to better care for it. It doesn't sound like she wants to get close to you, so that'll keep her from demanding a visit. But if she does want to see the cat again, invite her to join you on a trip to the vet."

Approving that plan, Cade stepped in with his own advice. "The cat and kittens will all need to be checked. You should get that scheduled right away."

When the kittens started mewling, the cat looked up, abandoned Bernard and hurried back to the box.

Covered in white fur, grinning ear to ear, Bernard strode over. "She'll need several things, but for now I can put together some food and better bedding. Tomorrow, I'll go to the store."

Madison gave him a hug. "I never knew you were such a big softy, Bernard."

That put his nose in the air. "I'm not."

Reaching out, Parrish plucked a clump of fur from his shirt. "You do an incredible impression."

Bernard shrugged. "I adore cats."

"Since when?" Cade asked.

"I was raised on a farm. My parents grew corn and soy, and we always had cats around." One thin hand smoothed his silver hair back into place, and in his usual lofty tone, he announced, "I've missed them."

Everyone stared at him.

Clearing his throat, Reyes took a step forward. "Look, the cat is my responsibility—"

Eyes narrowed and mean, Bernard took a step, too. "She's staying here." The challenge was clear—a first for Bernard.

Taken off guard, Reyes retreated, hands up in surrender. "Fine. No problem. I appreciate the help."

"Oh my," Star breathed.

Cade glanced at her, then followed her gaze to where the mother cat sat by Bernard's feet, a kitten in her mouth.

Bernard went comically mushy all over again. "You're bringing me your babies?" he asked in a high, silly voice. "Oh, you precious, precious thing." He sank down and accepted the little bundle. "I'm overwhelmed."

They all shared another look. Star couldn't hold back her grin, and it got to Cade. After the melancholy following the sting, she was happy again.

Relieved, aware of several strong urges, he pulled her to his side.

Madison leaned against Reyes, patting him in sympathy. After all, he'd gotten, and lost, a pet in record time. "I have some leads we can follow based on where the women were grabbed."

Jumping on that, Reyes asked, "All from the same area?"

"Very close. I've configured a map and I have a few ideas."

"It's getting late." Stressing that it was time to take a break and regroup, Parrish gave a pointed look at Star, which luckily she missed.

Knowing the toll it took to do their specific jobs, Parrish was keen on physical and emotional health.

Star, being new to it all, would especially be affected, so Cade gave his father a nod of appreciation for understanding and not pushing her.

"We can plan our next move tomorrow—" Looking down at Bernard, Parrish shook his head. "I was going to say over breakfast, but now I'm not sure."

"There will be breakfast." Bernard cuddled all three kittens in his arms, and he looked deliriously happy. "Just don't expect anything fancy."

Cade wasn't about to miss that perfect segue. "Star and I are heading downstairs. We'll see you all in the morning."

She was still trying to say her goodbyes when Cade led her from the room and to the stairs.

"Why are we rushing?"

"Because the way I need to kiss you, I figured you'd prefer we were alone."

Warmth entered her dark eyes and humor lifted the corners of her mouth. "Too impatient to wait?"

"Something like that."

She took the lead, passing him by, making him laugh out loud, until they reached his rooms. After securing the door, she started undressing—on her way to the bedroom.

"Wait up."

"Found your patience, huh?" Her T-shirt hit him in the chest and she kept going, her hands busy on her jeans. "Well, I don't want to wait."

With his longer stride, Cade caught her before she got her jeans down any farther than her knees.

Lord help him, how she looked bent over, her perfect ass on display, was enough to test his strongest convictions. But she'd been hurt, and whether or not she'd admit to the ache in her head, he wouldn't forget it.

Pulling her upright, he slid an arm under her hips, scooped

her into his arms and went to the barrel chair adjacent to the dresser. Sitting with her again in his lap, he took her mouth.

He meant to be gentle, but she already had her slender fingers clasping his jaw, keeping him close while she consumed him. Her warm tongue stroked, her sharp little teeth nibbled and, yeah, he lost it.

"I want you," she groaned, shifting around so she could grab his shirt, peeling it up and over his head. Her scorching gaze traveled over his chest, and she leaned forward to lick a tattoo.

He wasn't made of steel. "Your head—"

"Is fine." Breathing hard, she leaned back to see him again. "It's my heart you need to worry about right now."

"Aw, babe." This time he kept the kiss short and sweet. "I will always protect your heart, I swear."

Emotion softened the lust, made her lips tremble. "My heart needs to feel you, around me, in me. Give me that. Please."

She'd easily outmaneuvered him, and Cade knew when to relent. Kissing her more deeply, he stood and carried her to the bed.

It felt good to have Cade hold her so easily, proof of his strength and his affection. Even better was how he carefully lowered her to the mattress, then stripped away her jeans and panties.

That compelling steel-blue gaze moved over her. "You'll tell me if your head—"

"Yes." She patted the bed beside her. "I'll tell you."

He stripped out of his own clothes, robbing her of breath with his remarkable body. Now, being turned on, his abs were tight above an impressive erection. Always, his body hair fascinated her, how it spread out over his chest, how that happy trail led down to his cock. Every single part of him, from his military haircut to his patrician features, his granite body down to his feet… She loved it all. So very, very much.

Not unaffected by her rapt attention, Cade snagged a condom, opened the packet and rolled it on.

The second he stretched out over her, her hands went exploring, relishing the warmth of his taut flesh, the flex of firm muscle, his indescribable scent that both incited and soothed her. A little overcome, Sterling hugged him tight with her nose in his neck, breathing him in.

Cade said nothing—not with words, anyway. He used his hands and lips, the stroke of his tongue and the press of his body to tell her how much she meant to him.

Now, after everything, she believed him. This was real. Solid. A commitment she could count on. Security she'd never known she wanted but relished so very much.

He kissed her, teasing at first, just brushing over her lips, tracing with his tongue—until her breath caught and she arched up against him.

Angling his head, he let his tongue sink deep. Hot, wet. Possessive.

Sterling's fingertips gripped his shoulders, and that seemed to fire his blood even more.

"You're mine," he rasped, reaching down between their bodies to find her sex, to slide his fingers over her warm wetness... to press in, fill her, make her cry out with escalating sensations.

Marveling, Cade breathed, "Damn, you're close already."

In agreement, she pulled him into another tongue-thrusting, molten kiss while tightening around his fingers, rolling her hips against him, needing and taking.

He pulled away, but only to readjust, and then it was his cock pressing into her. Braced on his forearms, his hands holding her head and his mouth eating at hers, he rode her hard.

And she loved it.

Their combined sounds of pleasure filled the room. Desperation grew. Pleasure coiled tighter and tighter.

The second the high, vibrating moan escaped her, Cade put his head back, jaw clenched in concentration, until she began to ease in the aftermath of her orgasm. Tucking his face to her neck, he growled out his own release.

For only a few moments, he gave her his weight. With limbs tangled, all aches and pains forgotten, misgivings shelved, Sterling felt entirely at peace.

When she sighed, he struggled up to his elbows again. "Hey. You okay?"

"Mmm. I think you've found a cure for headaches. I'm blessedly numb."

The smile showed in his eyes, if not on his mouth. "Is that so?"

"Don't look so pleased. You already knew you excelled at *everything*."

Something else joined the humor in his eyes. Affection. Love.

"Look who's talking." Rolling to his side while keeping her tucked close, Cade heaved a big breath. "We both need some sleep."

She did, but she didn't want to sleep yet.

As usual, he seemed to know her thoughts. While stroking her back, her hip, he asked, "Something on your mind?"

Never had she thought to be in this place—a place of satisfaction and contentment. Admitting to the fears that had always plagued her seemed incredibly easy, at least with Cade.

"Star?" He lifted his head. "What's wrong?"

"I've always assumed a normal life wasn't possible for me, and I was right."

"Hey." With the edge of his fist, he nudged up her face.

She pressed a finger to his lips and spoke around the choking emotion. "I was right, but this, with you, isn't normal."

The tension in his shoulders eased a little. "It's exceptional."

"Very much so. You've given me what I didn't think I could ever find. A place to fit in." The damn tears spilled over, but this was Cade, so she didn't mind. "I never used to cry."

"Not on the outside," he agreed, and his hand settled under her breast. "But here, in your heart, I think you were very sad."

How could he know her so well? Easy—he loved her. Well, it was time she opened up, so she smiled and said, "I appreciate how you trust me, how you recognize what I can do...and what I can't."

His mouth touched hers. "You can do anything, babe."

Love swelled her heart until there were no hollow corners left in her soul. "No, I can't. And now I don't mind that. We complement each other, you and I. I feel safe with you when I'd forgotten what safe felt like."

His eyes went a little glassy, too. "I will always protect you."

"I know. Just as I'll protect you."

He smiled and said softly, "I know."

With her newfound freedom and confidence, Sterling said, "You love me."

"More than I knew was possible."

That seemed like enough. "I want to live with you," she stated.

"I want to marry you," he countered. "Naturally we'll live together."

Marriage. It had always sounded like the standard norm, a normal she'd never have.

Now it sounded like *them.*

Sterling hugged him, letting his scent surround her, his strength cradle her, and knew she'd found the most incredibly perfect man—for her. "I love you, too. So damn much."

"Will you marry me?"

"Yes, please." Giddy happiness consumed her. "As long as we don't live here—not permanently, anyway."

Cade grinned. "I think it's time I showed you my house."

"Tomorrow," she whispered, already comfortable against him. "You might not have noticed, but I had a trying day."

EPILOGUE

Everyone was in the breakfast room when they finally made it upstairs. Cade was surprised they'd waited on them, or so he assumed, until Bernard came in looking harried.

He carried a large tray of dishes…with his hair uncombed and his shirt untucked.

Cade shared a look with Star, who appeared equally boggled, then glanced at the others. Madison hid a smile. Parrish looked harassed.

"He's already been out," Reyes complained with a glare at Bernard. "Buying things for *my* cat."

Going rigid, Bernard paused by the table. "Her name is Chimera."

Left eye twitching, Reyes said in a soft, lethal tone, "You named my cat?"

Nose up, arrogance in full force, Bernard glared at him. "Better than calling that beautiful creature *Cat*."

"Beautiful?" Reyes leaned forward, his elbows on the table. "She has mismatched eyes and looks like she was run over by a mower."

"Her eyes are *stunning*, and now that I've bathed and brushed her, her fur is gorgeous, as well."

Astonishment dropped Reyes's mouth open. "You—"

At the head of the table, Parrish cleared his throat. "Enough on the…"

Bernard stabbed him with a look.

Parrish quickly amended, "Chimera. Food would be nice, preferably before it gets cold. Or did you only plan to stand there and let us smell it?"

The tray clattered to the table. In rapid order, Bernard set out scrambled eggs, muffins, fresh fruit and a plate of sausages.

Before he could leave, Star said, "Thank you, Bernard. I don't know how I got by so long without your cooking. You're a master."

Smug, Bernard sent Reyes a look. "Thank you. It's nice to be appreciated."

That earned a round of protests from everyone, but Bernard wasn't moved. For a moment there, Cade thought he'd flip them all off as he exited the room in his lofty way.

They dealt with a lot of crazy shit, but Bernard in that particular mood? Strangest of them all.

The stillness lasted all of three seconds before everyone started laughing. Madison pushed back her chair. "I'll go soothe the beast." She nudged her brother. "And you—stop needling him."

Reyes grinned. "No can do. The more I complain, the more determined he is to care for that… Chimera."

Cade snorted. "Good save. He did seem adamant about her having a name."

Even Parrish chuckled. "I've never seen him so rattled. He went out bright and early, buying everything from food and dishes, to catnip and toys, to bedding and brushes. He rushed back, afraid Chimera would miss him."

Star laughed. "She probably did."

"Didn't sound like it, given the racket she made while he

bathed her. He had to change clothes, but then Madison came in, and shortly after that, Reyes showed up, so Bernard didn't have a chance to properly spiff up. You know he's fanatical about having food ready."

Plate already filled, Reyes settled in to eat. "I had no idea what I'd do with the cat, but Bernard has offered the perfect solution."

"There are still three kittens," Cade pointed out.

"And I have two siblings. Problem solved."

As if someone had just handed her a million dollars, Star squealed. "I get a kitten?"

"When they're old enough to be weaned—though I imagine Bernard will demand visitation rights."

Cade was smiling when Star turned a worried frown on him. "I'd love a kitten, but it's your house we're talking about, so I'll understand—"

"It'll be our house."

That got everyone quiet again. Reyes even paused in midchew with his mouth full.

Madison returned with Bernard in tow. He still looked frazzled, but he'd at least smoothed his hair. Or maybe Madison had done that for him.

Now that they were all present, Cade decided to make an announcement, before Reyes stirred Bernard up again. "I asked Star to marry me."

All eyes turned to her. Wearing a cheek-splitting grin, Reyes said, "I'm guessing you said yes, or he wouldn't be looking so pleased."

"Of course I said yes. I'm not a dope."

In seconds, Madison was right back out of her seat, circling the table to grab Star in a hug. Appearing pleased, Bernard lifted his orange juice in a toast. "Welcome to the family."

Even Parrish smiled, saying to Cade, "Finding the right

woman for you is the greatest gift you'll ever receive. I'm happy for you."

That sobered them all. It was a stark reminder that Parrish had found his love—and lost her to violence. That loss had determined how he'd raised his children, and how they lived their lives.

Seeking justice.

Because of that, he'd met Star.

Such a lifestyle shouldn't have been conducive to a prolonged relationship, much less love or marriage, yet if it wasn't for his sharpened insights, he might not have noticed Star right off.

Knowing he owed Parrish a debt of gratitude, Cade looked at him, an older version of himself, and said simply, "Thank you, Dad."

Star leaned into his side, smiling, happy. "Yeah, thanks. For a bunch of stuff, but mostly for raising such an awesome son."

Being an ass, Reyes asked, "Do you mean me or Cade?"

Bernard threw a napkin at him, and Parrish protested the disruption. Ignoring them all, Madison opened her laptop while eating.

Star turned to Cade, grinning. "Don't tell them I said this, but your family is truly awesome."

As Cade looked at each of them, old resentments faded away. He'd been coerced to this life, but because of that he had Star. They were still nuts, but they were his. He hugged Star tight. "I agree."

★ ★ ★ ★ ★